THE PRINCE
WHO CHARMED HER

BY
FIONA McARTHUR

HIS HIDDEN
AMERICAN BEAUTY

BY
CONNIE COX

WITHDRAWN
FROM
STOCK

D0865410

A mother to five sons, **Fiona McArthur** is an Australian midwife who loves to write. Medical Romance™ gives Fiona the scope to write about all the wonderful aspects of adventure, romance, medicine and midwifery that she feels so passionate about—as well as an excuse to travel! Now that her boys are older, Fiona and her husband, Ian, are off to meet new people, see new places, and have wonderful adventures. Fiona's website is at www.fionamcarthur.com

Connie Cox has loved Harlequin Mills & Boon romances since she was a young teen. To be a Harlequin Mills & Boon author now is a fantasy come to life. By training, Connie is an electrical engineer. Through her first job, working on nuclear scanners and other medical equipment, she had a unique perspective on the medical world. She is fascinated by the inner strength of medical professionals, who must balance emotional compassion with stoic logic, and is honoured to showcase the passion of these dedicated professionals through her own passion of writing. Married to the boy-next-door, Connie is the proud mother of one terrific daughter and son-in-law and one precocious dachshund.

Connie would love to hear from you. Visit her website at www.ConnieCox.com

THE PRINCE
WHO CHARMED HER

BY
FIONA McARTHUR

MILLS &
BOON

Leabharlann

5745543

All the characters in this book have no existence outside the imagination
of the author, and have no relation whatsoever to anyone bearing the
same name or names. They are not even distantly inspired by any
individual known or unknown to the author, and all the incidents are
pure invention.

All Rights Reserved including the right of reproduction in whole or
in part in any form. This edition is published by arrangement with
Harlequin Enterprises II BV/S.à.r.l. The text of this publication or any
part thereof may not be reproduced or transmitted in any form or by any
means, electronic or mechanical, including photocopying, recording,
storage in an information retrieval system, or otherwise, without the
written permission of the publisher.

This book is sold subject to the condition that it shall not, by way of
trade or otherwise, be lent, resold, hired out or otherwise circulated
without the prior consent of the publisher in any form of binding or
cover other than that in which it is published and without a similar
condition including this condition being imposed on the subsequent
purchaser.

® and TM are trademarks owned and used by the trademark owner
and/or its licensee. Trademarks marked with ® are registered with the
United Kingdom Patent Office and/or the Office for Harmonisation
in the Internal Market and in other countries.

First published in Great Britain 2013
by Mills & Boon, an imprint of Harlequin (UK) Limited.
Harlequin (UK) Limited, Eton House, 18-24 Paradise Road,
Richmond, Surrey TW9 1SR

© Fiona McArthur 2013

ISBN: 978 0 263 89885 9

Harlequin (UK) policy is to use papers that are natural, renewable
and recyclable products and made from wood grown in sustainable
forests. The logging and manufacturing process conform to the
legal environmental regulations of the country of origin.

Printed and bound in Spain
by Blackprint CPI, Barcelona

Dear Reader

I've always wanted to write about a dashing prince, a fairytale royal wedding and a heroine who deserves to live happily ever after.

Monaco made a big impression on me when I was lucky enough to visit last year, and I was always going to have elements of the romanticism and glamour of that fabulous tiny principality in my story. Then there is the mythology of Greece...

Which brings us to the island of Aspelicus.

Prince Stefano Mykonides has never met anyone like Dr Kiki Fender. An unexpectedly torrid love affair in far-off Australia was not kind to them when they first met...but, goodness me, do sparks fly the second time around!

So we have a cruise ship, a fabulous Mediterranean setting, medical adventure on the high seas—and then the world seems to crash for our newspaper-shy prince and his unwilling Dr Kiki.

I really do hope you enjoy visiting my fairytale countries and their romance-challenged royalty as much as I loved writing their story.

Warmest wishes

Fiona xx

Find me at www.fionamcarthur.com

Also by Fiona McArthur:

A DOCTOR, A FLING AND WEDDING RING
SYDNEY HARBOUR HOSPITAL:
   MARCO'S TEMPTATION**
FALLING FOR THE SHEIKH SHE SHOULDN'T
SURVIVAL GUIDE TO DATING YOUR BOSS
HARRY ST CLAIR: ROGUE OR DOCTOR?
MIDWIFE, MOTHER...ITALIAN'S WIFE*
MIDWIFE IN THE FAMILY WAY*
MIDWIFE IN A MILLION

*Lyrebird Lake Maternity
**Sydney Harbour Hospital

**These books are also available in eBook format
from www.millsandboon.co.uk**

**Praise for
Fiona McArthur:**

'McArthur does full justice to an intensely emotional
scene of the delivery of a stillborn baby,
one that marks a turning point in both the characters'
outlooks. The entire story is liberally spiced with
drama, heartfelt emotion and just a touch of humour.'
—*RT Book Reviews* on
SURVIVAL GUIDE TO DATING YOUR BOSS

Dedicated to my prince, Ian xxx

CHAPTER ONE

DR KIKI FENDER gazed across the blue of the Mediterranean to distant houses that clung like pastel limpets onto the cliffs of Italy and breathed in the beauty of the day.

It wasn't something she'd done when she'd first boarded the ship, but it was easier now as she listened to the delight of the newly embarked passengers.

These first few hours sailing along the Italian coast was her favourite time. But duty called so she brushed the hair out of her eyes and turned towards the hospital below. Four months of shipboard life had brought the purpose back into her life and she was so grateful for that.

Her smile slipped when she remembered it was only five days until the date she'd so looked forward to would be behind her, and then it would get even easier.

One deck down, Prince Stefano Adolphi Phillipe Augustus Mykonides tried not to think of the worst-case scenario as he rolled the unconscious wife of his brother into the recovery position. With immense relief he noted the blue of her lips improve slightly as her airway cleared.

He'd hoped Theros could stay out of trouble this week, on his wife's birthday holiday, but it seemed it wasn't so. With a sigh, the eldest son of Prince Paulo of Aspelicus, a tiny but wealthy principality in the Mediterranean

Sea, knew it was his fault his brother had done something else stupid.

When he looked up at Theros his brother was as helpless as ever, his handsome face twisted in distress. 'Get the ship's hospital on the phone. Tell them it's an emergency,' Stefano said.

Theros's mouth worked silently, like a child's, and he looked shocked and incredulous as his wife began to turn blue again.

Stefano lowered his voice to a stern order. 'Now! Tell them it's a reaction to latex. To bring adrenalin.' He said the words slowly and enunciated clearly.

Theros blinked and stumbled to his feet as Stefano began to strip Marla of her skintight rubber playsuit, cursing under his breath as her breathing became even more laboured, but thankful that at least Theros had had the good sense to call him in time.

His concern lay in removing the offending clothing as fast as possible—before his sister-in-law stopped breathing. Not an easy job—which he gathered should have been half the fun. What he would have given for a scalpel...

Ten doors away Dr Kiki Fender jogged down the hallway to the largest suites, running over in her head what she knew about latex allergies. In truth Kiki was the on-call doctor for crew—not passengers—and she hoped her boss would follow quickly in case the patient was *in extremis*.

She'd hate to lose a patient on departure day, and royalty at that—very poor form. Terrible luck that Will had been on a cabin visit when the call had come in, so she was it till he came. She didn't even bother to try and imagine where this latex exposure had come from.

She'd tossed the usual personal protection gloves out from the emergency pack and donned latex-free ones, reminding herself they should use them in the whole medical centre in this current climate of escalating allergies, and had packed extra adrenalin ampoules. She carried in her hand the Epi-pen which made administration much quicker in such emergencies.

She prayed the patient's airways wouldn't have closed completely by the time her boss arrived with the rest of the equipment.

When the door opened she barely glanced at the distressed man in black shiny underwear and glanced ahead to the woman on the floor. Another man was bent over her as he struggled to extricate her legs from skintight latex leggings.

There was something oddly familiar about the shape of his head, but the woman was already unconscious and her skin was blotched with a paling red rash.

Kiki spoke to the dark hair of the man kneeling on the carpet as she bent down beside him. 'Is she breathing?'

'Just.'

Kiki glanced at the man's face and recognition slapped into her like one of the ocean white caps outside the window.

What the hell was Stefano Mykonides doing on her ship? *Lock that away, quick-smart,* she chastised herself, and quickly pinched the woman's leg to inject the adrenalin. Her eyes skimmed the almost naked woman for tiny rapid rises of her chest, aware that the movements would tell if the medication was helping. Most times with this type of shock recovery was dramatic, because the drug turned off the body's flooding allergic response like a tap.

But a tiny section of her brain was still suggesting that the Stefano she'd known was the last person who needed a threesome with a dolly bird in latex to fill his day.

She heard her boss and the nurse arrive with the emergency stretcher as Stefano leaned towards her.

'Of course I expect you to remain discreet about this event.'

She could see the pulse beating in his strong neck and a part of her responded involuntarily—and that increased her dislike. She met his eyes and tried with only some success to keep the contempt from her face. So typical. The woman was fighting for her life but it was all about how important the good name of the Mykonides family was.

She could say a few things about his good name. Instead she nodded at her patient. 'Of course, Your Highness.'

Stefano turned back to extricating Marla's foot. He was in shock—much like poor Marla without the benefit of the drug's reversal. Kiki Fender was *here* and to see her like this... As a saviour to his family, dynamic, confident of her skills as he'd known she would be. But it was not these things he remembered the most. Nor the woman who looked at him with distaste and called him Your Highness.

Before he could think what to say Marla groaned and stirred, and his sigh of relief escaped silently as Kiki leant over and spoke near her ear.

'You're okay. Take it easy.' She looked at him and silently mouthed, *name*?

'Marla,' he said quietly, just as thankfully the last of the trouser leg came free over her foot with an elastic snapping noise. He slid the rubber suit under the seat of the lounge chair out of sight as more medical staff approached.

Kiki saw him do it and rolled her eyes at his priorities as she turned back to her patient. 'I'm going to put another needle—a cannula —in your arm and tape it there, Marla, as a precaution, but I think you're improving every second.'

The cannula slid in easily. Always a relief.

'Like I said, this is only a precaution,' she said to the

dazed woman, 'in case you need further medication or intravenous fluids.' But within herself, Kiki thought the response appeared adequate from the initial dose—often the way—and it seemed the crisis was over.

She felt the trolley being manoeuvred in beside her and Stefano stood up.

He said, 'Please take my towelling robe,' and handed it to Kiki to cover the patient with.

Her nod of appreciation wasn't only for the gown for Marla, but because with him gone there seemed so much more air around the patient—and herself—more distance. Funny, that, and funny that she wasn't in the mood for laughing.

She had always had a respiratory awareness of him— like her own damned anaphylaxis—but she'd thought herself desensitised against that response after what she'd been through. Later, on her own, she would worry about that.

'Hi, Will.' Kiki glanced at the senior ship's doctor as he knelt down beside her. 'This is Marla. Severe reaction to latex. We've removed the causative agent.' She flicked an ironic glance at Stefano before she turned back to her boss.

Dr Wilhelm Hobson leaned over and took the woman's wrist to feel her pulse. 'You've given adrenalin?'

'Two minutes ago.' Kiki finished taping the intravenous cannula in place.

Marla groaned and opened her eyes more positively. 'Where am I?'

'It's okay, Marla. You're in your cabin. Just close your eyes and rest. You'll feel better soon.' She rested her hand over Marla's in sympathy. She and Wilhelm looked at the welts on her arms that seemed to be fading before their eyes. 'Good response, as you see.'

Will nodded, then wrote the pulse-rate, dose and time

down on his scribe sheet while Kiki took the blood pressure cuff from the nurse and wrapped it around Marla's arm. As expected, the pressure was very low.

'In shock.' The nurse nodded as she adhered cardiac dots to the patient's skin and the sound of a racing heartbeat permeated the room. They began to assemble an intravenous line to increase the pressure in Marla's blood vessels with an extra fluid bolus.

Confident now that their patient was stable, Will stood up and faced the two men in the room. *This'll be good,* Kiki thought, and though she didn't look away from her patient her ears were tuned for their explanation.

'And who is responsible for this woman?' Wilhelm's tone was deadly serious. But then he was serious most of the time.

Stefano had watched Marla wake up with relief and now he refocused on the room. Kiki, down on the floor with Marla, ignored him—as she should. He glanced at the man in charge—a stocky blond-headed man with a South African accent and air of command. A ship this size would need a competent senior. One who knew how to be discreet.

Then he looked to Theros. His brother stood, twisting his hands across his body, suddenly aware that he looked strange in those ridiculous shorts. His mouth worked but, as usual in times of stress, nothing came out.

Stefano sighed and stepped forward. Of course he was responsible. He had been since the moment of Theros's accident all those years ago. It did not occur to *him* to feel vulnerable, dressed only in swim-trunks, and he glanced coolly at the medic. 'I am.'

Kiki flinched when she heard Stefano's voice and realised she'd hoped otherwise. It shouldn't have mattered. Didn't matter. She'd always expected him to be more than he really was. A prince who lied and made promises he didn't keep.

She didn't wait to hear the rest. 'Okay, Ginger,' she said to the nurse. 'Let's help Marla up onto the trolley and we'll take her down to the hospital for observation.'

Fifteen minutes later Stefano paced in front of the window in his brother's suite. 'Please get rid of those ridiculous shorts,' he said. Stefano moved very slowly, with rigid control, frustrated at his brother's propensity for disaster and his own for not preventing it—and at the fruitless urge to ask why he had to deal with this. He knew why.

At seven Stefano had pulled Theros from a deep ocean pool on their island and saved his life with a boy's rough and ready resuscitation. Unfortunately Theros had been left with an injury to part of his brain from its time without oxygen. After that Stefano's young brother had not been the most sensible of boys, and later had become a handsome and lovable but childish man.

But that had not stopped Theros from diving into mischief and danger whenever he could, and as often as he was able Stefano would be the one to rescue him.

'Trouble. It will find you in the dark. Or in this case broad daylight. Is sex so tedious with your wife that you must risk her life with latex?'

Theros wrung his hands. 'No. *No*. One of her friends gave the suits to us for her birthday... We were playing. Laughing. Suddenly she could not breathe. I did not know Marla was allergic to rubber.'

'Latex.' Stefano squeezed the skin under his nose with his fingers in a pincer grip to stop himself from losing patience. He never lost patience with Theros. His father had been right to say that if only he, Stefano, had been faster at getting help perhaps his brother's brain would not have been damaged.

It was a legacy of guilt he could not shake. The job of protecting the family and Theros from ridicule had fallen to Stefano, and he had protected his brother well for many years—because he'd been willing to take up the mantle and carry it regardless of the impact on his own life.

His foray into medicine—the vocation that should have been Theros's—had stemmed from that guilt, from his father's distress and disappointment, and from his own lack of ability to prevent such a sequela for his brother. Even at such a young age he had vowed if such a situation ever arose again he would know what to do. Unexpectedly, medicine had also provided a true vocation, and something that soothed his soul.

His father, Crown Prince Paulo III of Aspelicus, had hired a sensible woman to supervise Theros while Stefano had been away at a medical symposium in Australia earlier that year, and to everyone's surprise his simple little brother had found true love.

At his father's urgent request Stefano had rushed home from the arms of Dr Kiki Fender—but too late.

Theros had already eloped. Then Stefano himself had been involved in a serious motor vehicle accident, and during his slow recovery months had passed.

To his unexpected relief Theros's sensible wife had proved helpful in steering Theros on a more stable path, but even the most sensible could make an unfortunate mistake. So any notion of Stefano being released from his duty of care was a misconception. Theros would always need him, and he could offer no life to a vibrant and intelligent woman like Kiki, who was not accustomed to the strictures of royal duty.

In the harsh light of reality he knew that as heir to the

throne he should let go of what had passed between he and Dr Fender in Australia. That was for the best.

But it seemed she had not forgiven him for his failure to return.

Theros coughed and Stefano returned to the present. His brother still waited for reassurance.

He took his fingers from his face and stared at Theros so he could be sure he was listening. Perhaps even absorbing the gravity of the situation.

'Marla could have died. Almost did.' He paused, let that settle in. 'One of you must carry an injection, similar to that which the doctor had, in case she is exposed to this product again accidentally.' He stared hard. 'You are her husband and it is your duty to keep her safe. Do you understand?'

'Yes, Stefano.' Theros chewed his lip. 'The doctor said she would be all right, though? They'll let her out of the hospital this afternoon?'

Not surprisingly, Theros had an irrational fear of hospitals—which hadn't been helped when Stefano had nearly died.

Stefano saw that fear, and his irritation with his brother seeped further away. His voice gentled. 'For the moment the danger is gone. Yes.'

Theros climbed into his swim-trunks and sadly handed Stefano his latex briefs. 'And she will be fine tomorrow, won't she? We're going to Naples to climb Vesuvius. You're coming with us.'

'My leg is a little painful.' Why must his brother love adventures that required exposure to the public? It would be so much easier on the island of Aspelicus, their island home off mainland Greece, and he had so many things that required his attention there. But his father had asked him to watch over them on this short cruise that Theros had promised his wife.

Ashore, his man could be with them. And while they were touring it would be a good time for him, Stefano, to reacquaint himself with Dr Fender.

After finding Kiki where he least expected her, he had pressing matters to attend to. First an apology for his non-return. Past ghosts to lay.

The problem was that the woman he'd left behind in Australia had stayed like a halo around his heart. He, of all people, knew it wasn't sensible to desire a woman who did not understand or deserve the ways of royal commitment. As heir, in his country's crises *he* was the one who was called.

But still he smarted from the thinly veiled contempt in her sea-blue eyes, because he remembered the warmly passionate, fun-loving side of sweet Kiki.

The gods must be laughing at this insult to his pride. If they had been destined to meet again this was not how he would have orchestrated the moment.

Less than an hour ago—still achingly beautiful, yet transformed—she'd hated him.

She'd always been confident, sassy, and so different from the women he was usually introduced to. Of course he'd been recklessly drawn to the young doctor during his Sydney study tour to promote ground-breaking surgery at his small hospital. What a week *that* had been.

He would admit he had not behaved thoughtfully during their intense time together. Neither of them had. Everything had progressed far too quickly. They'd immersed themselves in each other for a torrid affair of incredible closeness, tucked away from the world in her tiny flat when they weren't at the hospital.

Until another crisis created by the man in front of him

had required his immediate presence on Aspelicus and he had left her bed and flown out that same night.

He had spent the last few months recovering from his own accident—months of rehabilitation after he'd almost lost his leg. He'd barely been able to look at himself in the mirror, let alone consider showing himself to a woman.

But that excuse had gone now and his treatment of Kiki Fender had recently made him feel ashamed. It was another burden of guilt he found he could not move on from, because it had taken him almost five months before he was able to rule his own life again. A loss of control he never wanted to experience again.

By the time he had begun to search for her, at least to attempt an explanation, she'd been untraceable.

At first he had tried the hospital in Sydney, then her home phone, mail to her old lodgings. He did not know her friends or family. She had disappeared without a trace. Ironically to this very ship.

Tomorrow he would finish this and then fulfil his destiny for his country. Seek her forgiveness, allow himself to let go, and move on to secure the succession.

But for the moment his man-boy brother needed reassurance. Theros was playing with the legs of the latex suit he'd found under the chair and Stefano reached out and took them from him gently. 'Manos will drive you to Vesuvius.'

'Oh, good. And Marla will come.'

Theros looked childishly happy and Stefano supposed it was good that *someone* was pleased.

Later that afternoon, in the ship's medical centre ten floors below the royal suite, Dr Hobson was ready to discharge Marla.

'You can go back to your suite.' Kiki helped her sit up.

'Your observations are fine, and will stay that way if you stay away from latex.'

Poor Marla blushed again. 'No more birthday gifts that almost end it all!'

'It was just bad luck.' There was a lot of that around at the moment. Kiki grimaced with her. 'Allergies can be to anything. It could have been peanuts.'

Marla smiled. 'I'm supposed to be the sensible one. But thanks for that.'

'Hey, it was your birthday.' Kiki grinned back. 'At least now you know latex sets up a reaction in your body and you can make sure that if you ever go into hospital the staff keep you latex-free.'

The young woman nodded and stared down at the little Epi-pen in her hand.

'And be careful with that.' Kiki smiled. 'You can get into trouble if you inject it in the wrong place.'

Maria nodded.

'True,' Will said helpfully. 'I saw a man once who injected it into his thumb trying to work the plunger. It's a powerful drug and it shuts down the peripheral blood flow. His thumb fell off with gangrene.'

Kiki's eyes widened as she helped Marla up. 'Imagine what a disgruntled wife could do?'

The senior medic held out his hands in horror. 'That's true. Don't go there.'

Kiki shook her head in amusement, because Wilhelm's seriousness always cracked her up. 'Is he scaring you, Marla?'

'Only because of my husband.' The girl laughed and shook her head. 'I will not let Theros near it. I truly can be sensible.'

'Not too sensible.' Kiki smiled. 'Still have a great birthday. It's such a shame this has marred your holiday.'

Kiki couldn't help but think that Marla wasn't the only one whose voyage had been affected. And this week of all weeks, when her emotions were already on a rollercoaster. Bummer. Bummer. *Bummer.*

Usually fair-minded, Kiki guessed she owed Stefano an apology—but it wasn't going to happen. She still didn't get why he was on his brother's holiday as his minder—on *her* ship—and was finding it hard to forget that somewhere above her head was the man she'd accepted she'd never see again.

She glanced at the ceiling above her head. Up there, larger than life and twice as disconcerting—because she might not have agreed to dress in latex for him, like Marla had for Theros, but she'd been just as weak, losing her common sense in the sensual haze they'd created together.

And as for her less than flattering thoughts of him earlier—well, he could jump off the owner's suite balcony before she'd apologise.

Ginger's offer to escort Marla to the suite was jumped on with enthusiasm. No way was Kiki going back up there. Because during the long weeks while she'd waited for his promised return, during the phone calls when she'd tried to contact him after she'd discovered she was pregnant, it had been too shameful.

There had been an unexpected lowness of her spirits when he hadn't called, and she'd been so sick and weak, barely able to function in early pregnancy, that she hadn't been able to motivate herself to do anything more about it.

By the time the first trimester had been over and she'd begun to feel more like herself again Kiki had accepted that Stefano wasn't coming back. He had clearly decided his royal status meant she wasn't good enough for him to follow up. Well, she and her baby didn't need him. All her life she'd been independent—the youngest sister to three brilliant sisters who didn't need her, with her doctor parents who were busy. The only person she'd felt connected to had been her big brother Nick. And briefly Stefano. But soon she'd have her baby and they would be a team. She couldn't wait.

But at eighteen weeks, when she'd already begun to create a nursery of tiny clothes and softest wraps, the pains had come and suddenly her baby was gone. Soon her baby's due date would pass and she would finally be able to move on. She'd promised herself.

The best thing she'd done was to come here to heal and move on to a new life.

Wilhelm wandered back into the main office. 'Marla seems very sweet.'

'She does.' Kiki blinked and came back to the present.

'Embarrassing for our royal guests, though.'

'Mortifying.' Kiki raised a smile. 'I bet her brother-in-law hated that!'

Even in the brief time they'd been together Stefano's avoidance of the whole topic of his royalty and his absolute hatred of the press had been obvious. At the time it had seemed sensible—she knew little of the life of a minor royal, which was the impression of himself he'd left her with. Not that she'd even thought about it much when they were together. As a man he'd been able to help her forget the world.

She dragged her mind back to Marla and Theros. 'It's Marla's birthday. They've been married less than a year. And Theros wanted to holiday on a cruise ship instead of their island like most of the family do.'

Will shrugged. 'So why is his brother here? Heir to the throne and all that. A bit high-powered for a minder, don't you think.'

Kiki tried for a careless shrug. 'Family name is very

important to everyone, so I imagine in a royal family it would be more so.' She wasn't sure who she was trying to convince—Will or herself. 'Apparently Marla's husband has bad luck with the press.'

'Bad luck, eh?' Will raised his brows as he waved Ginger off duty on her return and shut the clinic door.

Kiki picked up her bag, but he put his hand up to stop her.

'One sec.'

She paused, looked back, and her stomach sank. She'd been afraid of this.

Will scratched his head. 'So what's going on between you two?'

'Which two?' She'd hoped nothing had been noticed. Nothing had been said. She hadn't even looked at Stefano as they'd wheeled Marla out.

Will waited patiently and Kiki felt the blush heat her cheeks. The silence stretched and she didn't like silence. That was her only excuse for being unable to extricate herself. 'You mean me and Theros's brother? Nothing.' How the heck had Wilhelm sensed that? 'I don't know what you mean.'

She switched off a computer she'd thankfully missed at shut-down. An excuse to turn away.

But the flood of memories she'd been holding back all day rose like a wave in her throat. Such rotten timing. She concentrated on her feet, firmly planted on the deck. She was *not* going under. Control re-established, she turned back to Will, who tilted his head and went on.

'Come on. I may be a bit oblivious sometimes, but the air was thick between you two and the guy was watching your neck like Dracula on a diet. Nick didn't mention you knew any royalty?'

Because she'd told no one about her stupidity—not even

5745543

her closest sibling, and definitely not any of her sisters. 'Nick has nothing to do with this.' Because her brother Nick would be out for Stefano's blood if he knew what the Prince had done to his little sister. 'Stefano is a surgical consultant I worked with him briefly in Sydney during my last rotation.'

'You worked with a *prince*?'

Will looked even more interested, not less, and Kiki could feel the walls of the little clinic begin to close in on her. She didn't want to think about that time with Stefano, let alone talk about it, but her South African colleague could miss the obvious sometimes.

He proved it. 'So what happened?'

'That's all there is.' To her horror her eyes filled with tears. Not because of Stefano, but at the thought of the sadness that had been building for this past week.

'Hey. I've upset you.' Will shook his head. 'Sorry. I just want you to know I'm here to listen if you need an ear.' He raised his hands in defence. 'I promised Nick I'd look out for you.'

Don't mention this to Nick. But if she said it out loud it would be the first thing he'd do. 'I'm a big girl, Will. I don't want to talk about it. Don't need to talk about it.'

Even she could hear the over-reaction. She sighed. Too vehement.

She turned away to wipe at the tear that had slid out against her will. 'Sorry—water under the bridge, that's all.'

'Well, if he gives you a hard time just let me know,' Will said gruffly, and she nodded and fled.

CHAPTER TWO

WHEN KIKI FINALLY fell asleep that night her dreams were filled with the sensation of being lost and alone, and always in the distance was Stefano, turned the other way and choosing not to see her.

When she woke she had tears on her cheeks, and despite the sun streaming in she was so exhausted she wanted to roll over and bury her head. Her shift didn't start until eleven but she wouldn't get back to sleep.

Through the open window she could hear the mooring crew as they secured the ship to the wharf in Naples, and she lay on her bunk and felt the ship creak and strain against its ropes.

And that made her think of yesterday's latex session gone wrong.

Unwillingly, she felt her lips curve—which wasn't a bad thing considering the night—and she knew at some stage she would have to share the story—names changed to protect the innocent—with her closest sibling. Nick would certainly enjoy the sense of the ridiculous.

She still didn't get why Stefano was on his brother's holiday.

From the brief mention Stefano had made of Aspelicus, Kiki gathered the island, once home to an ancient Greek school of physicians, a splinter school similar to the one on the more southern island of Asclepius, was a beautiful cliff-edged principality, with a harbour originally on the trade routes as a safe haven.

She'd spent hours online and discovered it had grown more Italian and French since its Greek heritage, and that its royal family were far more famous than she'd realised.

She'd been a fool. Of *course* Stefano had not returned for a brief fling he'd once had in the Antipodes.

His family had developed a stronghold in spices and teas from China, and the tiny monarchy had become incredibly wealthy. Now it was thriving on the sale of gourmet olive oil from the trees that dotted the hills, its cash flow supplemented by high-roller casinos and its own world-famous horse race along the lines of neighbouring Monaco's, which had its Grand Prix, and a borrowed idea from its neighbour to become a tax haven for residents.

On the other side of the island a sprawling low-rise hospital had gained international recognition for reconstructive surgery, with Stefano as its director.

The royal family could be traced back a thousand years, but somewhere each generation held a physician who had been available for the poorer people, as well as those who could pay.

It had all sounded incredibly romantic even from the few facts Stefano had shared with her.

She had waited for him to return.

But he hadn't.

She could remember as if it were yesterday when she'd applied for the job on the *Sea Goddess*, her brother's old ship.

Kiki had always idolised her gorgeous, crazy showman of a big brother—the only one of her high-achieving siblings who understood her.

She never had found out what had precipitated Nick's escape from reality but for herself it was wanting something totally different from the empty nursery she'd created for a child that would never come.

She'd never shared her loss with anyone. She hadn't been able to share with the absent Stefano, and she'd thought an ordinary cruise ship the last place she would find him and reopen wounds.

Unlike her older sisters, Nick had seen she wasn't herself and cheered her on. So she'd started on the hospitality side of the ship, which had forced her to return to her usual outgoing self, the person she'd lost for a while, and she'd even started to forgive the male of the species, to laugh with Nick's friend Miko and the waiters.

Until she'd begun to miss medicine.

When the opportunity had come she'd switched roles, and the last three months had been good under Wilhelm's guidance in the ship's hospital.

It had all been fine—*until now.*

Maybe it was time to find her real calling. Hiding from the world had proved fruitless. But why couldn't this have happened next week, when she just knew she'd be stronger? She sighed.

Stefano was here and there was nothing she could do about that. It was time to move on. She'd go and see Will and ask how hard it would be for her to be replaced.

With that thought crystallising in her mind, Kiki rose from her bed and walked to the window with new purpose.

She'd put her notice in and leave as soon as they found someone to take her place.

There were still the next four nights to get through, but she'd manage that if she had a plan. She'd foolishly succumbed to ridiculous attraction last time he'd entered her orbit and that would not happen again.

* * *

Stefano woke with purpose. Today he would deal with what he should have dealt with months ago. Laying this admittedly delectable ghost was well overdue.

He'd discovered the opening times of the ship's hospital and by the time Theros and Marla had left for their day-trip the clinic was almost due to close, which suited him perfectly.

He descended the stairs almost at a jog—foolish when his hip would kill him later, and he reminded himself it was not fitting to appear too eager.

The nurse greeted him with a smile. She was the same one he'd seen yesterday, and he inclined his head at the obvious approval he read in her face. She was a handsome woman, of the type he'd used to dally with a lifetime ago, but, like a stamp on the front page of his passport, no matter where he was, Kiki had dampened any desire on his part to consort with other women.

'I wish to see Dr Fender. I am Stefano Mykonides.'

'Of course, Your Highness, I know who you are.' She smiled at him coyly, fiddled excitedly with her collar, and blushed.

Stefano smiled back blandly, curbed his impatience as the woman went on.

'But Dr Fender isn't on duty until later this morning.'

A door across the waiting room opened and the senior doctor ushered his patient out.

As the young boy and his mother walked past them the nurse said, 'Perhaps Dr Hobson?'

'No.' Stefano inclined his head at the doctor, but before he could leave Hobson crossed the room and held out his hand. They shook hands briefly.

'Ah, Your Highness. Good morning.' He turned to the

nurse. 'Can you run those blood samples up to the courier, please?'

He turned back to Stefano. 'I hope all is well with your sister-in-law this morning?'

Stefano tried not to show his irritation, but he was trapped. And where was his quarry if not here? 'Yes. Thank you.' He was over discussing Theros's disasters.

Hobson glanced at his watch. 'How can we help you?'

Stefano picked up nuances and wondered why this man felt Kiki needed protection. From him. 'I had hoped to thank Dr Fender personally, for her timely assistance yesterday. I did not have the opportunity at the time, of course.'

'Of course.'

Hobson smiled non-committally and Stefano felt like gritting his teeth.

'I could convey your appreciation?'

Very pointed, Stefano thought, but he held his temper. 'Thank you, but I wish to do so myself. I will return at another time.'

Hobson didn't shift. 'I'll let her know.'

Stefano could see that the good doctor was in protection mode. He wondered just what kind of personal relationship he had with Kiki and had to admit he disliked the idea very strongly. His hand tightened on the room card in his pocket. The card bent. Disliked very strongly. He examined the doctor more closely. He was a well-muscled man, almost as tall as himself, and no doubt attractive to women.

He tested the water. 'Or I could surprise her.'

Hobson's smile appeared frozen on his face. 'I think she has had enough surprises.'

Stefano had to give the man respect. Loyalty was a good thing, and despite his own misgivings he could not grudge Kiki her friend's championship. Though his cousin, who owed Stefano many favours, *did* own this shipping line.

His fingers loosened. *Relax. Let it go.* He, too, cared that Kiki was not upset. 'It is not my intention to distress her.'

Hobson met his gaze head-on. 'Good.'

Enough. His day had soured and the pain in his hip from his reckless descent down the stairs was annoying him. 'And good day to you, Dr Hobson.'

Stefano pressed the button for the lift with remarkable restraint, not stupid enough to brave an ascent of twelve floors despite his sudden frustrated desire for explosive energy. The lift doors opened and, as if conjured, Kiki stood waiting to alight.

'Just the person.' Wonderful how good humour could be instantly restored. 'One moment, please, Dr Fender.' He could not believe his good luck—finally—and gestured for her to wait. With a relief he was careful not to show he stepped in beside her as she hesitated.

Kiki couldn't believe her bad luck. So close to being safe. 'What if I was on my way to work?'

He shrugged those shoulders that still made her weak at the knees. Damn him. It was so hard to not to stare and just remember.

'I have been told you are not working for a few hours.'

His voice always had made her mouth dry, and now was no exception. What was the scientific reason for that? She searched a little desperately for distraction as she watched him press the lift button for the sixteenth floor.

Of course he had looked for her in the hospital. If only she hadn't run down for a quick chat with Will.

The doors began to close and for a moment she did consider diving out before the doors shut, like some female secret agent with a barrel roll in her repertoire—but she'd just look awkward, and probably get sandwiched by the doors.

Or, a hundred times worse, he'd put out his hand and touch her, and she wanted to avoid that at all costs. That was what had happened the first time. He'd laid his hand on her arm to help her from the car and she'd woken up in bed with him. And stayed there for a week.

That left the smart mouth as her only defence. 'So where are we going?' As if she didn't know.

He didn't reply, and she remembered that. The frustrating habits of a man used to answering questions he felt inclined to and ignoring the rest. A prince with his own agenda unless it was for his family. Lucky him.

She stared straight ahead at the doors of the lift as if they'd magically open and she could float out to safety somewhere in the stairwell. She could feel his eyes on her.

'Why are you on this ship anyway, Your Highness?'

She heard him sigh. 'Do you call me that to annoy me?'

Now she glanced at him. Sugared her voice. 'Is it working?'

He looked at her from under his own raised brows, and then in the ultimate retaliation he smiled. Blinded, she felt it rip open the wound she'd healed so diligently over the last months aboard ship. *Blast, blast and double blast.* She needed to get away.

She'd fallen in lust with him the first time she'd seen him. Only lust. Love wouldn't have ended as it had.

Stefano had smiled at her then, as if they shared a secret, when she'd been late for her last surgical day in the operating theatres because of car trouble. He'd been a guest consultant of her boss, and should have chastised her like all the other consultants would have done, but instead he'd shown her surgical techniques she'd never thought to witness.

Later, he'd bought her coffee, plied her with cake to replace her missed breakfast, and invited her to ride home with him at the end of the day. When his hand had touched hers she'd been stunned like a landed fish, all big glassy eyes and floppy with desire.

And she knew where that had led.

The flicker of the number lights speeding upwards brought her back to the present and her sense of impending danger grew exponentially. This wasn't sensible. Or safe. Though she wasn't sure who she was more afraid of. Him or herself.

'I don't want to go anywhere with you.'

She thought for a moment she'd actually hurt him. There was just a flicker behind his eyes... But that was a joke. Instead he sighed as if she were a troublesome child, or probably just a troublesome subject.

'I will not keep you long.'

'Well, I know *that*.'

This time he did flinch. She saw it. Good, he felt guilty—even though he didn't know how guilty he *should* feel. But she was tired of scoring points or second-guessing his intentions. She just wanted to forget she'd seen him again and re-grow the scar tissue so she could complete her healing.

When the lift stopped she planted her feet more solidly on the spot. He waited for her to pass him and when she didn't lifted his hand to direct her. She stepped out of his way and back against the wall so fast his hand fell.

'No.' She licked dry lips. 'Goodbye, Prince Stefano. Have a good life.'

There. She'd said it. What she hadn't had a chance to say nine months ago. Now it was done. Finished.

Except he didn't get out, and the silence lengthened.

Without direction from them the lift doors shut and the chamber began its descent to another level.

His voice was mild. Slightly amused. 'So, are we to ride up and down in the lift all day until you wish to get out?'

She stepped further to the left of him. 'Leave me alone, Stefano.'

He didn't lift his hand again, but his voice reached out to her. She tried to imagine a soft ball of cotton wool jamming her ears to mute the sound—it didn't work.

'Is a few minutes of your time so much to ask? A chance to apologise, explain a little, and then we may part as friends—or less, if that is what you wish.'

She didn't know how much more of this power struggle she could take before those damn tears she could feel prickling behind her eyes made their escape.

She could get out on another floor, stride away, and then spend the day dreading what could be over in a few minutes if she just faced it. Over and done with. Great theory, but what if it wasn't? She still wasn't sure who she trusted least.

The silence lengthened. The lift stopped and began to go down further. 'For goodness' sake. Must you get your own way in everything?' She stepped forward and stabbed the light for the sixteenth floor. The little button rattled with the force. 'Get it over with.' The lift whooshed upwards again.

Stefano winced. This was not how he had expected it would turn out. A polite thank-you, a question as to whether she was well, an apology because he had had to leave so abruptly the last time they'd been together, and—most importantly—he would see that he was not as attracted to the flesh and blood woman as his imagination had assured him. Then he could move on to his duty.

In fact, to his discomfort, the desire for Kiki back in his arms, and most assuredly in his bed, was growing stronger by the second.

Perhaps he should have stepped out of the lift on

his own after all. But how was that going to help his predicament?

The lift doors opened again and he extended his arm against the doors to hold them. 'After you.'

'Are you? Not again, I hope,' she muttered, and he had to bite back the smile.

This was the woman who had captured his attention over that long-ago week. With her tiny rebellions that always startled him out of his self-assurance, the rapier wit that amused him with its irreverence, the unpredictability of Kiki with the crazy name and so alluring body.

He was in trouble. But, then again, so was she.

CHAPTER THREE

KIKI PRECEDED HIM into the suite and glanced around. Very grand. Split level. She hadn't noticed much yesterday—too many other things had been going on. Like a woman critical with shock. Like Stefano reappearing beside her. Like a hundred memories she didn't want to remember.

She kept her back to him. 'Must be cosy, sharing with a married couple.'

'Their suite is very similar. Next door.' Kiki could hear the smile in his voice. The lock clicked. 'This is mine.'

Why did she feel there was emphasis on 'mine'? She squared her shoulders and faced him. Why did he have to look so damned amazing. 'So let's have our little conversation and then I'd like to leave.'

He ignored that. The ignoring thing again. He prowled over to the drinks cabinet. Turned to face her and asked mildly, as if they did this every day, 'Would you like something to drink?'

No, but she wouldn't mind something in her hand she could fiddle with—or throw in defence.

Kiki circled the plush sofa and sat on an upright armchair. 'Thank you. Soda water.'

He smiled. 'You were always so confident.'

She ground her teeth. 'Until I met you and thought the sun shone out of your tailbone.'

Of course he ignored that too. 'You always had fire when roused.' They both heard the echo of a similar word. Was that *a*roused?

He held out her drink and she took it carefully, so as not to touch his hand. Again his gaze met hers and she looked away. Knew his gaze never left her face. She could tell even with her fierce concentration on her glass.

His voice drifted over her like a wraith, encircling her, pulling tighter. 'But still there is more. Yesterday you were incredibly efficient. Practised. Calm. Capable. All things I knew you would be.'

She didn't want to hear this. She wanted out. 'Why don't you cut to the chase, Stefano? Why are you here on this ship?' And, more to the point, 'Why am I here in your suite?'

He stepped closer. 'The truth?'

She shrugged, trying hard to disguise the fact she was getting more spooked by the minute. 'Novel idea, I know.'

He came to stand in front of her chair. 'I could not forget you.'

'Spare me.' *Please don't say that,* she pleaded mentally. 'It took you nine months to figure that out?' She winced. Unobtrusively she eased back in the seat to create a little more space. Now she could inhale his aftershave, just a wisp, and it was true: the sense of smell was the one true memory.

He looked down. Apparently sincere. 'I did search for you.'

'Then you're not very good at it, are you?' She'd still been in the same flat for the next five months. Waiting. Hoping he'd at least call back. Until she'd woke up to reality. 'Tell me. When did this fictitious search occur?'

Thankfully he stepped across to the window that looked out from the stern of the ship and she could breathe again. The glorious picture window framed the blue of the ocean, the trail of the wash from their ship, and the haze of land off to the east. And the outline of Stefano's magnificent frame.

'It was many months before I could begin. Only now, through chance,' he added more thoughtfully, 'or fate, have I found your whereabouts…'

He'd waited *months*! Not in a hurry to find her, then. Four weeks after he'd left she'd discovered she was pregnant. Another fourteen weeks and she'd been desperate for him to call so she could share her confusion, share her joy at the promise of finally feeling as if she belonged to someone, share her fears and hopes with the father of her child. Instead she had been completely alone.

But not as alone as she'd been when her baby had slipped away one silent night. The doctor had said her baby had a cardiac malfunction, a missing part so the growth could not progress, and she had accepted that— with grief, like the lacking in the relationship it had come from. The grief had been worse because in the beginning she had been ambivalent about its coming. Had thought more of the complications than of her own child until it had been too late for fierce regrets.

And the due date was next week.

The ever-present ache squeezed in her heart. It was time to go before her control let her down. 'Great. Thanks for that.' She stood, glanced at him up and down. 'You look well. Don't seem to be pining. I think you'll survive.'

He stepped back into her comfort zone. 'Is Hobson your lover?'

They were standing chest to chest, a pulsing fission of air between then, and she almost missed the question.

What? Where did this guy get off? But stoking up her anger was a good idea. Much better than sadness. Anger made her feel less trapped. Less baited by his need for control at this moment. Less weak.

Flippantly, with an airy wave of her hand, she said, 'He's one of them.'

The flare in his eyes stunned her.

'Then his position has become vacant.'

She blinked. 'Don't be ridiculous.' She sat down again in shock. Any other man and she'd think he was joking. 'You can't do that.' Wrong thing to say. She knew it as soon as it was out of her mouth.

He didn't even have to say it out loud. Of *course* he could do it. The power of the Mykonides in the Mediterranean had never been in doubt.

Her turn to back-pedal. She'd suspected he had this side, had just never been shown it before. 'Of course Will's not my lover.'

Stefano cursed his temper, something he usually had an iron control over, and wheeled away to look over the sea again. The sea was unpredictable today, like his feelings for Kiki, and just as dangerous. More bad behaviour on his part. But despite that he felt his shoulders relax a little. He had not believed Hobson was her lover, but the concept had been gnawing at him since his visit to the ship's hospital this morning.

So what else had she said that was not true. 'Is there a man in your life at the moment?' He could feel the beast within him stir at the thought, and it didn't escape his notice that he had no right to ask such a thing.

She opened her eyes wide. 'Is there a man in yours?'

Little witch. 'Why are you baiting me?'

She glared back at him. 'Because apologies and good wishes haven't appeared on the menu and that was what I was promised.'

She had a point. And again he was behaving badly.

Why did this happen with the woman he wanted to liaise honourably with?

He paced and came to stop in front of her. 'I sincerely apologise for leaving without explaining my reasons.'

She nodded. 'And the phone calls you didn't return?'

Those he could not remember? 'I did not get them.'

'Perhaps not.' Her tone said she didn't care any more and she put her glass down. 'I accept your apology. Thank you for my drink.' It was untouched.

So that was that. The degree of disappointment seemed out of proportion to what he'd expected. The wall between them was too great for them to part amicably but his expectations had been optimistic. At least he knew where he stood. It was time to move on. To duty.

She stood again. 'Goodbye, Stefano.'

But as she passed him his hand reached out of its own volition and captured her wrist. Her skin was soft and supple and so fragile. She froze and lifted her eyes to him. Limpid pools. He'd forgotten how her emotions changed their colour from brilliant blue to dark violet when she was aroused. Or angry. Which was it?

His thumb stroked the pulse on the underside of her wrist. 'Dine with me. Tonight.'

'No.' She tugged in slow motion, as if already unsure if she wanted release or not.

'Tomorrow?' He stared into deepening violet and between them the fire flickered and stirred and the wraith encircled them both.

'I'm working.' Almost a whisper.

He stroked her wrist again. 'Then it must be tonight.'

Huskily, With another brush of her tongue over her lips, she said 'What part of no don't you understand?'

But for Kiki it was too late. Too, too late. He'd touched her.

His hand held her wrist, his skin was on hers, and the

two receptors were communicating, entwining in their own matrix of reality. The warmth crept up her body, wrapped around her in tendrils of mist, and in slow motion he drew her forward. Subconsciously she swayed like a reed towards him.

His other hand came up and tenderly brushed the hair out of her eyes. 'You have grown even more beautiful.'

With worship his fingers slid across her cheek and along her jaw as his mouth came down, and she could do nothing but turn her face into his palm and then upwards. To wait.

As he had with their first kiss he took her breath, inhaled her soul as she did his, and the sometimes comical, sometimes cruel world disappeared.

Her hands crept up around his neck and his hands slid down, until he cupped her buttocks and pulled her in hard against him. With the taste of his lips on hers, she could feel all of him, rock-solid against her, familiar, and then his mouth recaptured hers in the way only Stefano's could.

She moaned against his lips, her mind blank in the thick sensuality only he could create. She forgot all her intentions, all her reservations, and when he lifted her shirt, swept it over her head, sighed at her lace-covered breasts, she gazed up in a sensual mist of buried memories at the man she'd dreamt about last night.

He carried her across the room and she hooked her legs around his hips. Her mouth was on his, starving for the fuel of life she'd missed, as they went up the stairs to the loft bedroom in a haze of heat and hunger and primitive surrender.

The fog parted briefly as he lay her down, stripped off his own shirt. She could see the muscled perfection of his chest, the fine sprinkling of dark hairs and the nipples erect with his desire. Quickly he protected them both. And before her brain could function sensibly he was beside her, stroking, murmuring his delight, kissing her mouth as if he would never stop, and she was lost again despite the insistent whisper that warned she would taste remorse later.

She felt a long ridge of unfamiliar scarring on his thigh, a myriad of smaller ones, and her hand stilled. But he swept her up again before she could investigate further and the moment was lost in the maelstrom.

Stefano felt the swell in his chest, the furnace of desire for this slip of a woman who, until he touched her, could hold her own. Then she was his. He sensed it. Tasted the victory he hadn't known he burned for until it was upon him.

Clothes had fallen away, skin melted into skin, and heat seared between them as they reacquainted, shifted, joined. Together they cried out, until the sound died in the little death and she lay beneath him, limp and spent in his arms.

Then he moved again, slowly, savouring every tiny moment, every gentle trail across pearl-coloured skin, every cupping of mounds and exploration of hollows. And always he returned to her mouth, her honeyed mouth that he could never have enough of, until the beat grew faster, the hunger more desperate, the climax more shattering, and again they collapsed.

Replete for now, in awe, still confused by the speed and urgency that had carried them both, he lay back with his arm under her, hugged her close, smiling and sated.

For the moment.

Until the drop of a tear landed on his bicep.

'You are crying?' Stefano felt the dagger of shame and turned to see her face. Kiss her hand. 'I have hurt you. God, no. I am a beast.'

Kiki was in shock. She'd done it again. One touch and she'd lost all will. How could that be? She was no young and foolish teenager, swept off her feet by a handsome man. She knew what he could do. Had wept buckets at his hands before. If she didn't get out now she would lose what shreds of self-respect she could gather from the clothes strewn around the floor.

'I have lint in my eye. It's okay.' She eased out from under his hand and inched to the edge of the bed.

He sat up, the sheet falling from his chest, his hand out. 'Let me help you.'

'No.' It was sharp and panicked, and she tried again in a calmer voice. 'No. Thank you. One moment.'

A plan. She had no plan except to escape. Not to let him touch her again. Her feet touched the floor and she scooped up her underwear on her way down to the bathroom, padding down the stairs in bare feet to where her shirt lay at the bottom of the steps like an abandoned child. She scooped it up. Hopped on one leg as she slipped on her panties.

God. What had she done? How had it happened? At least he had used protection—but then they had done that last time. She would get a morning-after pill. Make sure.

All stupid thoughts when really she should be worried about escape and remaining undetected by a ship full of people who knew her. She opened and closed the bathroom door noisily, yet didn't go in. Instead she hurriedly pulled on her bra and her shirt and slipped out through the door as soon as she was dressed.

Outside she pulled on her sandals and smoothed her clothes. To top everything off if somebody saw her leave the suite of a passenger her job would go. And she was due at work in an hour.

On the crew level she passed Miko, her friend from her first early days on the ship, when she'd been more than a little lost. He was another of her brother's confidants, and the restaurant manager on the *Sea Goddess*.

She ran her fingers through her hair. *Nooooo*, she must look a sight. Miko raised his eyebrows, smiled sardonically, and walked on without saying a word. Did she look like a woman who had just left a man's bed? Kiki hurried to her cabin in the crew's quarters and as she went she groaned.

Stefano groaned too.

She'd gone. He knew it. And now, instead of finding resolution, they were in deeper trouble than before. What the hell had happened? He pushed the heel of his hand back into his forehead. *Idiot!*

It had been like this the first time he saw her. She'd arrived breathless, like a beautiful, vibrantly exotic bird, grabbing his attention so that he'd barely been able to concentrate on surgical technique. Her fierce intelligence had shone joyfully out of the most beautiful eyes in the operating theatre, like the Mediterranean Sea at sunrise, and he'd been lost.

His time with Kiki in Australia had blurred into a golden haze of laughter and loving and lust, and even his responsibility to Aspelicus had faded for a brief while.

When duty had called he'd fully intended going back to reassess it all properly—discover where it led. He had thought it would be a matter of days before his return, but first there had been the accident, then the months of rehabilitation, when the chance of losing the use of his leg had hung in the balance. It had all kept him away. As if the gods had intended they should both suffer for too perfect a match.

By then she'd disappeared. And more crises had arrived. Slowly his mind had been torn from her as well—except for that tiny halo in his heart.

But it was bad that he had hurt her. Profoundly. He could

see that now, and deeply he regretted it. The trouble was that it seemed if he had an opportunity to hold her again he had no choice but to take it. Hold her. Lose himself. This had to stop. This was not healthy. Not wholesome. Because the way he felt at this moment he would destroy them both before he could stop the way he wanted her.

The next morning, as the ship moored at Civitavecchia for Rome, the clinic was quiet.

'You okay?' Will looked at Kiki with concern.

She forced a smile. 'I must have eaten something that disagreed with me.'

Like a morning-after pill that sat on her stomach like a rock. She couldn't rid her mind of the distant warning that this had been the only chance she'd had to carry Stefano's child again. She hated that thought.

'Take the day off sick. I've got nothing planned. We'll manage.'

'No. I'll be better with something in my stomach, perhaps. It's fine. I'll stay.'

'Why?' Will gently propelled her out into the empty waiting room and towards the door. 'Go. Lie down. Read a book. You're allowed five sick days a year and you haven't had one.'

She didn't want to go back to her cabin to beat herself up. To go over in her mind relentlessly how she'd allowed herself to be seduced, had reciprocated in the seduction. It was an even tougher pill to swallow.

But she did feel miserable—and not just mentally.

'Okay. But I'll swap a day. I'll do one for you next week.' She looked at Will's concerned face and felt bad, but relieved. 'Thanks. I'll see you tomorrow.'

'Do you want me to get them to send up some food?'

'You're a sweetie.' She offered a wan smile. 'No. I'll wander. See if anything looks appealing.'

At least she needn't worry about running into Stefano in the public dining rooms. Far too plebeian for a prince. Though, to give him his due, he just avoided public places himself—he had no grudge against them.

Stefano had never played on his royal privileges or his power with her.

Except yesterday, when he'd thought she was sleeping with Will.

That had shocked her. There had been real possessiveness in that threat, and she didn't understand why.

If he'd wanted her, truly wanted her, then surely he would have moved heaven and earth to get back to her. How hard was it to pick up a phone? E-mail? Even a stamped addressed envelope would have been nice.

That was the crux of everything. She hadn't meant enough for him to follow through and say he wasn't coming back. Though, looking at what had happened between them yesterday, maybe he'd just expected to drop in every couple of months or so and be back in her bed.

She groaned and climbed the stairs to her room. As expected, when she got there it closed in around her.

Nope. She couldn't stay here.

Swiftly she shed her white uniform and stood in front of her small wardrobe. Brightly printed sundresses made her want to shade her eyes, and she winced her way along the rack until she came to black. Perfect. It suited her mood. Suited her intentions if the absolute worst happened and she came across him.

CHAPTER FOUR

STEFANO HAD LEARNED from last time. When he telephoned the hospital, as expected, the nurse answered.

'No, Dr Fender is not working today. In fact she has just left to get something to eat.'

She thought perhaps in the main dining area.

Stefano had not been through the main entertainment and restaurant areas. Apart from an early-morning swim in the lap pool just before Marla's unfortunate medical crisis, he'd avoided the other passengers. A discreet perusal of the common areas would not hurt him.

Kiki looked at the array of food, grimaced, and chose a banana. She knew they were good for hangovers and, while she hadn't had any alcohol, the Stefano hangover left her all kinds of miserable. Her belly rolled and she glanced at her watch. Not time yet for her next anti-emetic. That was the problem with morning-after pills. The nausea that accompanied them was pervasive.

As she wandered back out to the pool area a redheaded pre-teenage boy scooted past, almost knocked her down, slowed, and called sorry over his shoulder. He spied his brother, obviously a twin because they looked so similar, closing in, and put on speed again.

FIONA MCARTHUR 45

To have that much energy… 'Hey, slow down,' Kiki called after him.

Just then his brother slid into sight, didn't make the corner, lost purchase as he rounded a post at speed, and before Kiki could tell him to slow down it was too late!

The second boy's feet flew from under him and, unable to save himself, he slammed his head of red hair into the steel pole.

Kiki stood, stunned, then her mind clicked into gear. She took two quick strides and fell to her knees to bend over him, but the boy had clearly been unconscious before he hit the ground.

Kiki hailed a passing waiter who'd missed the action and sent him off speedily to summon further medical aid. Apart from him there were very few people near her.

Until the last passenger she wanted to see appeared and strode over.

For the boy's sake she was glad. For herself less so. She ignored the surge of nausea as Stefano approached, and forestalled any comment other than on the present. 'Did you see him hit?'

Stefano nodded. 'If he has not fractured his skull he is very lucky. I will take the neck as we roll.'

Stefano placed his hands either side in case of spinal injury, and together they turned him carefully onto his side to keep his airway clear.

Just then his brother reappeared around Stefano's shoulder, his freckled face screwed up with fright. 'Is he okay?'

Kiki recognised him with relief. 'What's your name?'

'Mikey.'

'And your brother's name, Mikey? And the number of the cabin your family's in?'

The terrified boy stuttered out that his name was Chris,

and the number, and Kiki repeated it to make sure she had it right.

'Okay. Go get your parents. I'm a doctor. Your brother hit his head and knocked himself out. We'll take him down to the ship's hospital as soon as the stretcher gets here and we'll meet you down there with them.' The frightened boy nodded and sped off. 'Slowly!' Kiki cautioned him, and she saw him reduce his pace to a jog.

Stefano's mind rolled back the years to a moment he'd never forget. A time when he too had been terrified at his brother's lack of response. The feeling of being powerless to prevent an accident, to prevent disaster. His father's constant reminder that *he* had been the responsible one weighed heavily even now. It was no wonder he needed to feel in control as a man. But he could feel that control slip away now, as this boy sank deeper into unconsciousness.

Kiki must have seen the sadness in his eyes, because she paled and he recognised the moment when she too felt the presence of impending disaster.

'You think he's critical?' she asked quietly.

'Theros was like that as a boy. Always rushing.'

She frowned, missing the context—for which he was glad. No doubt she was impatient with his latex-loving sibling right now.

She shook her head and concentrated on the boy. 'I heard the impact. Horrible. Wilhelm should be here with a stretcher ASAP, but he'll need to be shipped out.'

'I agree.' Stefano lifted the boy's eyelids one at a time to see his pupils and frowned. 'If we are that lucky.'

Will and Ginger arrived and Stefano helped them ease on a spinal collar and slide the boy onto the stretcher on a spine board. Within minutes they were all crammed in the lift on their way to the hospital, and Stefano could feel his own heart-rate increase as he watched tiny ominous changes in the boy. A flicker of a tremor in one finger. The shudder of an indrawn laboured breath. Nobody spoke as the doors shut and they all watched their patient.

He saw Hobson look at Kiki. 'He'll need to be shipped out immediately.'

Stefano checked the pupils again. 'There may not be time. Already one pupil is dilating.'

Will shuddered. 'So fast?'

'It happens.' He glanced up at him. 'Do you have the equipment for burr holes here?'

'Craniotomy? I guess so.' Will looked at Ginger, who nodded. 'But I've never done it. Cranial surgery's not a common thing on cruise liners. We should chopper him out from the wharf. Faster than an ambulance.'

Stefano shook his head. 'The preferred option is retrieval, but I do not like the look of this. It should be considered just in case.' They all knew even that took time.

'Kiki says you're a surgeon. If it's burr holes will you stay? Supervise?' Will asked.

Stefano nodded. He could not leave and never know.

'Of course.' Then he saw the limbs on one side of the boy begin to tremble, faintly at first, and then with greater intensity as he began to convulse. Stefano helped Hobson hold him desperately to keep his cervical spine stable until the seizure ended.

Chris's breathing slowed, stuttered, and the boy's condition deteriorated further even in the short time it took to descend to the hospital. Stefano's heart sank. To them all Chris's prognosis had begun to look horrifyingly bleak.

Kiki fought back the horrible feeling they would be too late and helped Ginger steer the trolley from the lift as soon as the fit ceased. That was when she realised the boy's parents had arrived before them.

Stefano hadn't seen them. 'The fits will get worse as the pressure builds.'

'What will get worse?'

A bluff redheaded man hurried across to them with his worried wife and Mikey in tow. Kiki gently guided them aside as the others pushed through to the hospital.

'Hello, I'm Dr Fender.' She took the man's hand. 'Is Chris your son?'

Worried grey eyes met hers. 'Yes. Mikey said he hit his head.'

Kiki nodded. 'It was a very nasty fall. I saw it. Dr Hobson and Dr Mykonides are going to examine him now. While they're doing that we need to know if Chris has any other illnesses, or allergies that we should know of. Has he ever had any operations?'

The father looked at his wife and she shook her head, fear huge in her eyes as she realised the gravity of Chris's accident. 'Is he going to be all right?'

Kiki could only pray. 'I'm sorry, I can't answer that. He's very ill. He may have fractured his skull and torn a vessel inside his head. It looks as though he is building a collection of blood that is pressing on his brain. Our first preference is to fly him out by helicopter from the wharf because his condition is so critical.'

She looked at them, deeply sympathetic, but sensible to the fact they needed to know what was going on.

'As soon as the doctors have examined Chris we'll know if we have time to transfer him. Dr Mykonides is a passenger, but also a very experienced surgeon. He will know what is best.' Chris's mother began to weep silently and Kiki drew them into the waiting room. 'I'll send the nurse out to see if she can get you something while I find out what going on.'

'Thank you, Doctor.' The boy's father drew his wife

and son under the shelter of his arms and Kiki felt the tears sting her eyes.

'I'll be as quick as I can.'

The father's voice followed her. 'Take all the time you need. We'll wait.'

She nodded, left and prayed as she hurried into join the others. Surely Chris would recover. She knew how she'd felt the pain of grief when she'd lost her tiny baby, but couldn't imagine the worry *they* must be feeling.

Wilhelm had booked the retrieval team but they would be thirty minutes before arrival at the earliest.

'We'll lose him if we wait.' Stefano examined the depressed skull fracture on the rapid X-ray they'd taken while Kiki read out the boy's blood pressure and pulse. He shook his head. 'I give fifteen before brain damage is irreversible,' Stefano confided in Kiki quietly.

Kiki agreed. 'Systolic blood pressure's rising, widening of pulse pressure, and his pulse is slowing.'

The pressure inside the head was compressing Chris's brain down towards the base of his skull. At some point it would do irreversible damage.

Will nodded. 'Let's do it.'

Kiki looked at Wilhelm. 'I'll talk to the parents, get consent, while you and Stefano get scrubbed. The nurse can get him set up in the suture room. We can make this happen fast.'

Chris's parents stood up quickly when Kiki hurried into the waiting room.

'A helicopter's on its way but Chris has pressure from the blood building very quickly on his brain. Already his blood pressure is high and his pulse has slowed right down. Dr Hobson and the surgeon, Dr Mykonides, agree it is imperative to operate now to relieve that pressure. I'm sorry to have to tell you there is a real risk Chris might not survive his arrival at the hospital if we don't do something now.'

Chris's mother put her hand over her mouth and hugged her husband, and Kiki saw the lump shift in his father's throat as he gathered his wife in. 'Then do it.'

Kiki passed them the consent form, and the father signed quickly. 'They're setting him up now. The object is to make small round holes in Chris's skull to let the pressure out and repair the bleeding artery before the brain is damaged. It's an emergency lifesaving procedure. We may be too late. Do you understand?'

'Just save him. And afterwards?'

'A medical team will arrive to stabilise him and transfer him to a hospital neurological ward.' She squeezed the mother's shoulder. 'Do you have any other questions?'

The father looked at his wife and other son. 'Not now. He's in your hands. Hurry.'

Kiki nodded and did just that.

By the time she was back in the tiny operating theatre Chris's skull had been shaved on the side of the fracture and draped to create a sterile field. Will and Stefano were preparing the area with an antiseptic solution.

'Consent signed. They'll ask questions later. Please go ahead.'

The ventilator machine was breathing for him, but no anaesthetic had been used because the boy was deeply unconscious. It would be Kiki's task to monitor that and Stefano handed Will a syringe of local anaesthetic for the skin incision just in case.

Will hesitated and Stefano waved him on. 'Let's go. Inject the site. Make a three-centimetre incision through the skin. Separate the fascia.'

Will did so and the boy didn't move. His breathing

sounded mechanically in the room and Kiki was glad they'd had time to intubate, because at least they could keep him going until the pressure on his breathing centre was released.

She'd never seen the operation before, and Stefano kept a commentary going as Will performed the surgery.

'Control the bleeding with the diathermy. Use the retractors now.' They could all see Will's hands shaking but Stefano's voice was rock-solid. 'Exactly. Yes. Now drill the hole with the hand drill two centimetres above and behind the orbital process of the frontal bone.'

Will's hands shook more, and Stefano leaned across and steadied him.

'This is good. You will be an old hand soon.' He glanced at Kiki. 'How's our boy going?'

'Holding his own, just. Pulse now forty. BP one fifty on forty.'

'We have a minute or two at the most. Faster drilling.'

Stefano's eyes looked even grimmer and Kiki wondered if he was frustrated by Will's nerves. She couldn't tell, and wondered if he might throw legality to the wind and take over.

Will continued with the procedure.

'Watch for the release of pressure.' Just as the words left Stefano's mouth a thin, powerful stream of blood shot upwards high off the table from the collection in Chris's head.

Will jumped back as it slowed to an oozing trickle and Stefano murmured, 'Good. Pressure is released.'

Will shuddered. 'No wonder his observations were going off.'

'Speed is essential. Now we find the bleeder.' Stefano pointed with tiny mosquito forceps. 'There it is. Tie it off.'

Will leaned in. Tying off vessels was something he was good at.

'Good. Now bandage for transfer.'

* * *

Half an hour later the emergency team loaded an almost stable Chris into the helicopter.

Stefano walked across to where the other boy watched the transfer of his brother. His red hair stood on end from his agonised raking and fat tears rolled down his freckled face. He knew the turmoil ahead and Stefano's heart ached for him.

Mikey looked up. 'It's my fault. I shouldn't have teased him. He wouldn't have been so angry.'

Stefano put his hand on the boy's shoulder, squeezed the bony ridge as Mikey dashed his hand across his eyes. 'It is hard to watch. Especially for you as a twin.'

Stefano sighed as he fought back his own images. He couldn't bear the thought that this boy would go through the remorse he had.

'My brother was sick like yours once. And I tell you it is *not* your fault your brother hit his head. Boys run and chase, and things happen we have no control over. It could have been you that fell and he would not have been able to stop it happening.'

Mikey looked away from Chris to the man beside him and he did not look so woebegone. 'You think?'

He knew. 'You did everything right by getting your parents to the hospital. We might not have saved your brother without them being there so quickly.'

Mikey sniffed and rubbed his nose with the back of his hand. 'I ran. I did what the doctor asked me to do.'

Stefano nodded and patted the boy's shoulder again before he lifted his hand. 'You did well. Your brother is strong and he has you.'

They watched the helicopter pilot start the rotors and soon it was in the air. Chris parents came across to shake

Wilhelm's hand and thank Kiki and Stefano, and then with Mikey they climbed into a waiting taxi that would take them to the hospital.

Will turned to Stefano and nodded. 'Thank you.' He sighed ruefully. 'Though I wish you could have done it.'

Stefano smiled grimly. 'No. It is better to have the experience. One day another boy may need your skills, and doing it yourself can never be replaced by watching. There were only seconds between the same result for you or I.'

Will nodded again and glanced at the ship that shadowed them on the wharf. 'I need to report to the Captain.' He glanced at Kiki, and then Stefano, but held his tongue. 'See you later.'

Kiki felt as if she'd been run over by steamroller now the tension had been relieved by Chris's transfer, and suddenly it didn't matter that Stefano was the only one left beside her.

She saw him in a different light. She'd watched him go out and talk to Mikey and hadn't been able to help overhearing some of his words.

Today Stefano had been kind, thoughtful, and a steady teacher. As much as she hated to admit it, he'd seemed like the man she'd fallen for. He'd been great with Will. And he obviously cared about the trauma to both boys.

So what had happened to them? Her and Stefano? Nine months ago? Didn't she deserve the same consideration that he now gave to an unknown family?

It didn't make sense that he'd stepped out of character and left her with no further contact after the week they'd had without a good reason.

Was there more she didn't know?

'Perhaps we should talk?'

Stefano smiled ruefully and she felt the mirror of her own response. 'Somewhere public?'

'Lord, yes.' No way was she going anywhere near his bedroom.

CHAPTER FIVE

STEFANO STEERED KIKI to the rooftop coffee shop and chose a corner table behind an exuberant fake palm. Kiki didn't mind because she was feeling particularly pale and not very interesting as nausea elbowed its way back into her consciousness now she had time to think about herself.

Stefano frowned as he noticed her pallor. 'Do you wish for something to eat?'

Kiki's stomach rolled and she winced. 'No, thank you. Just black tea.'

'You are unwell?'

He leaned towards her and again she recognised the tang of his cologne. This time, unfortunately, it wasn't her stomach that reacted. Something much more visceral stood up and waved.

She leaned back. 'Something I ate.'

'Strangely, my appetite for food is also absent.' His eyes darkened and she hated that—because she could feel herself weaken...and waken.

There was that damned glint in his eyes that she couldn't help but smile at. 'Stop it.'

He shrugged those shoulders and she looked away.

He said, 'So, I admit it is good to see you, Kiki.'

She wasn't falling into that one. 'No comment.'

His brows went up teasingly. 'So comment on something else.'

Umm. Something safe. 'Do you think Chris will be okay?'

He shrugged, not with unconcern—she could see that—but with a glimmer of hope despite the contrariness of life. 'I will keep in contact by phone, but I think the surgery should have done the job before damage, and his vitals maintained perfusion. Tomorrow will give a good indication.'

She'd known that. But still it was good to hear the hope in his voice. A silence fell. She could feel his eyes on her.

'I think there is more you wish to discuss with me.'

Well, he was right there. She should get it out and finished with. Dispel the questions that were beginning to eat at her all over again. She drew a deep breath and looked back at him. 'Why didn't you contact me after you left so hurriedly?'

The waitress arrived, took their order, smiled and batted her eyelashes at Stefano. He allowed her to walk away, and when she was out of earshot he leaned forward and said the last thing she'd expected.

'I was in an accident. Unconscious and then physically disabled.'

He had her full attention as she searched his face. Now she could see them. Tiny lines that hadn't been there before, a few strands of silver through his black hair at the side of his face. She had a sudden memory of that ridge of scar on his hip she'd fleetingly discovered yesterday. Her fingers fidgeted with the salt shaker, tensed, ached to reach across and touch his hand in sympathy. But luckily she wasn't that stupid.

She let go of the shaker and retreated her hand to the edge of the cloth. 'What kind of accident?'

'Motor vehicle. I spent several months in hospital. By the time I was discharged and could begin to sort what needed to be sorted you were gone.'

He laid his hand palm up on the table, as if to signal he knew she wanted to comfort him with touch. Like a coward she shifted her hand into her lap, and his fingers closed over themselves emptily as he sat back.

When she didn't say anything he said, 'By the time I could look, I could not find you. I thought perhaps you wished it that way.'

He watched her face and she saw the moment he understood that she had, actually. By then.

So would she tell him about her own little visit to hospital? No. She couldn't go there now. It was all too painfully close.

'I was on ship. Had my own family stuff happening. My brother got married. I made friends here.'

He sat back further, as if to illustrate the distance between them now. 'Life went on?'

She nodded, as if everything was sweetness and light. Not the way she was feeling. 'As it does.'

'But now we meet again.'

His voice dropped like that cloak around her shoulders and she mentally shook herself at the spell he could weave just by words and cadence and his very presence.

Harden up, she reminded herself, and sat straighter in the chair. 'Life is still going to go on, Stefano. You'll get off the ship. I'll sail away.'

He leaned forward. 'It does not have to be that way.'

'Yes, it does.'

She wasn't stupid. She'd learnt her lesson. Yes, he'd been sick for a couple of months, but that had been months ago. No contact after that because she didn't count enough. Well, she deserved better than that.

'Because we're from two very different worlds.'

It would always be that way, which was why she wasn't going to put her heart out there to be stamped on again. Or be seduced into his bed for the next few convenient days.

Now his voice was more formal and his expression more difficult to read. 'So are you always going to be a ship's doctor?'

But she didn't need to read him. She just needed to get out of here. 'No. I'm ready to move on.' Now. Literally. She glanced at him. 'Funny how I feel so unsettled today,' she said dryly.

'And where would you move on to?'

She shrugged. This whole scenario was surreal. They were like two acquaintances, chatting over a cup of tea. 'Maybe I'll go for experience. There's always the other extreme to this—foreign aid medicine. My brother's wife worked in a tent city in the Sudan. Or I could move into family medicine with Nick and his wife back in Australia.'

He nodded. 'It is very beautiful there.'

'They're having twins.' She shut her mouth with a snap as hurt from the past rose in her chest.

Her eyes prickled. She did not want to talk about expected newborns with Stefano.

She looked away hurriedly, in case he saw something in her face, then went on brightly as she drained her tea. 'Or I could go back to Sydney to another hospital. The family home's still there.'

'I see you have put some thought into this.' He looked pensive.

She didn't like to tell him it was only since yesterday. His fault. All she had to do was resign.

The nausea rose unexpectedly and she stood up. 'I'm sorry. I have to go.'

He rose also, his forehead creased with concern. 'Let me see you to your cabin safely.'

She could almost smile at that. 'I'm in the crew section. Out of bounds for passengers. So you see...' she leant on the table and pushed herself away from him '...I will be safe.'

Stefano watched her hurry away. Was she really nauseated? She looked pale—or was she upset? Did she hate him that much? All questions he would like an answer to, he mulled as he walked back to his suite. There was more going on than she had explained, he was certain of it, because deep in his gut he knew she was hurting—and he had caused it.

It seemed it was his lot in life to hurt the people he loved. But how to ensure she would at least talk to him?

Perhaps it was time to take the Captain up on his offer to inspect the bridge.

Will sent Ginger to check on her around four. 'Will wants to know if you're up for dinner in the officers' mess tonight. Captain's request.'

Kiki sighed. 'Bloody Stefano.' She didn't think she'd said it out loud but apparently she had.

Ginger looked suitably shocked. 'Kiki! I haven't been here long but I've never heard you swear.'

Stefano hadn't been here then. 'Sorry, Ginger. But stick around for the next three days and you might hear more.' *Oooohhh,* she'd kill him.

Ginger sighed dreamily. 'He must really like you.'

Yeah, right. 'He liked me before. For a week.' Indiscreet. She shouldn't have said that. But she guessed most people could tell they knew each other a little. Even Wilhelm had noticed. 'Stefano's bored and he thinks he can amuse himself before he disappears back to his little island.'

Ginger laughed. 'You can't really call Aspelicus a little island. It's got mountains, and flat lands—and casinos, even. And it has this massive village on the side of the volcano, a gorgeous palace, and a fab hospital.' She rolled her eyes in ecstasy. 'It's the most amazing place.'

Kiki had to laugh. 'You've obviously been there?'

'Last year. I was knocking around with the in crowd with my on-again off-again boyfriend—gossip columnist, long story—and we ended up there for the Prince's Cup.'

'A horse race?'

Ginger nodded nostalgically. 'Magical horse race they do there every year along this spit of sand at the edge of the island. Raises squillions for the hospital. And there's balls and cocktails and champagne lunches. I swear I put on ten pounds over five days.'

Ginger grinned.

'Anyway, Stefano looked pretty amazing as the host. So I guess I have a soft spot and can't get over the fact you don't want to play with him.'

Kiki rolled her shoulders and rubbed the wooden block full of tension that was her neck. 'Because after the fun and games I'm left picking up the pieces.'

'He really hurt you.' Ginger must have heard the truth because her expression changed to one of sympathy. 'I'm sorry. Want me to tell Wilhelm you're not up to dinner?'

Kiki knew she'd have to go. 'It was a request from the Captain. I can't decline just because I want to avoid his guest.'

Ginger was still new. 'Why not?'

You just didn't do it. 'Because Stefano will blow it all out of proportion, I'll find myself in sick bay, and Will doesn't deserve the hassle.' She sighed. 'What time?'

'Seven.' Ginger twisted her hands. 'The nurses have

been invited as well. Umm…do you think you could introduce me to that dishy Miko if you get a chance?'

Her friend Miko, who smiled as if he knew more than Kiki was saying. 'He's a heartbreaker.'

Ginger shrugged. 'I need someone to take my thoughts away from my ex. I'm not here for marriage. And I heard he was fun.'

Kiki grinned. 'He's fun, all right.'

When Stefano saw Kiki enter with Hobson the rest of the room faded. He thought she looked less pale than earlier, which was what he'd wanted to see. Or that was what he told himself.

'Ah, the medical staff are here.' The Captain smiled. 'But of course you have shared high drama with them already. Dr Hobson tells me your advice was invaluable.'

Through his contacts Stefano had been updated hourly on Chris's condition and the boy was improving steadily. 'Dr Hobson and Dr Fender were instrumental in saving that boy's life. And the nurses, of course. You have a brilliant medical team on your ship, Captain.'

The Captain visibly preened. 'I'm glad to hear it.'

'Of course Dr Fender and I are old friends.' His companion straightened with interest and Stefano chose his words carefully. 'We met during a consultancy I held in Sydney last year. I fear she is concerned someone might think she's consorting unprofessionally with a passenger if she's seen too much with me.'

The Captain was eager to dispel such a thought. 'Not at all. Fraternisation does not apply with previous acquaintances.'

'I thought not,' Stefano said smoothly, 'but of course I'm glad to hear you say so.'

'No problem.' The Captain stepped forward to meet

Wilhelm and Kiki as a waiter circled with a tray of champagne.

Kiki knew the Captain and Stefano were looking her way and were talking about her. Her ears were practically on fire.

'Soda for me,' Kiki said, and took the glass with a thank-you nod at the waiter as Stefano and the Captain approached. She should have asked for something with a kick. She plastered a smile on her face.

'Prince Stefano has been singing your praises, Kiki. All of the medical team, in fact.'

Kiki could play that game. Nice and impersonal. 'We were lucky to have such a surgeon to consult with, sir.'

'Prince Stefano tells me the boy is improving consistently. There is real hope he will make a full recovery. And no threat of the parents suing my ship.'

She didn't care if Stefano saw how much that news improved her evening. It was worth coming just for the information. 'That is wonderful news about Chris, sir. And of course your ship.'

The impulse to share her joy with Stefano meant she couldn't avoid looking at him any longer. Of course he was watching her when she did sneak a glance.

She searched manfully for a topic to deflect the pink that was rising in her cheeks. 'Your brother and his wife are not here, Your Highness?'

She saw his brows lower at her mode of address. 'Theros and Marla are watching the show tonight.'

The Captain nodded eagerly. 'The show is excellent. Of course the crew's pageant will be on in two nights. You must not miss it, Prince Stefano. Kiki and Miko dance.' The Captain sighed nostalgically, glanced around and gestured the restaurant manager over. 'They tango brilliantly.'

Kiki distracted herself by watching Miko cross the

room. All the women smiled as he joked and nodded, more of celebrity than the actual Prince. Kiki couldn't help her smile. He was such a hoot.

'Sir.' Miko saluted and the Captain introduced Stefano.

'I think you have not met our royal guest—Prince Stefano of Aspelicus.'

Miko made a very creditable bow and Stefano nodded his head.

Oblivious, the Captain went on. 'I was just saying how much I enjoy watching the crew pageant and especially your dances.'

Miko gallantly turned to Kiki. 'It is all because of my beautiful partner. She is a feather.' He lifted Kiki's fingers to kiss her hand with consummate grace. 'You look ravishing as always, Dr Fender.'

Kiki grinned and pulled her hand away. Something made her glance at Stefano, who had narrowed his eyes at the interloper. All trace of good humour had disappeared from his face and she remembered the way he'd reacted to her quip about Will.

Kiki decided discretion was the better part of valour. 'I have someone who wants to meet you, Miko. Excuse me, Captain, Prince Stefano.' And she drew the playful restaurateur away before more damage could be done.

'Ho-ho, if looks could kill,' Miko whispered teasingly in her ear.

Kiki relaxed against him. 'You are a menace.'

Miko's voice dropped even lower. 'And you have been sleeping with the Prince.'

'Stop it.'

He shrugged. 'You have known him before, perhaps? He is very jealous.'

Jealous, or a dog in the manger? 'That's his problem.'

'And mine if he thinks you care for me.' But Miko

laughed. He wasn't stupid. 'And also a problem for you too.' He shrugged as they moved out of sight. 'So why do you fight this great attraction?'

Survival. 'Because we are from different worlds and he has hurt me before.'

'And Nick knows of this?'

Kiki felt like stamping her feet. 'Why does everyone think my brother has to know about my life?'

Miko shrugged. 'Because he will kill us if anything happens to you. So it is purely selfish on my part.'

She had to laugh. 'You are so shallow.'

'That is true. But it's also true that is what you love about me. Come. Introduce me to this woman who wishes to meet me and I will let you go back to your brooding Prince.'

Kiki poked him. 'I'm sticking with you and I'm going to spoil your chances of seduction.' Kiki stopped when she found the nurse. 'Ginger, I'd like you to meet my friend Miko. I'm sure you've seen him around.'

Miko bowed. 'It is a great pleasure to meet you, Ginger. I believe this is your first cruise with us?' Miko lowered his head over Ginger's fingers and while his vision was obstructed Ginger winked her thanks.

The Second Officer approached and as Miko straightened he glanced at Kiki and grinned. 'Kiki? You are leaving us? I fear the Captain has placed you at his table.'

Next to Stefano.

The men stood as she approached and Stefano frowned away the waiter who'd moved to hold her chair.

As she slid into her seat she murmured, 'Seated by a prince. I am lucky,' and sat demurely with her hands in her lap. Stefano settled in next to her.

'Behave or I will not sit next to you.'

'You arranged it.'

'True. Because I can.' He changed the subject. 'I realise we have not danced.'

What had brought that on? Dog in the manger? 'Apparently you have to go out in public to do that.'

He sat back in his chair and regarded her. 'Not always, but *touché*. Of course I am happy to meet your conditions.' He gestured with his hand. 'After this, perhaps?'

Not likely. 'I'm afraid not.'

Silkily he said in her ear. 'And why are you afraid?'

Thankfully the entree arrived at the same time and she didn't have to answer. She turned to the person on her right.

Stefano was not altogether displeased. So she was afraid of her own response in his arms? A healthy respect for the severity of their fierce attraction was wise. Not fear of him, but of herself, for he had never sought to inspire anything but lust in Kiki's beautiful breast.

Stefano hid his smile and turned to the lady on his left.

The Captain's wife was Sicilian and had visited Aspelicus before. She was very pleased to be seated next to the Crown Prince. Stefano knew it would amuse Kiki to see him cornered, so he paid such flattering attention to the good lady he doubted he would be allowed to eat in his suite again.

Thankfully the Captain's wife enjoyed her food, and when the main course arrived he could turn to his other companion.

'The Captain tells me you are off duty tomorrow when we dock. I will be flying out to Aspelicus for the day on a matter of state that will not take long. Perhaps this could be a chance for you to see my homeland.'

Before she could decline he went on.

'We would have time to visit my facial reconstruction

clinic before we leave. It has facets of treatment that may interest you.'

She shouldn't be tempted, but his genuine passion for his work was clearly evident and it called to the vocation in herself. 'How far is Aspelicus that you can fly to do business and come back?'

He clicked his fingers. 'A mere hour's fight.'

The Captain's wife leaned across. 'You should go, dear. It's fabulous. And the Prince will look after you.'

Kiki muttered under her breath. 'That's what I'm afraid of.'

CHAPTER SIX

THE NEXT MORNING, as the ship docked in Livorno, after a night of mental flogging because she'd weakened, Kiki had to school the shock from her face when Stefano arrived at the gangway to disembark.

Dressed in a designer suit as black as his hair, with his royal chain of office flashing gold and precious stones in the sunlight, he looked nothing like the man she could lose herself in.

Her first taste of royal bling and she had to admit he wore it well. Too well.

The passengers leaning over the ship's verandas seemed impressed too, if the flashing of cameras was anything to go by.

His man opened the door of the official car and gathered her in. It was a discreet luxury sedan, so hopefully people wouldn't gawk and point at them as they drove along. She slid across the seat, suddenly glad she'd worn her best trousers and a camisole with a jacket, because even though she was off the ship it looked as if this was a day when she'd need everything she had to keep her head above the water line.

'I'm sorry to have kept you waiting.' Stefano slid in next to her, and despite the gap between them on the seat she could feel the shimmering energy field as he settled.

'You made quite an entrance.'

He narrowed his eyes at her as if perplexed. 'How so?'

And didn't she wish she hadn't started *that* conversation? 'You look very princely.'

'At the risk of being simplistic, it is my job.'

Well, she'd asked for that. But he looked so overpoweringly regal she was feeling threatened by her own insignificance. Not something she'd ever felt before. And what would it be like when they arrived at the palace, where he held considerable power?

Just the thought of feeling inferior made her spine stiffen. 'You said you have matters of state to deal with? What will I do while you attend to those?'

His gaze softened as if he sensed how unsure she was about their arrival. 'I had thought Elise, my housekeeper, could show you over the palace if you would like. She will no doubt burn your ears with her historical fervour. Elise is very proud of the island's heritage.'

So she was to be diverted to the housekeeper. That should keep her out of the way. 'She sounds interesting.'

He didn't turn to face her. 'She is, but if you are not in the mood for a history lesson you could relax in the library and browse. We have an extensive collection of original books collected by my mother.'

'Both options sound appealing.' But the history more so. She could sit in libraries any day.

Now he turned to her. Searched her face. 'I should not be long. It is a matter of signing papers that should have been ready a week ago, and the settlement of a matter which has caused my father some concern for too long. Hence my decision to be done with it today.'

The car drove onto the tarmac of the airport and eased smoothly to a stop.

Stefano glanced out of the window. 'I hope helicopters do not worry you?'

'Not that I've noticed in the past.' *Never been in one.* She was quite pleased with her nonchalant tone, but seriously, how many people chose helicopters as their basic transport?

She'd been psyching herself for a sleek little Learjet at worst, but there was not much she could do about their mode of travel now.

'I'll be fine.' Though it looked more like a large bumble bee than an aircraft.

To top it off Stefano had climbed into the pilot's seat and the lump in her throat tightened. His man opened the rear door. 'I'll sit in the back, shall I?' she murmured to herself, and allowed him to bow her into the helicopter with its royal insignia, her reluctance disguised because she'd always prided herself on her sense of adventure.

This definitely rated as an adventure. She'd bet there were hundreds of girls who would have changed places with her, and she wondered again why Stefano had manoeuvred her into accompanying him on this excursion.

As soon as the pre-flight check was complete Stefano turned and assured himself that she was strapped in before he started the engine.

As the roar grew louder the little cabin began to shake and she resurrected the deep breathing exercises she'd learnt long ago during her obstetric term. Calmness at take-off seemed a great idea.

In through the nose all the way down to the base of her lungs, hold for three, and ease out through the mouth before breathing in again. She didn't care that the breaths seemed loud in her ears and that Stefano's man must be looking at her strangely.

Thankfully after six inhalations the flutter in her chest

began to ease, and when she opened her eyes that were three feet above the ground and going up fast.

Everything happened very quickly after that as they rose and turned and soared away from the helipad towards the Mediterranean Sea. The shimmer of the waves below made her squint and reach for her sunglasses in her bag, and away to her left the hull of their ship overshadowed the docks.

Islands dotted the horizon in tiny volcanic outcrops, some with soaring peaks and others quite low to the water. After nearly an hour, during which she'd begun to enjoy the bird's eye view over the waves. she realised they were approaching a larger island, shaped almost like a whale, with the hump of a volcano in the middle and three separate areas of inhabitation. A long beach on one side edged a magnificent horse racing track, and she guessed that was where all Ginger's action had happened.

They approached the soaring volcanic cliffs and flew towards a turreted castle perched in a position impossible to assail without permission. As she looked down at a ribbon of winding road that circled the cliffs she guessed that was the way to the gate. And when she saw the even tinier toy cars that clung to it she wondered if that was where Stefano had had his accident.

To the left were rolling hills with what looked like miles of olive trees and scattered small villages, and on the other side of the island it seemed there was a small city she barely saw before the sight was cut off as they approached the castle.

Her stomach rose and fell as they landed on a brightly painted H on the castle forecourt with a tiny bump, and then Stefano had lifted his headphones and turned back to her with the flash of a white smile. A man who enjoyed his time at the controls. Why would that surprise her?

The door beside her opened and she fumbled to release her seat belt as fresh mountain air rushed into the little helicopter. Her companion was already out, and Stefano had waved away the person in front of him and waited with hand outstretched to help her from the cabin.

'Welcome to Aspelicus, Dr Fender,' he said formally, but the twinkle in his eye showed he was pleased to be able to share this moment with her.

She had no choice but to lay her hand in his, and of course when his hand closed around hers she couldn't help the smile she returned. She really needed to learn to avoid physical contact with this man.

'Thank you, Your Highness.' She gathered her own control and looked around. 'Your castle is very beautiful.' The words replayed in her head. Even the conversation was surreal.

'I think so.' He turned to a tall grey-haired woman who had crossed to his side. Her eyes were warm and kind and she obviously adored Stefano. 'Elise, this is Dr Fender. Please care for her this morning, until I can return.'

'Certainly, Your Highness.' She inclined her head, obviously happy to do whatever he wished.

Stefano nodded and strode off towards another stairway, surrounded by suited figures, before Kiki realised he was going away.

So much for goodbye, Kiki thought. A bit abrupt in the leave-taking department, to her mind, but maybe she was being childish to expect anything else.

Elise waved her hand gracefully towards the main sweeping castle steps. 'This way, Dr Fender.'

Feeling a little like an unwanted package, Kiki lifted her chin. 'Please, call me Kiki.' She smiled at the older woman. 'And may I call you Elise?'

'Certainly. Welcome to Aspelicus.'

They turned and began to climb the wide stone steps. Sections of the stone had been worn away by feet over the centuries.

Kiki glanced around. Everywhere the castle was meticulously maintained, from its flowerbeds to lichen-free stone. 'The castle looks old but very beautiful.'

'Some form of the castle has perched here for over a thousand years, and thankfully all generations have continued to treat it with respect and care so that it remains as strong today as it has ever been.'

Elise glanced around and Kiki had no doubt that any fault found would be swiftly acted upon.

'And has Prince Stefano's family always been the ruling family?' She couldn't believe she was talking about the man whose bed she'd left only yesterday. At that thought the heat rushed to her cheeks, and she stopped to examine a particularly ugly gargoyle and breathe back control.

Elise's voice drifted over her shoulder as she, too, paused. 'Indeed. Which is rare. They have been fortunate in that their sons have been most virile and capable of siring many lines.'

With a pang of loss, Kiki knew she could believe that.

'Now, with Prince Theros happily married, there is even more surety of the line continuing. And I'm sure Prince Stefano will marry before the year is out.'

Kiki frowned at that little pearl of information. 'Do you mean he *has* to marry?'

Elise inclined her head. 'It is by royal decree that the heir to the throne must marry by the time he turns forty.'

So Stefano must be thirty-nine. Ten years older than her. She hadn't realised there was such a gap, but then when had they sat and discussed mundane matters like his needing to be married by the time he was forty and only having a year to do it? Instead they'd made love. Often.

Her mind darted like the birds swooping outside the windows and she had to remind herself to be in the moment. It wasn't every day she had a private tour of a palace. So she tried to concentrate as they walked through into a vaulted main entry with impressive tiling in glorious Italian marble that seemed to shimmer with light. Their footsteps echoed away to the gold-trimmed ceiling that soared to a huge dome adorned with age-darkened seascapes in turbulent oils.

During the next hour Elise opened doors to lush apartments filled with gilt furniture and more framed artwork. Some of the paintings were so huge they covered entire walls, while the floors glowed with the subtlety of magnificently woven rugs from the Orient.

The throne room proved the most regal, with red silk walls, two huge portraits of a man and a woman, and an extremely ostentatious fireplace that seemed to be made out of solid gold adorned with the royal crest.

'This is where the current Prince, Paulo III, was married. That is the late Princess Tatiana.' Elise sighed. 'She was a wonderful woman.'

Kiki looked at Stefano's mother and saw her regal son in the same hooded yet beautiful grey eyes. 'And very lovely. Everything is magnificent.'

Elise nodded and led her back to the main hall. 'It is a mission I take on gladly to keep it this way. But these formal areas are not the most comfortable to sit in. These are state apartments, for formal gatherings and the hosting of foreign dignitaries.' She gestured to a side stairway. 'If you would like to follow me we will go through to the family apartments, where it is easier to relax. Perhaps a cup of tea would refresh you?'

'Thank you. Lovely.' An overused word, but Kiki couldn't help feeling a little overwhelmed.

The idea that Stefano had been so comfortable in her little two-room flat seemed ludicrous and hard to imagine. No wonder he sat blasé amongst the furnishings on board the ship. It was nothing compared to his home. And yet when they'd been alone together she'd known there was nowhere else he'd wanted to be than with her.

'The upkeep must be horrendous?'

Elise frowned. 'It is a duty and a privilege.'

Oops. Of course it was. That's what royal families and their subjects did.

They went through a set of large stained glass doors and suddenly the light and warmth of a much less formal area lay before them.

'Oh, this is gorgeous.' Kiki could see a conservatory to the side, overflowing with lush green plants, and to the left a sunken lounge with a handful of plush cushioned lounges and chairs. There were flowers everywhere, and even the artwork was modernistic and lighter, but no less magnificent.

'The late Princess, Prince Stefano's mother, refurnished this.'

'She had lovely taste.'

Elise sighed with pleasure. 'Our tiny country is fortunate that its ruling family is wise in the ways of fashion and finance.'

Kiki glanced around. *They'd have to be.* 'Very wise.'

'Yes. The family fortune has built since not long after the Doges of Venice began amassing their own fortunes. Before the family became the Aspelican monarchy one distant uncle was even friends with the famous Venetian Marco Polo, and the island became an outpost on the routes of trade and gathered the riches of silk and spices.'

Elise waved at a wall full of glorious pottery from all over the world.

'But since early Greek times always the family has held physicians. The Crown was bestowed on the first Prince of Aspelicus because he saved the eldest son of the Italian King during a fever that all had thought would carry him off.'

Elise really did love her history, Kiki thought with a smile, and encouraged the woman to go on.

'In every generation one of the family becomes a physician, and I understand Prince Stefano will be showing you his hospital this afternoon.'

'He did mention that.'

'Prince Stefano does great work.'

There was an extra thread of emotion in her voice that had Kiki turning back to look at the woman.

'Personally for you?'

'My son. After many miscarriages I bore a live child, but he was born with a lip and pallet deformity. Prince Stefano reconstructed his face.' The woman's face seemed to glow. 'It is a miracle.'

Many miscarriages. Kiki could only imagine the pain. 'That's wonderful, Elise.'

The woman nodded eagerly. 'And his work is not confined to those who know the family. He will repair any child, and do what he can for the damage that affects peoples' lives. He is a great man.'

No wonder Stefano had wanted her exposed to Elise. The woman hero-worshipped him. Kiki would hold judgement until this afternoon, but it seemed Stefano had had many reasons apart from his accident for not contacting her when she'd needed him.

There was so much to learn about him and yet so little time. And he had shared barely anything with her of his life here. She wondered if her exposure to Elise was the most he could do to open up.

By the time they had drunk their tea and eaten the tiny pomegranate cakes a maid had brought the glass doors opened and Stefano strode in. Suddenly the huge apartment seemed smaller.

'Ah, here you are, and I see you've had tea.'

Elise jumped up, wreathed in smiles. 'And cake. Will you join us, Highness?'

He'd changed into less formal dark trousers and an open-necked shirt so she could hopefully assume his royal duties were over.

'No. Thank you.' He glanced at his watch and then at Kiki. 'I hate to rush you, but flights are easier to and from the island the earlier in the day we travel. Air currents become stronger as we go into late afternoon. Are you happy if we leave for the hospital soon?'

Rough air currents on the way home? Excellent. 'Of course.' She tried to sound upbeat. 'Are we flying?'

'No.' He smiled as if he knew it was an act. 'We will be driving across as I wish to give you a brief glimpse of the scenery on the island. But we must get back to the ship as promised.'

Their trip to the other side of the island started with a winding descent from the castle—an exercise in S bends with the cliffs falling away to the side and the sea below. Not dissimilar from being in a helicopter, really.

Stefano drove a little convertible with total disregard for the precipice, and despite a few gasps on the whole Kiki knew she was safe. Strange.

'I hope this isn't where you had your accident?'

He laughed. 'Nothing so impressive. I hit a cow on the way to the hospital.'

At the bottom of their descent they drove parallel to the beach, and Stefano pointed out the famous race track where the Prince's Cup would be held the following week.

She remembered what Ginger had said. 'A nurse on the ship says you have quite a social event with your race.'

He smiled. 'It is popular with the sophisticated traveller and with philanthropists, and we raise more than enough money to cover the hospital's costs for that year as well as for several health research projects. Last year we raised money for a gynaecological wing which opens in a few days.'

'So it's not just a party?' She liked that.

He shook his head. Twice. 'It is a week of tedious social engagements which I would prefer not to have to attend, but the good it achieves makes me appreciate the generosity of those who come.'

'Poor sad Prince. So you don't have any fun?'

He flashed a grin at her. 'Sometimes. The race is fun. If you would consider joining me I think I could have more fun?'

She'd bet he would. 'While you make a fortune?'

'That too.'

Not a sensible idea. 'Sorry. I'm a working girl.'

He flashed another grin at her. 'I thought you might say that.'

There was something in his voice that made her frown, but just then they rounded a bend and turned away from the sea. Now they drove through rolling vistas of olive groves with grey-green leaves that glittered like stars in the sunlight and stretched away to the base of the mountain and a third of the way up its sides.

'We grow only three varieties of olive here and Aspelicus is famous for the gourmet oil it produces. One of my ancestors proclaimed that every family must plant three olive trees a year. We have many thousands of them now.'

'So when do you pick the olives?'

'We harvest in November. It is all done by hand.' She

raised her eyebrows, and he laughed. 'I admit. Not *my* hand.'

'But it doesn't hurt to have the Royal Seal on the bottle?'

He grinned. 'Not at all.'

The largest village, though really it seemed almost like a city, was clustered above the last of the olives and clung to the southern side of the mountain, its red-tiled houses and larger official buildings secured to the rock with Aspelican determination.

She could see the spires of several large churches, and the main belltower of a cathedral soared above the rooftops.

'I love the narrow stone streets. I'll bet the roads are cobbled and cool in the summer up there.'

He glanced where she pointed. 'If you come back I will show you. It is serene and very special. Most families go back hundreds of years.'

'And yours a thousand?' She was teasing him, but she was beginning to see that he had a heritage he was responsible for.

He tapped his forehead. 'Elise has been giving lessons again.'

As if he hadn't known she would. 'Wasn't that the idea?'

He shrugged innocently, and she had to smile when he said, 'I wouldn't dream of boring you.'

'You knew you wouldn't.'

The rapport between them was undeniable, and Kiki could easily have pretended he'd never been away. There was danger in that. Real danger. Because it wasn't true. He *had* gone away, and left her to face the worst time in her life alone. The sparkle seemed to drain from the day.

'Why am I here, Stefano?'

Stefano sighed. He could not but be aware that there was a distance between them that might never be breached, and still he was not sure how to repair the damage. All he knew was that he wanted back his rapport with Kiki. That after months of feeling flat suddenly he was alive again.

'When I saw you I had an idea.' He shrugged and the movement tightened his hands on the wheel. 'A thought to show you my work. Perhaps for you to consider a change in your medical direction. Even to consider coming here and working with me for a time.'

She shouldn't have been surprised. He'd already said they should spend more time together. So he'd been plotting to entice her to his island with the carrot of working with him in surgery...

Unfortunately the idea was attractive, because the tiny fragment of surgery she'd seen him perform in Sydney had been incredible. And she knew he was a good teacher. Further evidence had been in his direction of Wilhelm only yesterday.

To have the opportunity to watch and learn from such a surgeon would be the dream of many a young doctor looking to expand her skills.

But those other doctors wouldn't be as fatally attracted to Stefano as she'd been once before, and she didn't trust him. She knew, fatalistically, that if she moved here and spent time with Stefano he would ensure she become more than an associate. She would become the Prince's temporary mistress.

She must have been silent for an extended time, because the car slowed and she could feel his gaze on her.

'Do not concern yourself. This discussion is for another day. Enjoy the moment without strain. Let me show you first. Not obliged or pressured to consider anything you do not wish to do. It is my foolish pride that wants to show you my work.'

He shrugged. 'Of course I do not like the idea of you

going off to live your life without the chance of at least sharing my own dreams with you.'

Life. Dreams. Chance. All dangerous words for Kiki. Empty words. What was he trying to do?

'Why me?' And how was she going to quiet her unsettled thoughts now that he had spoken?

His attention returned to the road. 'Why anything?'

He was giving nothing else away.

Their snaked their way up a final hill and against the backdrop of more marching rows of olives a modern building sprawled elegantly over several acres, two-storeyed, and painted olive-green to blend into the countryside.

The closer they drove the more attractive it became. Now Kiki could see vine-covered verandas running around both floors, and the windows winked with white wooden shutters latched back against the olive walls.

'It's so pretty.' Gorgeous, really.

'My mother's design.' Pride was unmistakable in the gesture of his hand and in his voice.

'You miss her?'

'Very much.' He kept his eyes on the road. 'She was the voice of reason and the one who did not hesitate to laugh at me if I became too serious. Perhaps that is why I find you a breath of fresh air.' He looked away. 'But then she could forgive me if I made a mistake.'

He looked thoughtful for a moment, shrugged and went on.

'She could not change my father, for he was trained differently, but she influenced me greatly with her humanity and sense of fairness.'

This unexpected insight into Stefano as a very young man touched her deeply. 'When did she die?'

He hesitated, as if it was physically difficult to talk

about himself. 'When I was a teenager. An unexpected aneurism. Before I began medical school.'

So he had lost his mother around the same age as she had. She knew that feeling. The devastation, the aching void in the family, the feeling of betrayal at being left an orphan. 'I lost both my parents in a car accident.'

He looked at her. 'I am sorry. I did not ask enough about you in Sydney.'

She grimaced to herself. 'No, you didn't. But I understand your loss.' And there had been little time between work and bed for conversation. 'I had my sisters and Nick to look after me.' To look after the nuisance youngest sister. Though to be fair Nick had never treated her like that.

'But it is not the same, eh?'

'No.'

But this was not what she needed to think about as her baby's birthday came closer, and she pulled her mind away from the fact that she'd finally felt complete at the thought of being a mother. That too she had lost. As she would Stefano when the time came—a huge reason not to risk losing her heart to this man again. She was sick of loss.

But Stefano's past? It was the last thing Kiki had expected. A royal tragedy—the loss of a mother he adored. Kiki began to wonder about the man who ruled this little principality—Stefano's father. A man who didn't forgive easily. Who'd been brought up differently from someone with a sense of humour, perhaps?

It made her wonder what sort of life it had been for the young Stefano and his brother after their mother died. How had his father reacted to her death? How had these events moulded the man she'd thought she'd known?

But they had arrived.

CHAPTER SEVEN

STEFANO STOPPED THE car and vaulted over his door to come round to hers. Flamboyantly he opened it and held out his hand. 'Come. Let me show you my work.'

Kiki looked at his fingers, outstretched, waiting, and handed him her handbag. Especially vulnerable after the recent disclosures, now was not the time to let herself hold his hand. But scrambling from a low-slung sports car was a little more difficult than climbing down from the helicopter. She achieved it, although not with elegance, and eventually stood beside him. It would have been easier to take his hand. She ignored the tilt to his mouth and allowed him to lead the way.

The foyer of the hospital was bright and airy, with serene watercolour seascapes and lush potted greenery. The receptionist appeared and bowed, and Kiki was reminded that this man was accorded deference. But not from her. He seemed to cope with that remarkably well, really.

They were met by an auburn-haired woman with bright green spectacles perched on a snub nose. She had a stethoscope poking from the pocket of her white coat. 'Your Highness. Welcome.'

'Ah, Dr Herore, I hope you are well?'

'Yes, thank you.'

He gestured to Kiki, who stood quietly by his side. 'This is Dr Fender.'

Kiki and the young doctor shook hands, and she could tell the woman was wildly curious about her, in a nice way, and that made it easy to smile.

Stefano strode forward and they hurried to catch up. His whole demeanour had changed again and it was easy to see he loved his work. 'How are my patients today?'

'Jerome has been very silly and picked at his stitches. He will not listen to me, but perhaps now you are here...'

'We will start there.' He turned to Kiki. 'Jerome is five.' He slanted a glance at her. 'An orphan, caught in a bomb blast. I have been reconstructing his face and chest. He has been very brave but is quite the mischief.'

They walked the length of the corridor and turned into another wing. The wooden floors glowed with the deep red of cedar and Kiki wondered where they'd sourced these building materials on an island this size. It was a warm alternative to the marble everywhere else.

In the children's ward teddy bears, bright red cars and happy circus animals adorned the walls. With his back to them, a little boy was hunched over a red fire engine. By the set of his shoulders he wasn't happy.

Stefano stopped and tilted his head at the solemn figure. 'Jerome, what is this I hear?'

The child turned and even in the shadows his surly face lit up when he saw Stefano. But the ravages of war were still apparent in the criss-cross of tiny sutures that mapped his mouth and neck as he jumped to his feet and limped towards them in his striped pyjamas.

'Papa,' he lisped in broken English, and Dr Herore bent down and hushed him.

'You must not call His Highness this.'

'All is well, Dr Herore. Until he finds his new family I

may be his papa. And how are you, my son? What is this I hear of scratching sutures?'

The little boy hung his head and Stefano tilted his chin with one gentle finger.

'No more of this. My good work and that of Dr Herore needs to be carefully nurtured. Like the plant you care for me. How *is* my plant?'

The boy looked up with worship and reached for Stefano's hand. 'See the plant,' he said, and Stefano allowed himself to be dragged towards the window. 'It goes well, and when it is strong I too will be strong.'

'This I believe—and see how pretty it is?' They both gazed at the robust olive seedling in a red pot. 'I wish this for you, too, so you must promise not to scratch your sutures.'

'I will not.'

'Good. Now, climb to your bed and I will wash my hands. This is my friend Kiki. She is a doctor too, and I would like to lift the bandages on your chest and show her how well you are healing. If that is all right with you?'

'Okay.' It seemed nothing could faze his good humour now that his hero was here.

Kiki could barely restrain her smile. There was so much pleasure to be had from their conversation, but even in short acquaintance she could tell Jerome was far too serious to laugh at. She had not expected Stefano's rapport with children. But then he had been good with Mikey too. It made her wonder why he had left having a family so late when he would obviously be a splendid father. The smile slipped from her face and she glanced away from the little boy.

'Perhaps we will be able to leave the bandages down today and the dressing will not annoy you so much?' Stefano looked at Dr Herore.

She crossed her fingers and said softly while the boy's back was turned, 'It would help. He has been very patient, but the bandage is chafing him and he will not let us touch it.'

When Stefano had donned the gloves that Dr Herore had laid open a nurse wheeled in a trolley with dressing equipment.

Stefano spoke to Kiki but his words were for Jerome even though he didn't look at the boy. 'It makes me sad when Jerome does not let my fellow doctors and nurses look at his wound, because when I telephone for his progress they cannot tell me.'

Jerome shifted guiltily on the bed, but Stefano continued to gaze steadily at Kiki.

'He has been brave and strong since he came here. Now we have repaired his face and neck and used skin grafts for his chest he will be as other boys his age when we have finished.'

'Except I will have learnt your English.' The boy held his head still as he spoke.

'It is not *my* English. We speak it here so that all you children may grow up with two languages at least. Now is the perfect time to learn.'

Jerome shrugged. 'I do not mind.'

Luckily Kiki's giggle drew a smile from the boy and not a frown.

'She's nice, your friend.'

'I think so.' Stefano was engrossed in lifting the edges of the thick dressing carefully. The little boy's fingers clenched on the sheet but he didn't move.

Kiki stepped closer and slid her fingers across the sheet next to his.

Jerome looked up with gritted teeth and tentatively reached out and held onto her fingers as if to draw strength.

Kiki's eyes stung as she studied the brave little face and saw his sheer determination to be good. When she glanced up she saw Stefano had stopped his easing of the bandages and was watching her.

'Did I not say he was brave? But we will count to five—' he wagged his fingers at Jerome '—in English, before we start so that he can be brave again.'

Gradually the extent of the chest wound was exposed, and Kiki had to fight not to dig her own nails into the sheet. Everywhere across the boy's sunken chest tiny sutures trailed over the livid skin like rows of tiny ants, pulling together what must have been an almost mortal wound.

'Ah. It heals well. Your big heart is safe again.' The wound was clean and dry, and the graft site looked well fixed. 'Dr Herore will check the donor site later today, when you have had a break from people disturbing your wounds but you are on the mend, my brave friend.'

When it was done Jerome let go of Kiki's fingers as if he'd never needed them and turned his worshipping eyes to his hero. 'That is good.' Then he broke into Lebanese.

To her surprise Stefano answered him fluently and the conversation flowed over her head.

While Stefano spoke with Jerome, Kiki was drawn to a cot in the corner of the room, where a dark-haired little girl with a bandaged hand heavily disguised by white crêpe sat quietly. The little girl turned big, mournful eyes to Kiki and did not return Kiki's tentative smile.

'And what is your name, little one?'

Dr Herore spoke from behind her shoulder. 'Her name is Sheba and she is from the nearest village. Her mother comes daily. Sheba's fingers were almost amputated in an accident, Prince Stefano has managed to reattach, and we have great hopes she will regain full use.'

'She seems heavily bandaged.'

'This one we cannot stop from pulling at her wound, so it needs to be well out of her way. We are still worried it may become infected.'

Just then a small-boned woman came into the room. Until she turned sideways to curtsey to Stefano Kiki didn't realise she was heavily pregnant.

'Ah, here comes mama now. *Bongiorno*, Rosa.'

The woman was panting a little as she arrived, and Kiki wondered if she was in some pain. Her face seemed especially strained, even though she smiled at Dr Herore.

'*Ciao*, Dr Herore. How is my little Sheba today?'

They all looked at the little girl standing on tiptoes in her cot, reaching out for her mother, and such was the anguish on her little face Kiki could barely watch.

'She misses you badly.'

'*Si.*' Rosa brushed away her own tears, heaved the little girl into her arms to comfort her and was almost strangled by the tightness of her daughter's grip.

Dr Herore dropped a hand on Rosa's shoulder. 'A few more days, until the risk of infection is gone, and she will be able to go home.'

'I know. She is so lucky to come here. And soon my new baby will be born and Sheba will be home.'

Stefano crossed the room and joined the conversation. 'Take care, Rosa. You are rushing too much at the end of your pregnancy. You must be well for this little one too.'

'Yes, Your Highness.' Rosa looked totally overwhelmed by Stefano and Kiki glanced at him, confused by the many facets of this man she had thought special but still a man.

The silence became a little awkward and Stefano settled it for everyone. 'Time passes.'

Though Kiki felt he was very aware he was disturbing the mother's time. He nodded kindly, brushed the shiny hair of little Sheba, and placed his hand on Kiki's arm.

'Come, before we leave I will show you the viewing window into our theatres. I am very proud of them.'

As they left Kiki glanced back at the children, at the warmth they all showed towards Stefano. As the distance increased she could just make out the mother and child locked in an embrace.

'How did Sheba hurt her hand?'

'A dog attacked her—thus the risk of infection has been very great. She has many intermittent antibiotics so she cannot go home yet, which is hard. Her mother will not miss a day and walks four miles to see her.'

'Can't you send a car to bring her?'

He smiled at her censure. Shook his head at the idea of doing so. 'I offered and she declined. I will get Dr Herore to ask again. But I must be careful of the old ways of the village.'

'The children love you.'

He shook his head. 'They are away from their families. It is easy to grow attached to an adult they think will keep them safe.'

She didn't think that was it at all.

They left the children's ward behind and turned another corner to climb a tiny spiral staircase with intricate ironwork. The steps were narrow, and looked incredibly old and frail for a new building.

Stefano saw her hesitate. 'As you see, these stairs have been restored. They are safe.'

'Okay. I believe you.' She was beginning to understand that Stefano took his responsibilities very seriously. And he didn't know he should have felt responsible for *her*.

He ran his fingers up the iron handrail and there was something so gentle and reverent in the way he touched the cold steel she couldn't help the memory of other times when she had watched his hands—on her...

When he spoke she almost stumbled, jerked from the past, and he put out his hand to steady her.

Luckily it was only for a moment, and his conversation remained on the steps. 'They are from a section of the castle that crumbled in a landslide and had become dangerous. I had them transplanted to this spot. They are beautiful, are they not?'

She ran her hand gently over the balustrade. 'I've always wanted a spiral staircase.'

He smiled down at her. 'Come work for me and I could call it the Kiki Stairwell.'

So now he would name a staircase after her? Tempting, but… 'You never give up. I'm sure the others who spend so much time here would not be happy with such favour.'

He shrugged. 'It is my hospital. I do as I wish.'

That was the man she knew was under there. 'How disagreeable.'

He stiffened, searched her expression, and then relaxed at the amusement on Kiki's face. 'Perhaps, sometimes, I am. Even need to be.' It was a fact—not an apology.

They reached the top of the stairs and turned onto a landing with windows on both sides of a narrow corridor. The outward-facing window opened over the roof and the lawns, and the inward-facing windows gave a superb view of a pristine operating theatre. Even from here Kiki could tell Stefano had every latest device for his patients, for comfort, and for the surgeon's expertise.

She couldn't help but imagine working there. Working with him. 'Wow. It's fabulous.'

Stefano looked quietly pleased by her response. 'I knew you would appreciate the promise of facilities like these.' He turned and his face grew more serious. 'Even in the few days I saw you at your work in Sydney, barely trained in operating theatre techniques, you had the potential to be a great surgeon. Yet I find you on a pleasure ship?'

'And you.' She was flippant. 'Ironic isn't it?' *Don't spoil the day*, she thought. But they'd always be skirting the edge of this discussion.

'So why did this irony occur?' Stefano watched her. He could see she would choose not to enlighten him and he stamped back his impatience.

She shrugged. 'Things happen. Life throws you something you don't expect and your path changes.'

He wished she would tell him something he didn't know. 'And what changed *your* path, Kiki. Or who?'

She turned her back. Stepped closer to the next window. 'So, tell me about the type of operations you have here. Is this the only OR you have?'

'*Bah!* You are like a clam.' She was the most frustrating woman. He would never have believed it before.

She shrugged. 'And you are used to getting your own way. Not this time.'

He looked at her. Her back was towards him. None of his people would have dared to turn their backs on him. It did not seem at all difficult forKiki to do so. But he would not have her different. He revelled in the difference.

'So we continue the dance.' *Bah* again.

Then he shrugged and went on as if the conversation had never happened. He saw the slight loosening of her shoulders. So she was more tense than she appeared. He would watch for that sign again.

'Operating theatres. We have two others—though one is really only used in emergencies.'

She turned to face him. 'What emergencies do you have?'

'Most often the sudden influx of more than one patient. It is word of mouth. I have a representative in most medical facilities in trouble spots where children are at risk. They contact my team and when information is gathered they can phone me any time. We discuss if the child or children will be strong enough to withstand the journey. To remove a child from all they know is no light matter.'

She could certainly see that. 'Of course not. So who brings them?'

Good. She was deeply interested. He relaxed a little as he let her into his world. The memories of many retrievals coloured his response.

'I have a team who fly in and out when we hear of a case that would benefit greatly from our intervention. There is also a political team who work with governments and organise extradition, and a medical team that goes in on the ground to source the patient from whatever hospital they are in and stabilise for transport.'

'Sounds efficient.'

They were paid to be efficient. 'Most times. Before they retrieve, my political team endeavours to trace parents and relatives, if we can find them alive, so they know the child has survived and is being cared for. We always leave a point of contact.'

He watched her lean her nose against the glass, and not for the first time today he wanted to turn her cheek his way and kiss those stubborn lips of hers.

'Your organisation sounds amazing, but still, a medical crisis for a child... Losing their families... The children must be terrified.'

'I am very aware of that.' Something crossed his face that made her look more closely at him, but he turned away and took a step closer to the viewing window, so that all she could see was his profile. *Back off, I'm royalty*, was stamped all over it.

It was his turn to use the window to escape. 'As you see,

the other theatres are along here—but perhaps we should go. It is getting late.'

She'd said something to upset him. The mood had changed, and it seemed there was nothing she could do about that now, as he marched her along corridors towards the entrance. In the distance she could see the children's ward, and she wished she could revisit again just for a short time.

But he had moved on more than physically. 'I have asked the helicopter to meet us here. We'll fly back to the palace for lunch—there is a group of people I must meet with—then leave for the ship straight after.'

As they took off and soared across the tops of the olive groves it seemed surreal that her pilot was a prince, and she was the reason they were flying across these paddocks. How did she feel about that? Honoured? Chuffed? Excited? Certainly not oblivious.

Well, she wouldn't be human if she didn't feel a little bit special. But it was only one day. She'd just have to be careful to protect herself, because her senses were going into overload with all this care he was taking of her.

She'd enjoyed morning tea in the intimacy of the family apartments, and she hoped, if she was lucky, lunch would be similar, only with Stefano present.

How wrong could she be?

Lunch was served in the formal section of the palace, and she could barely see him at the head of the table, let alone need to worry about accidentally touching him. It seemed her escort—what a joke—was in great demand, judging by the procession of dignitaries that kept interrupting any attempt on his part to address his food.

There'd been a brief flurry of attention when everyone in the room had looked at her as she had been introduced to his father—a shorter version of Stefano, with bushy white eyebrows and scarily piercing blue eyes—and her composure had taken a beating as the older man had stared right through her.

Stefano had moved her on and then handed her over to Elise again, so she'd felt transformed back into parcel mode, and the island's hero had disappeared even faster than before. She'd begun to have an inkling as to how busy his life was when he was home and just what might have happened to thoughts of her when he went away.

But that still hadn't prepared her for lunch.

To say the lunch was formal was an extreme understatement.

She'd half expected a servant to bring in a whole pig, complete with apple in mouth, but they didn't. Not that they didn't have the silver serving dishes and a multitude of crystal glasses down pat. And this was *lunch*. About as intimate as a hotdog at a football game.

The woman beside her constantly complained about how far down the table she was while the tall, good-looking man on her other side quivered with mischief. There was something about him that reminded her of Miko, the charmer of the ship. There was no decision on who she'd rather talk to.

She held out her hand. 'My name is Kiki Fender. A pleasure to meet you.'

He took her hand in his with studied gallantry. '*Bongiorno, signorina*. Franco Tollini.' Of course he raised it to his lips instead of shaking it.

His kiss lingered on her fingers. Kiki kept her grin behind her lips but unfortunately for the first time since she'd sat down managed to catch Stefano's eye. How amusing—for her, at least. The Prince seemed less than happy. She turned back to her companion, who had no intention of letting this opportunity go by.

Franco reluctantly gave back her hand. 'I am part of the Prince's team. We transfer the children home to their parents when they are well enough to return.'

'So do you have a medical background, as well, Franco?'

'*Si*. Dr Tollini.' He shrugged with self-deprecation. 'I am a specialist in rehabilitation, but since coming here I have been performing some surgery.'

'Ah. The hospital. You obviously enjoy your work.'

He smiled, and thankfully Kiki could see it wasn't just in appreciation of her. He did love his work.

'The children are incredible. And it is my job to take them back to their families after they heal and help them settle.'

She couldn't help but think of Jerome. 'What if their parents are not there?'

His dark eyes flashed with fervour. 'Then they are adopted into families that will take very good care of them. Our mission is not to lose them entirely. We ensure their schoolwork is well catered for, and more often than not they will have better learning when they return, with opportunities for further study provided if they wish.'

Why hadn't she heard more about this place? 'It seems a fabulous cause.'

Earnestness shone from Franco's eyes. 'Prince Stefano is a great humanitarian and a great surgeon.'

Another fan. She was surrounded by them. 'I have heard the Prince is also a good teacher.'

'Spare my blushes, Kiki.'

They both looked up as Stefano sat elegantly down on her other side, like an unhurried lion settling to watch his prey. Goodness knew what he'd done with the person who'd been there a moment ago, Kiki thought, and had a sudden vision of the woman being thrown into a dungeon by Stefano merely because he'd wanted her seat.

'Hello there, Franco.'

'Your Highness.' Strangely, with Stefano now beside her, Franco seemed to shrink and become a little less boldly defined. Again Kiki realised the Stefano she'd thought she'd known was a totally different person when in his own pride. There was that lion analogy again. She could almost see his aura of power, which grew more apparent despite the gentleness of his tone.

Stefano went on conversationally. 'I've just been showing Dr Fender over the hospital.'

Franco looked at her, and then at the Prince. He swallowed. 'I was just telling…' he paused nervously '…Dr Fender, about our work. She has not had a chance to mention she knows you or that she's seen the hospital.'

'How remiss of her.'

Kiki had had enough of this. She turned to Stefano. 'And how unfortunate that you interrupted our conversation.'

His eyes flared but his voice remained even. 'My apologies. But the helicopter awaits and we must return—or should we be delayed until tomorrow?' He let the question hang.

Kiki blinked, decided she needed to be on the ship, and pushed back her chair. One of the waiters nearly broke his leg, trying to get to her to help, but he was still too slow for Stefano. The Prince assisted her sardonically.

The sooner she left here and returned to the real world, the sooner her head could try to sort out the hundreds of different messages she was getting today.

'Goodbye, Franco. Nice meeting you.' Deliberately she held out her hand, quite sure Franco wouldn't kiss it this time, with Stefano watching.

She was right.

Franco also stood. 'Goodbye, Dr Fender.' He bowed deeply. 'Your Highness.'

'You were really obnoxious.'

Stefano nodded and smiled as the dignitaries bowed as they departed. He ignored the hiss from Kiki beside him and kept her hand firmly in his. To hell with what the gossips said.

It had been a very unusual day. He supposed he should really try and curb his desire to run through any man who spoke to Kiki, let alone those who actually kissed her hand, but he wasn't sure it was worth the effort.

He was beginning to understand the pirate tendencies of his ancestors when they'd captured women and dragged them off. His mother would have been horrified. Then he smiled and remembered something she had once said to him about his father's courtship. Perhaps his mama would not have been so horrified after all.

When they reached the helicopter he waved the pilot into the front with his man and climbed into the back with Kiki.

When she said, 'I think I'll sit in the front...' he laughed out loud and helped her fasten her seat belt.

When he looked again at her face she was shaking her head. The struggle on her face suddenly gave way and she smiled too.

They grinned at each other, and his relief was a warning about how much this woman's good opinion mattered to him. That and having his arms around her. He'd been fantasising about that all day. Not his usual *modus operandi*. It would be better if he kept Kiki in his bed—that way she would not mess with his head, just his skin. Even at this brief thought his body stirred.

But his prestige would suffer if others heard the way she spoke to him. He really needed to do something about that, but he wasn't sure what. He had a feeling that a direct order would give her the excuse to walk away.

She straightened her face and pretended to frown at him. 'I'm not happy with you.'

He inclined his head and threw caution to the wind rushing by outside the helicopter. 'And there are things I need to discuss about *your* behaviour. Perhaps we could examine this over dinner. Privately. Say seven? My suite.'

'Six-thirty, if you don't mind. I work tomorrow. And the restaurant will be fine.'

Kiki wondered if she'd gone too far. She'd been very surprised when Stefano had decided against piloting their way back to the ship, and disappointed she wasn't going to have the cooling-off period she needed to recover from his grabbing her hand like that and marching her onto the helicopter.

It had certainly surprised a few people—not least her.

The problem was as soon as he'd touched her she'd been captive, and it had nothing to do with force. She glanced down at her fingers in her lap. She wouldn't have been surprised if her hand glowed like one of those luminous fish in the deepest depths of the ocean they were flying over right now. It felt irradiated with his touch, still warm from his warmth, and she was still subdued by the leashed power she had felt.

She wriggled her fingers until his hand came in over hers and stilled them. She glanced up and saw the devil-ish gleam in his eyes grow. *He knew.* Her face flamed and she pulled her hand away.

Stefano smiled. 'You may choose the restaurant this time.' He turned to look out of the window.

* * *

They landed back at the airport without too many of the bumpy updrafts Stefano had mentioned. There were a few minutes' delay while they waited for the pilot to give them the all-clear to alight, and then their transfer by car back to the wharf beside the ship took no time.

Kiki could feel herself tense as she waited for the vehicle to stop. Suddenly everything was awkward, overwhelming—the gulf between them, the hundreds of different examples of how Stefano's life and upbringing were so different from hers. She was a fool to think anything could come of falling in love with this man. She should never have agreed to dine with him.

'Thank you, Your Highness, for an interesting day. Excuse me if I rush off. I must check in with my colleagues.'

He leaned towards her and spoke over the noise of the ship's loudspeakers. 'Liar.'

She forgot her recent revelation and glared back at him. 'Bully.'

His eyebrows rose. 'Two hours' time.'

Thankfully someone opened her door to help her out and she could escape.

For the next two hours Kiki felt as if a huge clock was ticking inside her head. Each tick was louder than the previous one as the hands crept closer to six-thirty. With an hour to go she'd tried and discarded a hundred excuses, each lamer than the last, and in desperation taken herself down to the sick bay to see what was going on there. Nothing. The place was locked and empty.

She declined to ride back up in the lift. It was the hour for pre-dinner drinks, and well-dressed men and women would be crowding the lifts for the next few hours, so she trod the stairs, hoping the exercise might burn off some of the nervous energy she seemed over-endowed with.

Nothing for it but to get dressed and get it over with. The problem was she still didn't know what she wanted.

If she was honest with herself there were many reasons why she would love to go to Aspelicus and work. Not the least that it was time to leave the ship, stretch her brain, learn new skills. But was it time to risk her heart again? And why this week, of all weeks, when her guard was down from a countdown she'd been dreading? Could she keep the distance she knew she'd need when she was feeling so fragile?

CHAPTER EIGHT

WHEN KIKI ARRIVED for dinner, she'd chosen black. The demure effect of her high collar was lost by the keyhole yoke neckline which allowed a glimpse of the swelling valley between her breasts.

Stefano rose smoothly, as did his libido, and one glance at the *maître d'* was enough to keep the man away from her chair.

'You look stunning.' He leaned over her shoulder as she was seated. Along with the subtle scent of spring flowers he always associated with Kiki the view was even more incredible from this angle.

He returned to his seat and looked across at her with a lightness of spirits he wasn't used to.

As he glanced down at the menu he wondered how she did it—lifted him from being immersed in business, too involved in matters of state, too focussed on his patients. She made him remember he was truly a man who deserved a life that was not always lived for others. It was this quality that so intrigued him, tantalised his consciousness, because *with* her he felt unlike he did at any time without her.

They had two days left —not enough to throw caution to the winds, but enough to convince her she needed to join his team. And then he could see if they had a future. Already it was at that stage.

When they had both ordered, and the champagne had been poured, he raised his glass. 'To an interesting day together.'

She bit back a laugh. *Interesting* didn't nearly describe it. 'Great word-choice.' He did make her laugh. *'Salute.'*

He leaned forward. 'So, what did you think of my hospital.'

Kiki felt her shoulders relax a little. He'd started with an easy one. Thank goodness.

She'd spent the last half an hour shoring up her defences. She needed a protective barrier around herself just in case he brought up the fact that she was like soft soap in his hands as soon as he touched her.

The easy stuff first.

'Your hospital is amazing. I love your work and the miracles you create.' *And I see you love children.* But she didn't say it. Couldn't say it. She just felt the gaping hole and smoothed it over before it could cloud her mind.

He smiled, and her heart ached while she smiled back. It wasn't fair. Why had she crossed paths with a man it would be so hard to forget?

He leaned towards her. His intense gaze captured her as easily as if he'd caught her physically, yet her fingers were tucked safely in her lap.

'And if I offered you a position there? On a surgical term, learning what I could teach you? Would you be interested?'

'Is that what you are offering?' Because she knew without a doubt that if she became his mistress again she would lose herself. One day she would regret it.

And she worked hard, believed in the good she could do, and deserved more self-respect than choosing that life for herself.

'It is a job offer. Yes. I believe so.'

'Do you?' She shook her head. 'If it was a stand-alone package, just that position, it would be hard to refuse.' These were dangerous waters and she saw the flare of triumph in his eyes. *Not so fast, buddy.*

She read his fierce intelligence, searching between her words, sifting for weakness, assessing his own strengths.

He took a sip from his glass and set it down. 'And what did you think of the palace?'

The palace. She thought of his father's cold eyes. The long formal rooms. Her own feeling of insignificance and his vast importance. Not a comfortable place. 'Your palace is very beautiful.' Now to the more difficult part. 'But I wouldn't want to live there.'

'So where *would* you live?'

'In the village. A walk across the fields would be a delight after a hard day in the OR. I could practise my Italian, or French, or whatever language it is they speak up there.'

'Italian.' He sat back with a smile. 'So you have at least thought about the position?'

'And its disadvantages.' She didn't delude herself that he would marry her, or even that she wanted to be a princess, watching her husband from the other end of a long, table of dignified guests. But that was far fetched.

He frowned. 'Disadvantages? I see none.'

The entrées arrived. As they ate she changed the subject. 'Elise said you operated on her son? Was the defect a difficult one?'

'Yes. Full thickness and requiring several operations.'

He explained in detail and drew on the table with his finger, outlining the sections that had required repair. Again he made it easy for her to understand why and how.

She would learn so much, the voice inside her insisted.

'His mother is pleased with his recovery,' she said.

'Elise has had a hard life. She would have loved more

children. Though with her husband passed away that will not be possible unless she remarries.'

'I can't imagine her leaving her position. She admires you very much.'

'She has worked for our family since she was a girl. For the last few years she's been my housekeeper and she expects perfection for me.'

Now, *that* brought up an interesting topic. 'She said you must marry before you are forty. Are you feeling the pressure?' Did she really want to know this? In case he thought she was putting herself forward, she hurriedly added, 'I'm sure there are dozens of perfect future princesses out there for you.'

'A few.'

He was watching her and she didn't know where to look. 'So what happens if you don't?'

He shrugged. 'I forfeit my royal inheritance.'

She frowned. He didn't seem too perturbed. 'Might it be hard to live as a subject again?'

He shrugged again. 'I make my own fortune. I spend it on the hospital. I would have more than enough to live on, and I would still be a prince. I could not leave my country for personal satisfaction.'

Her stomach sank and her appetite drifted away. 'So you will marry?'

'Yes.' He smiled, but there was no humour in his eyes. 'My father has several women he approves of.'

She knew one his dad wasn't so keen on. 'Congratulations.'

'Are not in order yet.' He glanced at her plate, seeing the signs that she had eaten all she wanted. 'Dessert?'

'No, thank you.' She folded her napkin and placed it on her side plate.

He lifted the bottle. 'More wine?'

She shook her head and took another sip of the mineral water she'd changed to before the main course.

'Good.' He signalled the waiter. 'Then if you have eaten enough perhaps we could go somewhere more private to finish this discussion?'

Kiki glanced around. The atmosphere was elegant, non-intrusive and discreet. Above all—safe. 'I think not. I'm very happy with the company we are in.'

If he was disappointed he didn't show it. He just waved the waiter away again, as if it was of no matter, then was straight back to the hunt. 'So, what is it you'd want from me if you took this position?'

He had brass, asking that. 'I could ask you the same question.'

'Ladies first.' He gestured with his hand.

'I think not.' She lifted her chin.

'So stubborn.' He glanced away and then back, and she couldn't read the expression on his face. 'So determined not to show me the respect I am used to.'

He was right, but she didn't think she could change. 'I do not intend to offend you. I respect you, but I will not give in to your need for control all the time.' *Because I would lose respect for myself.* And in the end that was all she would have left. *Herself.*

'Well, let me see.' He ran his eyes lingeringly over what he could see of her and smiled. 'The idea of working with you, watching your surgical skills grow, feeding your desire to repair intricately and restore function, to watch you blossom into the surgeon I know you could be—that is enticing.'

Kiki could admit the concept was very attractive. 'And for me also.'

His voice wrapped around her. 'As well, I wish to show you the beauty of my homeland with its depths that you can only begin to imagine. Celebrations like the Prince's Cup, the galas held after the harvest season, the saints' days and the markets...'

He opened his hands and she couldn't help but be enthralled with his passion for his island.

'In my palace are long tunnels from the castle to the sea, works of art nobody views, buildings so old and manuscripts so holy and so fragile even the Pope agrees we do not move them.'

She did appreciate his deep pride, and the responsibility he took with his position, and she was not immune to the honour he spoke of bestowing on her. 'That would be wonderful.'

'And...' He left it hanging.

'Is there more?'

Of course there was more that he wanted. And that was what she was so afraid of.

'Yes. Then there is the heart of it.'

His eyes darkened and his voice took on a quality that made the gooseflesh rise on her arms.

'Then there is the woman who makes me understand the baser instincts of a bygone age. Who makes me remember I am a man not to be trifled with. A woman I burn to protect and long to conquer. I want the lot—and I don't want you staying half an hour from my bed in the village.'

She shivered. It was there. Plain speaking, as she'd asked. There was no doubting his intent—nor the fact that every nerve in her body leaned towards him as he said it. She'd asked for honesty and got it. With a vengeance.

He shrugged his shoulders, as if he'd been discussing the weather. 'But I understand your dilemma.'

Holy Dooley—what could she say to that? 'I don't think you do.'

He tilted his head. 'So tell me.'

Where to start? With her mind blown by the fantasy he had conjured she was starting from way behind. 'I appreciate your honesty…' *Sort of.* She paused. 'And I will try to reply with my own.'

'See…' He smiled and looked at her as if she was a wonder of the world. 'This is why you hold me.'

She shook her head, not willing to be diverted from saying her piece while she had some structure in her head. 'Strictly business. My own residence away, from the castle—preferably in the village, if possible—and set work hours.'

He shook his head. 'I do not find that possible. A single woman living in the village would be prey to gossip and perhaps even harassment.'

He shook his head again, but she ignored him with a smile. 'The harassment I'm worried about lives in the castle.'

He stared her down, dark eyes full of wicked amusement. 'It is not me you are afraid of, Dr Fender. It is your own base instincts and the fact that we spontaneously combust when we are alone.'

Didn't she know that? 'Exactly. But I did not interrupt you—perhaps you could show me the same courtesy?'

He straightened, only half joking when he said, 'You are speaking to a *prince*.'

But she wouldn't be shut down. Not now. Not by him when so much was at stake. 'And that's why you like me.'

It was Stefano's turn to laugh. 'So what am I to do? See you through the day, toss in my lonely bed at night, only to be exposed to your unreachable womanly wiles again the next day? I think not.'

She spread her hands, borrowing his favourite mannerism. '*Impasse*. Your choice.'

He sat back further and a slow smile crossed his face. 'I will sleep on it. Though I will not sleep.'

She gathered her purse. 'Well, I have to sleep because I have work in the morning. Which reminds me—if you meet my requirements, I would need to give two weeks' notice.'

He glanced away. 'I will see that the cruise line does not suffer, if you leave with me it will be when the cruise ends in two days.'

By the time Kiki made it back to her cabin her knees were shaking. What had she talked herself into? When she'd left this same cabin two hours ago it had never been going to happen and now, after one meal with him, she was negotiating contracts. *Crazy, foolish woman*. She needed serious advice.

She didn't know who to turn to. Now would be the perfect time to talk to Nick, but her brother had his own life, and anyway they were at sea so her mobile wouldn't work. She couldn't talk to Ginger because of the risk of her capturing the scoop of the week for her ex-boyfriend's gossip column, and Wilhelm, while a great boss, just wouldn't understand.

But when she went to work the next morning, as the ship docked in Monte Carlo, everyone already knew. Because Prince Stefano Mykonides had put in her notice for her and a replacement doctor was arriving tomorrow, when the ship returned to Livorno. So, not only would tomorrow be the day before the one she was dreading for emotional reasons, now she would be out of work and out of her home.

Ginger's eyes were wide with a grudging respect for Kiki's new notoriety, which didn't help at all.

She looked at Wilhelm and her stomach sank at the worried expression on his face. She couldn't believe Stefano had been so arrogantly sure of her decision—plus so high-handed that he didn't think there would be repercussions.

It was a classic example of his privileged lack of thought. How could he not realise this would send her back the other way?

'It's not true,' she said, conveniently forgetting that she had already decided to finish work on the ship regardless of Stefano's offer.

Wilhelm patted her on the back. 'Well, the new guy's coming and your resignation papers have been drawn up without the need for any notice.'

She looked for inspiration or explanation but there was none on Wilhelm's face. 'How could he *do* that?'

Wilhelm shrugged again and rubbed his hands together awkwardly. 'Easily, apparently. It's by order of the cruise line's owner.'

Kiki stared at him and through him, trying to see an answer. 'Can I reverse it?'

Wilhelm sighed. 'Apparently not. I already asked, because I figured it was something like that.'

She could feel incredulous anger building. 'Well, thank you for that.' She could not believe this was happening. At least Will had had some faith in her. 'Of course I wouldn't resign without telling you. I can't believe he's done this. Is he insane?'

Wilhelm rubbed the underside of his jaw. 'No. Just used to power. Owed favours by the owner.'

She needed to get out of this small room before she exploded. This couldn't be happening. 'I'll be right back.'

'You want me to come looking for you if you aren't?' Wilhelm was beginning to get the idea that this man played hard.

She was about to say yes, then thought about the repercussions that didn't just involve her. 'No. I can handle it.

You stay out of the firing line. He has just bought more trouble than he knows.'

Kiki fumed all the way up in the elevator. Halfway she briefly wondered if perhaps she should have taken the stairs, to at least try and calm down and heighten the chances that she would act rationally when she arrived.

That thought was vetoed.

As each floor flashed by on the control panel of the lift she couldn't remember ever being this incensed, but the annoyingly persistent voice in her mind was suggesting again that this headlong course of action might not be the wisest one.

Well, to hell with that. He deserved a blast. A quick in and out might not save her job on the ship, but it was going to make her feel a whole lot better.

When the suite door opened she let him have it. 'How dare you—?'

Wrong man. Blast!

She scanned past the shoulders of the bristling man in front of her and spied her prey at the windows of the suite. She took a step, but came up against the surprisingly solid bulk of Stefan's manservant.

'Let her in, Manos.' Stefano's voice was even. 'Then leave.'

Which only served to incense her more.

She threw daggers at him as she waited for the hulk to get out of the way. 'You might want to keep him around for protection.'

'I think not.'

The man hesitated as Kiki swept past, but Stefano waved him on and the door shut silently after him. When she glanced behind her he'd gone. Kiki kept walking until she was a hand's breadth away from him and glared into his face.

'I've upset you.' Stefano watched her with a wariness born of unfamiliarity with this kind of scenario.

'Brilliant deduction, Sherlock.'

He blinked.

'As I was saying—how *dare* you hand in my resignation without my permission?'

He stepped to the side and picked up a half-filled glass of juice. 'Don't you think you are overreacting?'

His voice was mild, but the thread of sudden amusement in it was a torch to Kiki's anger.

'Not yet, I'm not.' There was probably steam coming out of her ears—not that he'd notice.

Unperturbed, he shrugged. 'I saw you were worried about giving the correct amount of notice.' He crossed the room and sat down on the lounge, crossed his legs and looked at enquiringly. 'My cousin owes me favours. I have merely taken the matter out of your hands.'

She spun and stormed across the room until she stood over him. 'Well, I want it back in my hands. And I'm giving you a straight refusal on the offer of a position while I'm at it.'

He remained impassive. 'Don't be foolish. What will you do for a job?'

She lifted her head. 'I have plenty of options.'

That wiped the smile from his face. 'I'm sure you have.'

'What's that supposed to mean?'

He put the glass down and she could tell his temper had slipped a little.

'Whatever you wish.' He rose and took a step towards her, his eyes drilling into her.

Alarm bells started to ring. She needed to get her piece said and go. 'Well, know this, Prince Stefano Mykonides. I'm leaving this ship tomorrow, and I'm *not* going to Aspelicus.'

Then she spun on her heel and got out of there while she still had her clothes on.

The door closed and Stefano stared at it. He should have caught her before she left, because the sex would have been explosively incredible. But in fact he had been in the wrong. Out of line. And to take advantage of her emotion would have made him more culpable, not less.

She was totally correct. He had no right to assume control. *Yet.* Difficult to remember when all his life decisions had needed to be made and he'd gone with them. Most times he chose the correct path. With Kiki it had been one false step after another.

Now he needed to win back her good graces. Because she *was* coming to Aspelicus.

Late that afternoon Stefano waited around the corner beside the lifts. He knew she would be out soon. He could imagine the headlines: *Prince Waits to Pounce on Innocent Doctor!*

The door opened and she walked across the foyer from the hospital to the elevator with a nurse, who pressed the button for the lift.

Kiki's hands were full. At least she hadn't tossed his flowers out, or left them in the waiting room.

It was a two-fold ploy on his part—to apologise in public with flowers, knowing if he made the bunch large enough she would have to take the lift to get them to her room. His plan to throw himself at her mercy would not work if he had to follow her up the stairs.

Amazing how devious he could be when he had to.

He waited until the lift doors began to close and then strode across the distance between them.

'Hold the lift, please.'

He pressed the button for good measure, in case she was quick enough to realise it was him.

He slipped in between them as the doors shut. 'I'm very sorry.'

'You can't buy me with flowers.' Kiki pushed the bouquet towards him but he was way ahead of her.

He took them and handed them straight to Ginger. 'Would you be so good as to hold these?'

Then he turned back to Kiki and lifted her hands in his, squeezed and kissed her fingers.

'Forgive me.'

Her hands and her eyes were cold. 'Done. Now leave me alone.'

The lift slowed. His plan had not met his expectations. Again. Why did that happen with this woman?

'It was a misjudgement on my part. I have withdrawn your resignation.' He hadn't, but he could do it very quickly if need be. He'd hoped for some response, but again she just looked at him coolly and that surprised him.

'I'm sure you haven't.'

How did she know that?

'But don't bother. If the cruise company can do that without my knowledge I don't want to work for them. And if you think you can control my life I certainly don't want to work for *you*. Not everything is under your control, Your Highness.'

The lift stopped.

He watched from the back of the lift as she stepped out, and as she walked away he heard her say, 'I'll see you at the show. Please keep the flowers, Ginger.'

CHAPTER NINE

MONACO WAS A great place to buy a sexy catsuit—even in a thirty-minute dash by tender after work.

The salesgirl had assured her it was latex-free—Kiki didn't want to brush up against Marla and start that whole scenario again—and the blatant sexual statement that she could wear what she wanted, in front of whoever she wanted, would annoy Stefano. She hoped. It was her last chance to do so.

An hour ago it had seemed like a brilliant idea.

The final night crew's pageant always proved popular with the passengers because it was more personal to cheer for their favourite crew member, waiter or cabin person while watching them perform on stage.

Kiki had been dancing at the pageant with Miko for almost four months, so there was little practice needed for their tango session. And this was the last night to end all last nights.

Tonight the theme was the *Lion King*, but any type of animal was acceptable. The skintight silver suit dipped low at the front and, with a sheepdog's tenacity, rounded her breasts up and pointed them in the right direction without the benefit of padding. She hoped it wasn't cold in the auditorium.

Now she was dressed it looked so much worse under

fluorescent light, and Kiki laughed with a trace of hysteria. All in all, the suit left nothing to the imagination, she thought as she stared at herself. Maybe she couldn't do this?

But this was her last night aboard. Kiki gulped one last time at herself in the mirror, then stepped out into the corridor.

The first man who saw her whistled.

It was lucky she trusted Miko to look after her, because this suit was designed to say one thing. *Come hither.*

Her shoes clacked down the hallway and she wondered why the heck she hadn't brought a coat. But it was too late now. Maybe it hadn't been such a good idea after all to flaunt herself, but it had seemed the most efficient way of annoying her nemesis for the last time.

Ginger had somehow discovered that Stefano would be in the Captain's box in the auditorium, so he would have a good view of what he couldn't have. That thought straightened her spine.

Unfortunately, once backstage, Kiki had a hard time fielding the ribald comments because Milo had been held up with a disaster in the restaurant. Finally she dragged Wilhelm to stand beside her so he could glower at anyone who dared to raise an eyebrow.

'Not so sure brother Nick would like this outfit, Kiki,' Wilhelm said in his measured way as he looked anywhere but at her.

Kiki felt as if she should pat his arm to comfort him. 'I'm a big girl, Will.'

'I hadn't realised quite how big,' he said, with a rare attempt at humour.

'Wilhelm. Don't you start.'

Thankfully Miko arrived, all suave black panther, and

took one appreciative look at her, bowed and kissed her fingers.

'I see we will be dancing for effect, my sweet. I will step up to that challenge.'

This was followed by a ludicrously wicked wink that had Kiki smiling again.

'Well, you only just made it.'

'Such is the drama of my position.' He squeezed her hand, noticed the chill of it, and rubbed her fingers between his own. 'Enjoy your last night. Be Catwoman for me. Hopefully I will not wake up in a dungeon tomorrow.'

Kiki's nervousness receded. Miko always made her feel better. Like a favourite cousin. Funny how she'd never fancied him and yet he was a delight.

'I promise we will have fun.'

She'd never see these people again, would never do anything like this again. She might as well give it everything she had.

She lifted her head and plastered on a smile.

Their turn. The red light came on.

How appropriate for her costume, she thought sardonically as Miko straightened and she put her hand on his arm.

He patted her shaking fingers. 'Good girl. Let's do it.'

Stefano conversed pleasantly with the Captain's wife. It was what he'd been trained to do. He'd promised to attend but he wished the night over, so he could return to his real world and decide on his next strategy for seducing Dr Fender.

His brother and sister-in-law were in very good spirits and had enjoyed their short holiday, and they had all survived without any further dire embarrassments.

The music changed to the unmistakable beat of the tango, and Stefano, like every other male in the auditorium, drew in his breath and held it when Kiki stalked onto the stage.

He heard Theros say, 'Is that the doctor?' but his eyes never moved.

Her ridiculous tail twitched, seductively sinuous and provocative, and the lights caught the skintight shimmer of her perfectly luscious body. Her breasts gleamed high and proud, shimmering with stardust. Stefano's mouth dried.

Mesmerised, he followed every sway and bend, each drift and spin. The woman in silver was heating his blood to boiling point, and never had he wanted her more.

Then he realised every man in the room had their eyes glued on his woman and wanted her too.

The flash of a camera from behind him made him grit his teeth, and he resisted the almost uncontrollable urge to reach back, grab the offending instrument and smash it into a million non-recording pieces. Instead he clenched his hands in his pockets and remembered to breathe, letting the air out slowly and with intent. He repeated the process, as if he would feel better soon. Unfortunately he didn't.

While he could almost admire the grace and precision of the dance, admire the rapport and impeccable timing between male and female, he would have given the crown jewels for it to end. He wanted her covered from head to foot at this moment, as his anger built, preferably bound and in the back of his helicopter heading for home.

How could she flaunt herself so?

As soon as the dance finished, to the most enthusiastic applause of the night, the rest of the cast came on for the final joint farewell and she flaunted herself all over again.

Stefano gritted his teeth as the crew sang their way through the final number. There was thunderous applause and he wondered grimly how much of it was for his little Dr Fender.

Finally he could excuse himself, and with Olympian control he strode to the stage door just as she stepped out in a group.

Thankfully someone had given her a coat. She was laughing as he approached, and that incensed him more, but he was no fool.

Miko was the first to notice his approach. 'Here comes retribution.'

He said it quietly in Kiki's ear but she heard and turned, plastered a smile on her face. 'Did you enjoy the show, Your Highness?'

'Most illuminating.' He smiled at the crowd, moved in next to Kiki, and laced his fingers through hers in a statement nobody could doubt. 'What a naughty suit.'

He stroked her palm with his thumb and her legs almost buckled.

This was not what she'd expected. Battle-ready, Kiki was confused by his soft tone, by the damned weakness she always had when he touched her, and the come down from the adrenalin of the dance. And that thumb, insistently vibrating at the core of her, in tendrils of heat from her palm, was blurring her mind so she couldn't think at all.

Still he hadn't looked at her.

'If you would all excuse us for just a few moments? I'd like to speak to Kiki. We'll catch up.'

She had to hand it to him. He'd asked nicely, but the projection that instant obedience was expected was miraculous—though Miko looked more than a little worried as she handed him back his coat.

How the heck did Stefano do that?

Maybe he didn't even care that she appeared almost naked in some lights. She sneaked a look at his face, saw his eyes and the penny dropped. Might be a good time to run after her friends...

Black pupils filled with sparks and his hand tightened on hers. 'I won't take up much of your time.'

If she could disentangle her hand she'd be able to think.

More people tumbled from the stage entrance and another camera flashed. Stefano swore softly—the first time she'd ever heard him swear—and let go of her hand to remove his jacket.

Kiki's mind began to clear the second they disconnected. She only had these few moments until he put his coat around her shoulders. The reality of the danger switched on like a light in her befuddled brain.

They were on the lowest level open to passengers, one below the gangplank, and there was no way he could get her to his suite unless she got into a lift. So she should be safe if she didn't.

'No lift!' At least she managed to get that out before he captured her hand again.

He nodded. Directed her to the stairs—innocuous enough. Almost as if he knew, his thumb circled her palm again, and her will weakened as a brief lull in the flow of passengers gave them a moment of privacy in the bend of the stairs.

He leaned her back against the wall, captured her chin and kissed her—not with force, he even started gently, though she could feel the tightly leashed control, the simmering emotion as he seduced her with implacable intent. He kissed her thoroughly until she could barely stand, would have followed him blindly over the edge of the ship into the water below.

Then he drew her up to the next level and into a packed but serendipitously waiting lift. It was as if even fate was against her. The whole time his fingers were linked through hers.

Her head began to insist she took note. She looked around and whispered, 'I said no lift.' She tugged on her hand but he didn't let go.

He whispered back. 'If that is the worst I do then you will be lucky.'

The idea was scarily attractive.

'Could you let go of my hand, please?' She said it a little too loudly but it had the desired effect. Everyone turned to look at them and Stefano dropped her fingers like a hot potato. 'Could someone press five, please?'

Her ears burned from the attention but to hell with it. She wasn't going to be monster'd by a royal bully even if she had pulled his tail deliberately. There was very real danger here—and not all of it was coming from him.

The lift stopped on her floor and she alighted without obstruction from Stefano. As the doors shut she refused to look back and took off, with her own tail in her hand, as fast as she could towards the crew's quarters.

The ship docked in Livorno at five a.m. Kiki woke after a restless night with her pillow screwed in a ball under her neck, her sheets twisted and creased and her body aching as if she'd done ten rounds in a boxing match. But worse was the mental exhaustion from duelling with Stefano in her dreams all night.

She crawled into the shower with a whimper, infinitely glad she didn't share her cabin with anyone else.

It was both an anticlimax and a blessing that she wouldn't see Stefano Mykonides and his entourage leave the ship. Because despite her resistance he had invaded her heart again, and now she'd have to re-banish him.

Today was going to be almost as big as tomorrow. She

had to say goodbye to colleagues who had been her friends, and she needed to find somewhere to stay tonight with all her luggage.

Then she needed to start forgetting the last week and sorting out a plan of action for work.

When she walked into the medical centre Wilhelm was talking to Ginger, and judging by the amount of gesticulating going on there was a problem.

'You guys okay?'

Ginger had tears streaming down her pale cheeks, Wilhelm was red-faced and angry, and both of them looked at her in varying degrees of distress when she arrived. Kiki felt her stomach sink.

'Tell her.' Wilhelm vibrated with emotion.

Ginger twisted hands that trembled as she turned to Kiki, but no words came out except a whisper that trailed off. 'I'm sorry...'

Kiki was liking this less by the minute. 'Sorry for what, Ginger?'

Wilhelm couldn't stand it any longer. 'She's sorry she e-mailed your story and a photo to her sleazy gossip columnist ex-boyfriend. You and the Prince will be splashed across every newspaper and magazine that can manage to change their lead article in Italy today.'

Kiki felt the cold seep into her bones. 'What story?'

'That you had an affair with Prince Stefano. That you flew to his island the day before yesterday.' Wilhelm dropped his voice and his eyes, unable to look at her while he broke the worst news. 'And that he didn't come to you when you lost his baby earlier this year.'

Kiki felt sick. And faint. And incredulously angry. 'How did you know about my pregnancy?'

Ginger looked as if she was going to be sick. 'My ex-boyfriend did some digging.'

Kiki's mouth opened and shut several times before words came out. 'And you sent my private life to a newspaper?' She looked at Wilhelm. 'And you knew?'

'No.' He shook his head vehemently. 'Ginger came and told me what she'd done this morning.'

Kiki could barely follow it. All she knew was that the whole sordidly tragic story, the pain and anguish she'd suffered alone, was now up for discussion by any busybody who fancied reading about her. Incomprehensible.

'How could you do that? Why would you do that?'

'I'm so sorry.' Ginger sobbed the words out. 'Last night I'd had too many drinks. Didn't think it through. Josh rang me. Asked for help. He said he was suicidal and he needed one good story to keep his job. I panicked. I love him, and I was scared he'd do it. So I gave him the best story I could find.'

'Mine?'

Ginger swallowed and then nodded. 'Yours. But I didn't know about the baby.'

Kiki sank back into a chair in the waiting room and shook her head, unable to comprehend just how public this was. That everyone would know a secret she'd kept hidden from everyone...most of all Stefano.

'Are you sure they'll publish it? The Mykonides family have a lot of power.' Didn't she know that? With the thought came the first hint of light. 'Of course they won't let them publish, and I'm not interesting enough to write about if his name isn't there.'

Wilhelm spun the computer screen around to show her. 'It's online already.'

That was when she saw the explicit glory of her catsuit, in full colour, and Stefano holding her hand. She looked like a call girl.

'That picture...' She put her head in her hands. 'My

family don't know about the baby.' She looked at Wilhelm, but all his sympathy wasn't going to help her now. 'Nick doesn't know, or my sisters.'

He sighed. 'Then you'd better ring him.'

'I can't.' She shook her head. 'I can't think.' An image of Stefano flew into her mind and she groaned. 'Stefano… His family… He hates the press.'

Running the gauntlet of the ship as she said goodbye was nothing compared to the reception the Italian newspaper journalists had planned for her when she stepped onto the wharf.

The flash of cameras and the surge of the bodies that crowded round her stole the breath from her lungs and she felt herself sway with the onslaught.

A car screeched to a halt.

'Enough!'

One voice, a whiplash of command, and four body-guards, hastily shielding a central figure. The crowd parted and fell silent in shock as Stefano strode forward, dropped his arm protectively around her shoulders and swept her back to his car. Her luggage was quickly packed into a second car by Stefano's manservant.

As she slid along the back seat the flash as the first pho-tographer recovered ignited others, and the din returned full force as Stefano slid in behind her.

The door shut and both vehicles pulled away. The guards followed behind as Kiki huddled in the corner of the seat, shaking, tears thick in her throat as she tried to re-gain her composure in a world that had suddenly gone mad.

She supposed she should be thankful he'd come, but she had no idea what to say to him. Where to start. What he thought. Her head still spun from the ramifications of such a private airing of her deepest pain. Many women had suffered such a loss but it hurt even more to expose it publicly. Not just the memory of the physical, the cramps and the loss of control, but emotionally it had been traumatic. And now the world was privy to that pain.

Stefano could barely see straight, barely think as he struggled with a feeling of betrayal greater than anything he had ever experienced before. This did not happen to him. He was careful. In control. Master of his own fate and no one else's—because his goal in life was never to be responsible for someone else's downfall again.

But control had been taken from him. This news had been waiting for him as soon as he woke.

His office had gone into disaster mode. His security staff had arranged a different departure point for himself, Theros and Marla from the ship, to avoid the inevitable press, and he had seen them to the airport and discreet safety. But he'd had to return for Kiki, though he wondered bitterly if she deserved it.

All this because he had terminated her employment. It was a smallness he hadn't expected. Fool that he was. He had been told many times, and even in the last few days by his father, that he should stay within the circle of people who understood the rules. And he had defended her.

Now all the world knew she had been pregnant. *His* child. Even when he had been in hospital she would have been able to reach him. His child had died at the time when he too had almost died. Another painful situation out of his control.

His anger bubbled and boiled. Or had it really been his child? Had there been any child at all?

He sifted through what he knew, what had been written, and tried to discern what was truth and what was fiction even as she who had caused this furore shivered beside him. He would find out. He would keep her close until this all died down and she could not spread more lies about him.

The hardest part was the fact that he had always been the one to protect his family from his brother's many scrapes. His way for making up the past, perhaps. By being the son his father wanted and Theros could not be.

Because of *him*.

But this—this was all his doing, and the woman beside him. They had brought shame to the royal house. Now he needed to be strong. Not weak. He repeated it in his mind. *Show strength not weakness.* The plan of action he had decided on was not the answer, but perhaps it would buy him time and stop the damage to his family until the truth could be ascertained.

Kiki could feel tension vibrating from the man beside her, emanating in waves, like a radioactive leak from a damaged core. Well, she guessed she had pierced his protective shell with the last news he'd expected.

Stefano's voice, coldly formal, as if he were talking to a bare acquaintance he disliked intensely, made Kiki feel even more alone.

'It seems you must come to Aspelicus after all. You will be safe there until all this dies down. The rest we will discuss later, when I can be sure I will not do something I regret.'

That stiffened her spine. As if *she* didn't have regrets. As if *she* had orchestrated the most public airing of her grief. Grief he hadn't even been there to share.

'Oh, it's all about *you*? Typical.'

He shot her a look of loathing and she returned it with interest. 'I am not informed. Yet you tell a newspaper.'

So that was what he thought. Again, typical.

'You think I would share my pain so publicly?' She

turned her head and stared at the swiftly passing streets. 'You really don't know me at all, do you?'

She couldn't believe he thought that. But then again why wouldn't he? It was all about him.

Now she was on her way to Aspelicus and too emotionally drained to fight it. Not what she would have believed possible less than twelve hours ago. The way she felt at this moment he could drop her off on the moon and she wouldn't care. In another world she would be waiting with bated breath for her labour to start. For her baby to be born. Instead she was the instigator of an injustice to him.

She just wanted to hide. And cry. But she wouldn't give him the satisfaction. Instead she stared unseeingly out of the window as they turned into the airport and drove onto the tarmac.

Before they got out he had one last thing to say. 'Your pregnancy. Was it really my child?'

Kiki turned her head and stared at this man she'd thought she knew, looked at him with such disgust he flinched.

At last he had the grace to say, 'I apologise.'

But it was too late. Of course he would think that. How could she have ever thought she loved him?

'Too damn late. It will never be unsaid.'

His implacable face stared at her. 'So when were you going to tell me you were pregnant?'

She could do cold. She should be able to, because she felt as if her heart had frozen over like those lakes in Switzerland she'd always wanted to see. Never more than at this moment.

'When you came back. But you didn't. So I tried to phone. But even then I didn't get the chance.'

Her car door was opened from the outside and the helicopter looked almost reassuringly familiar. It was funny how things could change in so short a time, and she was glad when he handed her coldly into the rear of the aircraft and climbed into the pilot's seat himself. At least she wouldn't have to sit next to his smouldering disapproval for the next hour.

Their ascent and the flight were a blur as her mind fought the paralysis this morning had left her with. It seemed only a short time later that they were landing on the forecourt of the palace, and she lifted listless eyes to the gathering that waited for them.

Stefano opened her door and shielded her from the waiting throng. 'For the moment, of necessity and to save face for my family, we are engaged. Perhaps some of the damage can be repaired. The engagement can be terminated when enough time has passed.'

His statement hit her like a blow to the chest. This day just kept getting worse.

'I'm not pretending any such thing.'

She would not be the outsider again, like during her whole childhood. She wanted to fit. To be loved, not tolerated. To be the centre of someone's universe, not a distant moon floating in his orbit until he was ready to evict her from his gravitational pull.

'It is not pretence.' He pulled a box from his pocket and lifted her unresisting hand, slid on the heavy stone. The ring hung like a shackle from her finger, a monstrous square-cut diamond, mocking her newly engaged status. 'It is temporary.'

'That's all right, then.' A semi-hysterical laugh slipped out. 'I'm used to temporary.'

His hand tightened on hers. 'Can you not see you have done enough damage?'

She felt so tired. What about the damage to *her*?

This time when he took her hand no sparks flew. Their

misery separated them completely and she should be grateful for that. What did she expect? That he would take her in his arms and weep with her, say he was sorry he hadn't been there for her? Unlikely. But it would have been nice.

He turned inscrutably to introduce her to those who waited.

She didn't understand any of this. How could a fake engagement help this situation? It would have to end some time. But she tried to smile as she mumbled, 'Hello.' Then she was towed across the forecourt to a line of servants, where another flurry of introductions was performed until finally it was over.

The wall between them must be visible to all who watched, but no doubt the loyalty of his people would colour it differently.

Once inside the palace Stefano dropped her hand and strode ahead, so she followed him up the inner staircase to the family apartments, more unhappy with every step.

They even passed the stained glass doors without opening them—so much for her favourite place—and climbed another staircase to a redwood landing.

He gestured her through some white doors and followed her in. 'These were my mother's rooms. It will be expected that you stay here. There is a turret if you wish for a quiet place to sit until I return. A place to gather your thoughts.'

He was just going to leave her here? Alone?

His face softened a fraction and she thought he was going to say something less harsh, but in the end he shook his head. 'This whole thing is a fiasco. I must see my father.'

And then he was gone.

CHAPTER TEN

MORE OF A tragedy than a fiasco.

Kiki stood, shivering, in the vast apartment with several doors that were closed, like strangers shutting her out. She didn't know what to think or do. She hadn't felt this numb and directionless since that night when her baby had left her.

Stefano strode away, but in the back of his mind was the picture of Kiki's white face and how small she'd looked alone in his mother's rooms. But he had to harden his heart to that because his weakness with this woman had caused all this. He must put aside the guilt that whispered to him that in truth he had not tried hard enough to touch base with a woman who had given him everything he had asked for.

And this new pain—this gnawing emptiness he had never experienced before—could it be the loss of something he had not thought would affect him so powerfully? But over it all was the disgust that he had let his family down again. That he could not forgive. He wasn't even sure where to start to repair the damage.

Kiki had fallen asleep on the sofa, and when she woke Stefano was back, sitting opposite, watching her with an unreadable expression on his aristocratic face.

She sat up, ran her hand through her hair and tried to straighten her clothes unobtrusively. Hard to gather her composure when he continued to stare.

'Do you feel better?' Not friendly, but at least the freezing tone of his voice had risen a few degrees.

She blinked and sat up straighter. 'That depends. Was it all a bad dream?'

He shook his head. 'It is still a bad dream.'

She sighed. 'Then I don't feel better.'

He almost smiled. 'So, I must apologise for assuming you told the papers.'

That was one bright moment in a bad day. 'You believe me?'

He had the grace to look away. 'I have the truth from your doctor friend, Hobson, who has been concerned for your safety.'

She sighed. 'Of course you didn't believe me.' She looked around then, hoping for a glass of water or a cup of tea. Anything for her dry throat. She saw the ring lying on the table where she'd taken it off. 'How long do I have to stay here?'

He too looked at the ring and his eyes narrowed. 'Is the apartment as well as the ring not to your liking?'

She shrugged. 'I haven't seen the rooms. And you haven't answered my question. In fact you've said precious little, and I've had just about enough of being kept in the dark.'

He said implacably, 'You must stay until I say you may go.'

She shook her head and stood up. 'That doesn't work for me.'

It was his turn to sigh. 'Again we are at loggerheads. And if I were to ask what *will* work for you?'

'I need to find a job.' She glared at him. 'Thanks to

you. Find a place to live. Leave this fiasco behind and get on with my life.'

He lifted his hand. Gestured to the room. 'All these things you can do on Aspelicus.'

She shook her head. 'I'm not staying in the palace.'

He shrugged. 'For the moment needs must. But in a few weeks perhaps you could move to the village through the week and stay in the castle during the weekends.'

As she lifted her head to dispute that he went on.

'You will be undisturbed in these apartments, of course, but for the next two weeks at the very least we must be seen together.'

She didn't understand. How could it help her, being here? She didn't want to be reminded every day that he hated her. 'Why perpetuate a myth that will be found out in the end?'

He stood and walked to the window. 'Because my father is old-fashioned. Because he and my people wish desperately for my heir and they are greatly distressed to think I would leave the woman who carried my child alone. The loss of that dream and the blow to my esteem has created a furore. If they think I am engaged to you then not all is lost.'

'Your father hated me from first sight. Let alone now.' The way Prince Paulo had stared her up and down the first time they met had promised little rapport.

'You imagine things. My father is very focussed on the good name of Aspelicus. He believes I should marry a woman of similar social standing, but this is my decision.'

'And mine. And I'm not marrying you.'

'But you will remain engaged to me for the time being, because you owe me that.'

Kiki felt as though her head was going to explode. 'I owe you nothing.'

But he was not having any of it. 'Is two weeks too much to ask? For the damage that has been done?'

She could feel the trap closing. 'Can't we just be seen together at the hospital? I can work with that.'

'In due course.' He stood up. 'For now, there will be a formal reception this evening. You are guest of honour. At seven I will come for you. The timing is poor, with the Prince's Cup next week and all the functions that require my presence.' He looked at her with a cynical smile. 'And now *your* presence too.'

She was sick of it all but too exhausted to fight. What did it matter? She looked down at her crumpled clothes. 'I'm going to look fabulous for the event.'

He stood. 'One of our local designers will take care of everything. She has several outfits she wishes to show you. Please try for a demure neckline.'

Her eyes glittered. 'Shame it isn't fancy dress. She might have a habit and I could go as a nun.'

'You look good in black.' His tone was less than flattering.

'With a wimple? So would you.'

He turned and left and Kiki stared at the closed door. What was she going to do? She had no idea how to survive what he was asking. Especially the way she felt at this moment.

And the wall around him was so thick she couldn't see the man she had once thought she loved. How had this happened? She was alone, held on an island where the ruling family decided whether she could go or stay. No allies except her family, and she didn't want to involve them until she could see her way out.

Before she could think of anything else there was a knock on the door and a maid brought in some tea and a cake.

Kiki decided the world might look less disastrous if she at least drank something.

By the time she'd finished her tea the designer had arrived and they discussed Kiki's fashion needs for the next two weeks.

It seemed there were mammoth requirements for the Prince's Cup. Shoes and handbags had been chosen, undergarments arrayed.

Of course Stefano hadn't mentioned the beauty technician who arrived to manicure, pedicure and mini-facial her before the hairstylist arrived...

It was perhaps fortunate that Kiki felt like a rag doll, able to be pulled this way and that, because her brain was whirring like a machine as she realised that she was truly officially engaged to a prince—albeit short-term—even if the world thought she had trapped him into it. And she would be expected to know what to do.

For the moment, she let them have their way. Perhaps externally she would look the part, and it required no mental energy from her.

To her surprise, all the attendants seemed genuinely glad to be of service to her, and she wondered why Stefano's subjects didn't hate her for putting him through the gossip mill.

But it seemed that despite what he had said to Kiki personally Stefano had cast her as the victim, not the offender. Shame he didn't believe it himself, because that shift would make this whole scenario so much easier to bear.

She didn't know if she could do this without his support. Her emotions were shot, and she had been getting more fragile every day—until here she was, on the eve of the day she had dreaded for months.

Never would she have believed it would be overshadowed by something else.

Even some direction on what she should do or say would be helpful in her current fragile state. How dared he not see how lost she was and how in need of support from him, no matter how pressing the affairs of state?

The only other person who might possibly be able to help her was Elise, but the housekeeper had been conspicuous by her absence and, given her extreme loyalty to Stefano, that was not surprising.

Just disappointing, because Elise was the one woman in the palace who would know what was going on. And maybe even understand how Kiki couldn't possibly be responsible for airing something so privately tragic. Elise might just understand because she too had lost her dreams of children.

At one o'clock the attendants had gone. A maid knocked and delivered a small salad and a roll for lunch, and a pot of coffee. Desperately Kiki stopped her as she was about to disappear.

'The housekeeper—Elise. Is she here today?'

'Of course, Dr Fender. Mrs Prost lives in the palace and is on duty whenever Prince Stefano is at home.'

She should have known. No surprises there. *That's how he'd like me,* Kiki thought cynically, *on duty whenever he wants.*

She nodded. 'Lovely. Then could you ask if she has a moment? I would like to see her, please.'

'Of course, Doctor.' The maid curtsied and slipped out through the door.

When Elise arrived, not many minutes later, Kiki wasn't even sure what she was going to say to the housekeeper.

One glance at her impassive face showed Elise was with-holding her own opinion.

Kiki needed this woman as her ally—she had to have at least one in the castle—and nothing but the truth was going to secure that.

'Please sit down, Elise.'

The woman perched uneasily on the edge of a chair. 'I hope everything is to your satisfaction, Dr Fender?'

The lines were drawn, then. 'I thought we were on a first-name basis?'

'That was before you became engaged to Prince Stefano. It would not be proper now.'

Kiki sighed. 'Fine. I need you to understand that I would never ask you to do anything that would harm Prince Stefano or the royal house of Mykonides.'

The woman's eyes flashed. 'And I would rather die.'

'I had already guessed that.' Kiki smiled. 'It is good to have that said.' She folded her hands in her lap. 'But I also need you to understand that I had nothing to do with publishing or giving the information that was printed by that newspaper.'

'So His Highness has said.'

She wasn't getting anywhere. The woman still dis-trusted her, and how could she blame her? 'Elise. I met Prince Stefano and we were very drawn to each other. As a woman who has lost her own children surely you can see that a mother would not share her grief with the world as has happened to me?'

Elise stilled, stared at her, and finally nodded.

Kiki felt the first glimpse of hope she'd felt all day and went on.

'I believe the Prince is a good man and is distressed by the news. Did you know I tried to contact him? I had no idea his royal duties were so arduous, or that his recent

accident was the reason he didn't answer me.' She saw the
moment Elise understood and finally sighed with relief.
'There is still a chemistry that neither of us thinks sensible. Now this has happened, and for the moment at least
I must stay here. Behave as his betrothed. I don't want to
let him down again. But I need help.'

Was that an imperceptible relaxing of her face? Was she
imagining just a little more warmth in the woman's eyes?

'I see.' Elise looked away to the tall windows for a moment and then looked back. 'And I am sorry for your loss.'
She nodded. 'Yes. You will need help. I will help.' She
added primly, 'Also, I can say there has been a retraction
in the paper, stating the fact that His Highness was gravely
injured at the time of your miscarriage, and that he found
you only a few days ago. Things do not look so bad when
the true facts come to light. Legal action has commenced.'

Kiki could almost spare a thought for Ginger and her
boyfriend. Almost.

Elise stood up. 'I can see that it will help if you sail
smoothly through the next two weeks.' She paused at the
door. 'I will return with your itinerary and discuss what
is required of you.'

For Kiki, at least, things improved after that. Elise's support, once offered, was beyond generous. By the time Stefano came to escort his new fiancée to dinner she knew
the correct curtsies, the names of the five most important
people she would meet, and the itinerary for the evening.
Even the menu.

It felt good to have a little more control.

And Elise's final suggestion had come in words from
her late princess—'God rest her soul.'

She'd told her, 'See only one person or the occasion will

overwhelm you. Look, speak and smile at one person and you will be in control of the room.'

Kiki nodded. Sound advice and she'd certainly try. Because it seemed that no help would come from the man who had let her down when she most needed him. *Again.*

Kiki wore a classic black floor-length gown, with just enough cleavage to say, *so this is why the man is smitten.* Her dark hair had been artfully piled on top of her head, and with her faultless make-up her composure appeared complete. Too complete. Because she felt like a figurine in a wax museum—incredibly life-like but numb to sensation. But she would get through this without his help.

Stefano didn't know what to expect when he reached the door to his mother's rooms. He hoped Kiki was still not slouched in the chair.

When he opened the door, for the first time in his life Prince Stefano Mykonides felt intimidated.

She looked at him with such indifference his blood chilled.

'I am ready, Your Highness.'

His Dr Fender looked like a film star.

The besieged and crushed victim whom he'd rescued from the press had been replaced by a self-assured young woman waiting calmly and coldly to take his arm.

He glanced around the apartment as if to see the other person he'd expected. This woman did not look out of place. The room could have been designed for she who consistently stunned him when he least expected it.

The grandmother clock in the corner chimed and he was jolted back into reality. Now was not the time to mull over questions that required thoughtful answers.

'Of course. Let us go.'

She put her hand on his arm without hesitation as he

led the way and her fingers did not waver. It was his turn to feel the wall between them.

All rose as they entered. Kiki smiled slightly and nodded—not effusively, but that was good. She curtsied to his father with such gracefulness that even the women of the court smiled and Stefano felt his chest swell just a little with pride. This morning he would never have dreamed that she would carry this off so magnificently. This morning there had been no pride to be had.

'She has presence,' his father grunted for his ears alone. 'But it remains to be seen if you have ruined someone else's life by your reckless actions.'

Stefano felt familiar guilt chill the pleasure he had gained in the moment and he glanced at Kiki. Something in her expression made him wonder if she'd overheard. He could only hope not.

When he seated her beside him she answered his questions, but there was still the distance that had been there since he'd collected her. A gulf so wide he could see no way of bridging it. He assured himself that was good.

She seemed to prefer to converse quietly with the Mayor, on her right at the table, and yet he, the more practised statesman, was too much aware of her. Probably just the upheavals of the day.

The evening continued to unnerve him. He had been prepared to protect her, gloss over the mistakes she wouldn't see, but she required no help.

Kiki nodded and smiled and held her composure with concentration. If she excluded the grandeur of the surroundings and the glitter of the people and concentrated on one person at a time she found her advice held good.

Especially if she blocked Stefano out.

Just in that first moment before they'd left, when he'd entered her rooms to escort her, he'd looked so tall and forbidding in black tails and the royal sash, with jewelled medals flashing, she'd mentally faltered.

But only for a moment, before she'd stoked up her anger. She'd concentrated on the person, searched behind the regalia and remembered the man who had left her without support and now expected her to fail in such unfamiliar and challenging surroundings.

That had been inexcusable, and the reminder had protected her from any connection that would discomfort her—until she'd heard that muttered judgement from Prince Paulo.

It had been a glimpse into Stefano's life and what he dealt with every day. She remembered his comment that his mother had been the lighter-natured of the two. She could see that now, and despite herself felt herself soften and sympathise with Stefano.

She glanced across to the old Prince and unexpectedly caught his eye. She glared at him, glad the engagement was a farce, because she didn't need a person like that permanently in her life. He blinked. Grumpy old man. She turned away.

If tonight's disapproval had been there all Stefano's life no wonder he could become tense with pressure.

She could sense him beside her now. Feel the awareness that seemed to inhabit the space between them even when they were not conversing. But she couldn't afford to lay her hand on his arm and express the sympathy she wanted to because she needed to stay focussed until she could return to the safety of her room. But perhaps she understood him a little more.

Luckily the gentleman beside her could converse easily, with little prompting from her. The Mayor of Aspelicus was one of the five Elise had mentioned, so she knew his role in the business, and that his son was in charge of festivities for the Prince's Cup. He did seem delighted with her knowledge and her appreciation of his heavy civil duties, and mentally she thanked Elise for her tutelage.

Eventually the older gentleman excused himself to answer a question from another table companion and Kiki had to turn back to Stefano.

He raised his brows. 'And how is my old friend Bruno Valinari?'

Kiki smiled, because in a lesser man he would have sounded almost petulant. 'He is well. And proud of his son—as he should be. And how is your dinner and your evening, Your Highness?'

His mouth came down level with her cheek and she tried not to inhale the subtle tang of his aftershave, because it floated too many memories for a state function. Tried not to look at the strong cheekbones and carved mouth as he drew closer.

'I am wondering if there is to be any attention from my fiancée.'

Subtly she drew back further. 'You'll survive without my attention.' She raised her brows. 'As I did without yours today.' She met his eyes. 'Did it occur to you I could have done with a little guidance from you?'

'My apologies. My duties constrained me.' His glance travelled over her. 'Though I see no lack in your instruction.'

'Gee, thanks.' She could play that game. 'How unusual for you *not* to see something.'

His eyes gleamed. 'So the cat has claws.'

Kiki sat straighter in her chair and even leaned a little to the right to increase the distance between them. She kept the smile on her face but there was none in her voice. 'I'm not duelling with you at this table.'

Actually, when it came down to it, she couldn't. She didn't have the headspace.

She glanced around for a friendly face and Marla waved her fingers discreetly from across the table. Kiki realised she did have another ally in the palace. When people began to circulate, perhaps she could excuse herself and cross over to Marla. The chance to seek out her supposed future sister-in-law would help enormously.

She changed the subject. 'I see Theros and Marla are here. They look happy.'

Stefano turned to look at his brother and his face became more guarded. 'Yes. It is good to see him not as restless as usual.'

That seemed a strange thing to say. 'So he is normally restless?'

He glanced around to see if anyone had overheard. 'That also is not for this table.'

No-go zones made life even more difficult, but what did she expect when in truth she knew little about his family? 'In that case it's your turn to start a conversation or I'll go back to Bruno.'

He smiled and inclined his head, and the appreciation in his eyes made the heat rise in her own face. She jammed the rising weakness back into its box.

'You look beautiful. And confident. I applaud you.'

Maybe he should go back to mocking her, because compliments played havoc with that very composure. 'Thank you.' She glanced at his father, who watched them both from under fierce white brows, and then back at Stefano. 'It could just be confidence from designer clothes and my own stylist.'

'Perhaps. Perhaps not. We shall see. Tomorrow you must meet the people. Two more critical children have flown in for surgery and I must go to the hospital. As soon as they are stabilised I will be in surgery.'

She wanted to ask more but he went on.

'Unfortunately the new wing—funded by last year's Prince's Cup—is to be opened. Now I cannot be there and my father's advisors have requested you attend with him.' He mocked her. 'Are you free?'

As if she had so much to do. And what if she said no? But just the idea of getting away from the palace made her feel better. She thought of the hospital and her spirits lifted. 'Of course. And could I visit the children as well?'

His eyes shuttered. 'I doubt there will be time.' He shrugged. 'You will be busy with your duties. It is only to be a short visit.'

The flattening of her spirits at his refusal did more to unnerve her than anything the glittering room could achieve. That he could so nonchalantly ignore the fact that to visit the children would give her pleasure seemed so out of character for the man she'd thought he was. It hurt anew.

Someone spoke to him from his left and she sank back in the seat. Sank back, not relaxed back, because foolishly she looked along the row of guests, most of whom glanced her way every few seconds, and knew this wasn't her natural habitat. She'd never get used to it—didn't want to get used to it, because in fact she disliked the grandeur, the formality, the opulence of it all intensely. At this moment she also disliked Stefano intensely, and this was where Stefano belonged. Not her.

When she glanced down to the end of the table a man smiled at her and she realised it was Dr Franco Tollini from the other day. She raised her brows and smiled and let her gaze drift away. Complications were too hard. Her head was above water—just—and she wanted to keep it that way.

She lifted her spoon and tasted the dessert but she didn't want it. Too much food.

How did Stefano keep so fit? He was all lean muscle and power…and perhaps she shouldn't let her thoughts drift there while she was being watched by a hundred eyes. Thankfully, Bruno turned to her and asked a question before she lost herself in remembering just how weak she was when he held her in his arms and how she had arrived at this moment.

Finally the long dinner was over. Nobody circulated, and Kiki had never felt more trapped. They bade goodnight to the Crown Prince, who glanced over them both coldly, and then to Kiki's relief they bumped into Marla and Theros. Stefano seemed reluctant to chat, but Kiki made a point of asking Marla how she was.

Before she could answer her husband chimed in with, 'Catwoman. Meow.'

Theros grinned at her and Kiki blushed. Stefano stepped in and took his brother's arm, steered him away. Kiki wasn't sure what had happened.

She looked at Marla, who smiled apologetically. 'I'm well.' She glanced at her husband and lowered her voice. 'He's an absolute darling but he has no social skills.'

It seemed a strange thing to say about a prince, but Marla went on warmly.

'What about you? I thought you were so brave, coming tonight.'

That made her laugh for the first time of the night. 'I didn't have much choice.'

Before she could enlarge on that Stefano returned with a subdued Theros, and Marla whispered, 'Let's catch up tomorrow,' before she caught her husband's hand and led him away.

Something wasn't right, and Kiki frowned after them, but all she could think was that perhaps the younger prince had had too much to drink.

CHAPTER ELEVEN

STEFANO STEERED HER in the other direction. 'Come. It is late and we both have a big day tomorrow.'

His hand was on her arm again, and she didn't know how much more of this hot and cold treatment she could take. Her physical awareness of him beside her only made her more cross. Judging by the way his hand came over hers on his arm, he might have picked up on the vibe that she was about to shake him off.

Stefano meant to leave her at the door and stride away. Because if he didn't there was a risk he would sweep her into his arms and forget everything. But he wasn't that man.

That man who had temporarily ignored the responsibilities of his station.

That one lapse.

Once in his life he had allowed his heart to rule his head and look what had happened. But he could not rid himself of the look of hurt in Kiki's eyes and his own heart ached in a way he had never felt before.

When he let her go to open the doors to her suite Kiki paused as he looked down at her. She stared at him, as if trying to see beneath his skin, and the moment stilled. The ever-present sounds of the grandmother clock faded and their eyes met and held.

Here they were, and for the first time that evening Kiki had time to feel like putting her head in her hands to mourn what they had lost.

How had they found themselves at such loggerheads? How had she ended up here, 'temporarily engaged' to the man she had tragically made a child with?

What series of events, trends of fate and plain bad luck had mocked them both and put such obstacles in the way of a woman and a man who were attracted?

'What happened to us, Stefano?' Kiki asked carefully.

Again he let her down. Just compressed his lips and shuttered his eyes.

'Almost everything. We must try to make the best of this disastrous situation while I deal with it.'

Her temper flared. 'I am not a "disastrous situation". I am a respected medical practitioner who has been kidnapped.'

She saw him glance around to check they were alone before he steered her through into the rooms, closed the doors and stood with his back to them. 'Please try and remember what happens when people overhear things they shouldn't.'

She was sick of worrying about what others thought. 'Why do you think you can shut me out? Why do you need to control everything? Do you think it actually changes fate? Life is learning to live with what happens.'

One of them needed to be honest.

She gestured to the room. 'Everything is different here. *You're* different. Especially now I've seen a small part of what your lifestyle entails and how it changes you.' She stepped up to him and he watched her with very little expression on his face. She wished he would react at least. 'This control freak is not the man I fell in love with.'

He blinked when she said she'd loved him.

'I need control.'

The words seemed almost torn from him and she stopped, arrested by the expression on his face.

Some nuance captured her attention, cut through her distress, sharpened her instincts. 'Why do you need control?'

He stepped away from the door, walked past her towards the settee she'd slept on earlier.

'How do you find my brother?'

She frowned. That was random. She almost said, *I'd look for Marla*, but she didn't want to talk about Theros. 'He seems nice.' She thought for a moment, and then a suspicion began to form in her mind. Something Marla had said. And Stefano had said Theros was restless. 'Is there something wrong with Theros?'

He sighed. 'You know Mikey's brother—Chris—he woke up. He'll be fine.'

Another random comment. Or was it?

'I'm glad.' She sat down beside him as he stared straight ahead. She waited.

Finally he began to speak. 'There was an accident when we were children. Theros almost drowned in an ocean pool. I managed to resuscitate him but not fast enough. He is a child in a man's body because of me.'

She lowered her voice. It all began to make sense. Guilt. Shame. Loss of control. 'How old were you?'

'Eight.' Still he stared straight ahead, and somehow she knew he had never spoken about this to anyone. She couldn't understand how he had kept it from being common knowledge.

'Eight years old?' Her stomach dropped and she wanted to take his head in her hands and kiss him for the years of pain and self-flagellation she could now see he had been determined to endure. Had probably been *encouraged* to endure, if she'd read his father right. But she needed to speak carefully if he was ever to have peace. 'And you resuscitated your drowned brother?'

He flexed his shoulders. 'Not quickly enough to prevent damage.'

She said, 'You resuscitated your drowned brother, by yourself, so that he breathed again?'

'Yes.'

She saw him blink. Consider. Finally use his powerful brain to think about himself. He closed his eyes.

She persisted. 'Would you have blamed Mikey if he had done the same?'

His eyes flew open and he sat straighter. 'Of course not.'

She stared at him, but he refused to meet her determined gaze with his own. She lowered her voice but knew he heard every word. 'Then perhaps it is time to forgive yourself.'

Finally he looked at her. 'I fear I am destined to hurt the ones I love.'

She nodded and took his hand, stroked the strong fingers that had held her through memorable nights, felt his pain and rested his fingers against her heart. She understood him so much more.

'And that is the dilemma. Perhaps it's time to let go that which can't be changed. Perhaps consider that happiness doesn't need perfection. Theros seems very happy.'

Stefano looked down at the slender fingers that stroked his and felt the weight of the years grow imperceptibly lighter. Just a little. He thought about his brother. Smiled at the thought. 'He *is* happy when he isn't in trouble with me.' He could acknowledge that if he allowed himself to consider it.

She put his hand back down and moved hers away. 'Then let it go. You can't control everything.'

How did she do that? Suggest gently and steer him towards peace when he'd carried guilt like a blanket made of lead around his shoulders for as long as he could remember?

The grandmother clock began to chime and neither of them spoke as the toll rang out until midnight was proclaimed.

Suddenly Kiki realised the day she had dreaded was here. But, despite his presence, Stefano wasn't with her for that.

She stood up. God, she was so tired. And there was so much to think about. Tonight she was going to try and do the same thing she'd told Stefano to do, because she'd promised herself that when this day came she would let go.

'Please leave. I'm tired and I can't think any more.'

She knew he could sense her withdrawal, so she was surprised when he asked, 'What if I don't want to go?'

She turned her back on him, because she didn't have the reserves to fight. 'I can't help that,' she said. And she walked away.

After an emotional discussion with her pillow Kiki slept fitfully. She was woken by Elise with coffee and croissants and a warning that soon the stylist would arrive to prepare her for a day of official functions.

Every time her mind wandered to the significance of the date she pushed it away.

The really bad news came with her breakfast. She must travel with Crown Prince Paulo in the official convoy.

She sipped her tea pensively. What the heck could she talk about? Or maybe you didn't talk to the Crown Prince—though an hour of disapproving silence would be like water torture.

By the time she was handed into the official car she was

feeling more sure than ever that she wasn't cut out for this life. And the royal scrutiny was such that she couldn't tell if he was satisfied with her appearance or not.

'Good morning, Dr Fender.'

'Good morning, Prince Paulo.' She slid into the car past the footman holding the door.

'Did you sleep well?'

Apparently he did talk, and Kiki felt herself relax slightly. She usually did after a big cry. 'It was a different sleep than on the ship.'

'Of course.'

He transferred his attention to the cobbled streets of the castle forecourt as they began their journey and Kiki sighed. That was that, then.

How had she ended up in a royal car with an autocratic old despot?

'If you don't mind me asking, why am I with you today, Prince Paulo?'

The Prince turned back to her. 'Because Stefano is not. Too often he neglects his royal duties for his passion with surgery.' He glanced back out of the window. 'And see where that gets him.'

Kiki's sense of fairness disputed that. Couldn't he see the good Stefano did? The depth of care and kindness his son showed his patients was admirable, even if that kindness didn't extend to *her* at the present time.

Kiki narrowed her eyes on the back of the Prince's head. 'Your son saves lives. Has there not been a physician in your family since the first Mykonides?'

That turned his head. Now he was every inch the monarch. His bristled white brows soared, his eyes narrowed, and in that moment she saw the dark eyes of his son at their most arctic.

'Who are you to presume to tell me my own history?'

But strangely Kiki wasn't afraid or uncomfortable. It was as if a calm voice whispered in her ear to let him bluster.

She should say *she* was the woman pretending to be engaged to his son to help the family's good name. But she didn't need this man as her enemy.

'My apologies, Your Highness.'

But they both knew she wasn't cowed by him, and she wondered if she could detect just a glimpse of approval in his eyes.

In a more conciliatory tone she went on, 'I'm saying his skills as a surgeon are a gift.'

The Prince shrugged and allowed himself to stop pretending he was enraged. 'So they say.' He turned to look out of the window and she heard him mutter, 'He should be more of a prince.'

Kiki turned to her own window as they began their spiral descent of the mountain. 'He could hardly be more.'

She heard the indrawn breath of the old man but she couldn't regret it. What could he do? Put her out of the car. Well, she was happy with that idea.

'So you champion a man who leaves you pregnant in another country?'

It seemed the old man had rallied.

They faced each other like circling dogs.

'Circumstances were not kind to us.'

'If he has any of me in him he will not be kind to you either.' He glared at her, and then slowly his gaze softened. 'You remind me of someone I knew long ago. She too was fearless.' He laughed without amusement. 'And stubborn. This may not turn out badly yet.'

Kiki had nothing to say to that. Now she felt less sure of herself, and wondered what had possessed her to take him on.

The drive through the olive groves passed silently and Kiki chewed on her lip as she worried what would be asked of her today.

Finally the Prince roused himself. 'I think you should address the women. The patronesses. It is a gynaecological ward we are opening. Thank them for their donations which have helped create the facility and they will be happy.'

Her worst nightmare. What should she say? 'Surely they would prefer your address to mine?'

'Ha! You are a woman.' He turned away. 'I have decided.'

Typical. Like father, like son, she thought with an unhappy sigh.

As Kiki came to the end of her speech—more of a lecture on meeting health needs as all women deserved—than an informal thank-you, and Prince Paulo seemed happy enough. It had proved less of a trial than she had anticipated. But it had been stressful, and underneath she seethed.

She'd had an epiphany. Here she was for these women, and today of all days Stefano, of course, was not here for *her*.

Kiki estimated there were about fifty well-dressed women, most of them around her age. With women's health so important she'd spoken from the heart, because that way at least she could be happy with what she said.

Until she asked for questions and of course the most difficult one surfaced.

Kiki looked at the woman and something warned her. Despite her designer clothes, her coiffed hair, she had sad, sad eyes, and Kiki knew this woman struggled in a dark place too.

The woman moistened her lips and Kiki leaned forward slightly to hear. 'Are you afraid of miscarrying again?'

Kiki sighed and nodded. 'But as a doctor I remind myself that one miscarriage, or even two miscarriages, does not mean I am more at risk. Yes, it crosses my mind, but I have to trust in the future.'

The woman smiled gently, closed her eyes and nodded. Then she whispered, 'I lost my baby last month.'

Kiki felt her eyes sting and stepped down off the little podium. The others parted to let her through, and the two women embraced. Quietly, but unashamedly, so it carried to everyone in the room, Kiki said, 'My baby would have been due today.'

When they drew apart and smiled mistily at each other Kiki knew she had found a friend, and for the first time she thought perhaps there *were* things she could achieve here if she and Stefano ever worked it out. But at this moment that seemed very unlikely. And the waste made her angrier.

Out of the corner of her eye she saw Prince Paulo gesture to the Mayor to conclude the event, and she mentally prepared herself for the trip back with the Prince.

Bruno directed her to the podium again and then turned to the audience. 'Thank you so much, Dr Fender, for your sincerity. We are all deeply appreciative of your presence today.'

Kiki stepped back, the crowd began to disperse, and she gathered her emotions and control. Just.

Until she saw Stefano arrive and cross to his father. She narrowed her eyes. Typical. *Great timing,* she thought, *when it's too late to support me, but in time to judge me.* Her anger stepped up another notch. Of all days she had had to do this and he didn't even know.

Stefano spoke briefly to his father and she saw Prince Paulo pat his son's shoulder in an unusual gesture of affection. He nodded in her direction, and with his entourage cordially turned away.

Stefano crossed to her side. He seemed bemused. 'My father said you did well. That the women liked you. Congratulations.'

Something snapped inside her. 'Gee, thanks.' She saw he didn't miss the sarcasm and was glad. How dared he? She 'did well'? So magnanimous of him. Was she supposed to be thrilled at his approval? And what if she hadn't done well? Would he have been here to support her?

His gaze narrowed. 'You're angry? With me?'

'Do you know what I told them?'

He shook his head warily, and she could feel emotion bubbling when she wanted to be ice-cold. Angry tears stung her eyes and she turned away from him, because the words wouldn't come. She wanted them to spill out, hurt him as they hurt her, but she couldn't make her mouth work.

He followed her as she walked blindly along the corridor back towards the entrance, and once he steered her gently when she would have taken a wrong turn.

Stefano didn't know what to do. He could see that Kiki seethed with emotion. Had he pushed her too far by expecting her to do this today? But he'd had to operate. He reminded himself that she hadn't been trained for these occasions as he had, and yet every time he asked something of her she responded magnificently. But at what cost?

She swept out of the hospital and he kept pace, nodding at those he passed as if it was his decision to continue this headlong race she had begun. She stopped at his car and spun to face him. The look in her eyes made him step back.

'Do you know what you asked of me today?'

He didn't want to know right here, right now, because

it was not going to be pretty. He opened her door. 'Please, first sit.'

She opened and shut her mouth, and with relief he saw she would do as he asked. When he slid behind the wheel her emotion was like a wall between them and he put up his hand as if to touch it.

'Can I ask you to wait a few more minutes? For the privacy you deserve, not for me. I wish to give you my undivided attention.'

Again she nodded, and he started the car and drove along the road until he came to a lay-by that overlooked the olive groves. He turned the engine off and faced her.

Finally the words spilled like bullets, and he winced.

'Since yesterday morning my life has not been my own.' She drew a breath. 'You have accused me of many things, all of them incorrect, and you have constantly thrown me into situations that were beyond my control.'

He knew it was true. Last night, when he'd finally stopped thinking about himself, he had begun to realise just what he had put her through. And yet still she had been there for him. The more he had considered it the more he'd been able to see how he had failed her.

He deserved every accusation for the mistakes he'd made. For the need he couldn't let go of to maintain control over his life. He wanted to say he was sorry for whatever he'd done, to hold her, comfort her. But the wall between them kept him back.

'Can you tell me what happened in there?'

She jabbed her finger towards his head. 'Can *you* tell me what happens in *there*? In your closely guarded mind that simply refuses to open to me. To trust.' She shook her head with frustration. 'You expect so little from me...'

'No.'

'Yes,' Kiki insisted. 'You would rather think I am a

woman who will fail you than a woman who can succeed.
I can succeed at anything.' She looked at him sadly. 'And
I can succeed without you, Stefano.'

'You have more than proved that.' And then he looked
at her. 'Not once have you failed me. It is the other way
round.'

'I know. Why is that?'

He had no answer. He watched her shudder against the
door as she leaned as far away as possible from him. His
hand clenched uselessly, because he couldn't mistake her
aversion to any movement towards her on his part.

She stared out through the front windshield. 'Today I
was there for those women in a way you have never been
for me. And it came home to me just how much you have
let me down. The waste when we could have been so good.
And, yes, it makes me very angry.'

She pointed an accusing finger at him.

'I gave more than I thought I would have to. Again without your support. In the last few days I have been forced to
publicly expose my pain again and again—and you know
what? I can't do it any more.'

She was right, and he hastened to reassure her. 'I won't
ask it of you.'

She turned towards him and he saw the tears in her eyes,
could feel her hurt in his own chest. She finally lifted her
chin. As always, her strength astounded him.

He could hear the control she clung to in her voice.
'You've missed the whole point of what I needed from
you. Especially today.'

The words captured him. Something in her voice...
'Why today?'

She didn't answer that right away, and he almost missed
the significance—again.

'Because it's heartbreaking to lose a baby. And today should have been about life. Not loss.'

'Today?' The full import of what she was saying finally seeped into his consciousness along with the anguish in her voice.

He read the confirmation on Kiki's face and realised he truly did deserve to lose not only his child but this woman. And just when he'd come to understand how much he needed her in his life.

That he didn't ever want to lose her.

Couldn't lose her.

He was so afraid he had finally completely driven her away?

Stefano knew it was time to battle his own demons. To risk everything. Because if he didn't he would lose the best thing that had ever happened to him. He reached for her, and to his shuddering relief this time she didn't pull away.

He slid his finger under her chin and gently turned her to him, so he could cradle her face in his hands, stare into her beautiful eyes. 'I am so sorry.'

He saw the reflection of his own sense of loss for what they'd had between them and ached to ease her pain.

'I am sorry,' he said again, and sighed. Why did he always do and say the wrong thing around this woman? 'What I have done to you is unforgivable.' He reflected over the last twenty-four hours and winced. His voice was bitter at his own stupidity. 'My bullying and my anger at the public scrutiny didn't take into account the cost to you.'

Mental screenshots flickered past like a horror film— the way he had dragged her to the palace, thrust his mother's ring on her finger, installed her in his mother's isolated rooms with barely an explanation. Left her alone to suffer while he'd worried more about others.

To make matters a hundred times worse he had then

forced her to attend a ceremonial function that very night—most probably because he had truly expected her to fail. Then he would have been able to tell himself it would never work.

How could she ever love the monster he had become?

He heard the rasp as she drew in her breath. Watched her blink away the tears that glittered on her lashes as she raised her head.

He had lost her.

'I was a monster to you.'

'Yes, you were.' But then she hugged him. 'All that and more.' She shifted her head back a little, so she could focus. 'Why?'

He had nothing left to give her but the truth. 'Because I was afraid.'

'Of me?'

'Of course of you.' He ran his hands through his hair. 'Of losing control of my life.'

She shook her head. He could see she didn't understand that he knew she was already gone. That he knew he'd knew left his run too late.

She said again. 'What are you talking about?'

'Already I have hurt you in so many ways because of my fears. I will take you back to the mainland this afternoon.'

'You still don't get it. I don't want to go. You've been horrible, but I'll survive.'

His hand lifted and one finger stroked her silken cheek. 'Of course you will survive. You are magnificent. Last night you rose and faced them all as if you had been born to stand head and shoulders above the world.' He was so proud of her, and ashamed of being the man who had subjected her to that. 'No thanks to me.'

She went on in the same hard little voice. 'And today I was there for those women in a way you have never been for me. It came home to me just how much you have let me down. And, yes, it makes me very angry.'

Her lips tilted, teased him, and his fear eased a little that she could still smile his way.

'Some things I *can* thank you for. You rescued me from the press at the dock.'

'Pah.' He snapped his fingers. 'That is nothing. I should not have left you. Well before that I was not there when you needed me the most.'

Stefano leant across and gathered her in next to him, felt her slight weight against him and wanted to protect her from the world. It had taken him too long to realise that was his mission.

'You are here now,' she said.

He drew her even closer. 'Is it true that our baby was to have been born today?'

She nodded her head against him. Whispered, 'Yes,' and his heart contracted.

He moistened his lips, prayed she would hear the truth in his words, and finally said what he should have said when he'd first found out that they had made a baby together. 'I am so sorry I was not there with you when our child slipped away from us.'

Her eyes shadowed as she returned to her most painful memory, allowed him to see through a small window to how it had been. She acknowledged his right to see, and he realised that was the greatest gift she had given him yet.

'It was night and I was alone.' Kiki pressed her lips together to stop their wobble.

He closed his eyes and breathed deeply, more ashamed than he had ever been in all his life. 'My poor, poor love. I wish I could have held you and shared your grief. I should have been there. Let me share it now.' He squeezed her to him as he felt the dampness of his own eyes. 'Please.'

Kiki turned her face into his chest and he stroked her hair as she remembered that night in the hospital. Her tiny, solitary room, dark and metallic, the loneliest place in the world when the pains had increased. Within minutes the bleeding had been so great that by the time a nurse arrived and rushed her off to Theatre her life had almost drained away.

She whispered into the silence between them, in a tiny sports car pulled over at the side of the road, on an island in the Mediterranean Sea with her prince beside her.

'I knew that when I woke up from the anaesthetic it would be gone. Not just our baby, but any link to you.'

And then the tears came, great gulping sobs, and the tearing of her heart that she could finally share with Stefano as she was wrapped in the very arms she'd needed so badly that night so many lonely nights ago. And at last, after far too long, the final healing could begin.

Stefano held her tightly against him, gathering her shudders of grief as he gathered her closer, inhaling the scent of her hair, stroking her over and over again with all the tenderness he had in him. He had never felt as close to anyone in his whole life as he did to this woman at this moment. Had never allowed himself to do so in case he lost himself. But now he wanted to be lost.

Lost with her.

Random flashes of his past with Kiki rolled through his mind.

The first time he'd seen her, like a ray of sunshine in his day, radiant, confident, joyous. A heroine on her quest to help mankind.

The first time he'd held her hand and sensed there was something between them that defied description yet was instantly recognisable—something he would never forget despite all the obstacles fate had thrown up against them.

And that magical week when she had opened her home, her arms and her heart just for him. Stefano the man—not Stefano the Prince. Even when he'd been away, recovering, she'd been like a shadow behind him that refused to be forgotten.

He would make it up to her. He would make it all up to her. He just hoped she felt the same about him, because now that he had her back in his arms he didn't think he could let her go. Ever.

Slowly her weeping turned to hiccups and her flood of tears to a trickle. He mopped her face and hugged her again and kissed her damp mouth gently. He wanted to repeat his apology, but he was afraid she would weep all over again.

But Kiki was made of sterner stuff than that. One last sniff, the hijacking of his handkerchief, and she wiped her eyes and blew her nose resolutely. 'I'm sorry. That was torrential. Thank you for letting me soak your shirt.'

The knot in his stomach loosened. 'You are very welcome.'

She sniffed again and smiled, with a tiny wobble still in evidence. 'Thank you, anyway. I think I needed that.'

He watched the old Kiki emerge and sat back on his side of the car with bemusement and wonder. Relief expanded in his chest as he realised she had already begun to forgive him. Now all he had to do was forgive himself.

Kiki screwed up the handkerchief after one last trumpeting blow. If he still fancied her after this then there was hope for them yet. But that thought and all it involved was terrifying.

'Thank you for listening, and for being here now.' She glanced around at the grove of olives across the road. 'But perhaps we should talk of something else.'

He didn't move.

'Or head back to the castle?'

The way his gaze moved across her face made her cheeks burn. His grey eyes were softer than she'd ever seen them, and he kissed her fingers and brushed her cheek with a gesture. More heat to her red face, and she looked away, embarrassed, suddenly remembering again that this man was a prince and she'd sobbed all over him.

'How was I so fortunate as to find you?' He shook his head in wonder, and as if unable to help himself reached and took her hand.

They both gazed down at the ring he'd insisted she wear. The huge square diamond flashed with reflected light even when there didn't seem to be any beams to catch. It wasn't hers. Not really.

He leaned forward and spoke very slowly and gently. 'So, my question is this. To the world we are already engaged. But the man who demanded this did not deserve you.'

He stroked the ring on her finger and drew it off. To her dismay, she felt bereft. So this was where they faced the truth. She drew in a breath and steadied herself for the end.

He raised her hand to his lips and caressed her knuckles with his mouth. 'May I start again?'

She blinked, not sure what he meant. A crazy, stuttering hope like a flame caught in a cross breeze tossed her into confusion. Start again? With what?

Stefano searched her face, saw her turmoil, and knew it was time to be brave as this woman had been brave. To lose himself for ever and hand her the power to destroy his world if she willed it. He'd never thought he would see this moment.

He drew a deeper breath. 'Do you know that I love you?'

Her eyes flared and she opened her beautiful mouth and closed it. Then finally she said, 'No.'

His tension increased as she shook her head. How to convince her? 'I love you and wish to spend my life with you. To respect and honour you. But only if this is what you want too.'

He saw the fear, understood she had glimpsed what that would mean and seen not all of it was good. None knew more than he that he asked for an enormous commitment. 'Will you share my life with me as my princess. Do me the honour of being my wife? Wear this ring always?'

She looked down at the ring in his hand. Remembered the weight of it. Could she? Rules and etiquette... Royal crises and functions... Their work at the hospital would keep them busy enough. She thought of the women, of the first of many friends she could make, of those she could help.

Then Kiki imagined a life never seeing Stefano again, losing her dream of dark-haired arrogant little boys like Stefano and tiny little girls in pink tulle, and there was no contest. She would not be alone. She would have Stefano the person. Not the heir to the throne. Just her gorgeous man. Stefano.

She leaned across and kissed him softly on the lips. 'I love you. Will always love you. And that's enough for me.'

He slid the ring back on her finger with immense satisfaction. 'Then that is a yes.'

CHAPTER TWELVE

KIKI'S BROTHER NICK and her sister-in-law had arrived to save her. Instead they accepted an invitation to the Prince's Cup.

This year, when the glitterati arrived on the Friday night before the race, a huge stage had been set in the centre of the racetrack with the sea as its background and festooned with a thousand lights.

There was to be a magnificent celebration for the engagement of Prince Stefano Mykonides and his bride-to-be Dr Kristina Karine Fender and the whole island was invited.

Open-sided marquees were provided for the guests to wander through, eat and drink, barbecue steaks, and strange Australian damper, while they listened to music from among the world's greatest musicians—including Kiki's favourite Australian band, flown over at the last minute.

As a gift and gesture of acknowledgment Stefano had set up a huge screen—a never-ending light show depicting the glory of his betrothed's homeland. From harbour to Outback, it showed soaring scenery, a bird's-eye view circumnavigating the whole coastline and across the continent. From Barrier Reef, to Uluru, the screen breathed life into a continent thousands of miles away, so that his people understood that he was a part of that world as his bride was now a part of theirs.

And through it all Kiki and Stefano walked among the people, shaking hands, smiling at each other and at the world. For Kiki, the magnitude of the spectacle had started as a challenge—but then she'd met people she knew: Dr Herore and her husband. Rosa's family plus Sheba and the new baby. Elise had brought her son, and to Kiki's surprise, Jerome. Stefano had whispered that Elise had asked for his thoughts on adoption.

She began to enjoy meeting the hundreds of people they spoke to, all eager to wish them well and ask about the wedding.

Kiki's brother Nick and his very pregnant wife, Tara, shook their heads repeatedly at his little sister's surprise rise to fame.

Wilhelm and Miko from the ship were there, and audaciously, Miko kissed Kiki's hand right in front of her fiancée. Kiki laughed and Stefano growled good-naturedly about it being his last chance to do so.

But finally, well after midnight, it was over, and Stefano kissed her as soon as they were through the door of their apartments.

'I have been waiting to do this all night.'

It felt so good to have his arms around her and feel the world just disappear.

She sighed happily as she lay back in his arms. 'When I marry you will the wedding be big?'

He laughed ruefully. 'Bigger than you can imagine. It will be a marathon. But at the end we will have each other.'

She leaned across and kissed him softly on the lips. 'Then that's enough for me.'

EPILOGUE

SIX MONTHS LATER, in the red silk-lined formal throne room of the palace, arranged in front of the huge gold fireplace and the soaring portraits of the current ruler and his late princess, in the presence of Prince Paulo, Prince Theros and his wife Princess Marla, a dozen dignitaries, and the bride's four siblings and their partners, a civil ceremony of marriage was carried out by His Excellency the Mayor, Bruno Valinari.

Kiki, dressed in coral-coloured Dior, sat straight-backed, her hands folded demurely in her lap, as she listened to the long legal discourse required before Stefano could legally make her his princess.

Finally the moment came, and without hesitation his voice decreed his intention. 'I pledge my life and legally bind myself to Kristina Karine Fender. My Princess.' And then softly, with joy and belief as he met her eyes, 'My Kiki.'

The Mayor said, 'For ever?'

'I do.'

Her eyes stung, but she knew she couldn't cry. She wondered if princesses were allowed to cry. She'd meant to ask Elise.

Then it was her turn, and she listened, minute after minute, to the legal jargon mixed with advice in the way of royal wedding ceremonies for the last five hundred years on this sovereign island discovered by pirates and ruled by physicians.

The longer the discourse went on the more nervous she became. Her heart began to pound. She would miss her cue, would stumble, would open her mouth and no sound would come out.

Suddenly she became conscious that tomorrow, in the cathedral, it would be a thousand times worse, with millions upon millions of television viewers. What if her words got stuck?

The Mayor's words seemed to join together in her ears, so she couldn't tell where one began and the other ended, and the lump in her throat grew so large she could barely breathe. Her mouth dried and she began to shake as a surge of adrenalin coursed through her body and made her want to stand up and run.

Finally she understood those movies where the bride bolted...

Then gradually, as if directed by a hand other than her own, she lifted her eyes to the portrait of Stefano's mother, which seemed to glow above the gold fireplace. The beautiful woman there smiled down at her.

My love to you both. The words were as clear as if she were sitting beside the mother-in-law she would never meet. *See only one person or the occasion will overwhelm you.*

Finally Kiki felt the knot that had tied her tongue ease and drift away as if it had never been. *Look, speak and smile at one person and you will be in control of the room.* Kiki sighed and closed her eyes.

When she opened them, the room had narrowed to the one person who mattered the most—the man she loved with all her heart and who would stand beside her anywhere. Joined to Stefano, she would never be afraid again.

All nervousness fled.

Finally the moment came, and she was so very ready. 'I pledge my life to you, Stefano Adolphi Phillipe Augustus Mykonides.' She smiled. 'My Stefano.'

The Mayor said, 'For ever?'

'I do.'

And they were wed.

When they stepped out onto the balcony of the palace the square below it was filled with Stefano's people—her people now—and the roar of the crowd swelled like the roar of a train, building in intensity and promising to carry her into a new life and new experiences.

Stefano turned her to him and she lifted her face for their first kiss as man and wife. As his lips touched hers the roar of the crowd doubled until they broke apart and smiled at their world.

On the morning of their cathedral wedding Stefano and Kiki lay entwined, heavily asleep, smiles on their faces and hands clasped.

Elise didn't want to wake them, so she sent Jerome in. 'Wake up!'

The young boy had a part to play today and he wanted to get started.

Four hours later in the bride's chambers it was time to leave for the cathedral. It was good to have Nick's hand to stop her trembling, but Kiki could see that today it seemed her big brother was the more nervous one.

Nick had told her that yesterday he'd thought she would faint from fright. He had been worried his little sister had chosen far too public a road for herself. But today she was a new woman, and she could see the look of love and awe on his face and it gave her even more confidence.

Her dress had been created by the principal of a famous Parisian couture house, with lace inserts from its high neck to under her bodice, and sewn with a thousand crystals and the fall of a thousand pearls. The train had her six attendants scurrying, and made Nick shake his head in male confusion.

And the veil… A thousand hours of stitching and twenty yards long, it was so thin and insubstantial it was like looking through a cobweb.

Nick scratched his chin. 'I have no idea how they're going to get this dress into the car.'

Kiki shrugged and twitched her sleeve straight. 'Don't worry. They'll have an expert do it. And it's a very long car.' Already she had learnt.

Her brother raised his brows, threw back his head and laughed.

'What?'

She did not want to be fashionably late. She couldn't wait to see Stefano.

Nick glanced at the open door held by a liveried footman and then back at his radiant sister. 'You've changed.'

She lifted her head. 'I've accepted and I'm blessed.'

She would take everything in her stride. One thing at a time. Because at the end of the day would be Stefano.

'I'm Stefano's wife. I'm going to be a very good one. And I'm not going to worry about the small stuff unless I have to.'

They did get the dress into the Rolls Royce. Just. With a hundred perfect folds so that it would leave the car as beautiful as it had gone in.

The streets were lined with flag-waving residents as Kiki and Nick drove slowly towards the cathedral. They passed huge screens set up on walls to televise the wedding to those outside. In the two cars behind, her six attendants followed: her own three sisters, Nick's wife Tara, two small royal flower girls and one little page boy, smiling so hard the scars on his face shone white in the sunlight.

Jerome's was the face of joy projected around the world which encompassed the celebration for the people in the streets. Finally their favourite prince had wed. They loved their new princess, and they were all invited.

Stefano arrived at the cathedral first, and the crowd roared their approval that he had shunned protocol and chosen to arrive first and wait for his commoner wife. He turned, waved, and entered the building.

Theros accompanied him nervously down the long red carpet to the marble altar at the front. Every red velvet seat was taken. Every foot of space was jammed with bodies and cameras.

Theros kept patting his pocket, where the rings sat. He and Marla had eloped to avoid this very spectacle. This was frighteningly huge.

Nervous of crowds, and frightened of the cathedral, he was diffident about following his brother, but his own bride had been so sure he could do it and he was determined he would.

Stefano recognised his brother's distress. 'Thank you for standing by me, Theros.' He looked around and spoke quietly, so the microphones wouldn't pick it up. 'I wanted to marry here. Mama is here, and I want her to meet my new princess.'

Then the music started, played by the minstrels in the gallery on golden horns: a serenade on the bride's arrival.

Stefano felt his heart trip. So much he had asked of a woman not born to this, and to every new challenge she had risen, teaching him so much about true inner strength. So brave was his bride, and he could not wait for her to stand here beside him and before God.

Then she was at the door, on the arm of his new brother-in-law.

She was a vision. An angel in white with her head high. Through the fine mist of her veil her eyes were searching, finding his, and the music swelled. But it was no match for the swelling in his heart as the woman of his dreams walked slowly towards him. Everything else faded. There was just this woman, fearlessly announcing to the world that she would love him for ever.

As he would love her.

* * * * *

HIS HIDDEN
AMERICAN
BEAUTY

BY
CONNIE COX

MILLS &
BOON

All the characters in this book have no existence outside the imagination of the author, and have no relation whatsoever to anyone bearing the same name or names. They are not even distantly inspired by any individual known or unknown to the author, and all the incidents are pure invention.

All Rights Reserved including the right of reproduction in whole or in part in any form. This edition is published by arrangement with Harlequin Enterprises II BV/S.à.r.l. The text of this publication or any part thereof may not be reproduced or transmitted in any form or by any means, electronic or mechanical, including photocopying, recording, storage in an information retrieval system, or otherwise, without the written permission of the publisher.

This book is sold subject to the condition that it shall not, by way of trade or otherwise, be lent, resold, hired out or otherwise circulated without the prior consent of the publisher in any form of binding or cover other than that in which it is published and without a similar condition including this condition being imposed on the subsequent purchaser.

® and TM are trademarks owned and used by the trademark owner and/or its licensee. Trademarks marked with ® are registered with the United Kingdom Patent Office and/or the Office for Harmonisation in the Internal Market and in other countries.

First published in Great Britain 2013
by Mills & Boon, an imprint of Harlequin (UK) Limited.
Harlequin (UK) Limited, Eton House, 18-24 Paradise Road,
Richmond, Surrey TW9 1SR

© Connie Cox 2013

ISBN: 978 0 263 89885 9

Harlequin (UK) policy is to use papers that are natural, renewable and recyclable products and made from wood grown in sustainable forests. The logging and manufacturing process conform to the legal environmental regulations of the country of origin.

Printed and bound in Spain
by Blackprint CPI, Barcelona

Dear Reader

When cruise ship doctor Annalise Walcott first sees celebrity surgeon Niko Christopoulos she thinks he must be a swimsuit model. But, like the ocean, Niko is more than he appears to be on the surface.

Annalise has her own uneasily buried secrets that only a man used to braving the depths of human tragedy—a man like Niko—can possibly bring to the surface.

Will love be enough to give these two the strength to survive the stormy wreckage of their pasts and build a bright future under the sun together?

Wishing you calm winds and gentle seas

Connie

PS I'd love to visit with you! Find me on Facebook: www.facebook.com/ConnieCox.writer, on Twitter: www.twitter.com/ConnieCox, on Goodreads: www.goodreads.com/Connie_Cox and on my website: www.conniecox.com

Recent titles by Connie Cox:

THE BABY WHO SAVED DR CYNICAL
RETURN OF THE REBEL SURGEON

**Available in eBook format
from www.millsandboon.co.uk**

CHAPTER ONE

DR. ANNALISE WALCOTT adjusted the two huge cases of medicines on her cart before she made the steep climb up the gangplank of the luxury cruise liner *Neptune's Fantasy*. While she'd had most of the supplies delivered straight to her onboard facilities, she liked to bring along the ones that needed refrigeration herself, just to make sure they stayed at the correct temperature. Not that she'd ever had a problem—Annalise avoided problems as often as she could.

Call her a control freak and she wouldn't deny it. She'd learned a long time ago that the only person she could consistently rely on was herself.

She trailed behind the last-minute stragglers, crewmates eking out the final seconds of shore leave before they boarded for the transatlantic cruise. They would be out at sea for over ten days straight before the first port of call, which meant a lot fewer breaks for the staff. And only a small percentage of crew got shore leave at each port. With rotating days off, most of them wouldn't have a personal day on land for at least four weeks.

One by one, they went through Security, a procedure that took forever but which, she had to admit, was a necessity.

A Gulf breeze made the afternoon pleasant despite the strong subtropical sun heating Annalise's back through her roomy, short-sleeved T-shirt. Thankfully, she'd slath-ered her arms and legs with sunblock before donning her shorts and sandals so she had no worries about her pale skin turning pink. Not a good example for a doctor to set when she warned others about avoiding sunburn.

"Need some help with those, Doc?" A bartender named Brandy pointed to the cases. Brandy sported a new tattoo, still red and slightly swollen.

Annalise hoped she'd had it done by a reputable shop. Illegal backroom bargains had consequences. She had long-lasting firsthand knowledge of that. If only hers had been as harmless as a tattoo.

"I've got them. Thanks, though." She moved forward another six inches in the queue, wincing as the corner of the cart dug into her ankle.

"Have a nice time on shore?" Bartenders were chatty by nature and Brandy was no exception.

Annalise had never learned the art of making small talk herself, beyond the few stock phrases she used to put her patients at ease.

"Just long enough to realize I'm ready to be back at sea."

Being on land in her home port of New Orleans always made her uneasy, even though all personal threats had long since passed.

"Didn't I see you with a friend on the patio at the Crescent City Brew House this afternoon? A male friend?"

"He was my study partner in medical school." They'd been more than study partners, but the bartender didn't need to know how he'd helped her work through her pain and grief all those years ago. "He's my *platonic* friend."

"Nothing more? Not even a friend with benefits?"

Annalise laughed, inwardly wincing as it sounded brittle and forced in her ears. "He's not my type." Not that she had a type.

"What kind of man do you like, Doc? I'll bet I can fix you up. I'm fairly good at that sort of thing."

Annalise wished it were that easy. "You bartenders are really cupids in disguise, aren't you? But there are rules against that sort of thing, remember?"

"I don't know about you, Doc, but the rule against fraternization gets old when I've been out to sea for a while. It's not natural to go without sex for such long periods of time."

Sex. Shipboard sex meant a shipboard relationship—or at least a shipboard flirtation. No way would she risk her career—or her peace of mind—for a fling.

To forestall the conversation, Annalise pulled the brim of her baseball cap down tight and deliberately looked up.

From where she stood, halfway up the ship's side with the ocean far below her and the top deck far above, Annalise felt the weight of such a huge amount of people, both guests and staff, dependent upon the ship's medical facilities. As usual, she was the sole physician on board, but she had plenty of trained medical professionals to help her, including a new physician's assistant. The P.A. came with great recommendations and Annalise was looking forward to meeting her.

Her only worry was the six-year-old girl on the manifest, Sophie Christopoulos, diagnosed with juvenile diabetes. But her parents had been wise enough to have the girl's endocrinologist consult with Annalise ahead of time and Sophie had an introductory appointment before tonight's first supper seating.

Sophie's insulin was in one of the cases on her cart. With precautions, the young girl should be able to enjoy her trip just fine.

A crepe paper streamer sailed down from the top deck

to drape itself across Annalise's shoulders like a boa. The makeshift fashion statement made her smile.

She looked up to see passengers on the foredeck already in full party mode and they hadn't even left dock yet. Cruises had attitudes and she could already tell this one was going to be a wild one. No peaceful, relaxing vibes coming from this crowd.

Brandy looked up, shading her eyes. "It's going to be one of those."

"The kind of cruise I enjoy most." While Annalise didn't partake of the party life herself, she enjoyed the energy.

"As long as they tip well." Brandy pointed to the sky. "Looks like a storm is coming in."

Annalise shrugged. "Typical late afternoon for New Orleans this time of year. It will blow through as fast as it's blowing in."

A thick bank of stormclouds dimmed the sun's brightness while a strong gust of wind brought chill bumps to her exposed legs. Sprigs of reddish-golden hair whipped into her face despite the baseball cap she'd plopped onto her head.

The layered cut had been a whim while she'd been on shore, a consolation prize after visiting her mother and finding her the same.

She'd thought short hair would be easier, but she missed the straightforward care of her ponytail. Now her hair was too short to capture with a rubber band and too long to stay out of her eyes without a lot of styling and primping. And primping had no place in Annalise's life. Why waste the time?

Her life was devoted to patching up people and keeping them healthy so they could enjoy their days under the sun. Stolen time away from the workaday world was precious and she wanted the passengers to be able to make the most of it.

Annalise knew the value of escaping the real world. That's why being the *Fantasy*'s onboard physician was her dream job.

A squeal of tires from the parking lot down below caught her attention.

A sporty black convertible with the top down slid into an empty parking slot and careened to a stop. Annalise squinted to see the dark-haired man behind the sunglasses pop his trunk, grab a suit-sized carry-on, a serious back-pack and a large rolling suitcase and make a sprint for the entrance of the cruise ship's land-based check-in facility.

She glanced at her watch. A quarter till five.

When the cruise line said to embark before four o'clock, they had their reasons—security checks being one of the most important ones.

Brandy shook her head. "There's always one who thinks the rules don't apply to him, isn't there?"

Annalise agreed. "He'll have to do some real sweet-talking to get aboard this ship."

Brandy gazed absently at the head of the line. "Some men are worth breaking the rules for."

Not any man she'd ever met.

Stormclouds moved into position overhead, blocking the sun's intensity but adding a couple of points to the humidity scale, making the moist air heavy to drag into her lungs.

The sooner she was out at sea, the better.

"Next," came the call from the front of the line.

As she moved forward, Annalise looked back at the dark-haired latecomer juggling his luggage to open the door to the check-in office.

She had to admit he had a face and body that could entice a saint to at least bend the rules a little.

He flashed a dimpled smile at her as he caught her staring.

She could feel a blush heating her face as she looked away.

She was no saint, but the man didn't exist who could tempt her. Sadly, she wished there were.

Dr. Niko Christopoulos leaned over the counter past the plastic *Closed* sign, giving the middle-aged receptionist a big dimpled smile. He hoped she liked the rugged, unshaven look. It couldn't be helped.

"I'm so sorry to be such a bother. I've been traveling for the last thirty-two hours straight to get here and my last flight landed late."

The receptionist, who reminded him of his Aunt Phyllis with her polite but no-nonsense attitude, pulled up his information.

"You're responsible for the party of twelve, right? The grandmother who thinks she's won the family cruise?"

Niko gave a quick look around the deserted lobby, as if any of his family might overhear. "That's right. Do you need to verify my credit card?"

"We've already done that. But I do need your passport, please." She held out her hand.

He handed her the well-worn leather folder.

"The Congo, Doctor? And before that Haiti? You're quite a world traveler."

Niko didn't talk about his charity work—ever. But if it got him on this blasted ship before it sailed… "Doctors Without Borders. An adventure every trip."

Her eyes softened and she picked up the phone. "Hold the ship for Dr. Nikos Christopoulos. He was unavoidably delayed and will be heading your way in just a moment."

"Thanks for waiting on me."

She gave him a sly wink. "I'm sure you're worth waiting for."

He returned the wink. "That's what they tell me."

"Do you need help with your bags?"

"Got it all here." He pointed to his military-sized backpack full of shorts and swim trunks and toiletries, his suit bag with his tuxedo and his one rolling bag, glad he'd packed for this trip and stuffed his clothes in his trunk before he'd even left for Haiti, for once planning ahead.

He was more of a go-with-the-flow kind of guy—which came in handy when making split-second decisions in the field. Life or death decisions were enough to worry about without adding the little things to the list. But this week he intended to surrender all decisions and worries and soak in the sunshine.

He needed these three weeks of enforced restful playtime. He had become soul-weary, the kind of tired a good nap couldn't cure.

Physician, heal thyself. He self-prescribed a big dose of fun and he intended to follow doctor's orders.

"Have a wonderful vacation, Dr. Christopoulos."

"I'll do my best." It worked. The charm his grandmother loved him for and his brothers taunted him about had gotten him where he needed to be once again.

Use the gifts you've been given, his grandmother told all of them. His brothers could all cook meals that would please the gods of Olympus. Niko couldn't boil an egg.

An easy way with words and a genetically pleasing appearance had been his gift—he just wondered if a woman would ever care enough to see past the exterior to the man underneath.

But then again, that would mean he would also need to look beneath her surface and that would mean getting up close and personal. A relationship was out of the question with the lifestyle he would soon be living full time. His ex-fiancée had made that perfectly clear to him. But that was yesterday's problem.

He would embrace today. Too many years ago he'd learned the hard way that that's all anyone could really expect to have.

As he headed up the gangplank, the calypso music put a kick in his step. This trip may have originally been planned for his family's benefit, but it was exactly what he needed, too.

Niko breathed in the tangy air and prepared to enjoy himself, no holds barred. And maybe he'd start with that cute little honey-haired woman in the baseball cap with the legs that went on forever. She stood at the end of the line apart from everyone else, looking totally unattached, which meant totally available, right? While long-term relationships were out, shipboard flirtations were definitely in.

"Those are mighty big bags for such a little lady. Prepared to dress for dinner, are we?" Niko jiggled his suit bag for emphasis.

Big drops started to fall from the clouds above. He moved closer to squeeze under the canvas canopy sheltering the ship's entrance.

The long-legged beauty tried to shift away but there was nowhere to go.

Just as Niko was considering stepping out into the rain to put her at ease, the line moved, giving her the space she obviously needed.

Then again, it seemed this woman claimed her own space. She looked down her nose at him as best she could, considering she was several inches shorter than him. "I'm on staff here. I don't do dinner."

Which wasn't quite true. Annalise helped out by rounding out the captain's table on occasion to even out the couples ratio. It was no hardship. Seated next to a partnerless passenger, usually an elderly gentleman or an awkward geek, she'd met some delightful people.

People like this stunning man next to her always had a date, or found one or two while shipboard. The ship's relationship rules definitely didn't apply to passengers like it did to crew.

Since she was a rule-abiding crew member, this man was not a threat. Even so, she found herself leaning away from him and his overpowering personality, even while she regretted the sharpness of her tone. She was definitely too much on edge today.

Brandy reached across her toward the guy with an open hand. "Hi, I'm—"

"Next," the security checker interrupted. He slid Brandy's ship's ID through the scanner. "You know the drill."

The tension between the security checker and Brandy crackled, proof that shipboard break-ups made for an incredibly uncomfortable environment.

Brandy turned to Annalise. "You know, Doc, this ship is large enough that a person could sail for a month without running into everyone on board. But no matter how big it is, when you're trying to avoid someone, no ship is big enough."

Annalise felt trapped, literally being caught between a man and a woman and their conflict. A clammy sweat started down her back as the old terror threatened to overcome her.

"Relationships. Not my thing," she managed to choke out as her throat tightened up on her. She tried to laugh but it sounded strained even to her own ears so she coughed to cover it up. From bad to worse.

Behind her, the late passenger took a step forward, concern in his eyes. "Are you okay?"

His voice was a low deep rumble. Masculinity personified.

She could feel the heat from his body as he crowded her.

Annalise took a deep breath as the unreasonable panic settled. It had been a few years, almost a decade, since she'd had a panic attack. But too many memories in too few hours had taken their toll on the solid, secure world she'd built for herself.

The sooner she put New Orleans behind her, the better off she would be.

"I'm fine. Thanks." She gave a numb nod and thrust her card at the security checker, careful to keep her fingers from brushing his.

The security checker took Annalise's card and slid it through. "Welcome back, Dr. Walcott. Need some help with that load?"

"Got it. Thanks."

The man behind her held his card out for inspection.

"Could you remove the sunglasses, sir?" the security checker asked.

"Of course."

Annalise had the strongest urge to turn around so she could look into his eyes but practicality took over. What she saw there would have no bearing upon her.

As she tugged her cart, it turned sideways, crashing into this man who made her feel things she didn't want to feel.

If she were only as graceful as she was independent. "Sorry." She meant for her gaze to skitter across his face but his eyes ensnared hers.

Tiger eyes. Amber golden with specks of brown, rimmed in a darker brown. Tiger eyes with a depth of... sorrow, perhaps, behind the brightness.

"No problem." He blinked, breaking their gaze and allowing her to blink as well. When he raised an eyebrow at her, she realized she'd been staring.

Flustered, she yanked her cart, banging into the counter and almost taking out the passenger scanner. He must think her a total klutz.

What did it matter what he thought? Odds were they would never see each other again unless he had a medical emergency. And he certainly looked healthy to her. Well-worn jeans and a wrinkled T-shirt couldn't hide his physical fitness.

She bumped into passengers all the time. None of them elicited a significant response from her.

Annalise overcame the impulse to check him out one more time.

What was it about him that made her feel… What? Aware? Self-conscious? Tingly? That made her feel anything at all?

As she fought the cart into submission, she heard the security checker say, "Welcome aboard, Mr. Christopoulos. Passenger stairway is to your left."

Christopoulos? That was the name of her patient with juvenile diabetes. What were the odds?

Annalise headed toward the staff elevators, grateful for the privacy and breathing room that safe little metal box promised.

"Hold the door, please." A large tanned hand inserted itself between the closing doors. If the man had seemed to tower over her before, he loomed now. "You don't mind if I ride up with you, do you?"

"Passengers are encouraged to take the stairs if they're able." Inwardly, she winced at her brusqueness. She had wanted to establish distance, not convey rudeness. Where was her balance?

"I'm nursing a leg injury." He gave her a lopsided grin, as if he were embarrassed to ask for special treatment.

Annalise wished a hole would open up and swallow her. "Of course, then."

She stared at the floor numbers as the door closed, not trusting herself to engage in polite conversation.

She needn't have worried about the man being chatty. He leaned against the back wall of the elevator, closed his eyes and slumped as if he would fall asleep right then and there. Except there was nothing relaxed in the tightness around his eyes or the brackets around his mouth or the squareness of his jaw.

Annalise took a moment to gather herself the way she'd learned in therapy so many years ago, rationalizing that her edginess had been provoked by too many triggers in quick succession, the worst one brought on by her own need to know that someone in the world cared.

When she'd knocked on her mother's apartment door while she'd been on shore leave, Annalise had half expected, even hoped, to be told that her mother had moved and failed to leave a forwarding address.

But she'd been there. Bright pink lipstick had leaked into the pursed lines around her lips and coated the end of the cigarette stuck into her mouth. Age spots showed on her chest and arms, exposed by her cheap orange tank top.

"Anna?" her mother had smoothed down her over-processed hair. "I hadn't expected…"

Scented candles perfumed the air. Annalise recognized the odor. Her mother had always thought men were turned on by heavy oriental scents. The smell made her stomach turn.

"I was in town and just thought I'd drop by."

The furtive look her mother sent over her shoulder to

whoever was waiting in the back bedroom was less than welcoming.

"I don't really have the time to come in and visit," Annalise assured her.

The relief was obvious in her mother's eyes. "Maybe another time."

Her mother had closed the door between them without saying goodbye.

It had been over two years. What was another couple of years between family?

Being in her home city, seeing her mother in the old apartment she herself had once lived in, consulting with the little girl's doctor in the same building where she'd attended those therapy sessions, and then meeting with her friend had been a bit much for one day.

And this man next to her, this man who exuded power and testosterone, this man who she was too aware of being just inches away from her, had her all off balance. Something was different about him.

The elevator bumped, threatening Niko's balance. He shifted his weight. From beneath his half-closed lids, he watched Dr. Walcott do the same.

Something was different about her, something that intrigued him. An air? An attitude? A challenge?

Only problem was, Dr. Walcott didn't seem interested. Could he change her mind? When had he last been challenged?

He rubbed his hand across his heavily stubbled face.

When he saw her eyeing him, he said rather self-consciously, "This boat has plenty of hot water, right?"

"The only reason you'll take a cold shower onboard this *ship* is because you take one voluntarily."

"I don't see that happening." He flashed his dimple.

She responded with the slightest of tight-lipped curves at the corners of her mouth. Polite, but just barely.

So much for winning her over with his innate charm. But, then, he wasn't at his best.

A shower and shave and maybe a nap first. Then he might seek out the good doctor on the grounds of professional curiosity. She'd give him a tour of the facilities. He'd buy her a drink. They'd have a private meal on his room's veranda and watch the sunset together—and maybe the sunrise, too.

"How is room service?"

"Very serviceable." She bit her lower lip then squared her shoulders and took a breath as if she were about to plunge into the deep end of the pool. "I use room service quite a bit. They are very prompt. You should try the salmon mousse."

"And maybe a bottle of pinot grigio to share with a new friend?" With the shipboard doctor, he wouldn't have to worry about expectations and entanglements.

"I've never tried it that way. But, then, I'm not very good at sharing." She glanced down at his bare finger. "I'm sure your girlfriend would enjoy the romantic gesture, though."

"No girlfriend at the moment."

She nodded her acknowledgement while she adjusted her grip on her cart, pulling it more decisively between them.

He'd gone too far, too fast. Message received.

He leaned back and closed his eyes, giving them both space.

He might be a romantic but he was a lousy long-term lover.

His ex-fiancée would be glad to expound upon that.

Impatient by nature, Niko had known there was some deep-seated, instinctive reason he'd never agreed to a wedding date. When she'd insisted he choose, either her or his work, he'd finally understood what that reason was.

Any woman who couldn't love him for who he was didn't love him at all. Sadly, after they'd both said their goodbyes, he'd realized he hadn't loved her either. He'd just thought he should because his family had insisted they were the perfect couple. And his family always knew what was best for him.

When it should have been a tragedy, breaking off their engagement had been a relief. It had also been the last tie to living the 'normal' life his family wanted him to live.

This trip was his parting gift, his apology for letting them down, his peace offering for following his dream when he knew that was the last thing any of them would want him to do.

But his lifestyle change was tomorrow's problem. Let tomorrow take care of itself.

The elevator jolted to a stop, putting the brakes on Niko's runaway thoughts.

"Your floor?"

Annalise jerked as his voice called her back to the present. She'd gone away in her mind to avoid an awkward situation as she had so often in the past. But she'd never let down her guard like that while in a confined space with a man.

He was still leaning against the wall, but one eye was cocked open. How long had the elevator been stopped with the doors gaping open?

Keep it together, Annalise. With that admonishment, Annalise pulled the tatters of her self-discipline around her, took a deep breath and determined to carry on. She gave him a sheepish smile. "Lost in thought."

"Been there, done that myself." He pushed away from the wall.

She tugged her heavy cart to get the rollers moving over the rough separation between the elevator and the hallway floor.

"Need some help?"

"No. I've got it under control." She was making more of this chance encounter than it really was, wasn't she? No man like that would be interested in a woman like her, would he?

"I'll be seeing you around."

Not if I can avoid it. She wasn't ready. Not now, maybe not ever, to feel an attraction to a man, especially a man as virile as this one.

"Enjoy your cruise."

He raised a suggestive eyebrow. "I already am."

She ignored the shiver that went through her. As she pulled her heavy load toward her clinic, she worked hard at dismissing the man who would forget about her the second the elevator doors blocked her from his sight.

Christopolous. If he was connected to her young patient, she knew all about how to keep her professional self apart from her personal self. *But was that what she really wanted?*

What she wanted was to have a normal reaction to a normal situation.

She couldn't help taking a look back.

He was watching her, appreciation on his face. He gave her a long, slow, deliberate wink.

Almost against her will her mouth quirked up at the corners, acknowledging—and enjoying?—his attention.

As she felt the ship's engines begin to churn far below her, she felt confused. She'd thought she was on an even keel, that nothing and no one could ever rock her boat.

Obviously, she'd been wrong.

CHOICE OF
TWO
GIFTS!

A **treat**
from us to
thank you
for reading
our books!

Turn over *now*
to find out more

Thanks for reading!

We're treating you to **TWO** fabulous offers...

2 FREE BOOKS

from your favourite Mills & Boon series plus
have books delivered to your door every month!

Find out more and claim your free books at
www.millsandboon.co.uk/bookclub

or call 020 8288 2888 and
quote BOOKCLUB today!

Plus **15% OFF** **

Your next order online with code
THANKSMAR at **www.millsandboon.co.uk**

*FREE BOOK OFFER TERMS & CONDITIONS

Accepting your free books places you under no obligation to buy anything and you may cancel at any time. If we do not hear from you we will send you up to 5 stories a month which you may purchase or return to us – the choice is yours. Offer valid in the UK only and is not available to current Mills & Boon Book Club subscribers to this series. We reserve the right to refuse an application and applicants must be aged 18 years or over. Only one application per household. Offer expires 31st March 2013. Terms and prices are subject to change without notice. As a result of this application you may receive further offers from other carefully selected companies. If you do not wish to share in this opportunity please write to the Data Manager at PO BOX 676, Richmond, TW9 1WU.

CIMAR13

**WEB OFFER TERMS & CONDITIONS

Offer valid online only at www.millsandboon.co.uk until 30/06/2013. This offer cannot be used in conjunction with any other offer. Discount excludes delivery charge. Exclusions apply including Offers, subscriptions, sale items and those with a 40% discount or more. Please see www.millsandboon.co.uk for full terms and conditions.

MILLS & BOON

* * *

Her little half-smile was more intriguing than the Mona Lisa's.

She was perfect. A woman in her profession would understand that any romance Niko allowed himself to indulge in would end when the ship docked.

Niko watched the good doctor walk away on her long, strong legs until the elevator doors closed, blocking her from view. This trip was supposed to be about family, about paying back all the sacrifices they'd made for him—even if they'd never know that part of it. But surely he'd find time for himself, time for a harmless shipboard flirtation, wouldn't he?

And if the good doctor wasn't interested, there were plenty more fish in the sea, right?

A wave of exhaustion overcame him. His long hours and primitive living conditions must be to blame. That sinking feeling certainly couldn't have come from the thought of possible rejection. His ego wasn't that big, was it?

If so, his brothers would soon set it to rights.

Niko opened the door to his home away from home for the next three weeks. While not a huge cabin, it was certainly bigger than the tent he'd been sharing with a nurse and an anesthetist for the last month.

The private veranda was big enough to dine on—and do other things on, too. Yes, this cabin would do just fine.

The quick shower he took refreshed his energy as well as his attitude. The restorative powers of hot water and a bar of soap were nothing short of miraculous. Fresh underwear was a close second.

He picked out the least wrinkled casual dress shirt and pants from his rolling bag, shaking out the mustiness. Not too bad. Packing was a skill he'd had a lot of practice with.

From the connecting door he heard a hesitant knock.

"Uncle Niko, is that you?"

"Yes, Sophie, it's me."

He finished with the last of his shirt buttons then unlatched and opened the door between them and immediately gathered up an armful of six-year-old girl. Her bouncy black curls smelled of baby shampoo and her breath smelled of sugar and spice. Too much sweetness? A hint of fruitiness? Juvenile diabetes sucked.

"Sophie, when was the last time you checked your blood sugar?"

Before Sophie could answer, a voice worn with age but sharp nevertheless, said, "What? Not even a hello first, grandson?"

He looked past Sophie, snuggled on his shoulder, to the four-foot-ten-inch paragon who ruled the Christopoulos family with an iron skillet in one hand and baklava in the other.

"Hello, Yiayia." He put down Sophie and bent to give a hug to the one woman who had always been there for him. "I've missed you."

"There's a way to prevent that. No one is making you stay away." Despite her prickly words, her hug was warm and comforting. She took a step back to look up into his face, keeping both her gnarled hands on his arms as if she could hold him in place. "Wanderlust, like your uncle and your grandfather. At least you have sense enough to keep yourself from getting killed. If I hadn't won this trip, I don't know when we would have seen you next."

Niko squirmed inside while he kept his smile brightly in place. "Livin' the dream, Yiayia."

His mercy missions meant everything to him. But his family would not be pleased if they knew he put himself in such danger, risking his life in areas where lives were lost in wars over water wells as frequently as they were from malaria. His thigh throbbed in memory.

The life of a an overworked, barely paid medical relief doctor was not the life his family had envisioned for him as they'd all sacrificed to send him to college and on to medical school.

He owed them so much. Could he do it? Could he follow his passion, leaving his family with loans and bills and kids to put through college—like they'd put him through all those years.

Yiayia pointed her bony finger at him. "The Christopoulos men are all lucky in love. Someday soon you will find the perfect woman and give me beautiful great-grandbabies."

"Maybe someday, Yiayia." It was easier to agree with her than to argue. And he certainly didn't want to start off a three week vacation on her bad side.

He was so unlike his three brothers in so many ways. Not being cut out to be a family man was the one that hurt the most. He'd dated his fair share of women and then some but he'd not found one he wanted to spend a week with, much less a lifetime.

He flashed the smile that always worked with her. "You've set my standards too high, Yiayia. No other woman can compare."

Yiayia reached up and pinched his cheek. "How can I stay mad at a face like this?"

Sophie had waited as long as she could. She jumped up and down to get attention. "I'm hungry. Ice cream, Yiayia! Ice cream!"

Yiayia's eyes sparkled as bright as Sophie's. "It's included in the trip, Niko. Did they tell you that? Any time we want some. And fine dining each evening, too. Such a dream come true."

It felt good to give back to the family that had sacrificed so much to give him his dream. They would have never accepted repayment for all the support they'd given him through the years. And they all certainly needed a break after the year and a half they'd just been through. If only he hadn't had to set up such an elaborate ruse...

"All right, little one. Let me get my room key." Yiayia turned to find the key.

Niko stopped his grandmother with a gentle hand on her arm. "Wait, Yiayia. What's Sophie's blood-sugar level?"

Yiayia had always made her little ones feel better through food and didn't understand why it had to be different with Sophie—which was one of the main reasons why Niko had agreed to oversee Sophie's care while onboard ship. All his brothers concurred that he had a way with Yiayia that none of the other three had.

"How do I know, Niko? You're the doctor in the family." She switched to Greek, a language Niko heard rarely and only among his grandmother's contemporaries who had immigrated to the United States when she had. But he understood the gist of it.

Yiayia was resistant to taking the disciplined stance needed to protect Sophie's health, thinking everyone was blowing it all out of proportion when her great-granddaughter looked just fine to her.

Niko gave her a stern look. "Where's her blood-glucose meter?"

"In my luggage. I haven't had a chance to unpack yet. She has to check in with the ship's doctor thirty minutes before supper, anyway."

Niko glanced down at Sophie, who was looking scared behind that pout she was sporting. The kid had been through even more than the rest of them.

In addition to being diagnosed with juvenile diabetes,

her mother had lost a baby and almost her life through miscarriage when their restaurant had had the kitchen fire. All the trauma had been straining a marriage that had been made in heaven. Sophie's home life had been tense day in and day out for a long time.

The only reason Niko's oldest brother and sister-in-law had let their daughter come without them was because they were on the verge of emotional exhaustion and Sophie's doctor had insisted it would be better for Sophie to be away from the stress and tension for a while. So they had stayed behind to keep the restaurant open and work on their relationship, knowing Sophie would be surrounded by aunts, uncles, cousins and Yiayia, who would all watch out for her.

"I'll take her, Yiayia." He checked his watch. "We're a bit early but we'll stop in and say hello to the doctor while you look for that meter."

He'd promised his brother he would take care of Sophie. Who could have known his solemn vow would have the side benefit of bringing him together with the good doctor? Niko knew enough about life to make use of good luck when it presented itself.

And now he intended to take full advantage.

CHAPTER TWO

ONCE SAFELY IN her medical suite, Annalise took a deep breath, the first one she'd managed since that man had crowded her in the line boarding the ship.

Surrounded by the tools of her trade, she found her inner balance. If she could relive those brief moments as she boarded the ship...

But, then, going back in time wasn't possible, no matter how hard she wished for it.

She dragged her clunking cases in front of the locked refrigerator reserved for medicines and inserted her key.

As Annalise put away the supplies she'd brought on board, bumping the bottles and boxes into uniform rows, she felt calm claim her. She pushed away the sheepishness she felt about overreacting. Emotional incidents happened on occasion, especially after such a trying day. Being ashamed of her reaction did nothing but undermine her success in coping.

The bell chimed, signaling someone had come into the medical suite. Officially, office hours didn't start until tomorrow morning, but she had scheduled a visit with her juvenile diabetes patient to make sure they started off on the right foot. She glanced at her watch. Better early than late.

"But I don't want to get stuck, Uncle Niko."

Annalise heard them before she saw them as they entered the anteroom of the medical suite.

"Can't be helped, Sophie."

Sophie—it was the Christopoulos child.

That was his voice, wasn't it? The elevator guy was with her little patient. Sometimes luck wasn't in her favor.

Still, she liked it that he didn't trivialize Sophie's fears.

She'd checked the manifest earlier—solely to see where her little patient's cabin would be and to verify that a small refrigerator had been moved into her cabin. She found it had been moved to the cabin next door, Niko Christopoulos' room.

The girl was staying in the cabin next door to the refrigerator with her great-grandmother, Olympia Christopoulos. Twelve people surnamed Christopoulos, all with adjoining cabins or family suites, were on the ship, which had made the odds good she might run into him again.

She thought she'd braced herself for that strange feeling he'd caused in her. But her stomach gave a little flutter, knowing she'd soon be face to face with him again.

Apprehension? More than that.

Fear?

No. Not fear.

Anticipation, maybe?

Before she could sort that one out in her mind she rounded the corner and realized she'd downplayed his good looks in her mind. How could a real flesh-and-blood man be put together so well without magazine airbrushing to lend a hand?

He'd changed. He wore a charcoal-gray boxy button-down made of a silky cotton so fine it slid over his chest when he moved. Even though she wasn't the touchy-feely type, she wanted to rub it between her fingers—purely for curiosity's sake. And his white linen slacks looked loose, comfortable, deceptive. She remembered the shape of him in those jeans.

As he filled her office suite, she felt as if an electric current rode just below the surface of her skin. Unsettling was an understatement. But also energizing? Good? Bad?

She wasn't sure.

Annalise stood a bit taller and smoothed down the lab coat she'd thrown over the chocolate-brown tailored slacks and matching loose blouse she'd changed into.

She felt acutely aware of herself as a woman, an awareness she always pushed down the list behind physician the minute she donned her lab coat.

What was happening to her?

Why now? Why him—okay, that one was easy. How could any woman not fail to go into immediate estrogen overload with him in such close proximity?

He held a notebook. The masculinity of his hand contrasted drastically with the notebook cover, which was totally overlaid with pink glittery stickers.

"Hi, again." He stuck out his free right hand. "Niko Christopoulos, and this is my niece, Sophie."

Sophie wore a baby-blue sailor dress with a large white collar and red cowgirl boots. Annalise could imagine the conversation between this little girl with the adorable stubborn jaw and the person who had helped her dress.

She took Niko's hand, long-fingered and large enough to engulf hers, and that fluttery feeling intensified to an erratic quivering that grew as the seconds ticked by.

Using all her willpower, she made herself hold tight when she wanted to jerk back.

Then he quirked his eyebrow and glanced at their bonded hands.

How was she going to handle this?

Her fallback answer. Professionalism.

She released his hand and used her best patient care smile she'd practiced so hard to perfect. "Welcome, Sophie. I'm Dr. Walcott."

"Uncle Niko is a doctor, too."

"Really?" That didn't surprise her. With his composure, Annalise was sure Niko Christopoulos could be anything he wanted to be.

Annalise squatted down to eye level with her patient, which gave her a good view of Niko Christopoulos' expensive shoes. "And what do you want to be when you grow up?"

"A cook, of course. That's what we all are—except for Uncle Niko." She said it as if becoming a doctor instead of a cook was the most rebellious thing a man could do.

Niko shifted, causing Annalise to look up.

His eyes were tense and his mouth bracketed at the corners. "That's not true, Sophie. Your mother is studying to become a nurse."

"And my dad says it's all your fault."

He gave a deep, sad sigh as he held out his hand to help Annalise stand. "Maybe I should start over. Niko Christopoulos, black sheep of the family."

Annalise wanted to make up an excuse to ignore his outstretched hand, but she couldn't bring herself to reject the man even that small bit when he'd obviously been rejected enough by his own family. She knew how that felt.

"Dr. Christopoulos, it's a pleasure to meet you." As she said the niceties, he wrapped his hand around hers again, this time with the slightest of familiar pressure as if they were comrades in arms. Between his strength and his warmth she felt cocooned. Before she could feel trapped, he released her.

"Call me Niko. Professional courtesy, right? And you are…?"

She was a woman who rarely gave out her first name to strangers, liking the barrier titles and surnames erected around her.

"Annalise." Saying her own name aloud felt so intimate, like a secret revealed. Trying to erase the uneasy feeling, she said in her most authoritative voice, "I understand you're in charge of your niece's blood-sugar checks while you're aboard. Do you understand how to balance her food and activity with her insulin? Are you comfortable giving injections? I can give you a refresher course if you like. I know some doctors don't give injections regularly."

"Got it down." His sister-in-law had emailed Sophie's requirements and he had studied them on the plane.

"I don't want a shot. I don't like Uncle Niko being a doctor."

Annalise shouldn't get involved in family relations but she found herself saying, "I think it's awesome your Uncle Niko is a doctor. He helps people feel better."

"Daddy says Uncle Niko makes people's noses smaller and his wallet bigger."

This time Niko grinned, his cat eyes sparkling. "Guilty." He gave Annalise a wink. "Although I can see my services are not needed here as you have a perfect nose. But we need your professional help, Dr. Walcott. We need to check Sophie's blood sugar."

Annalise had a huge moment of doubt. "You don't know how to use her meter?"

Sophie looked down at her red boots. "Yiayia might have forgotten my blood-sugar meter in the car."

Niko kept his smile firmly in place to hide his disappointment with Yiayia. She couldn't seem to understand how important it was to monitor Sophie's condition. Juvenile diabetes could get out of hand in a heartbeat.

"It's hard for some family members to accept their

young ones needing such continuous care," Annalise said sympathetically.

Apparently, she saw behind his smile. He must be slipping. He *was* beyond tired. Could he catch a nap on deck after supper? A few moments of solitude would go a long way to preparing him to facing three weeks with his raucous family *en masse*.

Annalise pulled up Sophie's charts on her computer screen. "When's the last time you ate, Sophie?"

Sophie shrugged, uncharacteristically shy, and pointed to the notebook her uncle held.

Niko turned to the last entry and angled it so Annalise could have a look at the meal listed there. Fast food at a burger joint. There were better choices—much better.

Sophie was young, but she would still have to be taught to be aware of what she ate.

Annalise asked in a different way. "What did you have for lunch?"

"French fries."

"Anything else?" Niko prompted.

"Aunt Phoebe made me eat my hamburger meat, but I didn't want to and Yiayia said I shouldn't have to because we were on vacation."

"Aunt Phoebe did the right thing." Annalise opened a cabinet and brought out a glucose meter. "Ready?"

Sophie folded her hands together behind her back and stuck out her chin. "No."

Niko's heart broke for her. Life wasn't fair.

What method of persuasion would work best with her?

Of all his nieces and nephews, Sophie was the most stubborn of the bunch. She'd often been compared to him. What would have worked best for him?

"Sophie Olympia Christopoulos, I'm not going to treat

you like a baby. You're too brave for that. Now stick that finger out there and prove it to me."

Niko could see the wheels turning in Sophie's little brain and knew he'd scored. She stood up straighter and held out a finger. Right before Annalise rested the meter against it, Sophie broke. "Hold my hand, Uncle Niko, so it won't go and hide again."

Niko looked up at the ceiling, trying to find the strength before looping his fingers firmly around her tiny wrist. "All right. Let's do this."

"Are you ready?" Annalise moved quickly, pricking in mid-sentence before Sophie had a chance to tense up more. "It's over."

Sophie looked surprised. "That's it?"

"That's it."

"When Daddy does it, it hurts more."

Niko could guess why. His brother probably let the drama build so high that the fear was worse than the prick.

It seemed a family meeting was in order.

The tug o'war that had been pulling at him all these months gave a jerk to his gut. He was the doctor in the family, the one they'd all sacrificed to put through medical school. The one they relied on for explaining these kinds of things. But he'd been out of town and out of touch more often than not.

And, if all went as planned, after this trip, he would be practically unreachable most of the time.

Guilt bowed his shoulders.

Annalise read the numbers then showed them to Niko. He hid his wince then checked his watch.

"We'll eat in fifteen minutes. It's about time for insulin, rapid and long-acting. Let's go with the same amount and I'll make sure she eats better this meal to balance it out."

"Sounds good. Check again a few hours before bedtime

to see if she needs a snack. Ask your waiter to bring apples and orange juice to keep in your room's refrigerator."

"Will do."

"Ice cream!" Sophie said. "I want ice cream. Yiayia said I could have—"

Niko cocked his eyebrow, stopping her whine in midsentence. "If you eat your meal, you can have a little for dessert."

While Annalise opened up her refrigerator and took out a vial of insulin, Niko paged through the notebook. "Abdomen for breakfast and lunch, thigh for supper, right?"

Annalise double-checked her notes. "Yes. And today is left side, tomorrow is right side."

Sophie's face clouded up as tears formed in the corners of her eyes. She looked so small and delicate.

Niko felt so powerless. Injections and a strict regimen were Sophie's fate for the rest of her life.

He picked her up to sit her on the examining table, giving her a big hug midway. "Sweetie, I would take this for you if I could, but I can't."

"If I don't eat, I don't have to have a shot, right?"

"Not an option, little one."

He took the vials from Annalise and filled the syringe to the proper marking.

"Hold your finger out like a candle, sweetie." He held up his own finger, showing her.

"I'm going to hold your leg still." He put his hand on her thigh. "When I say, 'Now,' pretend you're blowing out the candle. Be sure to blow hard."

She gave him a confused look.

"Trust me." He focused on the injection site. "Now."

While Sophie blew, Niko took advantage of her distraction and injected the insulin.

"Good girl. All over." He jotted down the particulars

in Sophie's notebook, taking a moment to appreciate the details his brothers and sisters-in-law were trying so carefully to document.

"You want to dig through the treasure chest, Sophie, and pick out a toy?"

"Okay." Sophie shrugged, not looking very excited. After all these months of doctors' visits she'd probably been rewarded with too many cheap toys in the past to make this one special.

Annalise helped Sophie down from the table then opened a huge plastic tub filled with monster trucks and snorkels and magic wands.

"I think there's a superhero cape in there somewhere. A real one."

Sophie began flinging plastic trucks and coloring books out of the box, digging for the cape. "Really?"

"Absolutely. I save the good stuff for the most courageous girls and boys."

Niko gave Dr. Annalise Walcott a long look. She was a smart one, reinforcing Niko's challenge to be brave with an enticing reward. Small things made big impressions with little patients. While he had the minimum of pediatrics training, he'd treated enough frightened children to pick up a thing or two. Apparently, Annalise had treated her own fair share of children, too.

"Found it!" Sophie triumphantly held up a bright pink cape along with the sparkling wand attached to it.

Niko quickly yanked off and crumpled up the tag that declared it a fairy costume instead of a superheroine disguise.

As she pointed the wand at him, he obligingly shrank back with as much mock terror on his face as he could muster. "SuperSophie. If I were a nasty villain, I would be quaking in my shoes right now."

"Let me tie it on for you," Annalise offered.

The pleased smile she gave Sophie made Niko think the good doctor really had picked out the cape herself. With her long legs she'd make the perfect bustiered and masked crusader.

Niko rubbed his hand over his eyes, clearing the vision. What was it about this demure doctor that had his imagination running wild? Had he been under so much pressure that he needed to resort to a fantasy life for relief? If so, what did that say for his stamina in the field?

Lack of resilience or desire to make a difference wasn't what sidelined most of the special mission doctors. Coping with the mental stress, knowing they were only making a small dent in the needs of so many was what broke most of them.

Then again, maybe Annalise brought out the creative imagination in him. Nothing wrong with that, was there? This was a fantasy cruise after all.

"You're really good with her, Dr. Christopoulos. I'm impressed." When she smiled, her gaze was honest, her voice sincere. It felt better than good to be appreciated.

"It's Niko." His own voice was huskier than normal.

"Niko." She licked her full lips.

Fascinating and, oh, so sexy with no contrivance or even an awareness of what her mouth could do to a man.

Niko reined himself in. It had been a while. Where he'd been wasn't exactly an environment conducive to lovemaking.

How did he ask the good doctor if she would like to share a drink with him under the stars tonight? How could he make himself stand out in a crowd when he bet every man on board this ship would like to do the same?

I don't do dinner, she'd said.

She'd been offputting on the gangway, but Niko could

understand why. She probably had to field invitations and propositions all day, every day from total strangers.

What made him different from them? And why did it matter so much that he was? There were plenty of women aboard this ship looking for a diversion. But he had no interest in pursuing them. Only her.

What made her different?

He didn't know, but he wanted to find out.

He searched for the right pick-up line but came up blank. What was the matter with him? He'd had no trouble knowing what to say to charm the opposite sex since he'd turned twelve.

"What? Do I have something on my face?" Annalise wiped away a non-existent blemish.

"How about sharing a bottle of wine tonight?" Nothing glib or witty or clever there. Just a straightforward request. "I thought, as colleagues, we could discuss medicine aboard ship. Strictly professional curiosity."

She was shaking her head before she even started to turn him down. "I don't really think…"

That's when he heard them coming. No one could ever say a Christopoulos didn't give you fair warning before arriving. From the sound of it, the whole family was in the medical suite's anteroom.

Annalise looked alarmed.

"Not to worry. It's not a mass emergency. Just an invasion of family."

Family. Wasn't that what he'd wanted when he'd planned this elaborate ruse, to spend time with family? Why was he even trying to strike up a shipboard romance with a woman who obviously had no interest in him?

He had to admit, paying attention to a beautiful woman sounded a lot more enticing than paying attention to his brothers as they droned on about the restaurant or to the

sisters-in-law as they expounded on the joys and tribula-
tions of parenthood.

As he and Sophie joined them he realized, as he had so
many times in the past, that he was a square peg in a family of round holes. Now he understood that no amount of
buying anonymous vacations was going to change that.

Seeing his sisters-in-law with children in tow, he also
understood that no number of casual relationships would
fill that hole of not having someone special to belong to,
like his brothers did.

Choices. Live every man's dream or live his own personal dream.

He would never again become involved with a woman
who made him feel the pain of having to choose.

Annalise.

The good doctor was safe, right?

At a glance, Annalise recognized the people in her waiting room as family. They looked—and sounded—exactly
alike.

Still, while the family resemblance was strong, Niko
stood apart.

One of the lanky teenaged boys jostled another, who
looked like an identical twin. "Of course we'd find Uncle
Niko down here, playing doctor with the nurse."

"I'd expect you to be out by the pool, Uncle Niko, checking out the bikini babes. When we walked by, there was
this one…" He raised his hands like he was holding coco-
nuts, or maybe watermelons.

Niko cut them both a harsh look. "Respect," he growled.

At the same time as one of the women gave the twins
a sharp look and said, "Boys, behave."

Amidst the chaos of the two women and smaller children throwing themselves into Niko's arms and the two men patting him on the back, Niko made introductions.

"Dr. Walcott, these are my brothers and their wives, with assorted nieces and nephews and my grandmother in the back. Family, meet Dr. Walcott. She will be helping us while we're here."

A tiny older woman, small in stature but big in presence, waded through three waist-high children and elbowed her way past the two tall boys to the front of the crowd. "I am Olympia Christopoulos. Everyone calls me Yiayia. We were all greatly relieved to learn the ship has its own doctor to help us with our little Sophie."

Surprising Annalise, Yiayia wrapped her in a big hug. Annalise flailed her arms, unsure what to do, who to be. Should she pretend to be the type of person who was comfortable with this type of thing? Should she hug back? Finally, the hug was over and Annalise could be herself again.

Too late, she wished she'd wrapped her arms around the old woman, just to see what having a grandmother might feel like.

The woman who belonged to the twin boys turned to Niko and patted her huge Hawaiian print tote bag. "I have the meter. I see you have the notebook. It's time for Sophie's s-h-o-t."

From the stricken look on Sophie's face she clearly knew what word the woman had just spelled out.

Niko gave Sophie a reassuring pat. "Already taken care of, Phoebe."

"You wrote it all down in the notebook, right? The time and the amount and her blood-sugar reading?" She turned to Annalise. "You know how men are. They don't always think of these things."

Who were these people? They acted as if they didn't

even acknowledge that Niko was a doctor in his own right. Or was that a good-natured tease? Maybe this was just a normal give and take of a normal family. Group dynamics wasn't her strong suit.

"Don't worry, sis. I learned how to chart in medical school." Despite Niko's self-deprecating smile, his tone held a hint of bite and his jaw held more than a hint of firmness.

His sister-in-law must have seen the same sparks in Niko's eyes that Annalise saw because she tried to excuse herself by saying, "Of course you did, Niko. It's just that you don't usually have children as patients and you have that big staff to do things for you."

Annalise envisioned a spa-like office suite with customized furniture arranged by a top designer, staff in matching trendy uniforms and coffee and tea with French names available to sip as the clientele discussed lifting brows, firming chins and reshaping cheekbones.

Her own utilitarian facilities would be stark in comparison. Still, her suite and her staff were top of the line, assembled to handle any emergency.

One of the men, older than Niko but definitely related, stepped forward. "Time to eat. Let's see how cruise-ship food stacks up to Christopoulos food."

A twin clapped Niko on the shoulder. "It'll be nice to be served instead of being the server for a change, too. But, then, you never had to do the waiter thing, did you, Uncle Niko?"

The tiny ancient woman reached up and tweaked the boy's ear. "If your grades were as good as Niko's, you wouldn't either."

Phoebe turned to Annalise. "Niko tutored during high school instead of working in the restaurant."

Annalise processed information, trying to fill in the

holes while simultaneously wondering why this family would reveal so much to a total stranger.

"Good thing Niko's so smart since he can't cook worth a flip," the other brother added. "Now, let's go and eat."

En masse, they turned and exited, carrying Sophie along with them but leaving Niko behind.

He raised an eyebrow. "Family. Gotta love 'em, right?"

No. No, you didn't. Annalise knew that first hand. But that was knowledge she had no intention of sharing. Sharing meant intimacy and intimacy was something Annalise didn't do, especially with a man who made her breath skip when he stood this close.

She fell back on her professionalism. "Enjoy your dinner. Bring Sophie back any time you need to."

"Thanks."

Annalise stood by the glass door and watched him walk away.

It wasn't that she didn't like to look at men—she just liked to look from a distance. Now she allowed herself to admire the breadth of his shoulders and tautness of his butt even while her medical training had her noticing the slight hesitation of his left leg as he climbed the short flight of stairs leading to the main hallway. He'd said something about an injury when he boarded the elevator with her, hadn't he?

Not her concern unless he sought out medical attention. She had to remind herself of that daily when she wanted to fix the world.

When her office was empty once again, it felt as if all the energy had been sucked out with the Christopoulos family.

No, not energy. They had taken joyous chaos with them when they'd left. The energy had gone with Niko, along with the impression of stability he projected of keeping that wild bunch under control.

Usually her haven, the atmosphere of the medical suite felt as cold as the stainless steel of the countertops and she felt restless, on the verge—but on the verge of what?

Underneath her feet the rumble of the huge engines reverberated as they churned through the waters of the Gulf of Mexico on their way towards the open water of the Atlantic.

She was being silly. The feel of freedom was all around her. Why, then, was she missing the anchoring sensation Niko had taken with him?

CHAPTER THREE

NIKO SAT AT the dining table surrounded by family, knowing he'd turned down his best chance of a family of his own.

His ex-fiancée hadn't asked him for anything extraordinary—only to give up his work, to give up his soul.

She hadn't understood. He hadn't been able to make her understand what Doctors Without Borders meant to him. That he'd never felt more alive as he beat the odds, winning out over a harsh world unlike any his family had ever seen and snatching the downtrodden back from the edge of death. What were the odds he could make his family understand anyway?

Misunderstood. Different. The story of his life. Was there anyone on the planet who could understand?

In walked Annalise Walcott. She'd shed her lab coat, exposing the silk blouse over her trousers. Classy.

She was the total package, wasn't she? Brains and beauty. Such a winning combination.

While he'd appreciated the shorts earlier on the gangway, now he appreciated the way her silky blouse moved across her...

"Uncle Niko, what are you staring at?" His nephew Marcus interrupted as the teen followed Niko's line of sight.

"Just taking in the scenery."

"You mean that brunette at that corner table? She looks like your type."

Niko checked out the voluptuous dark-haired woman sitting alone. Big hair, big earrings, big bone structure, everything he usually liked in a woman. He even liked her interesting nose, more aquiline than fashionable, but it suited her. "She's okay, I guess."

Beside him, Yiayia was taking a keen interest in the conversation while trying to appear as if she wasn't.

"You're not talking about Dr. Walcott, are you?" Marcus asked.

"Absolutely."

His nephew gave him a quizzical look. "She's not Greek."

"It's not like I'm going to marry her."

Marcus laughed. "Everyone knows you're not the marrying kind, Uncle Niko. We all live through you vicariously, even Dad." Marcus elbowed his father next to him to get his attention.

Niko's brother Stephen gave him a somber frown. "You've got to settle down sometime, Niko. We all liked Melina. Maybe if you talked to her? Apologized for whatever you did. Or even if you didn't do anything—"

"My broken engagement is none of your business, brother."

Stephen narrowed his eyes, but backed down and looked away when Niko continued to glare, using refilling his wife's wine glass as his excuse to turn away.

The eight years that separated them in age also separated them in values. Or maybe they were just too different. His brothers were so much like the father he could barely remember, while he was his own person.

If only he didn't have to keep reminding them of that.

Marcus spoke barely loud enough to hear. "It's true, isn't it, Uncle Niko? The Christopoulos men are destined to be family men, aren't they?"

"You've been listening to Yiayia too much." Niko could see a lifetime of family tradition shackling his nephew, just as it tried to shackle him.

"Every man has to find his own purpose. Family is a very good purpose—just not for everyone." Knowing what he was about to do was tantamount to anarchy, Niko leaned in and pinned his nephew with his stare. "Promise me, Marcus, that you'll take some time to think about what *you* want—not what anyone else expects from you."

Marcus swallowed hard. "Not everyone is as strong-willed as you are, Uncle Niko. I envy that about you. But someday…"

Niko thought of all the trips he took abroad with Doctors Without Borders, the trips his family thought he took for leisure. They thought he was gallivanting to tropical paradises, giving his wild side a long leash before settling down while his partners carried his load.

He encouraged them to think that. What would they think if they knew his partners admired and supported his perilous service work? And how would they feel about him if they knew family wasn't on his radar?

Not providing grandchildren was the second-biggest sin in the Christopoulos family Bible, right under "Don't live dangerously."

It was a rule he wasn't very good at following. Neither had his uncle or his grandfather. But, then, his parents had both been killed in a car wreck while on a trip to the store. Playing it safe didn't mean a person would *be* safe. And following the family rules didn't mean he would be happy like they were.

How did the good doctor juggle her family with her

medical practice? Working on a cruise ship, she was separated from her loved ones more often than not, wasn't she?

Because he was staring, and because she turned and caught him at it, he stood and walked toward her to invite her over.

She looked around, as if she were looking to see who he was approaching.

He brightened up his smile a few notches.

She gave him a nervous smile back, shook her head and started to turn away. And his ego took the well-aimed shot to heart. Of all the women in all the world, why did he have to find this one so fascinating?

Then fate worked in Niko's favor. The captain, coming up behind her, helpfully pointed out that a guest was requesting her presence.

"Good evening." As the ship rocked, the captain politely rested his hand on Annalise's back, effectively keeping her still and steady. "Are you in need of our doctor?"

Niko had the strongest urge to push away the captain's hand, replacing it with his own.

Need. Yes, he was in need of her. Just standing next to her made endorphins flood his brain. What was it about her? And what excuse could he use to keep her close to him?

"If you have a few seconds, Dr. Walcott, I could use the reinforcement when I explain once again to Sophie's grandmother why Sophie can't have late-night snacks."

The captain dropped his hand and Annalise took a breath and an automatic step back from Niko, trying to find her comfort zone. But nothing about this man could be described as comfortable. As soon as the captain was out of earshot, she called him on his excuse. "I've seen you with your family, remember? When you speak, they all look at you as if every word was gold. You don't need any help from me, Doctor."

"But I do." His tiger eyes glittered. "You might notice I'm the only unmarried brother left. My family would like to change that. You'll keep me safe from their matchmaking, at least for tonight."

Too aware that everyone at Niko's table intently watched them, Annalise hesitated.

"Please?"

Annalise had never been able to turn down a plea for help—at least, that's what she told herself as she said, "Okay. But don't make a habit of this."

As she wove in and out, past the other diners, she questioned herself but could come up with no reason why she hadn't made her usual polite escape whenever a man took notice of her.

Was it the sincerity in his voice? What about him made her feel ready to respond to the interest in a man's eyes?

All the Christopoulos men stood as Annalise approached their table. Their good manners made her feel self-conscious and very feminine.

With Sophie now cuddled in her Aunt Phoebe's lap, it left an open seat between him and Yiayia.

As Niko pulled out the chair for her, he leaned in and whispered, "You're blushing. Nice."

"I'm not used to such..." She held her hand out to the standing men, speechless.

"A show of good manners," Yiayia finished her sentence. "Take it as your due, dear. You deserve it."

What would it be like to be a part of a large family where she was loved and respected on a daily basis?

A warm glow deep inside vied with the chill of nerves prickling along her skin.

Conflicted. Was she doomed to always be conflicted?

"Wine, Doctor?" A server held the bottle of merlot for her inspection.

Normally, Annalise would say no. While she enjoyed an occasional glass of wine with a good book, she never drank in uncomfortable social situations. But she found herself saying yes instead.

"And you, sir?" the waiter asked Niko.

He started to shake his head, but his brother Stephen was nodding instead.

"Give the man another drink. He's a doctor, you know? Under stress all the time. Look at that strain around his eyes. You need to cut loose every now and then, Niko, or you'll be looking as old as me before your time." Stephen held his glass out. "And pour me another one, too, will you?"

Niko knew his brother's remark was a dig at his supposed frivolous lifestyle, which Stephen was both jealous of and proud he'd played a part in providing. Niko should have never let the misunderstanding lie between them for so long.

But so much had been happening when he'd left for his first mission. The restaurant fire, the miscarriage that had threatened his sister-in-law's life and Sophie's diagnosis had rocked the foundations of his very strong family.

Leaving his family at their time of need had been the hardest decision he'd ever had to make.

He wasn't good at raw emotion. Just being there for his loved ones had made him feel trapped and helpless—made him remember too much.

He'd had to take action. Do something. Fix something. There had been nothing he could do for his family to make them any better.

But he'd had the medical dossiers of a half-dozen children in his briefcase—children who could die without his medical care. He'd decided he would only be in the way if he stayed around.

He'd reasoned that there was no sense in adding to everyone's worries if Doctors Without Borders wasn't for him. Now that he'd made his decision, he wouldn't put a damper on this trip, but he would tell them at the end that working for Doctors Without Borders would be permanent.

He had already made arrangements to begin the sale of his share of the partnership as soon as he returned home. But for now he would keep pretending, for their sakes.

"Everything okay?" Annalise's hand fluttered over his arm, as if she wanted to touch him but felt he was off limits.

Niko pasted on his brightest smile. "I'm sharing a glass of wine with a brilliant, beautiful woman. What could be better? Except maybe a bit of privacy."

While he didn't know her well, he read her eyes with ease. Concern turned to disappointment. It seemed that's all he did lately, disappoint the women in his life.

But, then, Annalise wasn't in his life, was she? She was a simple, uncomplicated diversion. In three weeks, walking out of her life would be as easy as walking off this ship.

He'd meant to be flippant, but he tempered it with truth. "I've got a lot going on in my head right now. I guess I haven't quite made the transition to vacation mode yet."

As the waiter made the rounds, Niko held out his glass after all. "To vacations."

The rest of the family held their glasses aloft and echoed his toast before drinking.

When the server would have moved away, Yiayia stopped him, holding out her glass for a refill.

"Just leave the bottle. We'll serve ourselves." Phoebe grinned at the young waiter. "We've had practice."

As Phoebe topped up the adults' glasses, Marcus did the same with the tea and juice pitchers for the children.

"A toast. To my grandson the doctor." Everyone held their glasses high then drank. Even the children downed their glasses in style. Bewildered at first, Annalise looked around and followed suit. Niko had to smile at her quick assimilation into his crazy family. If he were looking for a woman...

But who said anything about finders keepers?

He gave her a wink before saluting the table with his glass. "To my family, who put me through college and medical school."

Annalise raised her eyebrows then drank with him as the rest of the family looked at each other, well satisfied with their sacrifice. His decision would be so much easier if they weren't so proud of him.

"And to my brother and sister-in-law who could not be with us today." Stephen, as second oldest, did the honors to acknowledge them.

As soon as Niko took the obligatory swallow, he leaned over and explained to Annalise, "Family tradition. We'll finish off the bottle this way."

As the young nephews and nieces started to droop, climbing into any available adult lap for a good cuddle, Yiayia began her bragging. "Dr. Walcott, did you know that my grandson has been on national television, on a talk show? Did you know that he operates on all the famous actors and actresses? But he won't tell us who they are. Confidentiality issues. It's all very mysterious. They bring them up through the hospital's loading dock."

"Remember that time you made your cucumber yogurt for that actress when Uncle Niko wired her jaw shut?" Phoebe turned to Annalise. "He still won't tell us her name, even though we've begged. He's very discreet is our Niko."

Under cover of their chatter, Niko said to Annalise, "You're very quiet. Don't wait for a turn to talk. Just jump in anywhere."

"I'd rather listen." She gave him a smug smile. "I'm learning a lot about you this way."

Niko was one part chagrined over his family's bragging and the other part overjoyed that Annalise wanted to know more about him.

"Then it's only fair I get to hear your life story, too."

When Annalise looked around the full table tensely, he quickly reassured her, "When we have time to ourselves. I'll want all your intimate details."

Visibly, Annalise shivered. While Niko would usually regard her reaction as a positive response in anticipation of time together, the way she held herself so tightly told him he'd overstepped the mark.

To break the tension, he refilled her glass even though she'd only been taking the tiniest of sips.

She took the glass, looking into it as if searching for answers. "I'm not much on pillow talk." Her voice was husky, hesitant and, oh, so sexy.

She was so much more intense than the women he usually dated, like the Greek goddess in the corner, laughing loudly and holding court with the ship's captain. Annalise wasn't his usual type at all. Whatever type she was, she'd captured his interest and he couldn't seem to let go.

He would need to go slowly with her, pace himself. It was a novel concept when he usually got what he wanted when he wanted. His brothers would find this strain on his ego amusing. He himself found it challenging.

Marcus leaned over his mother to tell Annalise, "Some big charity wants to auction off a date with Uncle Niko. He did it last year and cameras followed him around all night, even when he kissed her."

Phoebe pushed her son back into place without jiggling the sleeping young nephew on her lap. "It would be good if you could bring your date back to the restaurant this year, Niko. We got a lot of publicity from that and we could certainly use it again."

He would have to tell them. No more celebrity stories. No more TV appearances. No more magazine layouts for the hottest catch in the Crescent City.

"Niko? Are you okay?" Stephen's concern brought him out of his thoughts.

He blinked, back in the game. "Fine. Just tired."

Yiayia was telling the good doctor about her own excitement in front of the media crew—a crew Niko had bought and paid for.

"And then this pretty little blonde girl handed me a huge check, just like on the television, and this man with a video camera asked how I felt." Yiayia told her sweepstakes story to Annalise. "I thought I would have a heart attack right then and there. And, of course, no doctor around."

She patted Niko on the shoulder. "My grandson is never home. Itchy feet, just like my late husband Leo. The places we would go when we were young… We travelled around the world before Leo brought me to America and that's the place that felt like home. Travelling is a good thing to do when you're young." She looked around the luxurious dining room of the cruise ship and smiled. "And good to do when you get old, too,"

That smile made all the planning, all the money and all the subterfuge worth it.

As his brother reached past him for the bread basket, doubt jabbed Niko. If he stayed with his practice, he could give his family many more trips like this one. His brothers could expand the restaurant, hire more employees, spend more time with their children.

Although he tried to stop himself, he couldn't help glancing Annalise's way. What would she think of him giving up all his family had worked so hard for on his behalf? Would she judge him to be as ungrateful as he judged himself?

But, then, this was a woman who called a berth on a ship home. Obviously, she was following her dream.

He couldn't help hoping she'd understand.

After escaping from the enthusiastic Christopoulos family, and one dynamic Christopoulos male in particular, Annalise took some time to recover.

Although she wasn't sure there was enough time in the universe for her to recover from the emotions Niko Christopoulos set off inside her.

Right now, all she could say was that she liked being treated with such respect. He had been attuned to every word, every movement she made. The experience had been nerve-racking but very flattering, too.

But, then, from what she gathered from his family, all women thought the same about him. Smooth talking was not an asset in her book.

It was a lot to think about. She was sure she wouldn't be able to sleep tonight.

With the sun still up this close to the equator, the evening was still warm so she slipped on her shorts and T-shirt from earlier in the day and took a good long stroll around the deck's track, thinking of the love packed into those sincere family toasts. Afterwards, she ducked into one of the onboard kiosks to make herself a cup of hot decaf tea with the hope of swallowing down her envy for a life she could never be a part of.

Now Annalise breathed in the sea air as she took the stairs up to the adults-only top foredeck, carefully carrying her hot cup of tea to keep from spilling in the roughening seas. Although the wind was picking up, the temperature was still balmy.

Pinks and yellows colored the blue sky as the sun neared the horizon. At this time of year it would hang there for a good forty or so minutes before it plunged into the ocean. Watching the sunset was her favorite way to unwind and the tiny top foredeck was the perfect place to do it.

Most passengers found this little deck too tame. There was no pool, no wet T-shirt contests, no band and no elevator access. The three flights of stairs put off most people even if the lack of entertainment didn't.

So she was surprised to see someone sprawled out in her favorite deck chair as she rounded the platform at the top of the stairs.

And not just anyone. Niko.

She recognized him immediately, despite the dark sunglasses covering his eyes. His shirt was off as he reclined with his long legs crossed at the ankles, socks and loafers tucked underneath the deck chair.

That chest. Those pecs. If she didn't know better, she would think he'd been airbrushed. Dr. Christopoulos obviously didn't spend all his time in the operating room, lifting eyebrows and tightening chins. He had to spend a great deal of time at the gym as well.

This was not what she needed tonight. She turned to leave, then stopped herself.

No man was ever going to keep her from going where she wanted to go.

What was it about Niko Christopoulos that stirred up so much confusion inside her head?

When she could tear her focus away from his physique, she noticed his face. While his body looked peaceful in repose, his clenched jaw and compressed lips told a different story.

He looked like a man in internal pain.

Suddenly he half sat up, contracting those magnificent abs, and looked over the top of his sunglasses, straight at her. His features calmed, as if he pulled a mask over his emotions.

Had she made a noise? She didn't think so but she must have.

"Want to join me?" he asked.

As he made to stand up, she swallowed down all but the simplest of emotions and quickly said, "Please, keep your seat." The old-world manners made her feel special, even though she knew she wasn't. She pointed to the stairs behind her. "How's the leg?"

He shrugged. "The climb is worth it for the view."

The way he studied her over his sunglasses, she could almost imagine he was referring to her.

She could say no and probably would have if he had come on strong. There were plenty of empty deck chairs. She could say she just needed a few minutes of alone time. He would understand. Wasn't that what he was doing as well?

But he had invited her and she found herself moving in his direction before she could decline.

She picked out the deck chair next to his and placed her tea next to the water bottle on the table between them. "Catching some rays?"

By the deepness of his tan, she knew it wouldn't be the first time. She couldn't imagine him in a tanning booth. Too artificial.

Hold on there, Annalise, she told herself. *This is a man who does artificial for a living.* Why was she assigning him qualities when she knew nothing about him?

He propped his chair up a few notches and reset his sunglasses on the top of his head.

The intensity in those tiger eyes of his mesmerized her so that she couldn't look away.

His voice was low, like a rumbling purr. "It's the wind. There's something about that unharnessed power, that cleansing force that attracts me." He rubbed his chin. "That sounded strange, didn't it?"

"Poetic." She held up her book, William Cullen Bryant. "I like poetry."

"Me, too." He gave her a grin and a wink.

He was flirting—with her!

There was a whole ship of beautiful women and he was coming on to her. But, then, there was no other woman around, which made her convenient, right?

She raised an eyebrow. "Really?"

Her reply was supposed to be a warning that she knew his game and wasn't playing. Instead, it came out as a tease, as if she was taking up his challenge.

"Yup. Used to write it, too, under the guise of song lyrics."

"So you're a doctor and a musician? What's next? You're going to tell me you were a rock star in a boy band?"

"Only on my own block." He reset his sunglasses over his eyes. "Some friends and I had a garage band all through junior high and high school."

"Lead guitar?"

"Sometimes. Mostly drums. Some bass guitar. We switched around a lot."

"Did you sing?"

"Sometimes."

"I bet you had a motorcycle, too, didn't you?"

"An old Harley. I rebuilt it myself. And a black leather jacket—a hand-me-down from one of my brothers. I was really into the vintage rebel look." His self-deprecating laugh revealed two deep dimples.

"I'll just bet you were." With his dark looks she knew he'd pulled off the attitude perfectly. Surreptitiously, she glanced at his bare chest. He still did.

She winked at him. "From teenage heart throb to successful surgeon. Charmed life?"

She expected a flippant response. Instead, he thought about it for a moment then nodded slowly. "I've got a lot to be thankful for."

She wished she could see behind the shades. The moment hung in time, making an uneasiness spread through her. She shifted away.

While he didn't move a muscle, she felt him pulling back, too. Or was she only imagining it? What did she know of this man, except he was a compassionate doctor with the soul of a poet who, by the looks of things, managed his money well?

As she took a calming sip of tea, determined to treat this evening no differently than any other, he broke her concentration.

"Thanks for coming to my rescue this evening. They mean well, but they also think they know what's best for me."

"They're like those made-for-TV families. Are they always so nice? So genuine?"

"Nice? My family has good company manners. Genuine? Absolutely, even when it hurts. But I can call anyone, anytime, my sisters-in-law as well as my brothers, and they would drop everything to be there for me."

"And you'd do the same for them?"

He rubbed his hand over his face but failed to disguise the tightening around his eyes and mouth. "I always have in the past."

"But not in the future?" Annalise immediately regretted her impulsive question. "I'm sorry. None of my business."

"It's not you. It's me." With a forced grin he shrugged away her apology as he spouted the classic meaningless cliché. "How about you? Judging by how quiet you were at dinner, I'm betting your family is a lot calmer than mine."

"No family. Just me." Her recent visit to her mother made her all too conscious of those bound together because of shared DNA. It wasn't a bond she willingly claimed.

"Here it comes." She pointed at the sun, resting on the horizon.

As if the big ball of flame had become too heavy to hold itself up, it plunged into the sea, taking with it all but a flat line of pinks and yellows and oranges to keep the sky separated from the water. Above that slim line of fading color, the night was dark and starry with nary a moonbeam in sight.

Around them, the deck's automatic twinkle lights began to glow.

Under the vastness of the night Annalise felt at peace with the world. She knew the feeling would be fleeting, with the responsibilities and decisions life would bring her, but she would enjoy that feeling while it lasted.

Next to her, Niko drew in a deep breath, held it then let it out again.

Having him near made her feel less alone than she'd felt in a very long time.

That surprised her. She had expected to feel like he was intruding on her special time. Instead, he made it even more special.

The serene minutes ticked away, giving her a false sense of permanence. When the squeaking and creaking of the pool boy's cart broke the silence, she wasn't surprised. Only sad that the moment was gone.

That's when she noticed the chill of the night air as it rushed over her bare legs. Reality. She'd been lucky to escape it for a few moments. To expect that kind of tranquility to last was unreasonable, wasn't it?

Reluctantly, Niko said a silent goodbye to the moment out of time he'd shared with Annalise.

He sat up and put on his shirt, socks and shoes. Normally, he would ask her to join him for a drink, trying to draw out the situation. But doing so tonight would only place expectations on a moment so rare it couldn't be coerced into lasting.

The good doctor lay with her head back and her eyes closed. The pose should be peaceful. Instead, he saw the tension that made the corners of her eyelids twitch and her involuntary jerk when the pool boy let the lid of his towel hamper slam shut.

He glanced at his watch. While he was certain his sister-in-law was taking care of Sophie as carefully as she took care of her own three children, he would check in on her.

Then maybe he would… He wasn't sure what he would do next. When was the last time he hadn't had a list of things in his head that he needed to do, all marked urgent?

As he climbed down the stairs, ignoring the burning in his thigh, he looked out at the dark, flat vastness of the sea. Three weeks.

Three long weeks with nowhere to be and nothing to do.

Why did he think of Annalise when he thought of how he would fill his time?

CHAPTER FOUR

DREAMS, WONDERFULLY WILDLY erotic dreams had made Annalise twist and turn all night. She knew they were normal, even healthy. While these were not her first, they had never been this vivid before.

Her lover had been faceless, nameless and frustrating since she awoke before he could take her where she wanted to go. If pressed, she was fairly certain she could name the source of those disturbing dreams. As disconcerting as they were, she was thrilled to be having them.

Annalise had put in many hours of therapy and self-assessment making sure she didn't stay a victim.

Those hours had not been in vain. She could fully appreciate sexual magnetism evoked by the sight of a good-looking male. A male like Niko Christopoulos, who was looking mighty fine this morning in his red baggy board shorts, tight sleeveless T-shirt and tennis shoes as he sat on a bench outside the medical suite, waiting for office hours to begin.

Irrationally, she wished she'd spent a little more time picking out her own clothing, which was silly. Her monochrome gray blouse and trousers were perfectly professional and practical, if not the cutting edge of fashion. But now they felt a little mousy.

Niko stared out at the ocean, lost in thought.

She cleared her throat to alert him she was there.

He blinked as he focused on her. "I didn't hear you come up."

"Is Sophie all right?"

"She's fine. Her blood sugar was low this morning when she woke up, but not too low. She barely protested when I checked it and gave her the breakfast insulin shot."

Last night's restless dreaming made her feel edgy when she asked, "Then why are you here?"

She winced when she heard herself. "Sorry. Restless night. Can I start again?"

Her problem was she knew how to rebuff male attention, but she didn't know what to do to encourage it. But maybe that was for the better. There were those ship's rules about fraternization to consider.

Still, a part of her, the wanton part left over from last night no doubt, wondered what would be so wrong with a bit of flirtation. Just to satisfy her curiosity. With an experienced man like Niko it would be all in fun, right?

"No apology necessary. I know all about restless nights."

Much more civilly, she asked, "Do you have a medical problem?"

He rubbed his hand through his dark hair, spiking it out of order. "Actually, yes." He looked sheepish. "I've got something I need you to look at."

"Okay." She glanced at her watch. Her staff wouldn't be in for another half-hour. She usually preferred to have another staff member present when treating male patients. But it shouldn't matter in this case since they were both professionals. "Come on in."

As she unlocked the glass doors to the anteroom, Niko pointed to an envelope that had been slipped under the door. "A woman wearing a bartender's uniform, the one I met when I boarded, dropped that off for you."

"Thanks." Annalise pocketed the note. Concerned curiosity burned a hole in her pocket.

Once inside, Niko hitched himself up on the examination table and rolled up the right leg of his board shorts. A half-healed angry red cut at least five inches long sliced the side of his thigh. The stitches strained against the inflammation.

"What happened?"

He swallowed, then said, "A knife."

She narrowed her eyes. "I did my internship in the emergency departments of New Orleans's charity hospital system. I know a wickedly deliberate cut when I see it. This isn't from a steak knife or the slip of a pocket knife."

"I was caught in the middle of a knife fight over a water well in Haiti. So the infection could be tropical or it could be bacteria-related or—"

She put a thermometer in his mouth, making herself look away so she wouldn't stare at his firm, full lips or the rugged beard stubble on his cheeks. She didn't need any more stimulus to make her feel things—risky things—just because those tiger eyes were so mesmerizing.

And she didn't need to satisfy her curiosity by asking for details of his knife fight. The less she knew about him, the more easily she could convince herself they were just like two ships passing in the night.

When the thermometer beeped, he took it out himself, saving her from feeling his breath on her fingers.

"Ninety-nine and a half," he read.

"What have you been doing for your wound?"

"Topical ointment."

"That's all?"

He shrugged. "Antibiotics are in short supply there.

I'm healthy, unlike the people I treat. I figured I could fight it off."

With that clue, Annalise couldn't stop herself from trying to put the pieces together. "You were treating patients when this happened?"

"I do a lot of medical relief work in developing countries." He looked down and away, as if he wasn't quite okay with himself for his charity work.

Annalise thought of the free clinics she visited and the donated supplies she delivered when assigned to various routes. She had been thinking hard about her volunteer service recently. "Any particular organization?"

"Doctors Without Borders."

"They really get into the trenches." She took a cotton swab from a sealed package. "I'm going to take a culture, but I don't want to wait for results so I'm going to give you a broad-spectrum oral antibiotic, too. Tomorrow, when I know what we're looking at, I can refine your treatment. Are you allergic to any medication?"

"Sulpha drugs."

"That limits us. How about penicillin-based drugs?"

"I'm good with those."

"I'll be right back." As Annalise left the exam room for the pharmacy closet, she took a deep breath. Success, brains, looks and heart. Being around so much perfection made her feel... She wasn't sure how she felt.

When she came back, he had rolled down the leg of his shorts and was standing in the open exam-room doorway. She handed him the bottle of antibiotic pills.

His fingers brushing against hers almost made her drop it.

"Two now, one each night and morning. Stay out of the water until we know what this is. Come back tomorrow afternoon for the test results."

"Thanks." He cast her a sideways look, half shy and half pleading. "By the way, my family doesn't know about the Doctors Without Borders gig. Please don't tell them."

"I'm very good at patient confidentiality. In fact, I swore an oath. They won't learn about it from me." Annalise stuck her hands in her pockets, feeling Brandy's note.

"I didn't mean any insult. It's just that…" He stopped and held the pills up between them. "Thanks again."

Secrets. Why on earth would he want something that noble to remain a secret from his family? It wasn't her business, though, was it?

Still, it bothered her. Secrets made her think of lies. Was he lying to her?

Annalise hated secrets more than anything else on earth. How many times had her mother whispered "Don't tell…" as she was juggling men in her life? Then there had been the man who'd whispered "Don't tell" as he'd crept into her bedroom when her mother hadn't been home.

Annalise pulled out the note and read it.

"Doc, I need an appointment, but I'm working during your office hours and I don't want my shift manager to know. Could I come in after hours? Drop by the bar and let me know, okay? Brandy."

Annalise sighed. No doubt her tattoo had become infected.

The bell tinkled, signaling patients in the lobby. She quickly filled out a chart for Niko—Dr. Christopoulos—as she readied herself for the next patient.

As Caribbean music played softly from the overhead speakers, Annalise reminded herself that her life was totally what she'd made it and so far she hadn't done half-bad. Just keep it simple, she reminded herself.

And simple didn't include Niko Christopoulos.

* * *

Simple obsession. That's the only reason that could explain why, on a ship carrying several thousand people, Niko caught her attention as she took her afternoon break on deck.

She'd thought about him all day. His playboy image. His love for his family. His compassion with Sophie. His work with Doctors Without Borders. There was nothing simple about Niko and no simple explanation for why her feet were now carrying her straight towards him.

On the first full afternoon afloat, the ship was alive with activity and the Christopoulos family was doing its fair share to add to the frivolity.

Niko stood contemplating the rock wall. His older nephews had their harnesses strapped on and were waiting. Niko was not one to turn down a challenge.

He felt her before he heard her. Even though they barely knew each other, he knew the warmth by his side was uniquely Annalise.

"It's going to be difficult to keep that wound a secret if you break open the stitches halfway up," she murmured, for his ears only.

"The voice of reason. Where have you been all my life?" He waved is nephews on. "I've found something better to do," he called to them.

Marcus looked pointedly at Annalise then jostled his brother and grinned.

Annalise arched an eyebrow. "Are you being presumptuous by meaning me?"

"Let's not call it presumptuous. Let's call it hopeful." He gave her his best puppy-dog eyes. "Want to watch for dolphins off the starboard bow with me?"

When she hesitated, he appealed to her medical side.

"You'll be keeping me from doing something stupidly injurious to my health."

"Are you sure it's not too late? I think you've already fallen on your head one time too many since you've chosen me to flirt with."

"Flirt?" He grabbed at his chest. "You've wounded me. I would never toy with your affections." Yet wasn't that exactly what he was doing?

No. No, it wasn't.

Annalise lived on a cruise ship. No permanence there. She would know the score. There was no serious romance involved, just a casual attraction that would end at their final destination.

"Of course you're not flirting with me. Why would you when there are plenty of toys in this floating toy box?" Although she smiled when she said it, Niko thought he saw a bleakness cross her eyes or maybe it was only a cloud crossing the sun.

Before he could decide, she blinked and the fleeting look was gone.

"Ready? The dolphins won't wait." She led the way, weaving in and out of the passengers on deck.

"Thank you for rescuing me from myself. When the twins dared me, I didn't have it in me not to race them up. If you hadn't come along when you did, I would be halfway up the rock wall by now and my thigh wound wouldn't have appreciated my bravado."

"You have a hard time turning down a challenge?"

"Challenges are just another word for thrills for me. And you?"

She stopped at the railing and looked out on the sun-sparkled sea. "Challenges bring out the stubbornness in me."

"I've always thought stubbornness was a very good trait to have."

"Others would disagree." Very subtly, Annalise shifted away from him. Niko doubted she even realized she'd done it.

"Those *others* don't understand how much determination it takes to get through medical school."

"Determination. Scholarships. Student loans. Lots and lots of caffeine." She rubbed her arms. "And, occasionally, the kindness of the few others who do understand."

"Or who support you even when they don't understand." Niko thought of all the sandwiches his brothers had brought him as he'd studied past midnight. Of all the twenty-dollar bills his grandmother had slipped into his pockets after she'd laundered his clothes.

"Like your family?"

"Like my family." The family who wouldn't be at all happy with his new career path. "So where'd you go to medical school?"

"Tulane. I went there for both medical school and undergraduate pre-med."

Niko raise his eyebrows at the mention of the exclusive private college in uptown New Orleans's Audubon Park district. "Wow! I'm impressed.

"Did you grow up in New Orleans? The Crescent City has a thousand accents, but I think I hear a hint of a traditional New Orleans drawl, don't I?"

Her mouth tightened at the corners before she answered, "Yes, I did."

"What part?"

"It doesn't matter. Hurricane Katrina wiped it out." She shuddered, as if she was shaking off memories, before she forced out a smile. "Your turn. Where did you go to medical school?"

"The local state university."

"Ah, home of the Tigers. Did you play sports?"

"No." He grinned. "Even though that's their reputation, not everyone does—but I did drink a lot of beer. And you?"

"Beer or sports?" She smiled back, her face lighting up like sunbeams shone on it.

Niko soaked in her glow. "Either."

"Neither. I was on academic scholarship. No money for beer and no time for sports. I held a couple of part-time jobs, so that kept me busy when I wasn't studying. I was rather boring back then, I'm afraid."

"You, boring? Not possible. More like admirable to make it through Tulane's medical school while working, too." Niko once again realized how much his family had given him. "I worked at the restaurant on occasion and did a few odd jobs here and there, especially during the summers. But generally I had it pretty good."

"One of my jobs was as a dog washer for a local vet. I really liked working with the dogs. It wasn't a bad job—just messy and smelly."

"Did you ever think of switching to veterinary medicine?"

"Nope. I'm allergic to cats."

"Not many cats on a cruise ship."

"Not a single one on this ship."

"There's quite a bit of difference between working in an inner city E.R. and working on a cruise ship, I'd imagine."

Giving him a thoughtful look somewhere between sunshine and shadow, Annalise answered, "I like a bit of challenge, too. New places, new people, a diversity of problems to be solved. The E.R. took care of two out of three, but a cruise ship takes care of all three."

"Itchy feet. I understand all too well that the thrill of adventure gets your adrenaline rushing."

"As far as adrenaline rushes go, I can't say a cruise ship compares to being airlifted into a developing country, but we try." She grinned, showing off a dimple as she shaded her eyes and scanned the water for dolphins. How could she be so unaware of her beauty?

"That's what the brochure said."

"So what thrilling adventures have you had this morning?"

He had spent considerable time watching a very enjoyable wet T-shirt contest with the twins but he decided to tell her about the starfish demonstration he'd attended with his younger nieces and nephews instead.

"I had no idea starfish could regenerate body parts."

"Fascinating." She gave him a wry look. "Anything else?"

"Lunch with the family. Dining with them is always a major event, for us and for everyone around us. My brothers had to have a taste of every kind of bread in the basket to analyze taste and texture. The little ones spilled one glass of milk and one glass of orange juice in quick succession. And Sophie decided she wasn't hungry. Making her eat to balance out her morning insulin shot was a real challenge."

"How did you do it?"

"Yiayia gave her the evil eye. It always works." He'd had a long talk with Yiayia last night about Sophie's juvenile diabetes. While she didn't understand everything, she finally did understand the importance of working with Sophie's caregivers instead of against them.

"Your grandmother is very special to you, isn't she?"

"She raised me. I owe her and my brothers everything." He rubbed his hand across his eyes. He didn't like to talk about it. So why was he about to tell Annalise?

"My parents died when I was young. The three of us were in a car wreck." He left out the details about being stranded in the car with them for hours while the rescue workers had tried to save them all.

"It's why I hate goodbyes." As if compelled, he found himself confessing, "Before they died, they both told me they loved me. I didn't understand. I had the chance but didn't take it. I thought, if I didn't say goodbye to them, they would live."

"How old were you?"

"Eight." He stared out at the vast ocean all around. "My brothers were sixteen, fourteen and thirteen then. They buried their grief, trying to help me recover from mine. They had to grow up so fast for me. Along with Yiayia, they've been taking care of me ever since. They've never once complained about their lot in life."

"Your family finds strength in each other. I saw that last night at the dinner table."

He gave her a wry look. "And then there's me."

"You're different?"

He nodded confirmation. "I'm different."

"How?"

"I love my family but I often feel trapped, smothered. Uncomfortable in my own skin." He'd never said any of this out loud. Not even to himself in the dark of night. Why now? Why Annalise?

Was it because they were complete strangers and would never see each other after this trip ended?

He'd had so much on his mind and in his heart for so many years. Recently, since he'd started to consider selling his portion of the practice, the pressure had been building more and more until he thought he would come apart at the seams.

"They've sacrificed so much to give me a comfortable lifestyle they'd never even dream of having themselves."

And he had been determined to succeed for them. To

give back to them. To show his appreciation by being all they wanted him to be.

"They're very proud of you. Even when your brothers tease you, they do it with pride in their voices. And your grandmother told me at least a dozen times how you have big-time celebrities for clientele." Realization dawned. "You're afraid of disappointing them. How could you? You've become everything they sacrificed for. You've fulfilled their expectations. They get to be in the limelight through you, and I think they're perfectly happy that way."

"But that's not me." He struggled with being that man they imagined him to be. The one who strutted onto talk shows to talk about celebrity makeovers or who attended black-tie affairs with a model on his arm. The whole time he sipped champagne and waved away expensive hors d'oeuvres he thought of those who didn't have the basics of clean water to drink or food to eat.

"The sparkle in Yiayia's eyes when she brags about my photos on the society pages of the newspapers can't erase the bleakness in the eyes of the mothers whose children suffer from cleft palates. Doctors Without Borders. That's where I belong. No fanfare. No glory."

No family. That part was too painful to say aloud. Giving up the happiness his brothers had found in the arms of the women they loved had been a decision he'd willfully made but he still couldn't stop wishing he could have it all.

But his wandering ways didn't make for permanent relationships. A woman needed things. A house full of knick-knacks and baubles, a steady group of friends, children. Permanence. All the things he couldn't promise her.

"You've chosen a tough path."

He nodded. "But I need it. I'm never more alive than when I'm cheating death. I need the deeply satisfying buzz of seeing blank eyes start to sparkle, of seeing hope come alive in environments and conditions that make living from day to day a challenge."

His world was not one where he would voluntarily raise a family.

"I can see that in you. I hear the passion in your voice." Her own voice quavered, as if she was hesitant to offer that much up to him. "Why medicine? There are a lot of professions you could have chosen."

He shrugged. "Most of my memories of the wreck are fuzzy, just a lot of hazy pain, emotional more than physical, I think. I broke my jaw but I don't remember it hurting all that much right then. They sent a helicopter. There were flashing lights and rain and loud voices over the police cars' speaker systems.

"But through it all there was this doctor who crawled into the wreckage and held my hand while they cut my parents out. He promised me he wouldn't let go until I was free and he talked to me the whole time. He was calm and sure when my world was in total chaos. He was my hero. I wanted to be just like him."

Niko wiped at his eyes with the back of his hand. "I've never told anyone—no one's ever asked before."

The silence stretched awkwardly as he looked out at the ocean, feeling the loss of his parents, remembering the hours he'd waited alone for rescue. Knowing how he often felt alone even now, despite the love of his family throughout the years.

Annalise startled him when she covered his hand with her own. She didn't say anything. She didn't even look at him. She just stared out at the ocean, too. But with her hand on his, he didn't feel so alone.

A movement against the waves caught his attention.

"There they are." With his free hand, he pointed at the magnificent mammals playing in the waves.

Annalise shielded her eyes with her free hand. "Four of them."

Two small dolphins played among the larger ones. "A family."

"Their families are called pods. It's a matriarchal structure." Annalise smiled as one of the dolphins broke away from the group and started twisting itself above the waves.

"I'm very familiar with that structure." Niko watched the baby dolphin jump and spin. "There's always one that's got to be different."

She squeezed his hand. "That's not a bad thing."

When the dolphin had done a half dozen jumping twists, he swam back to his pod, where the other dolphins bumped noses in greeting.

The wind blew Annalise's hair into her face. He reached up to brush it back, but something in her eyes made him hesitate and he wrapped his fingers around the railing instead.

She released his hand to push the errant strands away herself. "That must be the dolphin version of a family hug."

She had given him the perfect opening. "How about your family?"

Her lips took on a wry twist. "In some animal species, the mothers eat their young."

She brushed off the hair on her cheek as she lost the brightness in her face. Her eyes looked bruised and sad.

Niko would do anything to wipe that sadness from her soul. But he had a feeling that would take a lot of time and patience and he only had a few weeks.

Then her eyes went blank, making him doubt what he'd seen just seconds before. She took a quick step away from him, glancing at her watch and clearly backing away from the intimacy they had shared. "I've got to go—"

"Back to work?" He said it for her, saving her the indignity of uttering the time-worn excuse. When he'd picked up Sophie's new insulin vial after lunch, he'd already been told the doctor had taken the early shift and was off for the rest of the day.

Obviously, he had mistaken the good doctor's compassion for something more. He wasn't sure what he'd wanted that "more" to be.

Even though she hadn't moved a muscle, he could feel her pulling away. "Niko, this is supposed to be your vacation, a time for fun and recharging."

"Not a soul-searching expedition." He felt rebuffed and more than a little embarrassed. Spilling his guts wasn't something he usually did with a woman—especially a woman he just met and had no intention of getting to know beyond these three weeks out of time. Just because he felt a pull toward her didn't mean she felt it too, or that she had to respond even if she did.

Her forced smile was so very different from her natural one. "Make sure your fun doesn't stress your wound."

This *was* a time for fun, not a time for deep reflection—most particularly about a woman he'd just met and would never see again after his fun was over.

His perspective restored, he nodded. "Sure thing, Doc. I've used work as an excuse myself a few times. I didn't mean to keep you from your patients. And I've got umbrella drinks to try. Maybe I'll catch you later."

Walking away was the right thing to do. Why was it so hard?

Because he never backed down from a challenge, right? That had to be the reason. But maybe this time he should. Life was too short...

From now on, when a woman flirted with him on deck, he would flirt back, buy her a drink, enjoy her company with the understanding they were both stealing a moment in a fantasy world that would come to an end when the cruise ended. He would take advantage of this time that had nothing to do with his reality and enjoy himself.

Then, during those long nights under mosquito nets, he would pull out the memories, have a smile, and find the energy to get back to work in the morning.

As he headed toward the big-haired brunette, the one that was supposed to be his type, he could feel Annalise's eyes on him, watching him.

When he looked back to be sure, he kept his sunglasses securely in place as he flashed her a cocky grin, deliberately hiding his reaction to a woman who moved him like no woman ever had before.

"Is this seat taken?" he asked the brunette.

She had more than enough appreciation in her eyes to soothe his ego, right?

She greeted him with a sweep of her hand to indicate the empty chair. "I've been saving it for you."

Niko let out a deep breath. This woman knew the game. Now to have some fun.

"What are we drinking?"

"I recommend the rum punch." She welcomed him with a raised glass and a gleamingly bright smile. "I'm Helena. Your grandmother said we should meet." Her Greek accent verified her heritage.

She was everything he should want in a woman, especially one who was only temporary.

If only he could be less aware of the reluctant little honey-haired blonde walking away from him and more interested in the eager brunette right in front of him, he would make a lot of people very happy—including himself.

The waiter brought over a tray holding huge glasses filled with enough fruit to host a luau. The paper umbrellas wilted against the condensation on the glasses. Definitely not his kind of drink. He thought about asking for a beer instead, but that would mean he'd have to stay around and wait for it to be delivered and he wasn't sure he wanted to stay that long.

"Your grandmother tells me you're single?"

Niko nodded confirmation.

"I'm divorced." Helen took a deep sip from the new glass and shrugged, as if it didn't matter, but her eyes said it really did.

Niko sipped his too-sweet drink and tried to look sympathetic. He'd heard so many domestic tales of woe that all he got from the conversation was validation that he was not made for marriage. "Sorry it didn't work out."

"Me, too. My ex-husband was a Texas oil tycoon. Sadly, after I turned thirty-five, he became more interested in drilling holes than in me."

"So you're going back home?"

"To visit. Maybe to stay. I'm not sure yet." The way she said it, she sounded like staying wasn't her first choice.

"We're on a family vacation. My grandmother is going to show us her homeland."

"I know. I met your Yiayia. She tells me you're a very successful cosmetic surgeon who's been on television and works on celebrities."

"Maxiofacial surgeon." He gave her his best smoldering look. Somehow, it felt more manipulative than usual. "I can see you don't need my services."

But Helen knew the game. She batted her eyelashes at him. "And here I was thinking you'd be good at popping a champagne bottle cork. Tonight? My balcony?"

It was the kind of invitation he'd hoped to get when he'd boarded the ship. But now all he could think of was sharing a sunset beer or cup of tea with Annalise on the foredeck again.

When he didn't answer right away, she gave him a hard look. "Not interested?"

"As much as I'd like to, I'm here for my family this trip."

"Sure." Her smile was bitter. "I guess my ex was right."

Yes, she knew the game well, fishing for a compliment to negate the ex-husband's harshness. He had a list of phrases he used in situations like this. Why couldn't he think of an appropriate one?

"I hope your homecoming is everything you expect it to be."

He left the drink on a tray, excused himself and determined to be anywhere she wasn't.

It wasn't Helena, who appeared to be perfectly perfect. It was him. He was so tired of playing the game.

Annalise didn't even know there was a game, much less how to play.

Niko suddenly felt very good about his decision. Helena was the kind of trouble he didn't need.

But, then, all women came with a certain amount of trouble, didn't they?

Why did Annalise seem worth it when all the other women didn't?

While he didn't believe in love at first sight, he now had first-hand knowledge that obsession at first sight was a very real phenomenon.

CHAPTER FIVE

ANNALISE DUCKED INTO an elevator and hit the button to close the door just as she began to shake. The intensity of emotion Niko had shared with her had caught her off balance. She'd wanted to reach out and hold him tight, to take away the pain in his heart, to make him all better.

But all she'd managed to do had been to touch his hand then make a hasty retreat before the conversation turned deep again. Sharing secrets about her own family would have been more than she could have handled.

As always, she hid behind her work, just like Niko had accused her of doing. It was all she had.

Annalise spent the rest of her afternoon off in the office, helping her new physician's assistant get settled into the ship's routine.

The work was familiar. Safe. Unexciting.

Unlike the way she felt around Niko.

As she worked, she couldn't keep herself from thinking of all she was missing, keeping herself apart and safe. And unexciting.

In fact, she would have to describe her life as downright boring.

For the first time ever, she craved a thrill down her spine, the kind of thrill she got when Niko was near. She wasn't sure what she should do about it but she was certain her lack of ability to handle her emotions had come across to Niko as disinterest.

That buxom brunette certainly had no problem projecting her interest, had she?

As she and her P.A. documented inventory and filed their charts, she was glad that the P.A was either in too chatty a frame of mind or was discreet enough to pretend not to notice her mercurial mood.

With only a fraction of her attention Annalise listened to her talk about leaving her fiancé at the altar.

"I figure I'll do this for a while, maybe a year. Then, when all the fuss dies down, I'll go back home."

While some did it for the adventure, the P.A. was one of many who had chosen to work on a cruise ship to run from bad history. She and Annalise had that in common.

Annalise responded, to be nice. "Better to break up before the marriage than after, right?"

She didn't add that it was even better to break up before the preacher and congregation were seated, waiting for the bride to walk down the aisle, like her new P.A. had done. That was an opinion better kept to herself.

But her P.A. seemed to be competent in her work. The way she managed her love life was none of Annalise's concern.

Then, again, with Annalise's lack of experience she really didn't have much basis on which to judge these matters of the heart.

Was Niko a love-'em-and-leave-'em kind of guy? From what his family said about him, she'd just bet he was.

"So what's your story, Doc? The contract office said you'd been sailing longer than any other doctor they had signed up."

This was not a conversation Annalise wanted to have. Her dread must have shown on her face because the P.A quickly followed up with, "They said it in a good way. That you were the best to learn from. But you've been doing this for a while, haven't you?"

"Yes, I have." The normal explanation would be that she was still running away, and maybe that was correct, but she had no intention of discussing her personal hang-ups with anyone other than her therapist. Hopefully, her tone would discourage any further conversation along this line.

Her contract was up when they made port in Malaga, Spain. She had an option to extend her tour of service to cover the extra week the ship would be looping through the Greek isles, but was thinking hard about whether she wanted to sign another contract at the end of this trip.

Regardless of her reasons, putting down roots in her home town of New Orleans, or in any one particular place in the world, held no appeal for her.

She'd been thinking about Niko and his charity work ever since she'd examined his knife wound. Maybe she'd find a private moment to ask more. It would be a legitimate reason to see him again instead of a trumped-up excuse.

And just maybe he wouldn't reject her like she had rejected him.

Tonight? On the foredeck? Annalise didn't believe in happenstance, but maybe this once she could allow herself to believe that if it was meant to be, it would happen.

Niko and his brothers and sisters-in-law had been hitting the "golf balls" made of fish food off the back of the ship for over an hour now. Watching the fish school to eat the "golf balls" made Yiayia and the children smile.

He teed up the fish-food golf ball and concentrated on swinging the club. Or at least he tried to concentrate on his swing. Even though he'd vowed to put Annalise from his mind, he hadn't been able to do it.

As he shanked his shot, he realized what had been nagging at him. That blank expression on her face when he'd asked about her family. He'd seen that look before—from victims trying to cope.

The thought of anyone anywhere hurting Annalise sent a burst of rage through him.

He teed up another fish ball and swung, hooking this one but sending it further than any of his previous hits.

Stephen put his hand on Niko's shoulder.

"Don't frown, little brother. I'll show you how it's done."

Marcus teed up his own ball. "Because we've been taking lessons. Right, Dad?"

Hearing his brothers' hearty laughter emphasized how much he had in his family.

And how much Annalise didn't have. As she had comforted him, he wanted to comfort her, give her a shoulder, let her know...

Know what? That he would always be there for her?

He couldn't promise that to any woman. The places he went, the things he did made commitment to a woman impossible. He was actually grateful to his ex for showing him the futility of trying to have it all.

"It's only fair that I pass on what I've learned." Stephen looked Niko in the eye, more serious than usual. "After all, thanks to my baby brother buying into the restaurant, we've been able to hire another manager so I can take the occasional afternoon off now and spend more time with my sons. I can never thank you enough for that, little brother."

"After all you've done for me, it's me that is in your debt." Niko grinned. "But I bet you a beer I can hit this next one farther than you can."

"I'll take a side bet on Niko." Phoebe grinned at them

both. "Don't you know that doctors know how to play golf? It comes with the diploma. I'll bet you play at all those fancy resorts you keep running off to."

"I'll take that side bet, Mom. I'll bet Uncle Niko doesn't play a lot of golf when he's out of town." Marcus gave Niko a strong stare. "Ask his ex-fiancée. He's not like most doctors."

What had his ex told Marcus now? Had she broken her promise to keep his charity work secret?

Phoebe patted Niko on the shoulder in case he needed comforting. "It will take a strong woman to keep our Niko's attention.

Annalise. Why did he think of her when he thought of a strong woman? He didn't even know her.

Could she live on canned beans and peaches for ten days straight because the supply truck had been hijacked? Could she sleep on the ground under a mosquito net because the wind was too strong to pitch a tent with a hurricane blowing in off the coast? Could she complete surgery as rebel gunfire threatened to overrun an encampment?

That's the kind of superwoman that would fit into Niko's life.

He had to grin as he thought of Annalise draping the superhero cape around Sophie's shoulders. Going from cruise ship to jungle boat would take a superhuman leap—a leap he could never expect anyone to take on his behalf.

He squared up to hit the last fish-food golf ball into the ocean.

Sophie jumped up and down and pointed at the splash he'd made. "Hey, look how far Uncle Niko hit it! He just beat everybody."

As one, his family turned and applauded him. That's

what the Christopoulos family did when you met expectations. They cheered you on.

He'd never let them down yet. What would happen when he did?

As Annalise was unlocking the etched-glass doors leading into the medical suite to accommodate Brandy's off-hours request, the bartender rushed up to her.

"Doc, you're here." Her face showed panic and her voice was on the edge of hysteria.

Annalise pushed open the doors. "Come in. What's wrong?"

"How could I forget? And now..." Brandy bit her knuckle. "Now I think I'm pregnant."

"You were fine when we boarded. What happened between then and now?" Annalise tried to put the pieces together. "Did you have unprotected sex recently?"

"No. Yes. Well, not within the last day or so, anyway." Brandy wrapped her arms around herself. "I can't have a baby, not the way I live. What will I do with it?"

A sympathetic knot formed in Annalise's stomach. She squelched it down, intellectually keeping her own personal experience safely dissociated from her patient's. Emotionally keeping her distance was more of a challenge. But overlying Brandy's circumstances with her own personal trauma wouldn't be good for either of them.

"Let's talk about it back here." Annalise ushered her back to an examination room, seated her in a chair and took out her clipboard with a fresh chart. "How many days has it been since your last period?"

"I don't know. I don't keep up with it, really, since I use the kind of birth control that keeps you from having one very often. But I've been feeling a little tired and my roommate says she's noticed I've put on weight." Brandy patted her gently rounded stomach. "I feel puffy and my breasts are really tender. Once my roommate pointed it out to me, it was obvious. All the signs are there."

"What type of birth control do you use?"

"The patch." Brandy looked down at the floor. "But I think I forgot to change it."

She looked up, desperation in her eyes. "What am I going to do, Doc?"

Annalise hated that question. She was duty-bound to discuss options, but she knew all too well all the choices would have life-changing consequences.

Annalise stared down at the blank form, using her analytical training to compose herself. "The first thing to do is take a pregnancy test. Test your urine first thing in the morning when the hormones will be more concentrated. If the test comes back positive, we'll do an ultrasound to try to determine how long you've been pregnant."

She took a pregnancy testing kit from an overhead cabinet and handed it to Brandy. Brandy hugged it to her chest like a lifeline.

"And then?"

"And then I'll give you some information and you can make some decisions." Three weeks. They would be out at sea for three weeks. So many things hung in the balance.

The wild look in Brandy's eyes worried Annalise. Even though she wasn't keen on personal touching, she felt compelled to cover the bartender's hand with her own.

"A strong support system will help you through this, Brandy. Your parents? Siblings? I can set you up with a ship-to-shore line and you can give them a call."

Brandy shook her head. "We're not that kind of a family."

"We can't all be that lucky, can we?" Annalise thought of the Christopoulos clan. Even though she'd only seen them in action a few times, she knew they would rally round one of their own, giving comfort and security.

Hesitantly, she asked, "What about the father? Would he be supportive of you?" When she thought about support, why did Niko come to mind? She'd barely met the man. Why did she cast him in the role of protector?

Brandy looked up at the ceiling, hugging herself tight and rocking back and forth. "I'm still thinking about that one."

"Promise me you won't do anything rash or stupid."

Brandy flushed as if Annalise had caught her in the act. She stood, hugging the pregnancy test box to her chest. "I promise, Doc."

"See you in the morning, then. Have me paged if you need me before that."

With a nod Brandy was gone, leaving Annalise with a quiet, sterile room and too many painful memories.

Needing alone time, Niko rushed through supper with his family. He loved them, each and every one of them. But they were so—so *there* all the time, like a litter of puppies, rolling over each other, playfully nipping at each other, never letting a littermate out of sight.

He settled into the lounge chair he'd claimed the night before. Board shorts, barefoot, beer in hand, now he could breathe deeply. He toasted the ocean, thinking of all the toasts his family had just saluted each other with. Too many of those toasts had to do with him finding the perfect woman, settling down, starting a family. They had drunk *to his future happiness!*

And to theirs, he'd toasted back, his lemon-twisted water standing out in stark contrast against his brothers' rich merlots.

He'd had enough wine the night before to last him a

while. Unlike his family's preference, wine wasn't his favorite. Just like attending tomorrow's tour of the cruise-ship kitchens was a field trip he'd opted to skip.

Only a few days out and he was already prowling the decks. This low level of activity wasn't good for him, tying him up in knots instead of letting him relax.

That sixth sense that had kept him safe innumerable times in the past told him she was approaching. Annalise.

"Is this seat taken?" Something in her eyes looked vulnerable, hopeful. Anxious. "Can I sit here?"

Something in his heart couldn't say no.

Waves of emotion surged through him. What he was feeling for her was more than the foam that short-term flings were made from.

He could so easily drown in the deep blue depths of her eyes.

The smart thing to do would be to explain his need for privacy. It was a valid answer. But he found himself saying, "I was saving it for you."

And he found himself realizing that's exactly what he had been doing.

She looked at him, looked hard enough he felt compelled to push his sunglasses to the top of his head.

"Hard day?" she asked.

He flashed her his celebrity smile. "I'm on a cruise ship. Is there such a thing as a hard day?"

Her eyes said it all. She was disappointed in him for skirting her question. He wanted to redeem himself very badly.

"I'm not used to doing nothing. It feels so…trivial."

"Tell me about Doctors Without Borders." Gracefully, she sank into the lounge chair without spilling a drop from the cup of hot tea she balanced on her saucer.

"What do you want to know?"

She leaned forward, as if she wanted to catch each word before the wind tore it away. As if what he said held great import. As if *he* were of great import. "Where was your first mission?"

So he told her about the trauma care facility in Northern Afghanistan and about how hours of operating made a person numb to the dangers around them.

"The real danger is becoming numb to the people around you. But there was always someone—a father or sister or friend—who reminded you that your patients weren't just bodies that needed medical attention but loved ones who needed medical care."

He couldn't imagine trying to explain this to anyone else, but with Annalise he could see the understanding in her eyes.

Her hands clenched and unclenched around her tea cup. "I was in my first semester of rotation in the E.R. during Hurricane Katrina. In my mind, everything runs together after those first forty-eight hours."

She took a sip of her tea. "What was your first assignment?"

"The tsunami."

"Tell me about it."

He talked for hours, longer than he'd ever spoken about his work before. And she listened, asked questions, nodded sympathetically and laughed at the humorous stories the human psyche needed to break up the horror of it all.

He fell asleep sometime during the evening and when he awoke with the stars gleaming overhead she'd covered him with a blanket against the night air.

CHAPTER SIX

SADLY, ANNALISE HAD had no erotic dreams during the night but she had fallen asleep with Niko on her mind and woken up thinking of him, too. She certainly wouldn't call her night restful. Who would have guessed such a heroic heart beat beneath that pretty boy rebel exterior?

Annalise went down to the medical suite as soon as the early morning yoga class on deck was dismissed. Brandy was usually in that class, but today she was a no-show.

It must have been one of the longest nights of Brandy's life. Annalise's heart went out to her.

When Annalise had realized she was pregnant she'd been almost as frightened as when—

The bell signaling patients arriving kept Annalise from going down a path she'd rather never travel again.

Like it always did, helping others took her mind off her own concerns. Annalise had a steady stream of patients with sunburn from strong tropical rays that took them by surprise and acid reflux from overindulging, both typical complaints at this point in a cruise.

Halfway through her shift one of her receptionists delivered a note, sealed and addressed to her, that had been left at the front counter.

Annalise opened the note. "Not pregnant. Relieved, but

kind of sad, too. Am putting on a new patch this morning. Brandy."

Simply apply a patch and go on with life. It was an uncomplicated way to handle a shipboard romance.

So why did Niko and complications pop into her head just as she was confirming her desire for the simple life?

After an hour of wandering around the ship, trying to accidently bump into Niko, Annalise finally spotted him wandering aimlessly around the main pool area. Instead of rushing up to him, she stayed back and observed him for a while. What was it about him that compelled her to watch him? Was it his natural good looks? Or the way his black wavy hair fell onto his forehead in that perfectly casual way? Or the way his T-shirt stretched across his muscled shoulders? Or was it the way he moved, strong and lethal like the tiger she saw in his eyes?

Or maybe it was the way those eyes lit up when he talked about fixing a cleft palate on a little girl and seeing her smile years later when he was reassigned to the same area.

She tried not to notice as she stood next to a high table near her favorite kiosk and dunked her tea bag into her cup of hot water. But as she stirred sugar into her afternoon tea her attention kept returning to him.

He sat at the bar for a while, ordered a beer, then moved toward the lounge chairs, but decided to look over the railing instead.

She had expected to see a playboy on the prowl. Instead, she saw a man alone who didn't know what to do with himself. She had the strongest urge to offer suggestions—suggestions that included her company.

As if he could hear her thoughts, he turned from the rail, scanned the crowd and found her.

"Annalise."

Through the noisy crowd she couldn't hear him, but she could read his lips. In the past, if a passenger wanted to get friendly, she would wave him off and move on, but she couldn't put Niko into the same class as just another passenger. So when he walked towards her, she stood still and waited for him.

"Hey, you." He pushed his sunglasses to the top of his head and gave her a movie-star grin that almost made her swoon. She barely stopped herself from looking around to see who he was really talking to.

If she had been diagnosing herself, she would have had to say her palpitations were the results a developmentally delayed teenage crush.

"Hey you back," she managed to say, pleased that she didn't sound at all bedazzled. "Just hanging out at the pool?"

"I threw a penny in the wishing well a moment ago. That thing really works."

"You got your wish already?"

"Yup. I wished a beautiful woman would come up and talk to me and here you are."

Self-consciously Annalise pulled down the hem of her new orange tank top, which she'd layered over her new bright yellow one, and wiggled her newly painted toenails exposed by her new beaded leather sandals. It was silly to feel self-conscious amongst all the string bikinis on deck.

"Thanks." She didn't need the glance in the glass doors that separated the cruise ship's interior from its exterior to remind her that she was showing a lot more skin than she normally did. She usually only wore tank tops under shirts or thin blouses. But something—or, if she was honest, someone—had inspired a shopping spree.

She might not be as sophisticated as that Greek woman but, still, she'd not done too badly, if she did say so herself.

He kept staring into her eyes. She realized she'd been staring back and blinked.

"So, what did you do today?"

He took a deep sip from the drink he carried. "I played bingo with Yiayia for a while this morning. I won a T-shirt and she won a key chain. Then I went to the kids Underwater Explorers' activity, where we learned about submarines. The twins are on the water slides, but my doctor grounded me from that. And the rest of the family is attending a pastry-making school. Can you believe it? They all cook for a living, but they go on vacation and now they're cooking again."

"I guess they love what they do."

"I guess so." He shrugged, giving her a crooked grin. "If the ship offered a seminar on reconstructing sinus cavities, I'd probably be in the front row."

The wry expression on his face made her laugh. "You should drop off that suggestion at Guest Services. They're always open to new ideas."

The smile he flashed reached all the way to his eyes. She hadn't realized how brilliant those eyes could be. They took her breath away.

But the sparkle didn't last long. "I was just wondering what to do next. Any suggestions?"

She consulted the flyer listing the day's activities, which she'd picked up after her pedicure, and picked the first thing on the list. "I'm going to the gourmet coffee tasting. Want to come?"

He leaned in close to read the paper she held. "I'll go anywhere with you."

The way he said it, so low and intimate, sent shivers through her. Practically, she wondered how many women he'd practiced on before he'd got that timbre just right.

He gave her a quizzical look. "What?"

"Just you and your pick-up lines."

"You don't like them?"

"I didn't say that." She looked up into those glistening eyes. "They just aren't necessary. I like you fine without all the swagger."

He pulled his sunglasses over his eyes. "But without the swagger, what do I have?"

Apparently, she'd hit a sore spot. This man-woman interplay wasn't her forte. She started walking toward the coffee shop.

The silence between them felt awkward and needed filling.

Annalise said what was on her mind, hoping her honesty didn't get her into worse trouble. "If you're fishing for a compliment, I can give you several. You're talented, according to your prestigious client list. You're generous. Brave. Good with children. Should I go on?"

She didn't know someone so deeply tanned—or so cocky—could blush as deeply as he did.

"If you keep it up, I'll have to hire you as my publicist."

"Do you have one?"

He gave her a sideways glance. "Uh—no. I'm a serious working doctor, no matter what you've heard from my grandmother."

"She's very proud of you."

"She's proud of all of us."

"I didn't hear her bragging about your brothers at supper the other night."

"Magazine covers and TV interviews impress her." He stopped outside the café's entrance. "It was all to build the practice. Thankfully, it worked. I keep telling my brothers they need to do the same to build up the restaurant, but they've resisted so far."

"Where's your family's restaurant?"

"In the city on Audubon Place. It's called Olympia's, for obvious reasons."

"I'll put that on my list of places to eat next time I'm in New Orleans."

"Just tell them you know me and they'll cut you a good deal."

"They'll probably charge me double, thinking that if I'm a friend of yours, I'll be trouble," Annalise teased.

Niko gave her a genuine smile. "Minx."

This was fun! In the past, when a man had flirted with her, she'd often thought of amusing retorts in kind but she'd never just blurted them out like this. She'd been too shy.

But with Niko she felt bold and confident. It was a good feeling.

"Want to sit here?" She gestured to a nearby table.

"Sure." Niko offered Annalise a hand to help her sit on the bar stool fronting the coffee bar. He probably did it without even realizing how chivalrous he was being. But Annalise didn't take the courtesy for granted.

His hand was big. Strong. Probably very nice. Still, she pretended not to notice as she climbed onto the bar stool.

As soon as he withdrew his hand she regretted not taking it. Maybe this time would have been different. After all, Niko was different.

He gave her a thoughtful look as he took the seat next to her, obviously not knowing what his personal touch would do to her. How could he know?

She'd never told anyone why she usually kept her distance. She'd never wanted to explain herself, never wanted a man to understand, until now. Maybe she should give him just enough clues that he'd know it wasn't him but her.

She swallowed. "Niko, I—"

The barista interrupted the moment and Annalise didn't know whether to feel relieved or disappointed.

She gave them the coffee-house spiel as she lined up six small cups of coffee in front of them.

"I recommend trying the samples from light roast to dark roast. Lighter is less acidic. Darker has more body." She put an icy-cold silver creamer and sugar bowl on a silver tray on the table. "Let me know if you want to try anything else on the board or if you have any questions."

Niko had lots of questions, but not for the barista. He wanted to know everything about the fascinating woman across from him. He especially wanted to know about the pain in her eyes and how to make it go away.

But by the way Annalise was avoiding looking at him, he knew this wasn't the time or the place.

He would enjoy the moment for what it was and do his best to make sure Annalise enjoyed it, too. There would be other opportunities. He would make sure of that.

After making generous use of the sugar bowl, he took his first sip and hid his wince. Coffee wasn't his favorite drink, but he would have agreed to share a bottle of absinthe if he'd had to, rather than turn down Annalise's invitation.

Annalise took a sip of first cup and grimaced.

"Not to your taste?"

"Not this one." She dumped cream and sugar into her next cup and gave it try. "Too much more of this and I'll have another restless night."

"Another?" Niko added cream to his cup, too, but hesitated before giving it another try.

"You know, Niko, I don't really like coffee. And I'm

thinking you don't either. Would you rather have a nice umbrella drink instead?"

"To tell you the truth, Annalise, I'm not very fond of those either." He leaned forward, knowing he was about to either breach a barrier or end this barely budding relationship at one go. "Instead of getting ourselves into something neither of us want, let's make a pact. Truth between us and nothing less."

By the wary expression on Annalise's face Niko knew he had his answer.

"All right." She laughed—a genuine laugh from deep inside. "You were expecting a different answer, weren't you?"

"Sadly, yes. Bad past experiences."

"About that—experiences, I mean. I'll be truthful, but I also reserve the right to not answer."

"Deal." He thought of the sweepstakes ploy he'd engineered for his family and, of course, his Doctors Without Borders gig. "Everyone has a few secrets they don't want revealed."

Niko caught the barista's attention and they placed their orders—a beer for Niko and a fresh cup of tea for Annalise because she had to check back in with her P.A. before the end of office hours.

"So…" Annalise licked her lips, making Niko yearn for a taste "…want to play Twenty Questions?"

"Sure." He couldn't have refused if his life had depended on it.

"Favorite color."

"I would have said blue before I saw you today. Now it's orange. Most definitely orange."

A rosy blush crept up her face even as her eyes sparkled. She ducked her head. "Thanks."

"What's yours?"

"Mine?"

"Your favorite color?"

She grinned. "Amber. Like your eyes."

Women had complimented his eyes before, but it had never mattered. Now it mattered. *Keep it casual, Christopoulos.*

He pushed the flattering remark away. "So you want to play that way, huh? Game on, girl. What do you want in a man?"

Annalise bit her lip as she tilted her head to the side and considered. Worry made Niko's heart pound faster.

From her expression, she was taking this game way too seriously.

"Kindness. Compassion. Strength enough to stand up for those weaker than him. Enough intelligence to hold up his end of the conversation." Very deliberately, she studied him. "And muscles in all the right places."

He spread his arms wide. "You might need to check me out for that last one, Doc. A physical exam would be so much more thorough than a mere visual inspection."

As she took a sip of her tea she looked up from under her lashes. So coy yet so direct. He couldn't stop staring at how she seemed to glow from deep inside when she was happy.

"And you, Dr. Christopoulos. What makes a ladies' man like you choose one woman over another? Give me a comparison chart, no names necessary."

"Comparison chart? Right now, you're the only woman I can even bring to mind."

"You're a glib one, aren't you?"

He put his hand over his heart. "Only truth between us."

"In that case, how long have you experienced this selective amnesia, Doctor?"

"Ever since I stood behind you when we were boarding."

"What about a certain buxom Greek heiress who needed sunscreen rubbed on her back?"

Helena hadn't even entered his mind. "Merely being polite. Are you jealous?"

"Nothing to be jealous about."

"You're right. You have nothing to be jealous about." He reached over to take Annalise's hand, but she checked her watch before his fingers could graze hers.

"I need to check in with my P.A." She looked down at her activities list and pointed to the next one on the list. "Look. They've got an origami towel-folding class starting in a few minutes. Would you like to try that?"

"Towel origami? Was it something I said?"

She looked at him, long and hard. "Duty before pleasure. You know the score."

"All too well." But something in her eyes didn't ring true. He was pretty certain he was getting the brush-off.

Still, he held out his hand to help her off the bar stool.

When she took it, giving his fingers an apologetic squeeze, he felt a zing go straight to his gut. This woman was different. Special.

And he loved a challenge.

"See you tonight on top?" he called after her.

She stopped and gave him a sexy look over her shoulder. "If you're lucky."

Annalise didn't show.

Niko waited until past midnight, tensing in anticipation each time he heard footsteps coming up the metal stairs, but he was disappointed each time.

He went over and over the conversation in his head. Had he come on too strong? Shy had never been his type before Annalise. But she had seemed to enjoy their banter.

And why did it mean so much to him? Why did he feel so at a loss? Feel such rejection?

As he unlocked his cabin door, he saw the blinking light on his cabin phone. Impatiently, he followed the lengthy button-pushing instructions to retrieve the text message that scrolled across the phone's display.

Medical emergency. How about tomorrow? Ice skating after breakfast? A.

Short. Cryptic. Exactly the kind of note he'd texted his ex when he had been running late. Now he understood why she hadn't always been satisfied with his terse communication.

Niko spent too many hours staring at the ceiling, thinking about relationships old and new, telling himself he should back away from this one before he fell too deep. Then, finally, admitting to himself he might have already fallen.

As he fell asleep he made the firm, sensible decision to skip the skating date, skip the moonlight trysts, skip all further encounters with Dr. Annalise Walcott. There was no future in it. He had enough goodbyes to say at the end of this trip. No sense in adding one more.

CHAPTER SEVEN

ANNALISE STUDIED THE contents of her closet and clothes drawers. While the ice rink wasn't too cold, her body was acclimated to the tropics. Usually, for ice skating she wore thick sweats, but she opted for her slimmer-fitting yoga pants this morning. Being a little chilled was worth the fashion trade-off.

She contemplated her oversized sweatshirt advertising the cruise line. Her other option was a T-shirt, which would be too thin no matter how much better it showed off her assets.

As she pulled the sweatshirt over her head, Annalise was not oblivious to the change Niko was making on her daily habits.

They definitely had chemistry together, but it wasn't only sexual attraction but also intellectual attraction.

Annalise's mother had often told her that she was too smart for her own good. That she intimidated men and she should try to tone down the brains. While she would have if she could have, she hadn't managed to do that. But with Niko she had no need to. He challenged her mind just as she did his.

Was he the right man? Or was this simply the right time? Even before she'd met him, she had been feeling the need for a change, thus her reluctance to renew her contract and her growing interest in medical relief missions. Even her unsuccessful visit to her mother could be seen as a sign that she was ready to move on from her status quo.

The right man at the right time.

Was she ready? How long was she going to let her past hold her back?

Dark secrets. Was she prepared to look at them in the light of day? It would take a very special man to help her breach the darkness and come into the light.

Did she want Niko to be that man? Would he even want to be that man once he found out about her past?

Secrets.

Niko watched Annalise walk toward him as he stood by the skate counter, fully aware how his pulse sped up at the sight of her.

So much for all his late-night contemplation.

He had no idea where this was going, but if it was leading to something serious… He surprised himself by wishing it could. But he would never be ready for a serious relationship. He'd made his decision.

Thankfully, Annalise was safe. She had her career, too. A career that harbored no expectations of a home and children and a husband who came home every night.

"Hey," he said as she came within earshot.

"Hey back at ya."

Niko grinned at how they had fallen into sync so quickly. He could get used to this. Warning bells went off in his head. Less than three weeks. No sense in getting used to anything about her.

Still, he could enjoy her company, couldn't he? She didn't just pretend to listen when he talked. She really *did* listen. They had well-informed conversations, give and take, back and forth. Yin and yang.

How often had he been misunderstood in the past? A parade of beautiful women flashed through his mind. He had to admit he had not always based his date choice on compatibility.

But with Annalise he had both beauty and brains in one package.

The only problem was—he didn't have her at all. She was her own woman with her own life that he only got to be a part of for the next two weeks and a few days.

This trip was supposed to be about relaxing, not about feeling the pressure of the clock ticking. Why did he do this to himself?

"Ready?" She raised an eyebrow at him in challenge.

Because he couldn't resist, he answered, "Ready."

As Niko bent to lace his skates, he rubbed his thigh, an absent gesture Annalise was certain he wasn't even aware of.

"How's the leg?"

"Fine."

Although she wanted to probe deeper, she practiced great restraint and let it drop. He was entitled to his privacy, just as she was.

"I'm ready to get rid of these stitches."

"I'll take a look tomorrow."

She watched him stand on the rubber map, his ankles wobbling. As soon as she stood, he grabbed her shoulder to steady himself.

Normally, she would shy away from such contact. But this was Niko. Instead, she reached out a hand to steady him.

"You really meant it when you said you wanted me to teach you to skate. You've never done this before?"

"Nope. Never."

"Keep your ankles firm."

"And then?"

"Then the first thing you need to learn is how to fall."

His grip tightened on her as he wobbled back and forth. "I'm thinking that lesson will come to me naturally in a very short time."

"Falling isn't inevitable."

"Except for falling in love," he quipped. Then he became very still. "At least, that's what Yiayia would say."

She was all too aware that they were avoiding each other's eyes. "That L-word can ruin a lot of friendships."

He nodded. "Then we won't let that happen, will we?"

Abruptly he sat on the bench behind him, craning up to look at her.

She sat next to him, putting them at the same height.

"Annalise?"

"Yes?"

"We can be friends, can't we? Even after this is over?"

She drew in a big breath. "Long distance? We can try. No promises, though."

He nodded. "No promises."

A group of teens rushed by, laughing and playing and reminding Annalise that life was full of fun as well as drama.

"Are we going to skate today, or hold down this bench for the rest of the morning?" she dared him.

"Let's skate." This time when he stood up he planted his feet firmly, not needing her for support.

"If you start to fall, lean back, tuck your chin in to protect your head and fall on your butt."

"Sage advice for life as well as for ice skating." He reached for her, brushing a strand of hair from her eyes. His finger lingered on the rim of her ear as he pushed the strand behind it.

The thrill made Annalise jerk away.

His lips were so close to hers she could almost taste them when he asked, "Ticklish?"

She took a step backwards, her skate catching on the rubber mat. As she windmilled her arms, he reached out to catch her.

They both lost their balance and he ended up sitting down hard on the bench with her in his lap.

Annalise jumped up.

"Sorry," she said, even though he should be the one apologizing. She hadn't been expecting that sizzling touch. She certainly hadn't asked for it either.

"I'm not."

Take it in stride, Annalise, she reminded herself. *This is flirting. This is fun. Nothing else. And nothing more.*

"Watch me." She walked in front of him. "See how I'm walking a bit forward and bending my knees?"

"Yes. I see."

The teasingly licentious tone of his voice made her grin but she didn't turn around and return it. Not this time. Too much had passed between them that needed some space.

She heard a scrape of blades once he came onto the ice, but no *kerplump*.

Turning, she skated backwards and instructed, "Just lean forward and bend your knees, like you're a superhero if you have to exaggerate it, until you get your balance."

Niko's black hair fell forward into his eyes, making Annalise think about how he could be her Clark Kent any day. Just not today. Too much, too soon.

Then again, this trip wasn't going to last forever.

Niko closed his eyes and took a breath, apparently finding his balance because when he opened them he said, "I'm ready."

And then he skated like he'd been born on the ice, taking long, sure strides and handling the corners with no problems for several laps.

He ran into the wall of the rink to stop.

He looked back over his shoulder at her. "Not graceful but effective."

Showing off a little, she demonstrated a hockey-style stop.

He raised an eyebrow. "Isn't there an easier way?"

"See the cleats on the blade? Drag your toe. They'll catch and slow you down until you stop."

He tried stopping a few times and then said, "Now I'm ready to do that thing you did when you turned around to skate backwards."

"Okay. Changing direction is best done while you're moving, not standing still."

She skated away from him, then crossed her feet and executed a smooth turn so that she faced him, skating backwards. It had taken her many hours of practice to be able to change direction so smoothly.

"Be patient with yourself if you don't get it right the first time."

"I'm not big on patience."

She skated towards him, turning again when she drew even with him. "I've sensed that about you."

Niko took a couple of strides, then crossed his feet, doing a complete circle instead of a half-one.

"It takes practice." Annalise turned back and forth a half dozen times in as many strides, enjoying what she was doing as much as flaunting her skills.

Niko frowned down at her feet, then nodded and gave it a try. Of course, he picked up the technique on the second pass. Was there anything this man couldn't do?

He dragged a toe, ending up a few inches from her, close enough she could see the golden flecks in his eyes.

"Now that I've done it, I don't understand the appeal of going round in circles. Maybe speed skating or doing those dangerous moves and jumps they do on television would make it more exciting." He skated backwards to Annalise's forwards.

"Always the extremes for you, isn't it, Niko?"

He looked sad. "It's when I feel most alive."

But that wasn't precisely true. Not anymore. He felt the same thrilling awareness of existence whenever he was with Annalise.

It wasn't a revelation he was happy to discover.

But he couldn't make a clean break of it. Finding an excuse to prolong this, he scratched at his thigh through his shorts. "No office hours today, huh?"

"Impatient man." Her smile was strained as she sat on the bench to unlace her skates.

Niko sat next to her, though not as close as he had before. Was there something more behind her bantering exasperation? He shouldn't want there to be more.

"Come by tomorrow morning and I'll take a look."

Tomorrow morning. Niko wanted to ask about tonight.

"Maybe I could just borrow a pair of scissors and tweezers." He gave her a practiced grin as he kicked off his skate. "I'm ready to try the water slides."

"You can always stop in and visit my P.A."

Niko thought about that, thought about how that was a very sound solution, then thought about how he yearned to feel Annalise's warm hand on his leg, gently tending to him. He decided he could put off the water slides until tomorrow.

He lined up his skates, one next to the other, and slipped into his tennis shoes, wiggling his toes at the familiar comfortable fit.

"See you then—if not tonight?"

"Tomorrow, for sure. Tonight?" She bent to unlace her second skate, effectively hiding her face behind her hair. "Maybe."

He wanted to ask what he could to do convince her, to insist. To make her commit.

Which would call for commitment on his part, too.

He checked his watch. "Family calls. I need to check on Sophie."

"Okay."

"See you then," Niko said again, restraining himself from clearing up the ambiguity. These things happened in their own time. If only he had that much time.

He grabbed both pairs of skates and headed for the counter to turn them in.

He couldn't help watching her as she walked away, her bottom perfectly defined in those form-fitting yoga pants beneath that huge sweatshirt. He'd bet each of those perfect butt cheeks would fit perfectly in his hands. How wise was he to want to prove himself right?

After filling the rest of her morning with grueling, hot yoga then a long swim in the pool after lunch, along with a trip to the video arcade to play a big-screen version of tennis, and a couple of miles on the treadmill instead of supper, Annalise should have been dropping from exhaustion. Instead, she found herself climbing the three sets of stairs to the top deck, a cup of hot decaf tea in her hand, anticipation in her heart.

The deck was deserted.

Annalise almost turned around and left but stopped herself in mid-step. What was she doing? A cup of tea on the top deck had been her habit ever since she'd started sailing on this ship. After all the cruises she'd worked, why would she let one man on one cruise change a tradition that gave her so much pleasure?

Hazy memories of the pleasures her dream lover had almost given her had her sloshing tea over the rim of her cup. It was a dream she would welcome again.

As she would welcome the man behind the dream?

Today, for the first time since she'd signed her first contract, the huge ship seemed too small. Like her P.A. had said, Annalise was a legend in the cruise line's history for her longevity of employment. Most people got tired of running from whatever it was, or found what they were running towards, after a few seasons of ship work. But she'd always been slow to make a change, hanging onto stability, to security.

Her yoga instructor would say that without change there was no growth. And without growth, death. At least in spirit.

Wasn't that what had happened to her own mother so many years ago?

Annalise was not like her mother. But, then, flirting with a man didn't mean selling her soul to him. That's not what a relationship, or even a casual encounter, had to be.

She had established her professional life on her own terms. She could certainly establish her love life on her own terms, too.

Right before the sun made its nightly plunge into the ocean, she heard Niko running up the steps.

"I didn't miss it, did I?"

"Even the sunset waits on Niko Christopoulos."

She'd expected that to elicit a smile or even a laugh from him. Instead, he settled down next to her, twisted the top off one of the two beers he held and saluted the pink and yellow horizon.

"To peace of mind." Although the strangle hold he had on the neck of his beer bottle told a different story.

She raised her tea cup in solidarity. "To peace of mind."

Niko lay back on the lounger with the last of the sun's rays casting shadows over his face, making him look tired.

She wanted to make it all better but they didn't have that kind of relationship. Silence was the best she could do.

As they lay within arm's reach of each other, attraction snapping between them like heat lightning, Annalise wondered how this would end.

CHAPTER EIGHT

NIKO WAS THE first one in her office. It was easy to do since he'd been up since before dawn. In fact, he wasn't sure he'd slept at all.

Annalise had been too much on his mind.

He hadn't spent a sleepless night over a woman in…in longer than he could remember.

Annalise bit her bottom lip, a worried line appearing between her eyebrows. "That knife could have sliced across your throat as easily as it cut into your thigh."

"Lots of things could happen that never do."

"You're one of the lucky ones. You have a family that cares. You could have died and they wouldn't have even known why. Closure heals a lot of hurts."

But acknowledging that something fatal could happen meant dealing with the emotions associated with that nebulous something. He didn't do family drama very well. "I'm going to tell them as soon as the time is right."

Niko felt Annalise's hand burning on his thigh. Her touch set him on fire. He couldn't deny it.

Just as he couldn't deny that he was a man of flesh and blood. If this had been more serious, if he had died, his family would never have understood. He would never have had the opportunity to explain. He owed them more than that.

Annalise was right. Soon. As soon as the opportunity presented itself.

Like that was ever going to happen.

Niko pushed that thought away, determined to squeeze every ounce of enjoyment out of this trip. He had almost two weeks left and he would make the most of them.

After Annalise confirmed that Niko's knife wound was healing well enough, he sat on the exam table and picked out his own stitches, using the tweezers and scissors Annalise lent him as she stood, propped against the wall, watching him.

She'd offered. He could have accepted. But her hand on his thigh would have led to an embarrassing situation that his baggy board shorts couldn't have hidden.

He looked up at her from under thick, dark lashes. "Are you as good at climbing the rock wall as you are at ice skating?"

She arched a brow at him. "Better."

"As soon as I'm done here, then, want to race?"

"I don't know. I might be taking unfair advantage." Annalise frowned as Niko tugged on one of the stitches to get it loose. "Living on this ship, I've climbed that wall a thousand times at least. And I've scaled real rocks, too."

"Yeah? When?"

"Before I was hired by the cruise line, I signed up for the emergency medicine residency swap program. So I gave New Mexico's emergency medicine program a try. I learned to climb there."

"You're just full of surprises."

She shrugged. "In New Orleans, I'd always lived around three feet below sea level in the inner city. I thought I'd try different terrain for a while."

"What did you think of it?" Field medicine wasn't for most doctors.

"I loved everything about it. The mountains. The desert. It was like the elements dared me and I was determined to win."

"Sweet Annalise in those rugged conditions. I've noticed you've got a competitive edge." The need to beat the odds was the attitude it took to be a good field doctor. More and more, he was learning there was more to Annalise than he'd thought at first glance. Although the first glance had been rather thrilling, too.

"You're doing it again." She rubbed at her cheek. "You're staring at me like I've got something on my face."

"Sorry. I must be losing my touch. That's supposed to be my intensely interested look. Obviously, I need to work on it."

"Honesty?"

"Honesty." He crossed his heart and held up his fingers like a scout. "When you smile like that, I can't help but stare."

She laughed, shaking her head at his compliment, not taking him seriously. "You and your flattery."

While he'd totally meant the compliment, he liked it that she wasn't too taken in by it. Annalise definitely stood on her own two feet.

"But a beautiful woman deserves beautiful compliments."

"Pretty is as pretty does." She gave him a sideways look. "You're good looking. Does that make you a better person?"

Her question, delivered quick and solid, caught Niko by surprise. "Of course not."

"Remember that next time you're throwing around random compliments."

Niko thought of the sinking feeling he always got when

he thought a woman was more interested in his appeal as an arm ornament than as a person. "Yes, ma'am, I will."

He flexed his leg, watching the healed skin hold true. "If you were in the emergency response residency program, I'm guessing you specialized in emergency medicine. So how did you end up here?"

"I applied for a couple of positions that would have set me up for emergency rescue work." She swept her arm around the exam room. "I was seduced by the glamour of all this."

He looked around in appreciation, catching a glimpse of the ocean out the high transom window. "It's a nice gig."

"I've had it for a while. And it puts me in the position of being an excellent rock-wall climber. Ready to lose to a girl?"

"Winner gets a back rub!" Niko didn't know why he'd said that. When he saw the shocked look in Annalise's eyes, he almost awkwardly retracted the prize.

But then she blinked and said, "You're on," and he was glad after all. Regardless of who made it to the top first, he was a winner.

And that's exactly what he was feeling, clinging to the wall as he looked up and over at Annalise's ankle, up to her calf, to her thigh and her wonderfully perfect butt.

"Hey, Uncle Niko, are you going to let a girl beat you?"

Why had he thought he was going to do this without an audience of family members?

The harness straps cut him in places where he'd rather not feel that kind of pain. To get some relief, Niko found the next toehold and pushed upwards. Because he was taller than she was, now he was even with her.

She looked over and met his eyes. "You haven't won yet, Christopoulos."

His fingers touched a plastic thing bolted onto the fake rock and he dug the tips of his fingers around the edge to pull himself up.

At the same time Annalise reached for the same plastic thing, covering his hand with hers.

"Oh!" She jerked her hand back. So he wasn't the only one that felt the heat when they touched.

Her eyes went wide as she swung her arm wildly, off balance. Then down she went on her guide rope. She fell at least halfway before the rope latch stopped her.

By the surprised but happy grin on her face she was fine.

Niko thought for a moment. He could slide down now, too, but that would mean no winner. And no winner would mean no back rub.

He gave her a wry look. "I like my massages with warm oil," he said, just loud enough for her to hear.

"You haven't made it yet." She swung back to face the wall, scrambled for a plastic thing and began climbing much faster than she'd climbed earlier, making him realize she'd been holding back and pacing herself to him.

The competitive spirit kicked in full force. Niko felt around with his foot, reached outside his comfort zone and found the toehold he was looking for. His healing leg quivered from fatigue as he willed muscle and sinew to lift.

It was a stretch but he could almost reach the next—

And then he was falling, falling, with his stomach flipping until the harness jerked him to a halt.

"Ow." The harness did unkind things to him. Good thing he hadn't planned on having kids.

Annalise paused her climb to look down at him as he dangled a few feet from the floor.

"You okay?"

"Just singing soprano now."

She gave him a wink then covered the last four feet of wall as if she were a spider. With great aplomb she rang the bell at the top.

"For form's sake," she called down to him as she planted her feet and descended in graceful hops as if she'd been born on the mountains instead of on the flat, soggy soil of New Orleans.

Niko worked at setting his own feet and pushing against the wall, descending until he finally touched the deck.

Annalise was only two hops ahead of him. By the time he'd unbuckled his harness, she had hers off, too.

Before the Christopoulos clan could totally engulf them, he leaned over close. With any other woman, he would be suggesting his room, but that didn't feel right with Annalise. She needed more finesse. And he was pleased to be the one to give her what she needed. Instead, he asked, "Tonight on deck?"

She nodded, adding, "I like my oil to smell like lavender."

And then she was gone, wading through his brothers and nephews and sisters-in-law and nieces as they gathered around to snap pictures and pat him on the back and tease him as only a brother could about his loss to a girl.

As he anticipated the evening activities, he couldn't help but grin. This was no loss. In fact, it was a pretty big win in his book.

Annalise made her way up to the top deck with equal parts of anticipation and trepidation. Maybe she should have let him win? Then she would have been more in control, touching him instead of him touching her.

Stop it, Annalise. It's just a back rub in public.

She wore her swimsuit underneath her shirt and shorts.

She'd thought long and hard about what to wear, giving it much more consideration than the situation merited.

Should he really go through the trouble of finding lavender oil, the modest one-piece exposed her shoulders and back and was easily washable.

If this back-rub thing started to become more than fun and games… Every time she imagined how his hands would feel, her mind skittered away.

As she rounded the corner, she saw he was already there on his favorite chair.

"Hey." His voice reached that place deep within her that her mind had been avoiding thinking about.

She rubbed her hands down her arms to rub away the prickles that danced along her skin.

She swallowed. "Hey back at ya." It was throaty, husky and entirely not what she had intended.

He had her chair decked out with a couple of thick towels and a bottle of oil with an expensive label she recognized from the spa on deck three.

He stood and indicated the lounge chair. "Madam, your masseur awaits your pleasure." With an exaggerated leer he rubbed his hands together then cracked his knuckles.

Before she could lose her nerve, she whipped off her top. "Just remember, you're a cabana boy tonight, not a chiropractor."

She thought about lying prone, but that seemed too intimate so she straddled the lounger instead. "So I can watch the sunset," she explained. *So I won't feel so vulnerable,* she admitted to herself.

"Okay." He swung his leg over to straddle the lounger behind her, thigh to thigh. "I like exploring new positions."

Annalise was too busy reacting to the sizzle along her nerve endings to think of a retort. *I want this,* she reminded herself.

At the first touch of his palms on her shoulders, her apprehension made her shiver.

"Relax," he crooned into her ear, which made her feel anything but relaxed.

His hands, slick with fragrant oil, slid along her shoulders until this thumbs found the knot at the base of her neck. With the right amount of firmness and gentleness, he made circular motions to get her shoulders to loosen.

Annalise tried to concentrate on the sunset instead of the man who sat inches behind her.

His hands stilled. "Okay?"

She wanted to be okay. With every cell of her body she wanted to want this, to enjoy this, to want more.

"Annalise?" It was a question wrapped in a worry.

A noisy crowd of five people scrambled onto the deck she'd foolishly begun to think of as their private nirvana.

She had a sinking feeling at the relief she felt to be interrupted.

"I— We…" What should she say? Sorry? Maybe next time? I wish things could be different?

"Look at me!" One of the intruders stood at the rail and held out her arms. "It's like I'm flying."

The others gave it a try, cackling with laughter and spilling drinks in the process.

Niko dropped his hands and blew out a sigh as Annalise leaned forward to grab for her shirt.

She pulled it on, grimacing when the back stuck to the oil on her skin.

Niko sat motionless behind her. She couldn't even feel him breathe.

Without a glance she got up and headed downstairs, down to her cabin with no windows, down to her dark little hidey-hole that kept the world locked out—but kept her locked in.

For the first time in years she cried into her pillow. Long, ragged, ugly sobs for all that had happened to her and who she wanted to be.

With her throat too swollen and sore to cry anymore, she made up her mind. She would not be a victim for the rest of her life.

Many hours later, as she lay in bed, reliving the scene over and over again, she kept up her litany, praying it wasn't falling on deaf ears. *Please. Another chance.*

CHAPTER NINE

NOT ALL PRAYERS were answered.

Her patient load was extraordinarily heavy with barely breathing room. Between shifts, Annalise tried to casually run into Niko but could never find him. She even made a point to look for the Christopoulos clan at their family dinner, even though she dreaded facing the lot of them. All that family happiness only contrasted with her own sad situation, reminding her how different she and Niko were. But her need for Niko overcame her unease.

She found out from their waiter that her courage was for naught. Apparently, they'd all decided to forgo formal dining in favor of an early picnic by the wave pool.

That evening, she sat alone on the top deck, watching a sunset obscured by stormclouds. Today was only the beginning of much rougher seas ahead.

Was Niko avoiding her? Of course he was. She couldn't blame him. He must think her the most fickle female on the planet.

But the next evening found her on the top deck once again, hoping. Praying.

After all, what better did she have do to and where better did she have to go?

* * *

Niko called himself all kinds of a fool as he climbed the stairs to the top deck. Some things just weren't meant to be so why was he trying so hard?

Because he couldn't get her out of his head.

He clenched his fists, remembering the feel of her skin under his palms. The energy that radiated through her into him made him feel so buzzed, so alive.

But she could turn it off faster than any woman he'd ever met. Maybe it was his imagination, but when she looked at him he thought he saw a wistfulness in her eyes. And he wanted to—had to—give her whatever it was she wanted. *Because he wouldn't be complete until she was.*

Niko rubbed at his eyes, trying to rub away that fanciful thought. With any other woman he would have walked away by now. But there was something—something that had him coming back to her.

He didn't know if that something was in her or in him. All he knew was that he was climbing these stairs because he couldn't think of any other place he would be okay about being in right now.

"Hey," she offered cautiously.

"Hey back at you." He set down between them the two cups of hot tea he'd brought up.

"Busy morning?" he asked.

"And booked until late afternoon, too. They come in—"

"Waves." He finished her sentence for her. "It happens that way, doesn't it? Biorhythms or something."

"I always blame it on moon phases." The conversation felt stilted, but at least they were talking.

She watched him add three packets of sugar to his tea. "Not sweet enough?"

He held up the cup. "Bitter. It steeped too long. But enough sweetener can fix anything."

Could she be fixed with enough sweetener? She hoped so. "I heard the Christopoulos boys closed the bar down last night." She'd heard it from Brandy at yoga that morning. She'd also heard Niko had turned down quite a few offers of female company before moving to the sports section of the bar to watch football with his brothers instead.

"We won." He hoisted his cup. "Go, Tigers. But, then, I think I cheered them on one too many times last night."

She grinned at his hesitant hurrah. "You're on vacation. You're supposed to be having fun."

Vacation. The fun wouldn't last for ever. And hers might be over before it even began if she didn't take action.

"I've had fun. I've especially enjoyed the ship's medical services. The cruise line employs a very fine doctor."

"Compliment accepted." She sipped her tea.

"I have to admit, though, while I've enjoyed my time aboard ship, I'll be glad to make our first port. I didn't realize these transatlantic cruises had so much sea time up front." Niko took a sip of tea and winced. "Only two more days, right?"

"Yes. Two more days until our first port of call, Isle de Paridisio."

"You've been there?"

"A few times."

He took a sip of tea. "At least I've got it drinkable."

"You could have always got another cup."

"I like this one just fine." He stared out at the ocean. "I know my family is a handful, but we would love to have you join us."

This was the opportunity she'd asked for. The one she'd prayed for. A second chance for her. She needed this so much. Such a double-edged sword.

"I'm sorry. I can't." Turning him down was one of the hardest decisions she'd ever made.

The ill and injured of Isle de Paridisio needed her more.

The cruise line fully supported staff volunteering at the various ports of call, often matching private donations and giving away tons of food to the shelters.

Annalise always offered her assistance to any of the medical clinics along the cruise ship's routes. So many of these tropical paradises had beautiful tourist resorts as a thin veneer over the destitution of the rest of the island.

During their stopover at Isle de Paradisio, the youth directors would visit a local orphanage to donate books and clothing and the kitchen chefs would donate food. Other staff would help, too.

Annalise would head to the refugee camp. So many refugees traversed the Mediterranean, making it only this far, with nothing but their lives to call their own.

She had medicine to deliver, donated by New Orleans charities, and she would lend a hand where she could while she was on the island.

The beeper on her hip buzzed. She squinted in the failing light to read the code, seeing that it signaled an immediate emergency.

"I've got to go."

"Of course. Duty calls. Been there. Done that." His mouth twisted into a wry smile. "Maybe later."

"Wake up, sweetie. Wake up for Yiayia." Hearing those ominous words float down the hallway of the medical suite, Annalise's heart sank like a stone and she picked up her fast walk to an all-out run.

There was Sophie, lying limp in her Uncle Stephen's arms.

Her other uncle, all her aunts and her cousins surrounded her. If love could fix her, she would be the healthiest little girl on the planet. Sadly, juvenile diabetes had no cure.

Her clothes were urine-soaked. Her little arm felt cold and clammy and her breathing was so slow as to be barely detectable.

"Did she vomit?"

The whole family started talking at once, but the general gist was that they didn't think so.

Annalise spotted Marcus. "Get your Uncle Niko. He's on the upper foredeck."

She would need him to run interference with his family as she helped the little girl.

"Bring her in," she directed Stephen, and pointed to the nearest exam table. "Where's her meter?"

Phoebe pulled it from her tote along with the notebook.

Annalise pricked Sophie's finger and the meter evaluated Sophie's blood-sugar level.

It was dangerously high.

Sophie's endocrinologist had warned Annalise that trying to balance blood sugar was more of a gut feeling than an exact formula. Drawing on her healer's instinct, Annalise grabbed a vial of fast-acting insulin and checked the charts. She filled a syringe conservatively and gave Sophie the injection. Now the wait.

Meanwhile, she wrapped a rubber tourniquet around Sophie's arm, trying to find a vein so she could draw a blood sample from her dehydrated little body.

Vaguely, she was aware of Niko herding out his well-meaning family members.

"Find out what happened," Annalise threw over her shoulder as she prepared to prick the vein.

Sophie fluttered her eyelids and feebly tried to move her arm away. "No. Don't."

It was a sleepy response, but still a response.

"Be brave, little one," Annalise murmured. Niko's big, strong hand came into view, gently holding Sophie's tiny arm still.

Sophie opened her eyes. "Uncle Niko?"

"I'm here for you, Sophie."

"I'm taking this to the lab. Stay with her, okay?" Annalise put the sample in the analyzer then rejoined them while the machine did its work.

Sophie's spark of defiance had been short-lived as she now lay still once again.

"What's the scoop, Niko?"

"Her aunt had given her permission to get a banana from the fruit bar. Apparently, Sophie figured out how to use the ice-cream machine next to it by herself. A helpful passenger boosted her up when she was too short to reach it. That inspired a binge. One of her cousins tattled and they found Sophie hiding under a dining-room table with a tray full of cookies and donuts and brownies. By the time they found her, it was too late to prevent this."

She handed Niko a water bottle. "Get her to drink as much as you can."

Annalise checked her watch. Almost twenty minutes.

This time Sophie protested the meter prick, which was as good a sign of her recovery as the blood-sugar level, which was slowly edging downwards. She gave Sophie and Niko a reassuring smile. "We're getting there."

The lab analyzer beeped and Annalise read the results.

Showing them to Niko, she pointed to the potassium levels. "Looks like we're okay here."

"Thank God." Niko bent down and placed a kiss on his niece's forehead. "I should have been there. I promised my brother I would watch over her."

"No, Niko. Stop it." Annalise hesitated, then touched

his shoulder. "Your family is saying the same thing. But they're only human. Do you blame them?"

"Of course not."

"Then don't blame yourself either."

He scrubbed his hand through his hair. "Little kids should be able to sneak an occasional ice-cream cone. They shouldn't have to get injections three times a day the rest of their lives. It's not fair."

"You, of all people, with all you've seen, all you've done, know that life's not fair and bad things happen. We do what we can to pick up the pieces and go on."

Niko looked into her eyes, searching—for what? Sincerity? Truth? She had that in spades.

Acceptance that they had to make peace with the unfairness of the world? No. She couldn't give him that.

"You understand, don't you?" He ran his finger down her cheek. "You understand the frustration of not being able to make everything all right."

She nodded. "I understand."

On the table, Sophie stirred. Her face screwed up in a scowl. "I'm wet. Who threw water on me?" She sniffed. "Somebody peed on me."

Niko shook his head. "You had an uh-oh, little one."

"I'm not a baby. I don't wet my pants." But the embarrassment in her face showed she understood that she had. To cover up, she pawed at the bandage taped to her arm, where Annalise had taken her blood sample. "This hurts."

Niko and Annalise both grinned at her irritability, a good sign of her recovery.

Niko raised an eyebrow at her. "This happened because of the ice cream and the cookies and the donuts, Sophie." He said it gently but firmly.

Annalise knew him well enough to know it was breaking his heart to deliver this lesson.

"But Phillip got some."

"You have to be more careful than Phillip. He doesn't get sick when he eats too much sugary food but you do."

"It's not fair."

Niko shrugged, a studied, calculated movement by the stiffness of his shoulders. "But that's the way it is."

Annalise did one more blood-sugar test, pricking Sophie's finger with the meter before she could protest. As Sophie glared at her, Annalise read the meter and found the level becoming more satisfactory.

She documented everything in Sophie's notebook and then wrote down her instructions. "We should be seeing normal readings in about another hour and a half. If not, call me. I'd do a check every hour for the next three hours or so. Then every two hours so both of you can get some sleep. Watch for it to swing. Going too low can look like sleep and be a coma instead. But, then, you know that, right?"

"It's different when the patient is family." Niko rubbed his hand across his face. "I appreciate your instructions. They help me keep my head on straight."

Not having family to speak of, Annalise wouldn't know that. "Call me if the levels are out of this range."

She wrote down the numbers in the notebook. "I can't recommend sleeping in. Keep her on her morning schedule of insulin and breakfast. Maybe a nap during the day. Come and see me tomorrow afternoon and we'll do a blood test to double-check that potassium level. Until then, no bananas and no tomatoes." She made herself look into Sophie's sad, angry eyes. "And no ice cream or cookies or brownies."

As tears welled in Sophie's eyes, Annalise steeled herself to keep from joining her. Niko put his hand on Annalise's shoulder and squeezed, comforting her.

Life was unfair but she would do what she could when she could. Perhaps someday she would learn to be content with that.

Until then it was nice to know that someone in the world understood.

CHAPTER TEN

IT HAD BEEN a long, sleepless night.

After assuring himself that Sophie's blood sugar had stabilized and that she had more than enough family members surrounding her, Niko spent the morning drifting in and out of sleep on deck.

Helena kept him company. Or rather she used him to keep a would-be paparazzo at bay. Somehow the man had figured out who Helena's rich ex-husband was and had been trying to interview her about their divorce ever since last night.

Niko didn't mind. Helena was comfortable with long silences. When they did converse, she was intelligent and well read. Her ex was a fool and he told her so.

And when the waves picked up, the nosy man, along with most of the passengers, retired to the interior of the ship, where the rocking didn't seem as pronounced if they couldn't see the splash.

Which left Niko pleasantly alone except for Helena but left Annalise incredibly busy. Which might be just as well.

They had shared moments, special moments that came from deep inside him, when she'd asked about his work with Doctors Without Borders, when they'd talked of his childhood and how important his family was to him, when they'd taken care of Sophie.

But maybe those moments had only been precious to him. Looking back, Niko realized that Annalise had dodged any questions about her own life before she'd become a cruise ship doctor. Had he forgotten his own rule? The one about shipboard romances?

When this cruise was over, so would be their relationship. Serious relationship and career choice didn't fit in the same sentence for him. Yet Annalise was not a woman to be taken lightly.

"You are frowning, *filo mu*." Helena adjusted her hat brim against the sun.

Filo mu. My friend. He knew for certain Helena would be his friend only until they docked and he was fine with that. Many people passed in and out of his life. Many more would come and go in the future.

But the thought of never seeing Annalise again—that was giving him a bit of heartburn and he wasn't sure what medicine to take that would offer relief.

Annalise had checked on Sophie throughout the day as often as she could. The child was resilient, as most children were. It helped that her young cousins treated her no differently than each other, even though the older family members tended to hover into the late afternoon.

If only the other passengers were so hardy. The waves and swells had picked up that afternoon as a storm moved in. Annalise and her colleagues had been handing out motion-sickness patches as fast as they could complete the examination. The patches took a while to work, though. Too little too late for most of the passengers.

The invitation to the captain's table tonight didn't surprise her. With this weather, he had probably received several cancellations.

Annalise wondered who she would be dining with this

evening. In the mood she was in, anything was better than eating alone. She was having a hard time keeping her mind off Niko and that Greek woman he'd glued himself to all afternoon.

Jealousy, especially unjust jealousy, was an ugly lump in her stomach she had never expected to experience.

In front of the mirror, she braced to keep from swaying with the rocking of the ship as she tried to arrange her hair. Ponytails swirled into ballerina buns were so much easier than this layered cut.

After twenty minutes of failure, she gave up on pinning the loose strands that drifted down and let them wisp around her neckline *au naturel.* She swiped on another coat of lip gloss since she'd eaten off her earlier application while trying to style her hair.

Mentally she reviewed the cases that had come through her office that day. The Christopoulos family seemed to be of robust stock, Sophie's diabetes notwithstanding. Not one family member had come to see her for seasickness.

A man like Niko wouldn't let a little thing like ocean motion interfere with his game plan. When she'd taken a quick break on deck to breathe in the fresh air, she'd seen him cozied up to that Greek heiress from Texas looking like he was her personal bodyguard.

Or maybe she had that backwards. The woman certainly looked like she wanted to guard Niko's body, keeping it all for herself. And Niko didn't appear to mind at all.

Annalise thought they'd shared something special— something unique just between the two of them all those evenings on deck. Then, the second she'd had to work, Niko had found another woman to tell his soulful tales to. Would any woman do for him or had that big-bosomed Greek goddess been able to give him something more than she could?

In the mirror, her cheeks were blotchy red. Time to take a reality check. The truth was, even though Niko had trusted her with his most precious secrets, she'd backed away whenever he'd tried to understand her. She'd shut down, just like she always did whenever anyone wanted to get close.

Annalise added more powder to her flushed cheeks then adjusted her cleavage, plumping it up to make more of it. She might not have as much going for her as the goddess, but she would make the most of what she had. And if she happened to run into Niko tonight...

What? What would she do if she happened to run into him? Promise not to leave so abruptly when the talk turned personal? Promise...?

That was the kicker. She could make no promises.

To the empty room, she said, "Who said anything about promises, Annalise? What's wrong with a little fun? No commitment required?"

Saying it aloud sounded bold and brave and beautiful, all the things she wanted to be, right? She would *not* continue to be haunted by a past that had been out of her control. She *would* live a normal life, a life that included a healthy relationship with a man.

She would look for opportunities. If not with Niko then with someone else.

That affirmation felt flat and uneasy. Try as she may, Annalise couldn't envision anyone other than Niko in her bed.

She looked at herself in the full-length mirror, reached up to adjust her halter-topped emerald-green dress for better coverage, then made herself drop her hand.

She was no more exposed than any other woman. She would hold up her head and be proud.

* * *

Niko twitched in his tuxedo as he was seated next to Helena at the captain's table. He'd dressed up for Yiayia but there she sat, across the room at a table for two. He would have to check out the little old man she was leaning so close to as they laughed together.

But now he apparently had a rich Greek heiress from Texas to entertain. He'd bet his passport his grandmother had had something to do with it.

The captain made the introductions. Mr. and Mrs. Smith, who were celebrating Mrs. Smith's seventy-fifth birthday. The ship's entertainment director. And Helena Grubbs.

"It's Artino now," she gracefully corrected him. "I'm going back to my maiden name."

"Helena. Always a pleasure." Niko murmured the polite response but ignored the hopeful question in her eyes. No. He wasn't interested.

The twins were right. She was his type. So why wasn't he more enamored of her when her big brown eyes freely offered so many possibilities? Because there was no spark. Only one woman on this ship held his interest. If only the feeling had been mutual.

"We keep running into each other," she said. "Destiny?"

He'd thought she knew where he stood. He hadn't been sending mixed messages, had he? Looking her straight in the eye, he made his intentions as clear as he could. "Maybe you're the sister I never had."

By the dimming of her expression, he saw that she finally understood.

"How about being my friend? A girl can't have too many of them, can she?" Clearly disappointed, she turned away to focus her attention on Mr. Smith.

Niko glared at his grandmother, who had put them in

this awkward position, but she was too intent on the man across from her to notice.

"Is anything wrong, Mr. Christopoulos?" the captain asked.

"Nothing. I've just never seen my grandmother dine with another gentleman before."

"Don't worry. He's one of our regulars, a widower. He makes trips with us several times a year," the entertainment director reassured him.

Mrs. Smith nodded knowingly from across the table set for seven. "Running from loneliness." She patted the arm of a man seated next to her. "Thankfully, I ran into the arms of a man who promises me I'll never be lonely again."

Niko felt the emptiness of the unoccupied chair next to him.

Then he saw her heading toward them. Immediately, he stood. How could he not in the presence of such beauty?

The captain made the introductions. "Dr. Niko Christopoulos, I think you might know our ship's doctor, Annalise Walcott."

"I've had the pleasure." On impulse, he reached for her hand. Surprisingly, she held it out to him.

He carried it to his lips, breathing in the scent of lavender lotion and Annalise.

As he pulled out her chair for her he had the strongest urge to whisper in her ear and tell her how stunning she looked but he wasn't sure how she'd take it, especially in front of the captain.

"Sorry to be late," she apologized to the captain and the table at large.

"Nonsense. I know your afternoon has been busy." The captain introduced her to the couple across from her. Mr. Smith might be elderly, but he wasn't too old to appreciate Annalise's cleavage.

Niko wanted to cover her with his coat or maybe the tablecloth.

"What?" Under cover of passing the bread, Annalise asked him, "Is something wrong?"

Rein it in, Christopoulos, he told himself. "No. Nothing." He forced a smile that strained his jaw muscles.

She lifted her eyebrow, not taken in by his pseudo-civility. "Where is your family?"

"I had expected to meet them here." He nodded toward this grandmother's table. "Yiayia tells me that Stephen and Phoebe are dining alone in their room while the twins watch over the little ones in the family suite. My other brother and his wife had a casual supper earlier and are on the deck, counting stars."

The no longer lonely Mrs. Smith leaned toward them. "Such a romantic set of brothers. Does it run in the family?"

Niko could feel himself blushing under her scrutiny.

"Yes, it does." Annalise answered for him. "I've seen him in action."

"And perhaps benefitted from his seductive side?" Mrs. Smith teased.

Annalise busied herself with buttering her bread instead of answering.

Thankfully, the captain chose that moment to make a toast—most probably to save his ship's doctor from the awkward moment. "To those who love the sea!"

Obediently, they all raised their glasses. The waiters followed up the toast by presenting plates of steak and stuffed crab for each guest.

Helena, seated next to the captain, had become incredibly chatty with him, requiring no conversation from him. Besides, they'd run out of things to say early in the afternoon. Funny, thought Niko, how he and Annalise had never run out of things to talk about, even though they'd spent hours together over the last few days.

For some reason, though, the discussions they usually shared seem too intimate to have at a table full of people. Not the subject matter, although the kind of medical discussion they had would probably bore the rest of the guests, but the conversations themselves.

The entertainment director was gifted in small talk, keeping the Smiths amused with funny tales of previous cruises, while they countered with narratives of their grandchildren. All parties involved seemed to be pleased to have new ears to listen to their old stories.

Conversation flowed around Niko and Annalise, leaving them in a cocoon of silence.

Annalise seemed to be lost in thought and he respected her enough to leave her to it as she picked at her food. Was it too much to hope she felt the same way he did about their private conversations? Or had she just had a long day and needed some down time? Either way, he was content enough to sit beside her. He didn't need any other stimulation. Not that he would turn it down if more were offered.

As they were served dessert, the entertainment director interrupted their quiet contemplation.

"Annalise, I hate to ask it of you, but the weather forecast doesn't look great tomorrow. Calm seas but rain. We'll need to have more activities below deck. Do you think you could participate in a staff talent show?"

It was an activity Annalise had never minded helping with before. Dressing up in costume, being someone else for a little while, was always a kick. But sitting next to Niko, she felt shy.

Taking a big bite of strawberry pie bought her some time.

"What's your talent, dear?" Mrs. Smith asked.

"I sing a little."

"She's got a voice that will rival any rock goddess," the captain bragged. "We've got outstanding talent on this ship."

She wiped her mouth with her napkin. Hadn't she learned a long time ago that the best way to face her fear was head on? "I'll be glad to, Captain. Dr. Christopoulos used to sing in a rock band. Want to join in, Niko?"

Before he even thought about it, Niko agreed. What was it about Annalise that called forth in him the need to make her smile at him?

Not only did she smile with those luscious lips, she smiled with her eyes. Sparkling in the way they were, those green eyes made him feel like he'd just fulfilled her greatest fantasy. Or maybe that's what he read in them because that's what he wanted to see.

Because as soon as the spark had come, it went out, leaving her eyes smoky and obscure.

And leaving Niko feeling chilled. What was it about this woman who blew hot and cold? Was it him?

He turned to Helena on his other side and flashed her a questioning smile. She flashed back, reassuring him she was okay—then put her hand on his shoulder.

"I think I'll skip dessert. It's not good to rumba on a full stomach and the captain has promised me he's quite an enthusiastic dancer."

The captain pushed back his chair, almost knocking it over. "Ladies. Gentlemen. It was a pleasure."

He pulled out Helena's chair. "Madam."

"It's mademoiselle." She took his hand and they were gone.

What would Annalise feel like in his arms? Niko wondered. "Do you rumba?"

"No. But thank you." She gave him a sideways glance. "Do you?"

He took a breath. "I'm not too bad at it. I could teach you. Or if you prefer ballroom dancing, isn't there a big band playing somewhere?"

Mrs. Smith nodded. "Yes, on the aft deck."

Annalise gave him a probing look. "You ballroom dance?"

"One of my part-time jobs during high school and college. Classes always have more women than men. One of my grandmother's friends owned a dance studio. She hired two of us. Quite coincidentally, the other guy became a doctor, too."

By her eyes, he could tell she'd gone somewhere else in her head again. Curiosity burned within him. This woman intrigued him like no other. Such complex intricacy. So many levels.

"I've always wanted to learn to waltz."

Niko had the strongest urge to hold her in his arms right then and there. But he reached deep and found the gentleman his grandmother had instilled in him. "Dessert first?"

She cast her eyes down. "If you want."

He wanted. But not food. "You're all the dessert I need."

There it was again. The sparkle as Annalise looked around the table at the other guests. "If you'll excuse us."

Niko tried to read the message behind the look the entertainment director gave him. He wasn't sure what exactly the man was trying to say but he had a feeling it had something to do with being very protective of his ship's doctor.

The director needn't worry. Niko would cut off his right hand before he harmed Annalise. He'd never felt like that with any other woman. Why did he feel that way now?

He had to remember that in a few short days anything between them would have to be over.

"Ready?" Annalise looked expectantly at him.

Ready? He wasn't quite sure what he was ready for. He only knew that if she was involved then yes. He was ready for anything.

CHAPTER ELEVEN

"LOOK UP," NIKO whispered in her ear.

Annalise looked up, away from her feet, to drown in those tiger eyes. She missed a step.

"Sorry."

"Don't be sorry. Everybody has to learn." As his breath warmed her ear, raising shivers along her nape, his big hand guided her in the right direction.

The deck was dark enough that the few couples on the makeshift dance floor were nothing but faceless shadows. The band was good—as was all the entertainment the cruise line provided.

The vastness of the night sky fell into the ocean, wrapping them in velvet darkness. Stars came and went overhead as clouds floated by. The moon was a gray crescent sliver overhead. The sea breeze was just enough to make Niko's body next to hers pleasurably warm.

She was acutely aware of his hand on her bare back as the pressure of his palm suggested a backward step.

"One, two, three," he counted for her. "Turn, two, three."

His words were like a litany that went beyond hearing, moving her body beyond her conscious control.

She felt like quicksilver, an extension of the music, part of the night.

"Exquisite," he murmured.

Annalise knew he wasn't talking about her waltz.

She was floating, floating with no concept of space and time. All she knew was Niko's body next to hers, floating, floating in perfect rhythm.

A lovely surreal mist surrounded her reality as she let her essence free.

As the ocean's waves and swells picked up, Niko held her closer, making their steps smaller and smaller until they were barely swaying.

"Look up," he murmured.

She did.

His mouth covered hers and she parted her lips, tasting, inhaling the scent of him, moving closer at the pressure of his hand on her back. She could read it through the energy he surrounded her with. He needed her.

She understood. She needed him. She answered his need, giving, taking, asking, demanding until she lost herself in his kiss.

Her world spun around her as she held onto Niko, secure in his steadiness. Right now, at this moment, he was the center of her universe, directing the moon and the stars. Directing each beat of her heart.

Annalise gasped, realizing she'd forgotten to breathe, realizing the music was now only in her head.

His voice rumbled through her. "Want to continue this in my suite?"

She blinked as if coming out from under hypnosis. The part of her that had ceased to think and could only feel said, "Yes." She sounded dreamy, drugged.

Then panic began to thin out the haze of her fantasy world. Old panic that should have long since been put to bed.

No. She wouldn't let that lovely floating feeling go that easily.

"Yes," she said again, wincing at the way her voice quivered, regretting that she was now anticipating the clamminess that would soon be rising up in her, the way it always did, wishing away a past that kept following her long after her assailant had been locked away.

No, she would not be a prisoner to another man's crime.

Niko placed the gentlest of kisses along her nape. One long finger traced down her spine and his hand splayed across her bare back, supporting her as she leaned away enough to look into his face.

Deliberately, she met his eyes. "Yes."

She sounded firm this time, sure of herself, bold and daring.

Intense desire swept through Niko, making his palms sweat and his heart race. Triumph!

He'd felt her hesitate. Then he'd poured on the charm, following his gut instincts to know what she needed from him, and it had worked.

Annalise. He would soon be running his hands over her, tasting her, feeling her respond—feeling himself respond.

And that's where the apprehension surfaced. Apprehension that this would mean more to her than...

No. That this would mean more to *him* than he was prepared for it to mean.

Logically, he knew he was being unreasonable. They had only met a handful of days ago under circumstances that were totally out of the norm for him. Circumstances that weren't made for anything deep or serious.

Hell, *he* wasn't made for anything deep or serious, no matter what the circumstances.

This was not a time for a game of cat and mouse with

a mouse who didn't understand he would be letting her loose as soon as he'd caught her.

That he'd sensed her pulling away was solid proof that this shouldn't be happening like this. Not without the full truth revealed between them.

He was a fool for asking her to join him in his suite. He was a fool for continuing to hold her in his arms when he should be putting distance between them.

Annalise did it for him. Putting her hands on his chest, she pushed him away. "What? I wasn't supposed to agree?"

Niko looked up at the night sky that only seconds before had been comforting in its cocooning darkness.

Now the vastness looked daunting, imposing and desolate.

He looked into her eyes, wanting her to see what he didn't know how to say. "I wasn't supposed to ask."

She darted a quick glance at his ring finger, then back up to his face. "You're not married, are you?"

"No." A raw, self-deprecating laugh worked its way through his chest. "No, I'm not the marrying kind."

"I don't understand." Tears welled, although Niko knew she was trying to hold them back. She was wounded, rejected, hurt. Her pain caused him misery.

"You're not the kind of woman to love and leave. You deserve someone who will stay."

Fire erased the tears in her eyes. "Who are you to say what kind of woman I am?"

"I'm the man who desires you with a want greater than any need I've ever felt before. But I can't take the guilt of feeling I might be coercing you into something you'd regret tomorrow morning."

"Coerce? As in force?" She gave him a wry smile. "Seduce maybe, but not coerce."

"Seduce then." He rubbed his hand through his hair. "I'm sorr—"

She held a finger up to his lips, not touching him by scant millimeters. "No. Don't say it."

He breathed in her lavender lotion, clenching his fists to keep from pulling her to him and kissing her until the shreds of his own good sense floated away on an ocean of pheromones.

Not trusting himself to speak, he gave her a parting nod and turned away.

But she caught his arm. Her hand on his sleeve held him still better than any pair of handcuffs ever made.

"What would it take—?" She stopped. Licked her lips and swallowed, then continued. "What would it take to convince you that a shipboard romance would be enough for me?"

"In the state I'm in right now? Not much." His mouth quirked up as he said it. Humor instead of hurt. It was what he did.

But then he pressed his lips together tightly and thought, respecting that she'd asked a serious question. "Come to me. No stars. No wine. No music. No romance." Niko knew his conditions would drive her away. She was too practical, too guarded, too astute to fall for a guy like him. "Come to me and tell me you want me. Then I'll know."

He turned his back on her and walked away.

With each step he took away from her, Niko felt he was going in the wrong direction. If he'd known it would be this hard, he would have never set foot on this ship.

Perspective, Christopoulos, he reminded himself. This trip was a slice of fantasy out of real time. Annalise would make a nice memory, maybe even a what-if memory. But she could never be his reality. He knew what was important to him and it couldn't include a cruise-ship doctor he would never see again once he disembarked.

What would it feel like when he walked away for good?

Reality made his head ache.

With a sigh Niko headed towards the neon-lit bar with music loud enough to drive throbbing thoughts from his mind.

Through sheer willpower, he kept putting one foot in front of the other until he ended up in a bar so overly loud, so neon flashy and so anonymous he could finally drop the mask of firm decision he'd donned to keep her safe—to keep them both safe—from foolish passion.

Instead, he dropped his head into his hands, not even looking up when he ordered a double Scotch, neat.

CHAPTER TWELVE

ANNALISE SWAM LAPS in the empty adults-only pool until Brandy, who was working the poolside bar, insisted she would grow a mermaid's tail if she didn't come out soon.

Reluctantly, she admitted that going back and forth without getting anywhere was not making progress, only making her exhausted.

How dared he? She scrubbed the excess water from her body then threw the towel into the poolside bin.

How dared he see through her bravado to the insecurities lying underneath?

Her legs quivered as she made her way back to her cabin. But her physical exhaustion did nothing to diminish her mental anguish or her sexual frustration.

Her body burned for Niko. For that nebulous release she'd heard about, read about, but had never experienced.

Finally, hours after she had pushed her alarm clock to the floor to hide the mocking numbers, she fell asleep.

Some time during the night she'd had fevered dreams that had left her soaked in sweat. When had that happened? When she had felt like her body was on fire?

She stripped off the oversized T-shirt and gym shorts she usually slept in, avoiding the mirror as she headed for the shower. But then she stopped herself as she realized her nudity, even in the privacy of her own cabin, made her feel uncomfortable.

Annalise gave herself a stern mental shake. If she wasn't comfortable with her own naked body, how could she be okay with Niko's?

Experimentally, shyly, she ran her hands down her curves.

Unknowingly, he'd dared her to explore her own femininity, to explore her own sexuality, to explore him.

And she *would* explore him, every nook and cranny.

Annalise realized she was standing in front of the mirror, her hands propped on her hips. After too many years of glancing away, she took a good, long look.

"Annalise Walcott, you are a fine-looking woman. A strong woman. A sexy woman—more than sexy enough for Niko Christopoulos. Now, prove it to yourself."

Her beeper startled her with a beep as it displayed the texted reminder, 'Talent show practice in thirty minutes.'

She had forgotten. Niko and she were to perform in tonight's talent show.

Annalise grinned. She knew exactly what song they would sing together.

Niko's late night and the predicted rain splattering on his cabin window lulled him into sleeping late. He awoke with a start, panic over needing to check Sophie's blood-sugar level sending his adrenal glands going into overdrive until he discovered that Phoebe had already taken care of the whole routine.

He was definitely off balance.

Headachy from his overindulgences at the neon bar, Niko looked over the lyrics he'd just been handed as he arrived at the theater two hours late to practice for the talent show.

You ain't no saint, I ain't your angel.

He knew the song. The melody was simple, the chords basic. Still, it had lots of room for drama. It was a good choice for a quick performance.

Apparently, Annalise had already come and gone. He would practice with a recording and hope they hit their cues right tonight. Thankfully, this selection had a lot of wiggle room to improvise and recover from mistakes.

After an hour and a half of getting comfortable with the finger progressions on his borrowed guitar and singing his part with a throat that needed a spoonful of honey to ease last night's excesses, he decided to spend a quiet couple of hours in the ship's library, reading and napping.

Before he could reach the literary refuge, his twin nephews found him.

Marcus gave him a speculative stare. "Uncle Niko, we were going to rent a couple of video games to play in the video-game room but the desk person said it wasn't authorized. They said we had to have your permission. What's the deal with that?"

"I'll take care of it."

"Or we could just ask Dad for his credit card."

That's all Niko needed this morning, to have to deal with his sweepstakes deception being discovered.

"Where's your dad?"

"He and Mom are hanging out in the adults-only pool area. Something about a hot tub and remembering their youth." Marcus shuddered. "I don't want to think about it."

"And everyone else?"

"Yiayia has the little kids in the kiddie theater, watching a movie. I think Uncle Theo and Aunt Chloe were going back to bed after breakfast." Marcus shrugged. "That's all I know."

"Which game did you want to rent?"

They told him and he promised to join them in the games room as soon as he had it arranged. Maybe blasting a few brain-sucking aliens and saving the planet was what he needed to clear his head.

Distracting himself in the games room was a good plan. It might have even worked if Annalise hadn't had the same idea.

Who would have known Dr. Annalise Walcott had a yen to be a kickboxer?

She barely gave him a nod as she kicked and punched, making the video version of herself teach a harsh lesson to the thugs and muggers of the unreal gamester underworld.

He wished he could be so focused as alien after alien blasted his video avatar into smithereens. Instead, he couldn't take his attention from Annalise, clad in a sports bra and bicycle shorts, virtually fighting her way through the underbelly of society.

To his nephews' exasperation, he wasn't nearly as successful in demolishing the invading aliens as Annalise was in dispatching society's scumbags. But the activity did make the time go quicker.

By mid-afternoon he realized he hadn't eaten all day. It was a good, if not quite valid excuse for his irritability. In the dining room he scarfed down a quick sandwich and a fruit plate then hurried off to costuming, hoping Annalise hadn't picked something totally ludicrous for him to wear.

A large crowd had been driven into the theater by the rain that was continuing to fall throughout the late afternoon. They had already sat through a half dozen acts of dubious quality and were getting restless.

In her white choir robe and feathery angel wings Annalise waited for her cue. Despite her nerves, she was ready to sing the opening bars.

While she could never have stood in front of a room full of people to deliver a speech, this was different. She was singing someone else's words, being someone else, being someone bold and brave and beautiful.

Niko would be entering from the opposite side of the stage. She could hardly wait to see how he carried off the costume she'd arranged for him—or to see his reaction to hers.

When she whipped off her angelic robe, she would be revealing a side of herself no one had ever seen. That made her extremely apprehensive. But she was no longer going to let fear stop her from going after the life she wanted.

And that life was quite a bit different than the one she'd been living. This life, this cruise-ship venue, had nurtured her when she'd needed it most but now she had grown past that need.

Doctors Without Borders. She'd been thinking about it for quite a while. She'd been delivering donated medicines and doing volunteer work for the poor of the islands whenever the ship dropped anchor ever since she'd started working for the cruise line, a practice she'd learned from her predecessor. The charity work had been the most rewarding part of her trips. After hearing the passion in Niko's voice when he'd talked about it, she was ready to make it her full-time work.

Since she would be leaving the ship at the end of this run, she would leave them with something to remember her by.

As the captain's personal stewards finished up their shaky barbershop quartet to politely enthusiastic applause, Annalise let out a sigh of relief. They wouldn't be a hard act to follow.

The curtain fell and the production manager gave her a nod along with a thumbs-up.

She hurried out to take her place next to the Styrofoam column that temporarily hid Niko's borrowed guitar. For some reason she'd never doubted he'd be up to the task of pulling off this act. He was the kind of man who inspired confidence.

As the curtain rose, her confidence fell. All those people clapping, waiting, listening for her.

With the floodlights in her eyes, she couldn't make out details, but she saw a movement at the edge of the stage. Niko.

She was not alone in this.

He strode out, tight jeans, black T-shirt and black leather jacket. His tiger eyes gleamed as he ignored the crowd and gave her his full attention.

He stood so close her wings brushed his midnight hair.

"Ready?" He grabbed his microphone from the stand.

She left hers in the stand, clasping her hands angelically instead. "Ready."

As the pianist played the intro lines, Annalise took a deep breath, held it, then belted out the notes right on key.

You say someday the right man will come along,
The man who will see my angel wings and hear my
angel song.
But I say to you, you're wrong.
Because that day has already come and gone.
And it looks like you're here to stay.

He leaned in close, so close she see the sparks in his eyes as he glanced her way then focused on the audience.

I may be here today, but I won't stay.
I'm the kind of man that plays then goes away.
You deserve a man who will never stray.

Niko grabbed the guitar and did a screaming instrumental of angry chords before cueing back to the lyrics.

I've got a wandering soul
And I'm not made to grow old
In one place, even if that place is heaven.

This was the moment Annalise had been planning for. As Niko performed the next guitar break, she unzipped the heavy, shapeless robe and wings and let them fall to the floor, stretching her arms wide to revel in the form and freedom of the tiny, shiny gold spandex dress.

Vaguely, Annalise heard the roar of the onlookers, but nothing spoke as loudly to her as the look in Niko's eyes.

If his tiger eyes were anything to go by, he was definitely feeling carnivorous.

She struck a pose, leaning in close and daring to look straight into those mesmerizing eyes as a dangerous thrill energized her like a bolt of lightning.

Plucking her microphone from the stand, she sang.

You ain't no saint. I ain't your angel.
I'm the woman who can match you, play for play.
Day by day.

She grinned, growling the words out.

And night by night.

Niko missed a beat as he swallowed. Then caught up with her.

Night by night
Day by day

You're the woman who can match me
Play by play.
And I'm the man that can match you, too.
Because I love you.

Together they sang,

Because I love you.

Annalise didn't even realize the curtain had fallen until it started to open again. From the dazed look on Niko's face he hadn't realized it either.

Amazingly, he looked away first, a bashful casting down of his eyes.

"Good job," she whispered as they took their bows.

He nodded, still not looking at her. "And you."

She grabbed his hand and almost dropped it again as heat travelled up her arm and throughout her body. Remembering who she wanted to be, she clasped it tighter as they took another bow and then she led him offstage.

Once alone backstage, he turned to her, searching her face. "Wow."

"Wow back at you."

And then the Christopoulos family interrupted, whooping and laughing and complimenting them.

How could she resent the intrusion when it was all too easy to breathe in the love, the cherishing and solidarity they gave Niko and, by extension, her, too?

What would it be like to be part of a family like this?

But they would expect more than she could give.

Niko lifted her chin. "What's wrong?"

"I need to change before these shoes start to pinch."

He eyed the high-heeled sexy shoes that made her legs look miles long. "That's a shame."

"Life's not fair." She shrugged, trying to smile through the truth. But the twisted feel of her lips told her she had failed.

When one of the twins said he was hungry, Annalise checked the clock. The show had run overtime and it was time for supper. Niko's brother Stephen nodded toward Sophie and said, "My turn," as the family gravitated toward the door.

Annalise knew that supper would be filled with joyous noise, kudos for Niko and endless toasts offered with unconditional love.

Niko called back to them, "Don't wait for me."

Annalise would not be the one to keep him from his family. "No, Niko. Go with them. I may join you later."

Sophie crossed her arms and planted her feet. "I want Uncle Niko to give me my shot. You hurt, Uncle Stephen."

Stephen sent Niko an apologetic look. "Maybe you can show me again."

Niko looked at Annalise as if he were seeking her permission. She nodded, releasing him.

"Sure, brother." He reached down and took Sophie's hand. "Let's show Uncle Stephen how brave girls do this, okay?"

Annalise watched the Christopoulos family troop out, looking and sounding so much like each other that anyone would know they were family. What would it be like to look into a child's face and see your own reflected there?

She could usually stave off her utter aloneness, the lack of a legacy to prove she'd left her mark on the world.

But today her future was harder to accept. One hand drifted to her damaged womb, which could never carry a child, and the other hand covered her damaged heart, which could never carry the love of a man.

She waited for the anger to well up within her, to burn

through the melancholy that always followed her reminder of reality. Waited to feel the remembered fear when her mother's boyfriend had loomed over her and she had shut her eyes tight no matter how loudly he'd shouted at her to open them.

She took a breath. Anger and fear and despair were ugly scars she didn't have to wear.

Instead, she thought about Niko. About being held in his arms as they swayed to the music under the stars. About feeling admired and respected whenever he looked at her. About how she would let her passion build and grow when they made love.

And they would make love.

She hung up the leather jacket Niko had worn. It was the only thing he'd needed from the costume wardrobe. The rest of the outfit had been all his.

With measured steps she trod onto the curtained stage.

Carefully, in the tight dress and high heels that she was so unaccustomed to, she stooped to pick up the heavy robe and angel wings from where they had fallen.

She'd tried to have a relationship before with her medical school study partner. They had become great platonic friends, with an easy way between them. When she'd asked, pleaded, for his help, he had agreed.

They'd both tried to make it work—she'd wanted it to work so badly. She'd wanted to prove to herself that her rapist wouldn't win in the end. He'd been kind, gentle and mercifully quick.

But all she'd managed had been distant numbness. Would it be the same with Niko? Would that fire in his touch, that tingling warmth that penetrated her thickest barriers, flame out when it reached her icy core?

Or would he be the one to unthaw her, heart and soul? She could walk away now. Never know. Never fail. Always think it might have worked out, while sanctimoniously congratulating herself on following the rules.

No shipboard romance. No knowing to what heights and depths this chemistry between them could take her. No having to say goodbye when this trip came to its end.

No guts, no glory.

Now was the time. Niko was the man. Tonight she would learn what it was to glory in being a woman, body and soul.

CHAPTER THIRTEEN

NIKO STOOD ON his veranda, his hands gripping the rail as he looked out onto the starlit ocean going past. He'd thought about spending another evening at the bar but muddling his thinking by drinking too many glasses of forgetful juice wouldn't solve his problem. Neither would going up to the top deck.

Would she come to him? So much depended on it.

He'd had it all mapped out, even to the point of accepting that his family wouldn't be happy with his decisions. He'd been so sure of what he wanted. But now…

Now he wanted more than he could have.

What if he loved her?

He shook his head. There was no *what-if.*

He couldn't imagine getting off this ship and never seeing her again.

What was he going to do?

Annalise knocked. Once. Sharply. Then turned away to flee back to the safety of her own berth.

The door opened and Niko reached out, catching her hand and pulling her to him. He bent his lips to her ear. "Annalise. You came." He breathed it like she was an answer to his prayers.

She inhaled his scent, wanting to hold it deep within her forever.

"About your rules, Niko. No stars. No wine. No music. No romance." She paused. "I've decided you don't get to make all the rules."

She set an ice-filled wine bucket on the counter then went to the wall of windows, looking out at the night sky where the last of the rainclouds were skittering away, exposing a handful of twinkling stars. "What's sex without romance?"

As he walked up behind her, she willed herself to stay relaxed.

Still, he noticed. "Problem?"

What should she tell him? "I don't usually…"

He moved a footstep away. "This isn't your first time, is it?"

Her laugh was much too harsh, much too revealing. "My previous experiences haven't been that great."

"Want to tell me about it?"

"Maybe another time." She closed her eyes. "Tonight I want something more than talk."

"Are you sure you want to do this?" He took another step away. "With me?"

"Yes." She didn't dare turn around, afraid she might show him something with her eyes that she would rather keep to herself.

He was silent for so long that a dozen stars had time to make their appearance. Annalise raised her palm to the glass, anchoring herself.

Ever so lightly, he rested his fingers on the nape of her neck.

She couldn't stop her instinct to hunch her shoulders and shrink away.

He dropped his hand.

"I can't—we can't do this with you being frightened." He backed away, sitting on the bed. "Annalise, you need to tell me what is scaring you."

For the longest time Annalise stood as still as a statue, staring out at the stars. Finally, she sighed deeply, looked at him, avoiding his eyes, then looked at the door.

Just when Niko thought she would go, she sat down next to him, her thigh touching his.

In the dark, in the silence, Annalise said, "I was sixteen when I was raped by my mother's boyfriend. I was afraid to tell her. Afraid she'd say it was my fault. Afraid she'd kick me out of our apartment. That happened to a girl who lived down the hall from us. She didn't even make it a week on the streets before they found her body. I figured one rape was better than a gang rape."

Niko felt such rage race through him he had to use all his concentration to keep his hand from squeezing hers.

"He got me pregnant. I tried to hide it from her but she figured it out when I was sick every morning for two weeks. She took me to this place above a bar and a stinky, greasy woman…she did things to me and I bled."

Bile rose in Niko's throat. He couldn't imagine what the sixteen-year-old Annalise had overcome. Few people, especially teens, would have had the mental strength. She had not only survived but thrived.

"She said the bleeding would stop after a while, but it didn't. Finally, my mother drove me to the hospital and dropped me off at the emergency-room door. She didn't come back for me."

Annalise was squeezing his hand so tightly his fingers tingled.

Niko had to swallow hard to ask, "Afterwards, where did you go?"

"At first I was in a home for wayward teens, repeat offenders in trouble with the law—not that I was one. It was the only place they had to put me." Her laugh was like sandpaper. "And I'd thought I was pretty tough."

"Then what happened?"

"The social worker from the hospital kept looking for a better place for me. She finally got a church-sponsored boarding school with an attached private high school to take me in. I was one of their charity cases. It wasn't bad and the education I received was outstanding. I was able to earn scholarships that paid for a lot of my college and medical-school expenses."

"Annalise, I don't know what to say." Niko wanted to hold her and protect her from all the bad things in life. But he was too late.

She brushed the tears from his face that he hadn't realized he'd shed.

"Hold me, Niko. Keep me safe tonight."

Could he do this?

His throat closed so that he could only nod. For the first time in his life he understood the healing power of being there. A gentle touch was all the action desired or required.

Annalise curled up in his bed and he curled up around her, cocooning her.

And they slept.

In the morning, she was gone.

Annalise hurried down the gangway, pulling her cart of donated medicines behind her. The island's refugee camp would be anxiously awaiting her delivery of supplies as well as her skills as a physician. Her charity work was one of the reasons she loved her job so much.

That's why, when she'd dropped her application for Doctors Without Borders in the outgoing mail packet early that morning, she'd been certain she'd made the right career-change decision.

She hurried, very aware that the camp would have been expecting her much earlier.

They'd docked sometime during the night and she'd planned to be off the ship at daybreak, but she'd overslept. She was certain she'd never slept so deeply in her life as when she'd been wrapped in Niko's arms.

If only every night's sleep could be as restful.

A wave of sadness threatened to swamp her but Annalise refused to dwell on what couldn't be.

A shipboard relationship, by its nature, was impermanent. With Niko, there were no expectations and no disappointments. She would just be sure to make the most of the little time they had left together.

Niko Christopoulos would always have a special place in her healing heart. Because of him there was a profound difference very deep down within her, like cleansing light had been shone into the dark corners of her psyche.

But it was better that way. Even if Niko was an adventurer now, she'd seen how much he loved his nieces and nephews and how much he admired his sisters-in-law. He would want a family of his own someday. And that was something she could never give him. The thought of being separated from him made her feet feel heavy.

"Annalise, wait up." Niko's deep voice startled her from her thoughts.

She slowed her pace and looked behind her to see him trotting toward her, concern on his face.

"Niko, what's wrong?"

"What's wrong?" He rubbed his hand across his eyes. "I woke up and found you gone. That's what's wrong."

She grinned, both relieved and flattered. "Not everyone is on vacation, Niko Christopoulos."

"You're working?"

"Volunteer work. This island has several refugee camps. People try to navigate the Mediterranean Sea and this is as far as they get sometimes. Different charity organizations have set up clinics. I do what I can when we come through this way." She started pulling the cart toward shore again, carefully concentrating to keep it from rolling out of control.

"I'll go with you."

"What about your family?"

"We've all had quite a bit of togetherness lately. I think we're ready to have some apart time." He commandeered the cart from her, easily keeping the pace steady.

"But you'll miss the tourist attractions."

"What I miss is practicing medicine. I'm not made to be idle this long."

"I understand. The few times I've tried to give myself a break from seeing patients between cruises, I've wound up being irritated with the world and itching to go back to my work. Being a doctor isn't just what I do, it's who I am."

Niko flashed her a brilliant smile. "You do understand."

"This one is not as advanced as some of the other free clinics on the Caribbean islands where we call," she warned him. "But working with Doctors Without Borders, you're used to a lot worse conditions, I'll bet."

"I've seen some primitive environments," he agreed.

Annalise thought about mentioning her recent decision and asking if he would mind if she requested to be assigned with him but now she was thinking that might be a bit presumptuous. If Niko could get tired of his awesome family, what would he think of being saddled with her, a virtual stranger?

Only Niko didn't feel like a stranger. He felt like someone she'd been waiting to meet her whole life.

Which meant that if they were assigned together, the arrangement could get complicated.

She should probably let fate take care of that little issue.

As Niko dragged the cart through the streets, past the brightly colored tourist shops and the clapboard houses with their white-picket-fenced yards, he asked, "What am I hauling?"

"Supplies. Donations from different charity groups. We have a nice collection of used eyeglasses. So many children and adults can't learn to read because they don't see well enough to make out the letters. The glasses are always a welcome donation."

Niko nodded. "Glasses are one of the sought-out donations on missions I've been a part of, too."

They weaved in and out of streets and alleys. The paint on the buildings became older and sparser until there were no buildings at all. A tent city sat on a span of vacant lots in front of them. Little more than a few strands of sparse weedy grass separated the tarps and quilts and stitched-together rags from each other.

For some, the hodgepodge temporary living quarters didn't appear to be so temporary but rather looked like journey's end. People of all ages sat outside their tents or walked aimlessly from place to place.

Annalise led the way toward the center of the encampment, where four sturdy canvas tents stood with their side walls rolled up.

"That one." She pointed to the tent on the far left.

And that's when they got busy. For the rest of the day, far into the late afternoon, Annalise and Niko saw patient after patient.

As Niko carefully lanced an eardrum, fluid-filled almost to bursting, on a toddler, Annalise said her good-byes to the staff. Most she had never met before as they changed so frequently. But a few she had known for quite a while. She explained that she wouldn't be back, but her new physician's assistant would come next trip if possible.

The staff took her departure in their stride. They had never known consistency. They just did the best they could with what they had.

As soon as Niko was done, she pointed to her watch. "We've got to get back to the ship. It's getting dark."

They walked in silence for the most part. Leaving behind such squalor for the luxury of the cruise liner, it always took Annalise a moment to adjust.

At the bottom of the gangway, Niko stopped.

"You were great today."

"You, too."

"Especially with the children. You'll make a great mother, Annalise."

No. She wouldn't. She couldn't. The botched abortion had taken away any possibility of her bearing children. "Not in the plan." It came out flippantly to hide her sorrow.

Niko gave her a long look. "I owe you an apology. I underestimated you."

"Most people do." Annalise shrugged it off then blatantly inspected Niko. "Good looks, expensive watch, attitude of nonchalance. I'll bet most people underestimate you, too."

"A man can be more than one thing."

"Like a good lover as well as a good doctor?"

He stopped walking. "What are you saying, Annalise?"

"I'd like to try it again." She licked her bottom lip. "If you're willing."

"With you, I'm always willing." The words were right but the tone was hesitant.

She put her hand on his arm. "Niko, please. Don't. Don't treat me like I'm fragile. I don't break."

"Tell me what you want, Annalise."

"I want to feel like a real woman, a woman who can make a man's blood run hot. I want you to make love to me because you think I'm sexy, not because you feel sorry for me."

"You trust me, don't you, Annalise?"

"I do trust you, Niko."

"Then believe me when I say I don't do pity sex."

"I'm trying."

"What can I do to prove it to you?"

"Make love to me like I was any other woman."

"Oh, no, Annalise. I can't do that. You're not any other woman."

"Because I'm different."

"Because you're special."

Outside his cabin door, he asked her once more. "Are you sure?"

"Yes, Niko, I want to make love to you more than I've ever wanted anything in my whole life."

He opened the door for her and followed her in.

Very quietly, he whispered in her ear, "Let's make this the first-time experience it should have been."

Annalise swallowed past the lump in her throat. "I would like that."

Slowly, gently, he reached up and touched her hair. She breathed in the scent of him as he ran his fingertips across her shoulders. Then he glided his fingers along the edge of her bra, barely brushing the side of her breast.

"Yes?" he asked, his voice throaty, needy, full of want for her.

"Yes." She turned in his arms, putting them chest to chest.

His hand traced her back through her thin T-shirt, leaving a trail of flame sizzling down her spine.

She lifted her mouth, needing to taste him. He met her lips with his own, teasing her mouth until she opened for him. Her knees weakened as the world around her began to blur, soft and hazy and out of focus. Niko was all that mattered.

His big hands brushed over her shoulders and down her arms, capturing her. A distant part of her mind waited for the flinch that would bring disappointment to his eyes. That's when the numbness would begin.

But she didn't flinch, didn't step back, didn't squeeze her eyes closed. Instead, her body leaned in as her instincts trusted Niko to bear her weight.

He carried her to the bed, gracefully sitting her in his lap as he leaned against the headboard.

"Niko." She said his name, soft and husky with an underlying plea for more.

"I'm yours for the taking." He'd heard her and was willing to give her what she needed. He spread his arms wide, giving her total access.

The moonlight through the open window gave the room a feeling of a black and white movie. He made a hell of a leading man.

The look of desire in his eyes emboldened her so she felt like his femme fatale.

Starting with his top button, her clumsy fingers pushed it free of the buttonhole. With her index finger she traced inside the open V. Under her fingertip his chest hair felt coarse while his skin was smooth.

He groaned, deep and long and soulful. "What sweet agony from my exquisite Annalise."

"Should I go faster?"

"No. Please." He kissed the tips of her fingers. "I want this to last forever."

She worked the next button free but couldn't stop herself

from going for the next and the one after that until his shirt lay open, exposing his chest and abs. She splayed her hands across his chest, feeling the twin peaks of his flat pecs respond to her touch. Experimentally, she rubbed them. He sucked in his breath like he'd been sucker punched.

She'd done that. She'd taken his breath away. A feeling of power rolled through her.

"Are you okay?" She couldn't keep the provocative pride from her voice when she asked any more than she could keep herself from flicking those sensitive peaks again.

"Vixen." The amusement in his voice caressed her while goading her to continue.

But her own body ached for his exploring touch.

"Tell me, Annalise. Tell me what you want."

"Take my top off." That had sounded demanding, hadn't it? "Please," she added.

"Absolutely." He reached for the hook at the nape of her neck. He pulled her T-shirt over her head.

The appreciated groan he gave her made the heat rise deep down inside that place that had never felt warm before.

She revelled in the way his eyes went dark when she reached back to unhook her bra.

So much appreciation. So much awe. So much desire.

Bare to the night air, her nipples peaked, aching for his attention. "Kiss me."

Obediently, he reverently suckled first one taut tip, then the other. The moan that escaped sounded like it came from the depths of her.

"Thank you." She sounded wispy, breathless.

"My pleasure." His voice was a deeply sincere growl.

"The panties match. Want to see?"

"Yes, oh, please, yes."

Smiling, she shimmied out of her shorts, revealing her newest purchase. No granny panties for her tonight.

In the gray moonlight, her black panties contrasted with the paleness of her skin, making her feel naughty and so very sexy.

She pushed Niko backwards until his knees hit the back of her bed. Fluidly, he lay back on the bed and she climbed on top of him.

Under her, Niko grimaced and shifted his weight.

Immediately, she lifted herself so she straddled him without holding him down. "Your leg?"

He grinned up at her. "No."

"Then what?"

"These jeans are getting a bit tight."

"Oh." Her own naïveté made her blush.

"Do you think you might want to take them off soon? Or at least unzip them?" Her hand hovered over the zipper as the intimacy of what she was about to do made her hesitate.

He grinned at her, his dimples deep as a cloud shifted and a moonbeam splashed across his face. "Please?"

Shyness won out. "You do it."

"Cover my hand." He waited until her hand rested on his before he unbuttoned and unzipped.

"Better?" she asked, even though she could see his jeans restricted him.

"Not quite." He lifted his hips, putting his rough jeans in contact with the sensitive ache that only the thin silk of her panties protected.

Beneath her, he pushed his jeans off his hips and thighs then kicked them free, all the while bucking underneath her, making her want… Oh, how she wanted.

She marveled at the throbbing that needed fulfillment. She had been sure such passion was only a myth made up for movies and books.

Niko drew in a deep breath. "You are so beautiful."

She stilled, realizing what a silhouette they made in the moonlight.

Quickly, she pushed down her panties. Just as quickly, Niko grabbed protection from the nightstand. His tip nudged her bud and she guided him inside her. They fit together as if they were made for each other. And somewhere in the joyous center of her soul she knew they had been.

She rode him, with her back arched and her hands braced against his chest. His lean body under hers responded to her pace and rhythm, faster and faster until they were both gasping for breath.

A throaty, wordless note of ecstasy came from her throat. Niko answered with his own deep roar of celebration. Together they pulsed in time with the universe.

After an eternity of bliss Annalise lay spent on Niko's chest as he brushed his hand along her back.

"Annalise?"

"Hmm?"

"Tomorrow morning we make port in Malaga. Whatever you have planned, I want to be part of it."

"No plans for Malaga." Annalise thought hard about what she was about to offer. Would it be more painful to experience what being a part of a family was like or more lonely to forgo the whole experience?

Better to have loved and lost than never to have loved at all. Poets were supposed to be experts at this sort of thing, weren't they?

"I've got the perfect idea for your whole family. Do you think—?"

"I think I want you all to myself."

"This is supposed to be your family vacation."

He grinned at her. "Now you sound like one of the Christopoulos women."

"If only you could be so lucky." Too late, Annalise realized what she'd implied.

Niko lost his grin. "If only…"

He said it low, but Annalise was too tuned in to his every breath to have missed it.

Only what would she do with it?

"Your idea?" Niko prompted.

"Malaga has some great bike tours. They even rent bikes with carriages on the back for Yiayia and the little ones. There's one tour in particular I've heard great things about that I think your family will enjoy."

Looking deceptively like a tame house cat, Niko turned those tiger eyes on her. But she'd seen them blaze with hunger only a short time earlier and was not deceived. "I'm sure my family will enjoy it, but what's in it for me and you?"

"I don't know about you, Niko Christopoulos, but I would love to spend a day with your family." Had Niko heard her yearning to experience being a part of a family underneath her light and breezy tone? She turned away in case her expression gave her away.

Niko came up behind her, giving her the lightest of kisses along her nape. "My family will love spending the day with you as well." Those kisses deepened as they travelled across her throat and down her breasts.

"How about room service tonight?"

"Your family—"

"Will have me all day tomorrow. Tonight I'm yours." He stopped kissing her a lip's width from the tip of her breast. "If you want me."

His breath on her sensitive skin made her ache so deeply she groaned her answer.

And Annalise found new pleasures she would never have imagined on her own. Much, much later, as she lay in his arms while he slept, she thought about all she had learned from Niko. The stuff that dreams are made of...

But who could go back to living on dreams of the heavens when she'd touched those glorious heights themselves?

Some time in the wee hours of the morning Niko felt Annalise shift, tidying up the bedcovers as if she were tidying up their relationship.

"Annalise?"

She laced her fingers through his. "The way you say my name makes me feel like the most special woman on earth."

"Then you've caught my meaning exactly right."

"Tell me what to do to make you feel special, too."

Niko had never felt so honored. "That you want me to feel that way does the trick for me."

She unlaced her fingers and sat up, letting the sheets fall to her waist. Moonlight showed her beautiful breasts full and perfect for his hands. He gave in to desire and reached toward her, cupping one, savoring the weight in his palm.

"So beautiful."

She reached up and brushed his hair from his eyes. "So are you."

"Tell me what you want, Annalise. Tell me what I can give to you."

"I want you," she said, shifting under him. "I want to feel your touch on every inch of me. I want to be so feverish with needing to feel you in me that I scream with desire."

"Should I start here?" Niko traced her ear then nibbled on the sensitive rim. "And should I taste you as well?"

"Y-e-s." She drew the word out, like she never wanted to let it go.

"And then move to here?" He trailed kisses down her neck, smiling when she grabbed his shoulders and pulled him closer.

"Now. I want you now." She wrapped her legs around him to pull him closer still.

As a gentleman, Niko complied.

And when they came together, each shouting the other's name, Niko had never had a more special moment in his life.

CHAPTER FOURTEEN

ANNALISE HAD BEEN to Malaga many times before, but seeing it through Niko's eyes made all the difference. When she'd recommended the tapas and wine bike tour for the family, they had insisted she come too.

For the first time in her life Annalise felt like she could understand the enormity of being accepted. Along with the whole Christopoulos clan, Annalise cycled along the tapas and wine tour route, eating, drinking and laughing. The younger nieces and nephews took turns riding with Yiayia in a carriage behind a bicycle, which the two older nephews were coerced into manning, while all the Christopoulos men opted for bicycles built for two with their women.

No one blinked an eyelash when Annalise paired up with Niko although she did catch a few winks behind her back.

It was a tour after the Christopoulos family's heart.

At their first stop Stephen raised his glass in a toast to Annalise, with great thanks for the suggestion of the bike tour. When Annalise followed it up with a toast to the strong backs and legs of the Christopoulos twins, the hardy laughs and cheers made her felt like one of their own.

Soon she was stuffed with olives and cheese and fried squid and was giddy from a bit more vino dulce than she was accustomed to drinking.

"This looks interesting. Want to try it?" She held a tapas up to Niko to taste.

He nibbled it from her fingers. "Mmm."

Stephen leaned forward and watched him chew.

"He swallowed it." Stephen high-fived his wife. "Annalise, you are some special lady."

Phoebe explained. "Niko is our picky eater. He won't put anything in his mouth without knowing exactly what it is first."

Niko smiled. "I'll eat anything from the hands of a goddess."

At every stop Yiayia charmed the chefs into giving her inside information, showing such appreciation for their skills that they were bringing the family their specialties to taste.

Cooking meant so much to them, especially to Yiayia and Stephen. It was a part of who they were even more than what they did.

Like medicine was to Niko and to Annalise.

Annalise rubbed her full stomach. The tapas bars of Malaga would not soon forget the Christopoulos family.

Annalise understood. A Christopoulos was not an easy person to forget. She was certain that, no matter what happened, she would remember Niko throughout eternity.

By the time they all reached their last stop, the beach at the fishing village of El Palo, the children were happy to build sandcastles while the adults and teens rested and watched.

The Christopoulos men procured beach towels and spread them on the sand, each trying to be more gallant than the others as they extended a helping hand to their women.

Annalise couldn't help pretending she was a part of this great loving family. She was so full of food and wine she could be excused for letting the line between fantasy and reality blur a bit, couldn't she?

Sitting on the beach, leaning back against Niko, Annalise had never felt more content.

Niko leaned forward and whispered in her ear, "I think this is the happiest day I have ever lived."

While he didn't say it, Annalise took liberties in thinking that his happiness was in some small part because she was there.

She knew he was the source of *her* bliss.

"Me, too," she said.

Her voice did things to him deep down that he would never have imagined were possible. His heart beat faster, his breathing deepened, and his hands itched to run along her arms and feel her silky-smooth skin.

He gave a quick look around to see if they had an audience, but his brothers were giving all their attention to their wives while Yiayia and the twins watched the little ones.

As shy as Annalise was in public, he took a chance and dropped a kiss on her neck simply because he couldn't help himself. Annalise leaned her head, giving him better access to drop a second one on top of the first.

Apparently he wasn't quick enough because Marcus gave him a thumbs-up. Thankfully, Annalise didn't notice or if she did, she no longer cared that his family saw their public displays of affection.

He was hoping it was the latter. All day he'd fought the urge to kiss her in front of strangers, which only made his anticipation of their time alone tonight much more intense.

He would have stayed there forever if not for the children becoming too cold and wet from the spray of the ocean.

Reluctantly they headed back to the ship. The only

thought that made leaving the beach bearable was the thought of Annalise in his bed.

His anticipation was rewarded.

Still shy with him, she asked permission to touch him here and there. Knowing what she was about to do then feeling her gentle, hesitant exploration touched him in ways beyond the physical.

Lying with his hands laced behind his head, he encouraged Annalise to explore. Whatever made her happy made him ecstatic.

She coasted her hands and then her mouth over him, eliciting the most wonderful pleasure he had ever known.

While the night started out for her benefit, her tender explorations quickly turned the tables, making it the most memorable night he'd ever had.

He had a strong feeling that each night with Annalise would be more memorable than the last.

As he was about to grasp a bigger concept, Annalise straddled him. Any logical thought patterns he'd been about to form completely fled his brain while a more primeval part of his body took over.

Softly, sweetly, she mounted him and they came together, swirling, swirling in a haze so rich with the rhythm of love Niko felt her whole body throb in tune with his.

As she lay collapsed on him, he ran his finger down her backside, loving the femininity of her curves.

Annalise soaked up the attention Niko gave her. She'd never had a man want to please her before. All too easily she could become accustomed to feeling cherished. Was it real? Or was it the Christopoulos charm Niko showed all his women?

Happiest day of my life, he'd said. She wanted to believe him. It had certainly been true for her.

But, then, the truth didn't matter, did it? This chance crossing of paths would soon come to an end.

Annalise thought of the enquiry she'd sent to the board of Doctors Without Borders. Maybe, if fate was kind, she and Niko would cross paths again. But Annalise couldn't count on fate.

It was time to practice some self-preservation, time to pull away before Niko left.

On the bedside table Annalise's watch beeped a warning.

Reality. Annalise reached over and checked the time. "I've got to go."

"Go?"

"I've got to dine at the captain's table tonight."

Naked, he stood behind her and turned her to the mirror. He ran his hands over her shoulders. "What can I say…" he gave her a sultry look "…or do to convince you not to go?"

What could he say? *I love you* would work. But he'd given no indication of that.

Lust. Tenderness. Gallantry. Niko had given her all that in spades. But love? There was a good reason for the rule against shipboard romances.

"Say no to the captain. Tell him you have plans with me." He flashed her his best practiced smile.

"Don't do that."

"Don't do what?"

"Don't get all plastic playboy on me because I can't stay and play. Respect me more than that." She had put in too many years of loyal service to want to leave on a bad note. And she needed a clean recommendation.

Plus—and it was a big plus—Niko had taught her to expect respect. Before she'd met him, before she'd seen how much he and his brothers respected all women, including her, she wouldn't have demanded it.

Niko blinked, as if he had been caught looking through her instead of at her. He backed off, leaving her to face the mirror alone. "Sorry. I've started thinking I have you all to myself. Forgive me?"

She turned to look at him, to read his expression. His face was like an open book. No smooth artifice. No practiced smile. Simply sincerity.

He could put more emotion into those tiger eyes of his than anyone she'd ever met. And she had to admit, his possessiveness *was* on the flattering side.

"Forgiven."

"Thanks." He dropped a chaste kiss on her head that left her wishing for more despite her resolve to put distance between them.

"Tomorrow in port?"

She shook her head. "It's my P.A.'s turn for shore leave. I've got to stay on board and handle the medical suite."

He blew out a breath, looking like a little boy who'd dropped his popsicle in the dirt. "Is it something I did?"

"I'm not on vacation, remember?"

"We're having a private birthday party for Yiayia tomorrow evening. I want you to come." His eyes sharpened, daring her to say no.

Annalise felt honored to be invited but, "It's for family. I don't want to intrude."

"Are you kidding? My family loves you." He looked into the mirror to shave off his five o'clock shadow. Annalise had suspected that with those dark looks he was a twice a day man.

He kept his attention focused on her reflection as she watched his. Seeing those eyes in the mirror gave her no reprieve.

She swallowed, determined to treat this lightly. "You've

got a great family. Everyone meshes so well together, brothers and sisters-in-law and all the children."

He lifted his chin to shave but still didn't break eye contact as if he wanted to judge her reaction. "They're a handful. Especially the nieces and nephews. But being the favorite uncle is the perfect deal. I get to cuddle and spoil them when I'm around, then leave them to their parents when one of us gets cranky."

Annalise had resigned herself to never having babies of her own, but being around the Christopoulos children made her wonder what her life might have been like if she could have been stronger and said no when her mother had marched her up to that filthy back room above the stripper bar and ordered the greasy haired woman there to "get rid of it". But at sixteen, with no means of support and her mother threatening to throw her out of her home, she'd been better at hysterical crying than rational action.

When she saw herself in the mirror, she looked incredibly sad. "They'll expect you to have babies one day."

"They have great expectations." Niko broke eye contact, looking at himself instead of her. That same expression he'd had the first day they'd met, the day he'd called himself the black sheep of the family, resurfaced. "They are destined to be disappointed."

"When you tell them about Doctors Without Borders? How can they be?" She reached out to touch him then dropped her hand as if the barriers going up around him were razor sharp. "Niko, you're a hero. A man to be proud of. The work you do is so important to so many."

She thought about telling him how he inspired her and that she was sending in her own application, but this moment wasn't about her.

He pulled a pair of linen pants from his closet. "The

price of these pants would feed a family of five for several months in some of the places I've been."

Annalise waited, knowing there was more.

"Sadly, improving lives isn't all about money. There's a lot of generous people out there. If all it took was throwing money at the problem, poverty would have been stamped out a long time ago. Education, health and developing strong leadership skills in the right people is the answer."

"And that takes time." Wrapped in a towel, Annalise inspected her clothes, wincing at the dirt and sweat from a day of bicycling.

He nodded. His time, his skills, his determination to make a difference were the most valuable contributions he had to give. "The cycle of poverty is so entrenched it all seems hopeless sometimes."

"I've read that burnout among the health-care specialists is a big problem."

He'd seen those who had given their all. War and disease took their toll on the workers, but burnout was a huge hazard, too. That's why trips like this were so important.

"Yes. Burnout is a big deal. I've given a lot of thought on how to deal with it. Vacations like this help."

He needed to remember the joys in life so he could deal with the tragedies. And right now one of those joys was joining his family, listening to the prattle of the little ones, seeing the hope for the future in his older nephews' eyes and knowing that love held the universe together as he watched his brothers and their wives make the world a better place just by being their happy selves and raising their happy families.

What didn't work for him was having a wife and kids at home who waited for the infrequent visits of a husband and father too involved in his work to give enough attention to his family.

Which was why there could never be anything between Annalise and himself beyond what they had now.

"What's wrong? Are you in pain?" Annalise scanned him, making him wish he was still naked. Making him wish for things he could never have, for the woman he could never have.

"I'm fine."

"You groaned and pushed your fist into your stomach."

He used his distracting smile. "It must have been that green stuff you made me eat."

Annalise narrowed her eyes. "If you don't want to tell me what's wrong, that's your business." Then her face went blank. "You're entitled to your privacy."

After being so intimate, the concept of keeping anything from each other seemed to make a mockery of their time together.

But how could he tell her his gut clenched at the idea of leaving her when he left the ship?

Niko turned away to give himself a moment.

Where he had been, what he had done, he had learned to live with loss, only it had never been so personal. And personal made the pain of loss excruciating.

He took another shaky breath, careful to keep his face hidden from Annalise. She could read him like no other.

When he had gathered his composure, he dug through his clothes and handed her one of his T-shirts and a pair of gym shorts. The T-shirt fit her like a dress. The shorts bunched around her waist when she tightened the drawstring enough to keep them from falling off her hips.

"You like?" She held out her hands and turned to model.

Niko caught his breath as he saw the hint of unfettered breasts under the shirt. The woman was breathtaking. "I like—and it has nothing to do with the unique style."

Her laugh brightened his world better than sunshine. "They'll get me back to my room."

"See you at the party tomorrow night?" He saw the hesitation in her eyes. "Please?"

She reached up and ran a finger over his lips. "Has anyone ever said *no to you*?"

"I've heard *no* on occasion and survived. But from you, it would be devastating."

"What would you say if I said the same thing to you?"

"Please, Annalise. It will be our last night on the ship." The implication laid heavy between them.

What could he do? What could he say? The reality of the moment ripped into him. "We can't leave it like this between us."

"Like this?"

"Unfinished." He refused to meet her eyes, afraid of what he might read in them. Which would hurt worse? Resignation or loss?

She nodded. "Closure is a good thing."

No. Closure meant the end. Inside, he screamed it, but he couldn't seem to say it. "Annalise…"

She reached up and cupped his cheek. "I won't go without saying goodbye."

She slipped away before he could answer.

CHAPTER FIFTEEN

ONCE THE DOOR closed behind her, Annalise had to run before all the pent-up emotion made her explode. With tears streaming down her face, she ran down the stairs to her floor. It wasn't that she didn't care who might see her, it was that she couldn't help herself. Running was the only way to keep the pain from overwhelming her. So she ran until her side ached and her lungs burned, her vision so blurry she could barely see.

But, no matter how fast she ran, she couldn't outrun the pain of knowing this had to end.

Then she had to stop. Standing before the door of her room, Annalise had to stop and face herself. Like too many times before, she had nowhere else to go.

She hugged herself, feeling Niko's encompassing shirt around her, smelling his scent rise from her own warm body. Remembering the depth of his eyes when he'd looked at her.

She'd been running away from looking inside herself ever since she'd knocked on Niko's door the first time. But now she'd run into a dead end and the nights spent together had caught up with her.

She had thought making love to Niko would change her inside. And it had, but not the way she had expected.

She had expected to feel braver, more secure, free

from her past. Instead, she felt invisible ties binding her to Niko—a man who lived his life without boundaries. What did ties mean to him? She only had to look at his brothers to know.

While she couldn't have children, maybe she could try to be a mother, for Niko's sake?

But what kind of a mother would she be when she really didn't want to be one? The kind of mother *her* mother was, she was afraid.

As much as she wanted it to work, she couldn't be the little woman, barefoot and pregnant, waiting for her man to return.

She couldn't be the woman for him. She couldn't give him what he needed. Family, children, stability to anchor him between missions, to refresh him and send him out again.

Annalise couldn't be that stability for him. Her restlessness was the equal of his. She had her own limits to push. As much as she wanted to be, she was not the home-and-hearth kind.

Niko, with his big heart, would forgo his own needs and accept what she could give, trying to make it work.

But she would know that she couldn't give him what he needed. Niko would always have a place in his heart for children to carry on his legacy, a hole only his perfect partner could fill. With her, that place would always be empty. She could never do that to the man she loved.

Tomorrow they would dock in Barcelona. While half the passengers would disembark then, the other half, including the Christopoulos family, would continue their trip for another week, touring the Greek isles before flying back home.

For the reduced passenger list, the cruise line didn't need both her and the P.A., though the captain and the cruise line had offered to let her stay on for the extra week without duties as a bonus for her long service. She had thought about staying, but now…

Now she thought about going. She had no future with Niko. More time together would only make leaving harder.

The only thing she knew for sure was that she would survive this. She would put her life back together, learn from the experience and go forward. That's what she did.

She was a survivor.

After a long hard night dining and then sleeping without Annalise, Niko had endured a long, hard day without her, too. If he couldn't get through eighteen hours without her, how could he live the rest of his life without her?

He now understood what his brothers meant. Love for the right woman made a man feel whole. Without it, he had an aloneness that not even his family could fill. In Barcelona, he had accompanied his family to a cooking school presented by one of the area's famous restaurants, had chaperoned the youngest nieces and nephews through the children's museum and had people-watched with the twins, which was usually one of his favorite pastimes but today felt boring beyond measure.

Niko knew the problem wasn't with his activities but with his lack of a partner. If Annalise had been with him, it could have been one of his favorite days of all time. That's what being with Annalise did. It made every day his favorite day.

Niko kept glancing at the door to the party suite, even when he willed himself not to.

Marcus elbowed him. "Looking for someone, Uncle Niko? Someone special?"

He elbowed Marcus back. "Always."

Marcus cocked an eyebrow. "That's a different Niko Christopoulos than the one I've known all my life."

"Just wait, nephew. Your time will come, sooner or later."

"In your case later."

Niko guessed he did seem old to a seventeen-year-old. "Better late than never."

That's what he'd tell Annalise when she finally arrived at Yiayia's party. And what he'd tell his family when he announced she was the one.

He glanced toward the door for the thousandth time in a minute. Where was she?

Niko hadn't caught a glimpse of her since last night at the late dinner seating when he'd sat with the family and she'd sat at the captain's table next to a computer nerd, smiling and nodding as if the twenty-five-year-old millionaire was the smartest man on the ship. Niko had to admit the kid probably was. Not that he had a right to be jealous, but...

If he only had that right...

Soon. Soon he would ask for that right.

Not that he would be the jealous type.

Had she really made a special effort to avoid looking at him, or had that been his ego aching, wanting her attention as she'd chatted the evening away with the computer nerd?

He would make sure Annalise never felt lonely enough to even want to talk to another guy *in that special way* a woman talked to a man.

But he couldn't be there for her, couldn't watch sunsets with her, if he was in some field operation with no way to communicate except by short-wave radio carried to the highest local mountaintop. Could he ask her to wait for him?

That's why he'd never intended to fall in love. But life didn't always turn out the way a man planned it, did it?

She wasn't going to show. Despair followed on the heels of the devastating thought he kept trying to push away. What if it was one-sided? What if this was only a shipboard romance? And if it was more—it had to be more—where did they go with it from here?

What if she didn't show? What if she didn't care? She did, though, didn't she? Hadn't he seen it in her eyes? Felt it in her touch?

Niko caught himself staring at the door as he remembered how her eyes had flashed then squeezed tight in ecstasy the first time they'd come together.

It wasn't only sex. Not for him. Not for her either. All those times together, all those sunsets had to mean more than a vacation fling. He was as certain of that as he was that he was going to take another breath.

As he desperately tried to keep his attention on his excited six-year-old niece telling her rambling version of feeding a talking parrot, Niko felt a tingle in the back of his neck. Without turning, he knew she was there.

Suddenly, all the pieces fit into place inside him.

Yiayia confirmed it when she called out, "Dr. Annalise, welcome to my party. Let me get you some cake."

Her sundress with oversized orange and pink and purple flowers fit her better than his T-shirt but he missed seeing her wrapped in something that belonged to him.

Yiayia gave her one of the prized corner pieces of cake topped with an icing rose.

"For our special friend." Yiayia added a hug with the cake.

Over Yiayia's shoulder Annalise caught his glance. Shadows colored her eyes the same shade of sadness he was feeling.

"Thanks." Annalise's smile, even clouded, lit the darkest corners of his soul.

Before she could take a bite, Sophie demanded her attention. "Dr. Annalise, look at my picture. I'm feeding a parrot."

Niko watched her with Sophie, giving the child a lot more focused attention than he'd been able to. Annalise blended into his family as if she'd always been a part of them.

She was so good with children. He'd seen that at the refugee camp as well as with his own nieces and nephews.

She deserved a husband who could give her a house full of them.

Something very ugly inside him cringed at the thought of Annalise with another man. But it didn't have to be that way.

He could be that man who gave her babies.

He hadn't finalized the papers to sell his part of the practice. He could give her whatever she wanted.

Could he give up his dream, his calling to be a part of Doctors Without Borders, for her?

Or his other option—could he get up every morning, knowing he'd never see her again?

And the biggest question of them all. Did she love him like he loved her?

"To Yiayia!" His brother Stephen began the toasting. "May she have another great eight decades."

"To my grandson Stephen, who had the good sense to marry Phoebe!" Yiayia toasted back.

"To all the fine Christopoulos children, that they may be as wise and gracious and noble as their great-grandmother someday."

The older kids saluted Yiayia and the younger ones quickly followed suit with a little coaching.

"That's how it is in our family," Niko overheard Marcus explain to Annalise. "Like the Musketeers. All for one and one for all."

"To Dr. Annalise, who has graced us with her wisdom and compassion," Phoebe announced.

That was a toast Niko was pleased to drink to.

The toasting went on for almost an hour until every single family member had been covered, except for him.

He cringed, dreading the toast that was sure to come.

His brother Stephen was the one to deliver it.

"To Niko, the slow one of the family." Stephen held his glass high. "May he recognize love when it bites him on the butt then marry the woman and give her a household full of children before she figures out he's so much trouble."

Under the guise of saluting them all with his glass, he noticed Annalise fail to drink. What did it mean? Anything? Everything?

Annalise couldn't do it. She couldn't wish Niko into the arms of another woman. Thankfully, no one seemed to notice.

Phoebe splashed more wine into Annalise's glass as Yiayia toasted her late husband, gone but not forgotten.

She made sure Annalise knew about his heroic exploits.

"My Leo, he was a brave and adventurous man. We travelled many places until we found the one that fit."

"Leo started the restaurant?"

"Oh, no, child. Leo couldn't cook any better than our Niko. He could never sit still either. Just like our Niko. Leo was a fireman. He died saving a pregnant woman. They called me to the hospital. He wasn't burned, at least not that we could tell, but the doctor said his lungs were too full of toxins. They didn't have all the fancy machines they have nowadays to save people. Two lives for one, he said, just before he died. Two lives for one." She looked sad but resigned and proud. "That woman's husband was a banker. He lent me the money to start the restaurant. My boys, Theo and Nicolos, they helped me after school. But then Nicolos became a policeman. We lost him in a bank robbery."

Yiayia glared at the Christopoulos men around her. "Until my grandsons, every generation has had a daredevil as far back as I can remember. But it stopped with my grandsons. I raised them to raise their own families, not to go and get themselves killed. It's a family tradition I'm proud to break."

Over Yiayia's head, Annalise shared a look with Niko, understanding too well his reluctance to tell her about Doctors Without Borders. What would it do to Yiayia when she found out about his work?

Yiayia waved away the conversation. "Enough of the sad talk. This is a party. Niko, bring Annalise a plate of grapes and cheese and crackers. She will need some meat on her bones when she settles down to have her own children."

Niko loaded up a plate as directed, bringing it to her with a blank expression on his face. She could imagine the turmoil under the surface and her heart went out to him.

When Niko spoke of Doctors Without Borders, the resonance of his voice as well as the passion in his words told her how much it meant to him. When he described the work by saying it was the only time he felt like he was truly fulfilling his purpose for being alive, she easily believed him.

She also knew how much he loved his family. If she had such a wonderful family, it would wound her beyond healing to know she had to disappoint them to live the life that meant so much to her.

While Annalise regretted not having a family to speak of, at least she had the freedom to make her own choices, guilt-free.

Annalise picked at the plate of food until Sophie called her to come look at how she could jump higher than her cousins.

Before the evening ended, Annalise was treated to at least one family story for each member of the Christopoulos clan, from the story about Stephen getting his tongue stuck on a block of dry ice to the one about how Niko hadn't told anyone about his motorcycle and how he'd been grounded for a week until he'd talked Yiayia into taking a ride on the back of it with him. Of course, she'd then forgiven everything and let him keep it.

Finally, Yiayia declared the party over when half the little ones were asleep on the chairs and the other half were running around in circles from being overtired.

All the brothers and sisters-in-law and their little ones hugged her goodnight, just like she was family. Annalise soaked it up. It would all be over too soon.

When they were the only ones left, Annalise asked Niko, "Want to go up top with me?"

"I'll follow you to the ends of the earth." While he'd meant it to be a teasing flirt, Niko had meant it from the bottom of his heart.

She grinned at him. "Tonight, the top deck will do for me."

"For me, too." Those moments alone with her each night gave him a calm serenity he'd never known before.

Tonight he needed that serenity to ease his angst. Niko had some deep thinking to do. If there was any other way...

But he'd heard it himself, verifying what he already

knew. Every woman wanted babies, a home, a husband she could count on.

His grandmother had survived the tragedy of having to bury both a husband and a son. She'd raised her sons and then her grandsons alone. It had been a burden he could never ask any woman to carry.

With the work he did, the risk was always high that he wouldn't make it back home. He was willing to accept the odds for himself but he couldn't accept them for the woman he loved.

Giving up Doctors Without Borders would be like giving up his right arm. But giving up Annalise would be like giving up his heart.

CHAPTER SIXTEEN

MARCUS WAYLAID THEM before they got very far. "Uncle Niko, could I talk to you? In private?"

Marcus looked serious, old beyond his years. Dread made Niko's gut feel heavy. Whatever this was about, it wasn't going to be good.

Niko put on his professional stoicism. Teenagers could be spooked easily so he intended to play this as nonchalantly as possible. "Let's see if the library is deserted."

Annalise gave Marcus an encouraging smile. "You two go ahead. I'll catch up with you later, Niko."

"Dr. Annalise, I was hoping you'd weigh in on this, too. I could use a woman's opinion on how to deal with the females in the family."

Annalise looked confused but reluctantly agreed. "I'm not sure how much help I'll be but I'll give it a try."

Marcus sent a surreptitious glance toward his parents, got a thumbs-up from his twin, who had obviously been assigned to keep them busy, and grabbed a folder of papers from under a chair cushion.

He led the way to a secluded alcove half-obscured by a big potted palm. Niko and he straddled a lounge chair each and Niko had to grin at how much he and his nephew were alike.

But the grin didn't last long. Marcus pulled out a magazine and plopped it in Niko's lap.

On the front cover was a coastguard helicopter, hovering to pick up patients on a sinking home-made raft.

Niko remembered that day well. He identified the sleeve of his own jacket. He'd been just out of camera range for the shot. The photographer had caught the anxiety in the coastguard officer's eyes as he'd checked the straps on the carrier before the patient had been lifted up into the helicopter.

Niko was all too aware of Annalise studying the photograph. Did she understand the danger involved? By the seriousness in her eyes he thought she might.

"That's what I want to do, Uncle Niko."

"Be a doctor?"

"No. A coastguard pilot." He handed Niko a sheaf of papers. "The recruitment office sent me this paperwork. I can sign up now while I'm still in high school and get preferential consideration for the coastguard academy when I graduate. But there's a problem."

Without Marcus having to explain, Niko understood fully what the problem was. Stephen and Phoebe. They would be adamantly opposed to their son choosing such a dangerous career.

"Your parents won't like it at first but they love you, Marcus. There is nothing that will make them stop loving you."

"But Mom and Yiayia… What do you think, Dr. Annalise?"

"The women in your life are a lot stronger than you give them credit for."

Niko glanced down at the magazine cover's headline. *"U.S. Coastguard Teams with Doctors Without Borders to Make Daring Rescue"*. "You want me to talk to them?"

"No. I don't need their permission. I'll be eighteen by the time I graduate. I won't need their signatures. But I need to get on the list now to take advantage of early enlistment." He handed Niko a blank form. "I want you to recommend me."

Niko blew out a breath. "Marcus, you know you've got my support in anything you want to pursue and I think you'll make a great coastguard pilot. But I won't go behind your parents' backs. Hiding things from your family is the wrong thing to do."

He was all too aware of the sideways glance Annalise shot at him.

With the way Marcus stared at him, apparently she wasn't the only one who knew he had something to hide.

"You mean like paying for this trip and saying Yiayia won it?" Marcus flipped open the magazine to a photo of Niko precariously balanced on the disintegrating raft as he started an IV in the arm of a child. "Or like being part of Doctors Without Borders?"

Niko looked away from his nephew's eyes and swallowed. "The wrong thing for the right reasons."

Marcus nodded. "You gave us this trip because it's something Yiayia always dreamed of doing but we couldn't have afforded it. You figured everyone's pride would be too great and they wouldn't have accepted it as a gift."

Niko nodded. "That's about the size of it."

"And keeping this a secret?" Marcus pointed to the magazine. "Because you didn't want to worry anyone?"

The dread of family drama built in Niko's stomach. He felt as helpless as a child—as an eight-year-old, to be exact. After all these years Niko realized he associated family turmoil with that time of tears and hysteria he'd barely survived.

Annalise put her hand on his shoulder, anchoring him and giving him strength.

Niko leaned into her touch as he looked into the eyes of the nephew who looked up to him. "It's time we came clean, both of us."

"You first?" Marcus challenged him.

"Me first." Niko threaded his fingers through Annalise's. "Come with me?"

"This is a family matter. They won't appreciate an outsider hearing about your financial ploy." Annalise unthreaded her fingers from his, leaving Niko feeling alone.

Usually she would be right, but his family had taken her in as one of their own.

"You're not an outsider anymore."

"Then what am I?" She crossed her arms, hugging herself. "No. I don't do families."

The guarded look in her eyes stopped him from saying more.

"Náste kalá." She reached up and kissed him on the cheek. *"Antio."*

As the two of them walked towards the party room, Marcus said, "You're going to tell them about paying for this trip and about Doctors Without Borders, right?"

"I'll tell them about the trip." Niko said aloud the decision he'd not wanted to face. "I'm resigning from the field."

"Why?"

"I want a—" Niko almost said *family*. But that was the easy answer, the answer he was programmed to give and Marcus was programmed to accept.

In the face of Marcus's honesty, Niko could do no less. "I can't ask a woman to take on my passion and travel with me or to stay at home and accept a part-time man in her life. So I'm giving up what I love most for who I love most."

"You're in love, Uncle Niko? With Dr. Annalise?"

Niko nodded.

Marcus cocked an eyebrow, looking so much like a typical Christopoulos male it made Niko smile. "The women in our lives *are* a lot stronger than we give them credit for. You should talk to her about it before you decide."

"Maybe I will, Marcus." Niko had to look away because he knew he wouldn't. Annalise would feel honor-bound to set him free. He would never put her in that position.

She would either tell him to go and she would wait for him at home—or she would just tell him to go. The first would wound her but he was certain the latter would kill him. While Marcus made arrangements with his brother to watch the little ones, Niko roused the adults and herded them into one of the family suites amid much confusion and speculation.

Once they were gathered, Niko tinged a half-full wine bottle with a fork to get everyone's attention.

"Marcus and I have some things to tell you." Niko took a deep breath, wishing he'd drunk the rest of the wine first. "I'll go first. Yiayia, the lady who delivered your sweepstakes check was an actress who owed me for medical work. I paid for this trip."

Thankfully, the suites on either side of his family's suite were no longer occupied as they all got uncivilly loud.

He told them everything—how much they meant to him for raising him and putting him through medical school, how he would be forever in their debt, how he deeply regretted disappointing them, but he had to be his own man. Everything had all tumbled out, as if the words couldn't escape him fast enough.

In the confusion and the turmoil Niko wasn't quite sure

how his confession came out so ungracefully. All he knew was that no matter how angry his family was with him, they still loved him, even if he insulted them by thinking he owed them anything. They did what they did for love—not for paybacks.

"Because that's what families do," Phoebe yelled at him when he tried to defend why he'd hidden his financial gift.

"Anything else you need to confess, Niko?" Yiayia asked. At his hesitation, his sisters-in-law added their own questions. Who could withstand the interrogation of the Christopoulos women *en masse*?

How he wished Annalise had been there to protect him when he said, "About those trips I've been taking..."

He made a full confession about Doctors Without Borders, even though he planned to resign for Annalise's sake.

Yes, Chistopoulos women were stronger than they looked.

They still weren't on board with Marcus's plan to make early application to the coastguard training academy. But when Stephen told Phoebe that at least Marcus was showing self-motivation and they wouldn't have to keep on him about keeping up his grades, Niko know they would eventually come round.

As always, his brothers forgave him everything, even expressing admiration, despite their wives' frowns.

Yiayia wasn't so kind about his involvement in Doctors Without Borders and his apparent bad influence on his nephew.

She wasn't speaking to him. In solidarity, neither were the other women. From past experience he knew their silent treatment wouldn't last beyond the night, and in the morning they'd be just as vocal as ever—which would not be a good thing if they were all still angry at him.

Yet he knew, when all was said and done, they were

family—his family—and they loved him as much as he loved them. That's how the Christopoulos women were.

It was a comforting feeling.

But he had another woman on his mind who was giving him heartache.

Niko took the stairs two at a time, needing to see Annalise, to touch her, to hear her voice. Needing to reassure himself he was making the right decision.

As he made his nightly climb, he heard voices from above.

The top deck was filled with passengers watching Barcelona grow smaller and smaller as they pulled away from shore.

But it felt completely empty without Annalise.

What was that she'd said when she'd kissed him on the cheek? *"Náste kalá. Antío."*

Be well and goodbye.

She hadn't meant…she couldn't have meant…

There was still too much unsaid between them.

Packing had gone quickly. Everything Annalise wanted to take with her fit in a single suitcase. The rest she left for the crew, as was the custom.

She now stood on the dock at Barcelona's main port, watching the ship sail without her. The single suitcase made travelling easier as she caught a taxi to the airport.

Her last-minute decision meant she'd be flying to Athens for her interview with the local office of Doctors Without Borders tomorrow afternoon, instead of arriving by ship. Otherwise, everything was going as planned.

Except she hadn't expected her heart to be shattering into a million pieces.

How had she fallen in love so hard, so quickly?

Saying goodbye had been the hardest thing she'd ever done.

But it had been the right thing to do.

Annalise had left the medical suite in good hands.

Should an emergency occur, Annalise had total confidence in her P.A. and the ship would be in port each day with easy access to the best of medical care. And Sophie was surrounded by her loved ones, who would take very good care of her, just as they would if she were at home, while the Christopoulos family spent the week among the Greek isles. The thought made her smile. Those islands would never be the same again after they left.

After meeting them—after meeting Niko—she would never be the same again.

The further the ship sailed from shore, taking Niko away from her, the deeper she felt the pain from the shards of her broken heart. How could loving someone hurt so intensely?

A tour bus pulled up and Annalise realized she was standing under their sign.

"You want a ticket for the Night Lights of Barcelona tour, lady? Special admission into the museums and other tourist attractions."

"Sure. Why not?" Anything was better than wishing for what could never be.

Touring the galleries of Barcelona by herself, Annalise had never felt so lonely. Before Niko, she'd preferred to explore alone, taking her time to enjoy what she liked most.

But a thousand times during the evening she wanted to turn to Niko and say, "Look. What do you think?" and see his tiger eyes, hear his deep voice as they shared something of awe or beauty.

Could she ever share anything with anyone again?

Checking into the hotel, she saw a father with his two children, a daughter and a son, and it made her smile.

The son had a dimple that flashed like Niko's. She bet the boy got whatever he wanted when he turned on the charm.

Niko was perfect father material.

That's the future Niko's family wished for him. That's the future he should have. The future she could never give him. Reality tore her in two.

She loved Niko with every cell in her body. She loved him enough to let him go.

In her hotel room she wrapped herself in blankets and tried to warm her cold soul with memories. She closed her eyes, remembering the heat of his hands on her, the healing fire he'd built in her heart and in her body.

Niko had forever changed her for the better.

Logically she should be grateful for that and move on.

Her heart clenched in agony. As hard as she tried to be practical, her emotions kept seeping through.

One breath at a time. That's how she survived.

Annalise knew that about herself. She was a survivor.

And she could help others be survivors, too.

She had skills to give the world and for that she would continue to move forward in her life. She would do it in honor of the man who had shown her what love was.

She wished she would have told Niko about her plans. Wished she could have told him how much he meant to her. Wished there had been a better way than simply walking away. But she might have found the limit to her strength. Saying anything more than goodbye to Niko might have destroyed her.

Finally, as dawn broke through the darkness, she boarded the plane that would take her to her new future.

* * *

Niko was not in a good mood. Not being able to find the woman you loved did that to a guy. He'd stayed awake long after midnight, thinking, hoping, wishing she'd come knocking on his door. It hadn't happened.

As soon as morning had broken, he'd searched the ship—their favorite kiosk by the hot tubs, the video arcade and the skating rink, their place on the top deck, everywhere he could think to look.

It was a big ship but he'd always been able to find her when he looked for her before.

Where was she?

They hadn't made plans to meet, but he'd taken for granted—

He'd taken *her* for granted, assuming she would be there when he wanted her.

Fighting down panic, he found her P.A. in the medical suite.

"I don't know where she went, Dr. Christopoulos. She didn't tell me."

The P.A. said Dr. Walcott was done with her duties, had finished her contract. No, she couldn't give out Dr. Walcott's private cellphone number. No, she couldn't give out her cabin number either.

The P.A. gave him a sympathetic shrug. "If she's still on the ship, I'm sure she'll show up."

Niko turned away from the medical suite, stunned. Confused. Lost.

He wandered the ship, bow to stern, for hours.

Desolate, with no appetite, he joined his family for lunch. The smaller passenger list meant only one sitting. He would see her there. It would all be a bad coincidence that they hadn't connected. They would laugh about it.

He would propose on the top deck. They would watch the sunset together. And his life would have meaning again.

But when he scanned the dining room, Annalise wasn't there.

The captain said he could give Niko no information. Then Helena took pity on Niko. She batted her eyelashes at the captain and asked sweetly on Niko's behalf. The captain agreed to have someone check the manifest to see if Annalise was still on the ship.

For now, all Niko could do was wait.

The meal with his family was as raucous as ever, reminding Niko what a misfit he was. While Niko barely mustered the will to swallow his soup, the rest of the family chattered around him.

As the wine began to flow, a steward came up to him, giving him a folded note.

Her contract with the ship is over. She vacated her quarters last night and disembarked in Barcelona. She's gone. I'm sorry, Helena

Niko waited impatiently for the ship to dock. His first stop in Athens would be the office of Doctors Without Borders. He would hand in his resignation and then search for Annalise.

He'd spend the rest of his life looking for her if he had to. And when he found her, he would do whatever he needed to do, be whoever he needed to be, to stay by her side.

Niko hurt deep down to the center of his soul. The ache was constant, like a thud on a hollow drum. He knew what it really was. It was the empty place where his heart used to be. Wherever Annaslise had gone, she had taken it with her.

Not that he hadn't given it to her freely. Only she had to be near him for it to go on beating, otherwise his life was just one day after the other with no heart in it.

Packets in hand, Annalise caught a taxi for her interview. If all went well, she would have a new job with Doctors Without Borders by the time she left Athens.

Once at their offices, Annalise signed the documents pledging herself for the coming year. The administrator gave her a genuinely grateful smile.

"You're perfect, Dr. Walcott. You've got emergency response training and emergency medical experience. You're used to making independent decisions and directing an ever-changing staff. You've even got all your shots."

Annalise gave her a rueful grin, remembering all the inoculations she'd had with the cruise line. "Sounds like I'm your woman, then."

"As soon as we finish all our background checks, we'll have your assignment for you. Not to worry, we'll put you with an experienced team leader until you're comfortable enough to be a team leader yourself."

Niko was a team leader. She had to grip her hands and bite her tongue to keep from requesting him. The wisest answer would be to specifically not ask for him.

It was a large, spread-out operation. What were the odds she would run into Niko on occasion? Would fate be cruel or kind?

In the end, she only nodded her understanding. "I'll be ready."

Emotion swamped Niko as he walked toward the Athens offices of Doctors Without Borders. Impatience overshadowed them all.

The sooner he got this excruciating decision behind him, the sooner he could begin his search for Annalise.

The doors opened and he blinked twice, sure his over-wrought brain was playing tricks on him.

"Annalise?"

"Niko?" All blood drained from her face.

If he stood still, she would come to him, right?

After standing frozen, giving her space, giving her time that seemed to draw out for an eternity, he could stand still no longer.

He took three long, quick strides, bringing him next to her. He wanted to reach out and grab her, hold her and never let her go.

But she stood there looking so brittle, he thought if he touched her she might break into a thousand pieces.

"Hey." His throat was so dry from nerves, his voice almost cracked.

"Hey."

"I told them. Told them all about paying for the cruise, about my work, everything."

"And?"

"And it's okay. They're my family."

"You're a lucky man."

"Yes." He thought about how he had been ready to search to the ends of the earth for her and here she was. "Yes, I am."

She swallowed. "What are you doing here?"

"Remember all those toasts my family gave, the ones about me and babies?"

"How could I forget?" She wrapped her arms around herself and stared straight up into the cloudless blue sky. "Go on."

By the way Annalise barely breathed her words, Niko knew how crucial this was to her.

"I'm leaving Doctors Without Borders. Trying to have a family life, expecting my wife to raise the children while I'm gone for months at a time, it wouldn't be fair."

"Your family will be pleased."

Niko expected to see joy and maybe even appreciation for his sacrifice in Annalise's eyes. Instead, her jaw was set in determination as if she was about to swallow a dose of bad medicine.

"And you, Annalise? Aren't you pleased?" He waved his hands at the building behind them. "I'm doing this for you, for us. For our children."

"No. Not for us. There can be no *us*." Pain made the words cut like glass in her throat. "I've joined Doctors Without Borders. I'll be leaving as soon as I receive my assignment."

"Annalise, I can't let you do that. It's too dangerous."

"You can't let me? Niko, you have no choice in this."

"I can't lose you."

"You never had me," she lied. A piece of her soul would always belong to him. But it was better this way.

"What are you saying?" Niko stared at her as anger tumbled with sorrow and churned with disbelief. "With all that has been between us, I mean nothing to you?"

She pressed her lips together and shook her head. "No."

Her eyes, brimming with tears, and her voice, shaking and thick, said otherwise.

"Only honesty between us, remember?" He reached out for her. If her body said the same thing her lips said, he would know.

Gently, as if she would break at his touch, he cupped her chin. The energy was there. That connection he shared with no other person on earth pulsed under his fingertips. "You say I mean nothing to you. Then why the tears?"

"There was damage. I can't carry a child to term." She blew out a breath. "I've never said that out loud before."

"Annalise—"

She reached out to touch him, but dropped her hand before she made contact. "I've got to go."

"No." He was fierce in his answer, frowning at her, blocking her way.

"You would be such a good father but I'm not cut out to be a mother." She took two steps back and wrapped her arms around herself. "Please, Niko. I'm breaking into pieces here. Don't make this any harder."

"I don't want children." He frowned. "I thought you did."

She wiped at her eyes with the back of her hand. "Why did you think that?"

He seemed genuinely puzzled. "All women do, right?"

Through her tears, she gave him a watery smile. "Has anyone told you that you sometimes have a chauvinistic streak?"

"So you were just going to walk away from me? Without a discussion?"

"I couldn't ask you to choose, babies or me."

"You couldn't ask me? What about my right to choose?" He wiped at his own eyes. "But, then, you just said the same thing to me about Doctors Without Borders, didn't you? We're two of a pair, aren't we? Except for me, there is no choice. Without you, there is no me."

She stopped him with a finger over his lips. "Someday you'll want babies, Niko. You deserve babies. I can't give them to you."

He kissed her finger before clasping her hand, keeping her at his side. "If that day ever comes, there's more than one way to have children. We could adopt."

"You would do that for me?"

"Don't you understand, Annalise? I would do anything for you. Even resign from Doctors Without Borders. Anything."

She put her palm over his heart. "You were going to give up what you loved most for me?"

He covered her hand with his, feeling it warm under his touch as he held it tight against his chest. "I love you, Annalise. What I love most is whatever makes you happiest."

"What makes me happiest is being with you." She gave a nod back to the building. "Think they'll assign us together?"

"They will if they want to keep two very good doctors on staff." He looked down into her eyes. "Is this what you want? I'll give it up for you."

"I would never want you to cut out a part of yourself for me. I love you, Niko. The whole package."

"The whole package. No more holding back. No more secrets—even if it is to protect the other person."

Annalise held out her free hand to him. When he wrapped his long, strong fingers around her delicate ones, she felt his strength surge through her. This was how it had always been between them. This was how it always would be.

"I'll make you a deal, Niko. I'll work on my communication skills if you'll work on yours."

He cocked an eyebrow at her. "It's going to take a lot of practice. A lot of togetherness."

She nodded. "A lot of patience and compromise."

"Sounds like a marriage to me."

"Are you asking?"

"No, I'm begging. Marry me, Annalise. Make my life whole."

"Yes, Niko. We'll be whole together."

A sneaky peek at next month...

Medical Romance™

CAPTIVATING MEDICAL DRAMA—WITH HEART

My wish list for next month's titles...

In stores from 5th April 2013:

❏ NYC Angels: Unmasking Dr. Serious — Laura Iding

& NYC Angels: The Wallflower's Secret — Susan Carlisle

❏ Cinderella of Harley Street — Anne Fraser

& You, Me and a Family — Sue MacKay

❏ Their Most Forbidden Fling — Melanie Milburne

& The Last Doctor She Should Ever Date
  — Louisa George

Available at WHSmith, Tesco, Asda, Eason, Amazon and Apple

Just can't wait?

Visit us Online

You can buy our books online a month before they hit the shops! **www.millsandboon.co.uk**

0313/03

Welcome to the world of the NYC Angels

*Doctors, romance, passion, drama—
in the city that never sleeps!*

Redeeming The Playboy
by Carol Marinelli
Heiress's Baby Scandal
by Janice Lynn
On sale 1st March

Unmasking Dr. Serious
by Laura Iding
The Wallflower's Secret
by Susan Carlisle
On sale 5th April

Flirting with Danger
by Tina Beckett
Tempting Nurse Scarlet
by Wendy S. Marcus
On sale 3rd May

Making the Surgeon Smile
by Lynne Marshall
An Explosive Reunion
by Alison Roberts
On sale 7th June

Collect all four books in this brand-new Medical 2-in-1 continuity

Find out more at **www.millsandboon.co.uk/medical**

0413/MB409a

***Join the NYC Angels
online community…***

Get all the gossip straight from the hospital on our
NYC Angels Facebook app…

- Read exclusive bonus material from each story

- Enter our NYC Angels competition

- Introduce yourself to our Medical authors

You can find the app at our Facebook page

Facebook.com/romancehq

(Once on Facebook, simply click on the NYC Angels logo
to visit the app!)

Special Offers

Every month we put together collections and longer reads written by your favourite authors.

Here are some of next month's highlights— and don't miss our fabulous discount online!

On sale 5th April   On sale 15th March   On sale 5th April

Find out more at
www.millsandboon.co.uk/specialreleases

Visit us Online

0413/ST/MB410

Save over £40

Join the Mills & Boon Book Club

Subscribe to **Medical** today for 3, 6 or 12 months and you could **save over £40!**

We'll also treat you to these fabulous extras:

- 🌹 FREE L'Occitane gift set worth £10
- 🌹 FREE home delivery
- 🌹 Books up to 2 months ahead of the shops
- 🌹 Bonus books, exclusive offers… and much more!

Subscribe now at
www.millsandboon.co.uk/subscribeme

Visit us Online

Save over £40 – find out more at
www.millsandboon.co.uk/subscribeme

SUBS/OFFER/M

 *Mills & Boon® Online*

Discover more romance at
www.millsandboon.co.uk

 FREE online reads

 Books up to one
month before shops

 Browse our books
before you buy

...and much more!

For exclusive competitions and instant updates:

 Like us on **facebook.com/romancehq**

Follow us on **twitter.com/millsandboonuk**

Join us on **community.millsandboon.co.uk**

Visit us
Online   Sign up for our FREE eNewsletter at
www.millsandboon.co.uk

WEB/M&B/RTL4